California Screamin'

The Rock & Roll Murders: A Rennie Stride Mystery

Also by Patricia Kennealy Morrison

Strange Days: My Life With and Without Jim Morrison

Son of the Northern Star (forthcoming)

The Books of the Keltiad

The Copper Crown
The Throne of Scone
The Silver Branch
The Hawk's Gray Feather
The Oak Above the Kings
The Hedge of Mist
Blackmantle
The Deer's Cry
The Beltane Queen (forthcoming)

The Rock & Roll Murders: The Rennie Stride Mysteries

Ungrateful Dead: Murder at the Fillmore
California Screamin': Murder at Monterey Pop
Love Him Madly: Murder at the Whisky A Go-Go (2009)
A Hard Slay's Night: Murder at the Albert Hall (2010)

California Screamin'

Murder at Monterey Pop

Patricia Morrison

Lizard Queen Press

On the Web:
pkmorrison.livejournal.com
mojohotel.blogspot.com
myspace.com/hermajestythelizardqueen

Jacket art and design by Andrew Przybyszewski

Book produced by James Allen Davis

Author photo by L.D. Bright

Book interior design by the author

"Oar", "Heart Don't Lie" and "Ozymandias" © 2004 by Patricia Morrison for Lizard Queen Music.

ISBN: 978-0-578-02470-7
Printed in the United States of America
May 2009

Author's Note and Acknowledgments

Although the Monterey Pop Festival of June 1967 and the Monterey area are of course quite real, I have taken liberties with both the local geography and the festival itself.

The Otter Point Inn is purely fictional, as are Otter Point, Mojado Hot Springs, the Mojado Valley and village of Mojado, and the Ramillies-Revels estate. I've also rebuilt the central California coast. (Just a little.)

The Big Magic Festival is a total invention, though at the time there had indeed been talk of an "anti-festival" — to be held at, of all places, Fort Ord, up the road from Monterey — for exactly the reasons presented here.

The framework of Monterey Pop, I felt, could easily support three fictional big-breakout acts, and I have slotted in Evenor, Turnstone and Lionheart where I felt they would have fit best. And where I would *so* much like to have seen them.

Thanks to Michael Lydon and Pauline Rivelli for the first-person memories they shared with me.

Thanks to the Monterey County Sheriff's Office and the Monterey Police Department for graciously answering my procedural questions. Particular thanks for the kindness and patience of Mr. Ted Brown (retired), Commander Tracy Brown and Lieutenant Randy Roach, who helped me get things right for the time frame; any inaccuracies are no fault of theirs.

Thanks to Richard Diehl for information on early portable videotaping equipment.

Thanks to the books and the authors, among them: *Flashbacks: Eyewitness Accounts of the Rock Revolution, 1964-1974*, Michael Lydon; *Trips: Rock Life in the Sixties*, Ellen Sander; *A Long Strange Trip: The Inside History of the Grateful Dead*, Dennis McNally; *Living with the Dead: Twenty Years on the Bus with Garcia and the Grateful Dead*, Rock Scully with David Dalton; *It Was Twenty Years Ago Today: An Anniversary Celebration of 1967*, Derek Taylor; *Bill Graham Presents*, Bill Graham and Robert Greenfield; *Go Where You Wanna Go: The Oral History of the Mamas and the Papas*, Matthew Greenwald; *Buried Alive: The Official Biography of Janis Joplin*, Myra Friedman; *Somebody to Love? A Rock and Roll Memoir*, Grace Slick with Andrea Cagan; *Long Time Coming*, David Crosby and Carl Gottlieb.

Thanks to D.A. Pennebaker for his brilliant documentary "Monterey Pop"(and all the cool DVD extras).

Thanks to all the acts who played Monterey, chiefest and favorite among them (in very particular order): Jefferson Airplane, Quicksilver Messenger Service, Big Brother and the Holding Company, the Byrds, the Grateful Dead, the Who, Buffalo Springfield, Country Joe and the Fish and Moby Grape—the iPod playlist to which I wrote.

Thanks to the acts who didn't but should have: the Beatles, the Beau Brummels, the Charlatans, Cream, Donovan, the Doors, Bob Dylan, the Hollies, the Kinks, the Rolling Stones, Steeleye Span, the Ventures, the Yardbirds and the Zombies—all also on the playlist.

Thanks to Black Pig Border Morris for "Coal Hole Cavalry" which I borrowed for Lionheart (and played endlessly) as the inspiration for "The March to Atlantis."

Thanks to Janis, Jimi and Otis. Still missed…

For Michael Rosenthal
friend, fellow artist, fellow grammarian

Oar

He's carried it about as far as he could
Started on the beach and headed inland
Vowed he'll keep on walking
with that odd-shaped piece of wood
upon his shoulder
never halting, never talking
till someone, bolder
or more curious than the day,
asks what's it for
and that is evermore
where he will stay

He'll put down deep roots
Wear leather boots
to tread on solid land
long leagues from seaweed strand
No deck beneath his feet
No swell to meet
the hollow hull
The wind spilled from his sails
Helm all a-lee
His back turned on the sea
and salting shore
He'll walk on waves no more

Fields of flowers
reign in summer
Seas of scarlet, waves of gold
Ships with keels and sails and rigging
Ballast in an empty hold

[bridge]

He walks away from the sunset
always with his foot above the tide
Bluewater sailor
Never before inshore to bide

Eyes scanning hills now, not horizons
that cloudwrack violet and gold bedizens
Renouncing coral sands
he'll sink the land in land
No more the topdeck battle slaughter
or, below, the nightquiet mirth
He'll never drown in earth
though he pray all gods to send him death by water

But every night he sails forever on
His dreams have not forgotten
the slant beneath his feet
the land-wind warm and sweet
rogue waves that bore him up
or beat him down
He knows in all his life
he'll never drown
(He'll never drown…)

Fields of flowers
rain in summer
Seas of scarlet, waves of gold
Ships with helms and masts and rudders
move across these tides untold

He walks away from the sunset
always with his foot above the tide
No ship will carry him to this last strand
He'll never drown on land
except in tears
He fears
he'll never drown

Fields of flowers
reign in summer
Swells of sorrow, surf of gold
Ships that found themselves a harbor
long before these oceans rolled

~ Turk Wayland

"You know what folding chairs are for, don't you?
They're for folding up and dancing on!"

–Bob Weir of the Grateful Dead
(or possibly Phil Lesh; reports differ;
hey, people were stoned!),
to the audience on the last night of Monterey Pop

<u>Prologue</u>

IN THE HAIGHT-ASHBURY DISTRICT OF SAN FRANCISCO *in the year nineteen hundred and sixty-seven, there is a huge explosion of what it pleases many people — usually not those personally involved in it — to call the hippie culture. Concerts, happenings, poetry, art, music, clothes (or no clothes), drugs, sexual freedom: it's all there, and ongoing, and has been for some years, with no outside interference and only a modest amount from within.*

But now mainstream America has picked up on it, and that spells nothing less than the Flaming Downward Death Spiral of Certain Doom. Everyone on the planet, pretty much, had seen the huge, dizzyingly colorful Human Be-in held in Golden Gate Park back in January, had viewed the magazine covers and newspaper articles and TV show about the happenings and happy hippie get-togethers, had heard the unprecedented glory that was the music. And so, you guessed it, here it comes.

Après nous le déluge. Suburban kids from all across the country are now clogging the Haight: infesting the streets, sleeping in the parks, hogging charity food right out of the mouths of those who really need it, panhandling spare change on street corners from people who don't have anything "spare" to begin with — people who work hard to get what little they do have, and who resent being constantly hit up for money by barefoot middle-class spoiled brats playing poor.

Those bright golden days hadn't lasted long. And though the music has never been better, the vibe is getting distinctly worse. There has even been serious talk of holding a wake for the scene, with a funeral procession and a coffin and everything, though like all else that takes place in the Haight it's also being treated as a significant goof.

But the goddess Nemesis is streetwalking in earnest now, grimly loitering under lampposts on every corner in the Haight, with a certain 'Who, me?' expression on her divine visage that isn't fooling anybody, and her girlfriends the Fates are busy with their thread and loom and shears everywhere you look.

And the change that they're handing out is about as far from spare as you can get…

Given all that problematic mojo, it's hard to tell why the thought has arisen in certain quarters that a big, open-air music festival would be a good thing at this particular point in time and space, but there it is, sleeting through the pot haze of the rockerverse: a free festival for and by free people, bringing the music back to its pure and uncommercial state. Yeah, right. As if anything like that had ever really existed for more than a couple of heartbeats.

All the famous big-name bands will play, the famous big-name organizers promise. It will be flowers and music. Peace and love. Acid, incense and balloons. The full blossoming of The Summer of Love. And this festival will be held not in San Francisco but in a place of unspoiled natural beauty and uncompromised spiritual excellence. For its sins, the coastal community of Monterey, a hundred or so miles to the south, draws the short straw, and there is much rejoicing elsewhere at having dodged that particular bullet.

To make sure the festival stays pure, it has unilaterally been decided by the not exactly hippest-of-the-hip originators that the artists should not be paid to perform at this festival, but instead should play for the clean, unsullied, commercially untainted virtue of the thing, and if there are any bucks to be made they should all go to 'charities' of the organizers' choosing, not to the artists who had made it all happen.

Exactly why the people who actually make *the music must do their jobs for free is never really satisfactorily explained. Particularly since money is apparently no object otherwise: first-class transport and hotels for all, side deals already on the bubble, TV and movies and soundtracks in mind. Big money will certainly be rearing its ugly head at some point, at least for some ugly big people.*

In any case, a festival that will largely rely on San Francisco talent has been hijacked out of the gate by Los Angeles promoters and self-promoters. Or at least that's the way the San Francisco musicians see it; the L.A. people, obviously, feel rather differently.

But no matter how anyone feels, very few who've been invited turn it down. People like Paul Simon and Cass Elliott and Paul McCartney, helping to organize, are contacting everyone they know: bands, solo performers, light shows, sound techs, those skilled in the arcane arts of bringing off big stage productions. Even Bob Dylan and the Beatles and the Rolling Stones have been approached, though for various reasons – drug problems, ego problems, just plain orneriness – no one expects any of them to show.

Everybody else, though, is coming: indeed, they're on their way. By plane from New York and London, by plane and train and car and chopper from L.A. and San Francisco, all heading to one of the most incredibly gorgeous chunks of

California coastline, or any coastline, there is. And they're bringing the music with them.

Coming to Monterey. Coming to play.

In the coastal hills a few miles north of Big Sur and a few more south of Monterey, at a lonely, lovely place called Mojado Hot Springs, a man in his thirties is sitting on the edge of a natural rock-lined thermal pool, deep in an old-growth redwood grove. He is bitterly arguing with a slightly-built, longhaired boy, very pretty and barely legal; the boy is half-submerged in the pool — they are both naked, bodies glistening from the steam and the spray. The nature of the argument is only too clear: the boy, weeping, wants very much to confront the man's wife about their relationship, the nature of which is also only too clear, and the man is equally desirous that he should not.

After a while, the boy's pleadings switch over to clumsy blackmail — not out of cunning, as he is far too young and inexperienced to know how to bring such threats off and make them stick, but out of desperation and pain. He's just a kid, a cute little groupie boy, miles out of his depth.

The man, however, has been in this situation before, and he knows exactly what emotional buttons to push; and after a while the boy's sobbing calms and he begins to nod his head, helplessly, apologetically, as if he agrees, as if he's sorry he's been so tiresome, as if it's all his fault. The man gathers him into his arms, lovingly, forgivingly, with relief — and also with something else, something less easy to figure out, something not very nice at all. Something maybe like triumph.

And someone standing very still in the shadows of the redwood grove, observing yet unobserved, listening, hearing, knows even more *about buttons.*

And all there is to know about how to push.

The Run-Up

Chapter 1

Sunday morning, June 4, 1967

"Summmmmerrrrr of *Loooove*," crooned Rennie Stride in tones of acid though still dulcet scorn. "Summer of absolute unadulterated godforsaken *hype*."

"You can't be talking about this music festival thing, can you? All you rock and roll riffraff invading Monterey couple of weeks from now?"

Rennie stretched until her toes reached down almost to the end of the wide brass bed, and scoffed at the man beside her.

"Why do you even bother to ask? You already know all about it. You police types always know. Indeed, that is *why* you ask, because you police types are always asking about *some*thing...it's what you do. And God is it ever annoying. Besides, I told you about it the last time you were here. Big huge music festival. At Monterey. Down the coast. Which I am so looking forward to."

Detective Inspector Marcus Dorner, SFPD, bridled — not an easy thing to bring off when you're naked. "I *know* where Monterey *is*."

"*Do* you! Well, Burke Kinney is sending me down there to cover it for the Clarion, of course, to be syndicated to the sister papers, and Lord Fitz ordered up a nice big pictorial feature for those new magazines he's starting up in London and New York."

"Well, your very clever editor and your completely insane publisher *would* want you on the job, wouldn't they. You being the queen of San Francisco female professional rock newspaper reporters and all."

"La, sir, how kind of you to say so! As I'm the *only* San Francisco female professional rock newspaper reporter, I sort of reign by default."

"There it is, then… Well, your rock and royal highness, who's going to be there? Not that, whatever names you might mention, I'd have much idea who they are."

"Oh, you have more idea than you think, copper. Prax, for one. With Evenor. You remember, the terrific and so far modestly successful band she put together after the murders last spring. Those murders she was accused of. The ones she didn't commit. The ones she was arrested for. But of course you won't have forgotten that, you being the one who helped arrest her."

Marcus sighed, as one who had heard it all before and didn't really want to be hearing it again.

"And I have apologized to Prax many, many times. She says she forgives me, and I take her word for it. And I've apologized to you too, even more times than I've apologized to her, though I'm still not sure why I should have to apologize to you at all. But give me *some* credit."

He lay back and looked up at the handsome ceiling moldings ten feet above his head, and recited as if by rote.

"Prax McKenna. Your best friend forever. Lead singer in a band name of Evenor, assembled after the Fillmore murders — for which I, yes, so very unjustly had her arrested on the obviously piss-poor evidence that she was present at both crime scenes and had known issues with the victims — from the ashes of the acid-rock group Deadly Lampshade and her own folk-rock former band Karma Mirror."

"Hey, not bad for the fuzz! But this isn't a test."

"That's what you always say. As for the bust thing, give it a rest, will you? I was wrong. You were right. You found the killer — oh no, wait, stop the presses, you only got *kidnapped* by the killer. *I* found *you* before he could add you to his multiply-murderous total and I rescued you and I carted the guy off to jail."

Rennie laughed and reached down to retrieve a pillow from the floor. "Oh man, get me rewrite! *I* found the killer, however inadvertently. *I* rescued me, in no uncertain terms. You just gave me a lift home. And a lecture to keep my journalistic nose out of police-type business from now on."

"And my words went unheeded, and my efforts were all in vain."

"I never promised."

"No, that's very true, you never did. Because what happened next but the murder at the Matrix Club last October, and the ones at the Golden Gate Park be-in back in January, and the one at the Carousel Ballroom in March, and there you were, yet again, right in the middle of things."

"And yet again I helped."

"If you like to call it that. At least you didn't get

kidnapped again."

"No. Not *kidnapped*, anyway. Still, it worked out."

"Luck." Marcus began to think about not getting out of bed, and of Rennie frying him half a pound of bacon for breakfast while he stayed in bed, and then of Rennie bringing him all that nice crisp bacon to *eat* in bed. "So tell me some more about the festival. We both know you want to."

"As I just now mentioned, Prax and Evenor are playing," she said promptly. "Could be their big break. At least their manager Dill Miller thinks so. And Tansy Belladonna and *her* new group, Turnstone, could be their big break too. You know Tansy."

"I do indeed. I'm very fond of both Prax and her, as you're well aware. Though Tansy is beyond a doubt the flakiest chick I've ever heard of, let alone met. Should work great for her as a rock star."

"Yes, well. Anyway, all of them are thrilled to pieces."

"Bless their hearts, who wouldn't be?" He wrangled the pillows behind him and resettled himself. "Anyone else besides your two closest personal friends and their bands?"

"Of *course*… It's going to be amazing. Just off the top, there's Janis Joplin and Big Brother. My darling Jefferson Airplane. The Grateful Dead. Country Joe and the Fish, Steve Miller, Quicksilver Messenger Service, Moby Grape. All Bay Area bands. The thing's only been under construction for about six weeks; it's very ad hoc, so who knows who will or won't show."

"That's a three-day weekend to fill up. Unless everybody plays four-hour sets."

"Which is not unheard of amongst that crowd, and which would be delightful in the extreme. But no such luck: the organizers are importing a buncha out-of-towners to fill the slots. Southlanders, mostly, more's the pity."

"Oh come on, you like *some* stuff out of L.A.! It's not entirely the invasion of the plastic people."

"Is it not?" Rennie dismissed the entire L.A. music scene with a wave of her fingers. "Okay, I do like some of what some of them do; okay, I like it a lot—but I am also of the opinion that it's on a whole other level from *our* music. A *lower* level. So: Byrds, Mamas and Papas, Buffalo Springfield—all confirmed. A few acts from New York—Simon and Garfunkel, Blues Project, Butterfield Blues Band, Al Kooper, Mike Bloomfield. So we, and by 'we' I mean of course our homegrown local bands, will carry this sucker and save the musical day. Days."

"Spoken like a true San Franciscan, transplant or not." Marcus began playing with her hair. "Anybody from England? I do enjoy some of those limey bands' records you play for me."

"Well, that's a bit more like it, and yes, some are coming over. Nobody really well known here. Yet. The big dogs can't come, mostly because of drug issues and not being allowed visas. But there's a few acts. This band called the Who—they're freaking *insane*, they smash up their amps and axes at the drop of a cymbal, but their music is incredible."

"Should be good, then."

"Should and will. And Lionheart, you've heard their albums right here in this apartment—big in Blighty but haven't really caught fire yet on this side of the pond. Oh, and this black guitar player who fronts a trio, Hendrix something. Jimi. Jimi Hendrix. Now this is interesting: he is in fact no true Brit but an American from up Seattle way. He's doing stuff so new and different that he had to go to London to get noticed, and *he's* supposed to be incredible too even though nobody's ever heard of him here in his own native land. Well, we'll just see about that."

"Actually, 'we' will." Marcus yawned prodigiously. "Not only have I heard about it, I'm going down there for it."

Rennie smacked his arm. "You let me go through all that and you're *going*? You might have said. But whyever for? You don't even *like* the music all that much."

"Not true, and you know it. Ever since you and Prax first dragged me into your crazy and sometimes homicidal rock and roll world, I've been a big fan. I don't like everything I've heard," he added candidly, "but I like quite a lot of it quite a lot."

He peered around the bedroom for his clothes, but he still didn't get up. "Anyway, it's strictly off-duty. An old friend of mine, Brent Gilmore, I used to work with him over in the Mission district, moved down near Big Sur a few years ago. Joined the Monterey PD and now works in the Monterey County sheriff's office. We keep in touch, and he asked me to come and give him a hand. The Monterey police chief is hiring as many off-duty deputy sheriffs and local cops as it can get to increase the law's presence at the festival, so Brent thought he could use some help too. So I got the call."

"To do what, pray?"

"Just advising on crowd control and general security, and of course, if the need arises, dealing with weirdos, which I've now had considerable experience with, thanks to you."

Rennie looked amused. "Glad I could be of assistance. I hear you're the go-to guy of record these days at the Hall of Justice, when it comes to weirdo wrangling."

"Guess so. Anyway, it's not an official paying hire the way the deputies are—I'll have no more legal authority than a rent-a-cop. Just a pleasant arrangement between friends: a backstage pass, a steak dinner at Nepenthe, Brent's Big Sur oceanfront-view guest cottage set among the pines to crash in for a week. I repeat, Big Sur oceanfront view. Not a damn thing wrong with that. Why does this surprise and annoy you?" he added. "Don't bother to deny it, I can tell it does, from that little pinchy expression you make when you're feeling those things. Yes, that's the one, right there."

She looked him straight in the eye. "Sure you're not going just to keep tabs on me, lest I find some cute musicians I want to go to bed with? Or in case I get into the kind of trouble I've been getting into for the past year and a half? That couldn't *possibly* be your reason, could it?"

"Goodness me! You have a vastly overinflated idea of your importance in my life. No, I swear, you got me genuinely interested in the music. That's all, folks! And helping out my friend, and getting a nice leisurely free week to kick back in Big Sur, which I happen to love. That's *really* all."

Marcus hesitated a moment, decided to go for it. "Heard from Stephen lately? You remember our Stephen? My cousin? Your husband? You don't mind that he seems to have found someone else?"

Huh. Talk about conversation stoppers...   A year and a half ago, barely ten miserable months after she'd married him, Rennie had left her still undivorced, adorable and adoring, extremely rich husband, Stephen Lacing, Marcus Lacing Dorner's second cousin, for a precarious yet gloriously independent existence in this top-floor pad in a Haight-district Victorian, and a career as a rock writer/pop culture reporter for the San Francisco Clarion, under her maiden name of Stride.

Then of course had come the Fillmore murders, and her meeting with Prax McKenna shortly before, and both Prax and Rennie subsequently being catapulted to national attention, as, respectively, the accused then vindicated murder suspect and the crime-solving journalist/kidnap-and-almost-murder victim. Sore at heart, Stephen had left San Francisco for Hong Kong after the murders were wrapped up—Prax being cleared and Rennie being safe—and he had spent the past year there cleaning out corruption in the Asian end of LacingCo, the Lacing family's multibillion-dollar business empire, of which interests he had just been given full control.

And as Marcus had just now pointed out, Stephen had indeed found someone else: a month ago, he had met a beautiful, brilliant French-Chinese girl named, rather spectacularly, Ling-ling Delphine de la Fontange, a gem expert from Hong Kong. Five years Rennie's senior, a year younger than Stephen, Ling was the daughter of autocratic French count Jean-Pierre de la Fontange—who ran LacingCo Asia in partnership with Stephen's father, General Lacing—and his wife Mei-mei, a Chinese aristocrat of imperial lineage.

By all accounts, Ling and Stephen were taking things very slowly and very carefully, which Rennie and Stephen had totally not. They'd known each other since childhood, their families had been friends for decades, and everyone involved had apparently learned something about whirlwind romances and disastrous elopements, which was how it had gone down for Stephen and Rennie. And of course this kind of thing was done very differently in Asia anyway: a year-long getting-to-know-you phase and a subsequent year-long engagement would be considered hasty even if Stephen hadn't still been a technically married man. But he wasn't pushing for divorce, and Rennie wasn't pressuring him; in fact, nothing in any way legal had even been filed yet. It was fine as it was, there was no rush, and they'd get around to formally ending the marriage in due course.

Now Rennie sat up in bed and stared down at Marcus. "*Mind*? That he met this incredible woman? Why would I mind? Not even a twinge. We've been living apart for over a year and a half. He and I were finished as soon as I set foot in San Francisco. Never should have gotten married in the first place."

She flopped back down again on the pillows. "From what he tells me, Ling could be absolutely perfect for him. She was born in San Francisco, lived in New York for years as a kid, went to college here, so she's as American as anything else. Her father has run LacingCo Asia for longer than any of us have been alive—as you know, being a major stockholder in the family firm. Obviously she knows what's required of a CEO's wife, and, unlike some other people we could mention, she seems to understand and actually be up for the challenge of being a future Lacing matriarch. I hope it works out for them, I truly do. He deserves somebody incredible. I haven't met her yet, but I've seen pictures—she's rrrravishing, and I hear she's really smart. They'll make some amazing babies to rule Lacingworld one day."

She saw his face change before he could control it. "I don't *believe* it! You're freaked out because she's half Chinese! What a racist pig—"

Marcus looked furious at the implication. "Not *me*!"

"Then—oh. *Her*."

Rennie should have known. She could imagine the scene in Hell House, the Lacings' historic Pacific Heights mansion that went by the name Hall Place to the world: her blondly cadaverous socialite mother-in-law, Marjorie Elaine Beldenbrook van Leeuwen Lacing, rending her garments (old worn-out unstylish ones only, of course; it would never do to trash something chic), wailing and lamenting because Stephen's at this point in time totally hypothetical children, the future

Lacing heirs, might possibly be, let's work it out now, shall we, oooh, a whole one-fourth Chinese.

"Unbelievable. That septic, bigoted bitch. Though if I were Motherdear, I'd be more hysterical about the French DNA than the Chinese… And Ling's parents have been tight with *les* Lacings *mère, père et frère* for, what, almost five decades? Stephen told me that *le comte* Jean-Pierre had been the General's older brother's roommate for years at prep school and Harvard, for pete's sake."

"Longtime friends and kin by marriage are two very different things where this family's concerned."

Rennie glanced down pointedly at their mutual bareness in her antique brass bed. "Kin by marriage didn't slow *you* down any."

"We've been down this road before, Rennie. I may be driving, but you're riding shotgun."

"Yes, I know, I recognize the trees, oh look, there's that little white picket fence again… How does it go: it's nothing but sex and we're not in love with each other and neither of us is serious about it and you would never have jumped my bones if Stephen had still been in San Francisco. And you still haven't told him we've been having it off."

"All true. You know it is. And be fair, you wouldn't have jumped mine back if he were. And you haven't told him either."

"Damn straight I wouldn't have! And didn't. And haven't. And yes, it is all totally and completely true."

It was, too, and neither of them had ever been anything but utterly honest and up front about it. She had gone to bed with Marcus out of every bad reason there was: boredom, curiosity, charity, plain old horniness. He was quite right: sex *was* all it was, and all it ever would be. She'd known it from the first, and she'd told him so long before they ever laid a hand, or anything else, on each other. It was pure selfish convenience and mutual use—though not without considerable affection. They were friends. It was easy and comfortable and safe. And damn good sex. He was there, and he wanted her, had been wanting her for quite a while, and she didn't have anyone serious in her life at the moment and he wasn't exactly repellent in any respect so why the hell not.

Once Stephen had left for Hong Kong last August, Rennie had found herself at an unexpected loss. She hadn't realized how much she trusted and relied on him as a friend and confidant, even though their marriage was over. It had never been a real marriage, no matter what they had deluded themselves into thinking. It couldn't have been; they loved each other, sure, but they'd never been *in* love, and they shared very few interests. He'd wanted someone he could mold, however unconsciously, to fit his world, and she'd just been dazzled that he wanted her at all. Truth was, they were ill-matched and unequal partners, and from the start they'd each been seeking very different things.

She'd been twenty when they eloped: a virgin, no serious boyfriends before him even, never out on her own, never lived in her own place, never supported herself. She'd gone straight from her parents' sheltering wing to her husband's very well-feathered nest. Because that was what nice middle-class girls did. Stephen, six years older, was already a successful financier-lawyer, helping his father and brother and uncles run their incredibly wealthy family's international business interests, and he'd courted her relentlessly and overwhelmingly, though she'd never been sure quite why he picked her, and still wasn't.

But no sooner had he carried her off to San Francisco and the ancestral Lacing digs than she knew she'd made a terrible, horrible, godawful mistake. She'd given it her best shot, she really had; but it had been a disaster and they both knew it. She wanted other things for herself, different things, not the things he wanted for them both, and she finally gathered up the courage to do what she had to do to get them.

So just before Christmas 1965 she'd moved out, into this very flat—the top floor of a gorgeous old Victorian painted lady across the street from Buena Vista Park, in the heart of the newly hip Haight-Ashbury district—and landed herself a job as the San Francisco Clarion's fourth-string rock reporter. The murders Marcus had just mentioned had certainly helped advance her career, and at lightspeed—she'd been seriously promoted twice at the Clarion, thanks to her literally noble publisher, and also thanks to him she was now writing for several other prestigious outlets as well and was even closing in on a book deal—but her personal life, though newly liberated and exciting, was a bit more problematic.

Okay, maybe jumping into bed with her husband's second cousin wasn't the greatest idea in the world, but she knew him, she could trust him, he was incredibly hot, it was no strings all round. So they'd been having a small, sporadic and rather surprisingly (on her side, at least) gratifying affairlet, sleeping together every couple of weeks for a few months now. So far.

For his part, Marcus had quietly lusted after her ever since they met, and only the fact that she was married to Stephen, who was more like a brother to him than a cousin, had stopped him from hitting on her before. Still, he'd decently waited a full six months after Stephen's departure before making his move, six months in which Rennie had begun to enjoy sexual freedom for the first time in her life.

Not that she was a tramp. Unless being with

eight or so different guys, four of them regulars, in a year and a half made you that, which she didn't think it did. But now that she was effectively if not yet legally available, Marcus had gone after her, not caring what the family repercussions would be if anyone found out he was sleeping with his cousin's wife; and she was lonely and bored and she didn't have anybody she was seriously interested in and she liked him a lot and, yes, lusted in her turn, so she didn't repel his advances.

It probably wasn't going to last much longer, though, let alone forever. In spite of the casual no-strings-ness he'd just affirmed, lately Marcus had been getting just a tad bit too uncomfortably possessive. And Rennie wasn't ready to be possessed again, not like that. Maybe she wouldn't be for a long time to come; maybe not ever. And again as Marcus had said, they certainly weren't in love. But sex was fine. For now.

She watched him as he got out of bed and began to pick up his scattered clothes and get dressed. He was really cute: six feet tall, straight Beatle-styled caramel-brown collar-length hair—acceptable to SFPD because of all the undercover work he did—great body, gold-flecked gray eyes. And smart. She liked that. Also he was much more aggressive and specific and demanding about what he wanted from her in bed, and what he gave her in return, than Stephen had ever been, and she really liked that. Plus he was a cop, and therefore armed and with his own set of handcuffs, and she *really* liked *that*.

But he was still a Lacing: his grandfather and Stephen's had been brothers, his mother and Stephen's father were first cousins, and he had been saddled with the same family baggage Stephen had to tote. And she *didn't* like *that*, no, she didn't like that one little bit.

"Come on," she said, slipping out of bed after

him, giving him a slap on the behind on her way to the kitchen, and receiving a pinch on her breast in return. "Bacon it is. I'm perfectly well aware that that's all you're really hanging around here for."

"Not all."

"So you say."

Chapter 2

Thursday afternoon, June 8

"WELL, IT'S BEEN A BUSY OLD YEAR in the small but mighty kingdom of Lacinglandia-by-the-Bay, hasn't it," observed Prax McKenna. "Eric and Petra having their fancy wedding, little Marjorie happy at last, turkey-baster baby already popped. And you just about the speck of dust on the Lacing horizon you've so longed to be and Marjorie has so long wished you were. Well played, I say!"

The eldest Lacing son, Stephen's brother Eric, and the gorgeous Petra Lawrence had been married late last summer, in a ceremony arranged at warp speed by Motherdear and her society-beldam cohorts, and the newlyweds had wasted no time buckling down to familial duty. Petra had gotten pregnant instantly, and the offspring had just been born, a boy, to Motherdear's endless and caroling delight. Stephen and Rennie had together attended the lavish nuptials, at which the bridal couple had been stood up for by their best friends, who were in fact their true beloveds and de facto spouses. Eric's longtime boyfriend, Thomas Copeland III, known as Trey, and Davina Shores, Petra's longtime girlfriend, immediately perceiving the sheer genius of the thing, had turned around and gotten married themselves.

The fact that all four parties to these unions were as gay as a bushel of rainbows was a fact known to almost no one in the family: Eric and Trey had long ago confided in Marcus, while Eric had told Rennie about himself when she came to live at Hall Place; and Stephen had known since their teenage years, the first person Eric had ever told. And Rennie, with Eric's permission, had let Prax, herself known to play for both teams, in on the secret. And of course all the couples' gay friends knew all about it.

But nobody else. Nobody's parents, grandparents, godparents or step-parents, brothers or uncles, sisters or cousins or aunts, friends or acquaintances or enemies or business partners. The marriages meant the social and family pressure was off: Mr. and Mrs. Eric Lacing and Mr. and Mrs. Thomas Copeland could have kids, even, and still be able to live with access to their true partners in an unaccepting, hostile, cold world that cut them no slack at all. If anyone wondered about it, it was usually just to comment enviously or approvingly on how lucky the two young couples were to have found such good and close friends in each other and spouses that got along so well together. And the two young couples just nodded and smiled and said Yes we certainly are.

Rennie rolled her eyes dramatically. "Yeah—I owe Eric and Petra big-time, for diverting Marjorie's hellhound attention from my fleeing steps across the swamp. Once the engagement was announced, she forgot all about Stephen and me in the throes of wedding arranging. I must admit, she made a good job of it on about ten minutes' notice: that reception in the Hell House ballroom was even more spectacular than the General's anniversary ball. But then, such things are what she lives for, and why the Lacings live in the kind of house they do."

"I was surprised to hear that they're living in Hall Place themselves, Petra and Eric," remarked Prax. "That pile wasn't big enough to hold you and Marjorie peaceably, as you and I both recall."

"The entire Indian subcontinent wouldn't have been big enough for that. But Marjorie absolutely dotes on Petra—the girl's a native San Franciscan of socially impeccable family and her mother has known Marjorie since finishing school, so both mums were over the moon about the wedding, little do they know—and Petra has a much better sense of humor about Motherdear than I could ever muster. They get along just fine. Besides, now that the sprog is here—and by all accounts no turkey basters were involved, so you needn't be so snarky—and being as the young master is the first male heir born to a direct-line Lacing male of this generation, Motherdear hasn't the time nor yet the inclination to torment little old miscreant me. O frabjous day! Plus Eric and Petra have already slated me as godmother to their first future daughter, which is going to get up Marjorie's nose so far it'll mess with her prefrontal cortex. If she has one. Callooh, callay, I chortle in my joy!"

The two friends were having a late lunch at Albino's, their favorite place in North Beach, a tiny Italian hole-in-the-wall they'd discovered when they were poor and struggling, and now that both of them were rather less struggling and considerably less poor they hadn't abandoned it. It was an excellent thing, they

thought, that they could now afford pricier dishes than
spaghetti and marinara sauce—meat and wine and
appetizers and dessert, even!—and the proprietor, a
lovely old Italian lady named Annamaria, was happy for
them and herself too that they could.

"They should be grateful you never touched a
cent of their blood money," said Prax severely, making
inroads on the outstanding house garlic bread, served up
hot in a small tin bucket. "Well, except for my bail. But
Stephen offered that; you didn't have to beg him for it."

"I would if I'd had to," Rennie promptly pointed
out.

Prax smiled. "I know, sweetness. But you've
never asked them for anything, ever, and I'm glad you
didn't have to make an exception on my account. You've
been so honorable about never taking a handout from
them. I'm very proud of you. I bet they expected you to
stand outside the gates of Hell House like the Poor Little
Match Girl, pressing your nose to the iron bars, all
ragged and starving in the snow. Drenched and freezing
in the fog, anyway. Well, you sure showed *them*."

"Yeah, Motherdear had her hopes up, all right,"
said Rennie, laughing. But, you know, if I'd ever been in
seriously dire straits, Stephen and I would have worked
out something that didn't shame either of us. As our
lawyer friend Berry Rosenbaum keeps reminding me, his
filthy lucre is my filthy lucre, since with all his worldly
goods he me endowed. But I didn't want to go that way,
however legally correct. Though I did hit the joint
checking account for that money for Ro Savarkin. All of
which she paid back once she got out of rehab and took
that job with LacingCo in New York, and which I then
paid Stephen back. So we're all square with Mammon."

"Have you heard from Ro lately? How's she
doing?"

Rennie negotiated a forkful of the house specialty

chicken that Annamaria had just beamingly placed before her.

"Doing just great. Had a letter from her last week — reconciled with her family, clean and sober, loves the job, has a new apartment and new boyfriend and everything. A good day's work there, by everyone involved. But that was the only time. About the money, I mean. It was really important to me that I didn't parasite off Lacing bucks but earned my own. It still is. I was so lucky after the Fillmore murders that I could — Fitz coming through when he did with those promotions."

"We love Fitz," remarked Prax, admiring her own plate of veal piccata. "Oh yes we do. If it weren't for him, we probably wouldn't be dining here right now. At least not so lavishly. We owe him. And, of course, he owes us. But luck had nothing to do with it. You *earned* all that."

The man known to all and sundry as 'Fitz' was Rennie's self-made gazillionaire publisher, the flamboyant and obligatorily eccentric Northern Irish presslord Oliver Fingal Flaherty Fitzroy, first Baron Holywoode. Pronounced 'Hollywood', and he was fully aware of the irony. He very much enjoyed being addressed as a lordship, of course — a *literal* press baron — but at his own insistence most everyone just called him Fitz. Ruthless, handsome, charming, frighteningly intelligent, he preferred people to perceive him as a typical British upper-class twit — he got away with a lot more that way. And he got away with a *lot*.

But Fitz was far from twittish, and his origins far from upper-class: born in Brighton, the son of a grocer and a teacher, he'd graduated from Cambridge, married a titled English heiress from a family half as old as time and twice as rich, and then proceeded to work his way into his current ownership of a score of British and American publications, with great riches and a nicely euphonious title of his own arriving along the way.

Hardly typical. He never asked for favors, though he wasn't shy about calling them in and he never, ever, wrote them off, and he gave them very sparingly indeed.

Thanks to her extremely sensational, way-up-close-and-all-*too*-personal first-person story on the Fillmore murders last year, Rennie had become one of Fitz's pet lambs; and also because of those murders — for two of which she'd been erroneously arrested, as Marcus and Rennie so exhaustively discussed — Prax had become a much better-known rock personage than she had been and had made great copy, so Fitz loved her too.

"Well, the way I reckon it up, we're pretty well even, Fitz and us." Rennie reached for another piece of garlic bread before Prax ate it all. "Paid in full. Anything from here on in is just gravy."

"Or marinara sauce."

They dined in silence for a while, paying serious attention to their food, which deserved it, and finally Prax sat back, replete for the moment.

"So, have you heard any more about Monterey?"

Rennie shrugged. "It seems to have already been co-opted out from under us by sneaky famous Southlanders."

"Yeah, so I'm told," said Prax darkly. "Famous John Phillips of the Mamas and the Papas and famous record mogul Lou Adler. The thing got started by two other people; then once Adler and Phillips heard about it, they stole the pig and away they run."

"They did buy those other guys out," Rennie said fairly. "And gave them seats on the board of directors. Right along with fellow directors Donovan and Jagger and McCartney and Brian Wilson and Jim McGuinn and Smokey Robinson. But basically it was, yes, a classic show-biz smash'n'grab. How'd you guys get hooked in?"

"Our glorious and excellent manager, Dill Miller. It started with a phone call he got from Lou Adler, all proper and correct, asking us to appear at this little beanfest. Dill said no on our behalf. All the major bands said no, at least at first: Airplane, Dead, Country Joe, Quicksilver, Big Brother. We don't like the L.A. crowd, and we knew they were only asking us because they desperately needed San Francisco musical cred. Then Dill got another call, this one from Papa John, as if from the top of Olympus, like *he* was doing *us* the favor of our appearance. Which, of course, he is, but we didn't like his attitude."

"Who would?"

"Right? Then after Dill gave them both the shove-off, 'cause he doesn't trust either of them as far as he could throw a Marshall cabinet, Phillips approached us directly, me and Juha, and the other bands too, earnestly promising all sorts of righteous charitable stuff, even enlisting Mama Cass and Mama Michelle and Pauls both Simon and McCartney to put the screws on. Especially Mr. Simon. They were all very persuasive. So we gave in and said yes—not really the least bit reluctantly, if you must know, though if you tell anyone I admitted it I'll claim you were drunk when you said it."

"No fear! But who could blame you for wanting in? Whatever it turns out to be, it'll be a great showcase for the bands that aren't fixed up yet."

Prax looked dubious. "Let's hope... Then, even as we up here all watched in impotent fury, it turned into the Phillips & Adler Show. 'Adlips On Parade', as I like to call it. All these plastic acts coming out of the woodwork: nightcrawlers from Vegas, has-beens, never-weres, complete unknowns, straight-out quid pro quos for powerful friends, you know how it goes. 'Put my no-name act on the bill and I'll lend my name to the proceedings and make sure my top gun comes to play.' Pure biz stuff. Though I say so who am still pretty much a no-name myself, and my band likewise. But they need to have the San Francisco bands on board. So that's why they're kissing our musical butts. But we're not so easily had. We'll be there, oh yes, and we'll play our best, but we're going to get what *we* want out of this, not just lie down and be run over by Adlips's big old personal agenda. Or their big old personal Rolls-Royces either."

Rennie reached for the dessert menu. "Let's *all* hope."

"So I hear you're covering Monterey all by your onesies, you clever old thing!" crowed Ned Raven, on the phone from London the next afternoon. Ned had been one of Rennie's regular boyfriends, transatlantic variety so not all *that* regular, maybe three times a year, on tour, and by now he was more like an ex-regular, though still a good friend: the dishwater-blond leader of Bluesnroyals, the incredible English blues-rock band that was making the Rolling Stones cast uneasy glances over their collective shoulder.

"That lot at the Clarion must really trust your reporterly chops," he added. "As well they should. But that's going to be a vast expanse of musical ground to cover. Rather less, of course, since my lads and I won't be there."

Rennie laughed. "And how you will be missed, you little perisher, not just by me. Didn't I tell you that your drug adventures would bite you in your adorable British bum? Or at least keep you from getting a work visa? I did. And did you listen to me? You did not. And so it has. God, it's so *boring* being right all the time! But no, I won't be entirely alone. Praxie will be there with Evenor, and Tansy and Bruno with Turnstone, and some of my fellow Fitz vassals from New York and L.A. to keep me company. Plus there's this new guy on the paper Burke wants me to break in, sort of. Nice, very. Funny. Really smart. Bit shy."

But that was short of the mark. Stan Hirsh was a reserved, brilliant, acerbically amusing young man a year or two older than Rennie. Brown-haired and owlishly bespectacled, he was newly arrived in San Francisco from his hometown of Casper, Wyoming, where he'd worked for a couple of years on the cow-town's local paper. Now, even more newly hired by Clarion editor Burke Kinney, Rennie's immediate boss, Stan had begun picking up rock reviewing duties as Rennie moved on, in her new station as pop culture reporter-at-large, to features and commentary and big theme pieces. He seemed glad and grateful for the gig and the work, and he passionately loved the music, as did she, but she had a feeling he longed for bigger things, and more. Which was perfectly fine, of course. So did she.

Ned listened to the Hirsh backstory with a critical ear. "Interesting. However on earth did he end up in San Francisco?"

"Back there in Longhornville, he'd always wanted to be a crime reporter, but it didn't work out."

"No talent?"

"Tons of talent. Just not enough crime. So he figured he'd come here, do this crazy fun rock trip, get some attention, then move on to better things. Or worse things, depending on how you look at it. He loves the music, but he prays and hopes for crime."

Ned chortled appreciatively. "And somehow you keep getting in on all the crime he covets, without having to lift one delicately manicured paw. He must be dying. So to speak. Maybe he's hoping to coast to crime-reporter nirvana on your hand-tailored paisley coattails. Listen, I'll bet you a pair of antique earrings against a bottle of vintage port that he will be totally seduced by rock and roll and forget all about crime and ten years from now he will take over your boss's boss Garrett Larkin's job."

"Not me to take over dear Mr. Larkin's job?"

asked Rennie, mock-hurt.

"Oh, sugartits, where *you'll* be in ten years? So very much better. You don't want Garry's gig. You want your own, the way *you* want it to be. And I have no doubt whatsoever that you are going to get it." He paused delicately. "So, does this Stan bloke have a bird? Or are you—"

"*No*, I'm *not*. I have quite enough trouble already in that area. As you very well know, having been a modest part of it. But that's the thing. No one's sure. He has this picture on his desk of an absolutely stunning blonde. He *says* her name is Marishka and she's from Brentwood in L.A. and is a theology doctoral candidate at Yale, but no one's ever actually *seen* her. The betting around the watercooler is that he's gay and he's completely making her up and he bought the picture in one of those frames from Woolworth's."

"How droll. But no, I get the vibe she's quite real. And good on him, I say! I'll take some of that action, if it's still going."

"Well, I've got my money on him too, if you must know..." Changing the subject, very firmly: "Hey, I hear your pals Lionheart and the Who are going to be playing Monterey. I've never seen either of them live."

"Oho! You're in for a treat, baggage, and you'll want to pay serious attention. I've known them all for years—we're all mates from our starving days and nights in grotty London blues clubs. Our *more* starving days and nights. They're both amazing bands, with amazing lead guitarists. Particularly Turk Wayland. And I say that with only the teensiest speck of envy. No, make that a lorryload of envy, he's just that much better than all the rest of us. Oh, and there's this young spade guitarist, too, Jimi Hendrix, one of you Yanks. I've seen him play in London, and I tell you now, you've never, ever, seen or heard anything like him. So check him out too. In a purely professional way, of course."

"Of course. Actually, I've already heard about Hendrix; I do read Melody Maker, you know, being a professional music-biz person... Any other advice?"

"Keep your nipples away from Keith Moon, Miss Music Biz Professional. And look out for flying guitar pieces."

After she'd gotten off the phone with Ned, Rennie curled up in her sunny bedroom window seat, casements wide open to the flower-scented air pouring in, and gazed out over the familiar view, endlessly spectacular in the clear twilight: Golden Gate Park, Golden Gate Bridge, dark looming Marin Headlands. It just floored her sometimes, how things had worked out. If she hadn't married Stephen, she'd never have come to San Francisco to live. If she hadn't left Stephen, she'd never have been doing what she was doing. Well, no, that wasn't true, of course she would, it was all she'd ever wanted, except it would have been very different and probably a lot more rugged. And it was only due to some very nasty stuff that nobody could have planned or foreseen that she was where she was at all.

As she'd remarked to Prax, last year's whole unfortunate murder situation and her first-person story about it had wrought good and mighty things for them both. And the deus ex machina in the case had been none other than Lord Fitz, who, not content with his British holdings, had bought Rennie's paper, the Clarion, and was busy buying up numerous other publications as well, pursuing visions of Atlantic-to-Pacific media grandeur beyond even the most lustful dreams of Beaverbrook or Hearst. As part of his empire's overhaul, he had been casting around for writers of caliber that he could lure away from other publications to work for him, and his unerring eye for journalistic talent had lighted on

Rennie Stride, young, gifted, smart, brave, pretty, and, what could be lovelier, already his employee.

So what if it had been her notoriety in the Fillmore murders — a story syndicated all over the world, much to the Clarion's gratification — that had first brought her squarely to her publisher's attention? He might not have noticed her for a long while otherwise, if at all. But it was her writing skills and not her affinity for murder that kept her front and center in his head: when Fitz found out that this Rennie Stride who was all over the headlines and had been instrumental in bringing a druglord serial killer to justice was intelligent and talented, and better still, he already owned her, he had ordered her promoted. And, over the past year, he'd begun sending stories and introductions her way.

As Rennie, guided and encouraged by Burke Kinney and Garry Larkin, had moved steadily onward and upward, encountering on her way four more murders to add to the first three, Baron Holywoode had followed her writerly progress and her body count alike, not in the kind and gruff avuncular way in which a powerful press lord would be aware of a cute, spunky girl reporter in a real-Hollywood movie story but in a true-life mutually exploitative way. Nothing in the least bit sexual, of course. God forbid. But they'd hit it off immediately, liking and respecting the other's vibe and head and attitude. Rennie was of course pleased and gratified, though she didn't see it as fairytale kindness, and much as she liked her boss, she didn't trust him for a heartbeat.

But Fitz had no problems whatsoever with her actually *making* news as well as merely reporting it. In fact, he heartily approved — anything that sold a few more papers was just fine with him, and he quite liked the idea of his own high-profile writer being notorious and widely read all over other people's front pages without him paying a penny for the privilege. And, indeed, himself being paid for it. Besides, she had serious social connections as well, even if she did seem to be hell-bent on kicking over the traces, and those were always useful.

None of this was lost on Rennie herself, who knew perfectly well that she had become flavor of the month because of the murder and kidnapping angle, not because of her seriously excellent writing abilities. She also knew enough to know that that would change: notoriety had its uses, sure, but it wasn't a stayer; you did not put your trust in it. That would be up to her; or more strictly speaking it would be up to her talent, and in that she had *perfect* trust.

She shifted in the window seat and lost herself in the lights of San Francisco beginning to come on, gold beads edging the green velvet of the Panhandle and the park. She'd done bylined features for over a year now, and full-page stories for six months, but Monterey was going to be her first big test. Oh, she had complete confidence that she could do it justice: not only did she trust her talent, she trusted her friends' talent. But what was she going to do for an encore—murder some *more* people?

Indeed, exactly that had been suggested to her, jokingly, or maybe half-jokingly, many times over the past year, by everyone from Prax to Janis Joplin to Ned Raven to Marcus to Fitz himself, and it made her nervous and superstitious every time she heard it. Be careful what you freakin' well wish for.

Chapter 3

Sunday morning, June 11

"CAN YOU REALLY COOL OUT in a hot spring? Isn't that, like, what's that big old smartypants word you're always flinging about like a cheap feather boa — an oxymoron?"

Prax put her chin on the back of the station wagon's front seat, raising winsome brows and looking hopefully for a reaction, but Rennie just laughed. The two of them, with two other members of Prax's band, Evenor — Chet Galvin, rhythm guitarist and current nonexclusive part-time bedmate of Rennie, and Juha Vasso, lead guitarist and current exclusive full-time bedmate of Prax, except for those occasional occasions when she favored girls, not guys — were driving south from San Francisco, heading to the mountains just north of Big Sur, for a little down time before the festival.

"Are we *theeeere* yet?" Prax mock-whined, reaching to tug at Rennie's long hair, grinning as her friend smacked her hand. "Tell me again why we're going down so early."

"You know perfectly well why. Because I have to write about Big Magic. So it's work. Insofar as any of this is *ever* work. And it's work for you lot, too. At least work prep. Because you have to practice before Monterey; there should be plenty of chances to sit in and keep your chops up or get your licks in or whatever the heck it is you people do."

"We're playing *Monterey*!" Juha exulted, for perhaps the twentieth time since the car trip had begun. "And our second album is charting."

"Yes we are! And it's ni-i-i-i-ice, having two albums out," Prax purred.

"Phalarope does seem to be doing right by you," said Rennie judiciously. "Good job Chimera merged with them after your first LP. Decent ad budget, couple of tours with support, promo boys doing their thing. Hot hit single, too."

Nods of deeply satisfied agreement all round: Evenor's first two singles on the Chimera label had done well, chiefly locally and in New York City and hip college towns, but the third one, on Phalarope, a rock-ya-sock-ya number called 'Severe Clear' — a meteorological term used by airplane pilots, meaning unlimited visibility in a cloudless sky — was twenty-six with a bullet in the national trades, and still climbing, and they were more excited about it than they cared to admit even to themselves.

Prax took a deep happy breath. "Yeah — but it was only a two-album deal. Chimera had the first one, Phalarope the second, and they're not renewing. I mean, they did offer, but we thought it wasn't enough, considering how we've done. And the offer seemed like an afterthought anyway. Too late the Phalarope. So we're up for grabs again now."

"Any prospects?"

"According to Mr. Randyll Miller III, manager extraordinaire, we've had a fair few nibbles," said Juha. "We're hoping for a really big fish to swim along and swallow us up, though, and so far that hasn't happened. Not Dill's fault," he added hastily. "He's been great, he'll get us signed. We're not worried."

Chet nodded. "That's why we thought Monterey would be so good for us. We'll be seen. And heard. Every record label exec and music writer in L.A. and New York and London will be there. If we pull off a really knockout show, maybe we could even impress somebody like Clive Davis of Columbia or Ahmet Ertegun of Atlantic or Pierce Hill of Rainshadow. They've got the money and the means to make it happen. If they like us. And we're going to play our fingers off to make sure they do."

"It's going to be a meat market! You guys realize that, don't you? Or a slave auction. Whichever is worse."

"We *want* to get bought by a big old rich established label, Strider. So does everybody who'll be playing at either Mojado *or* Monterey. You know that." Chet sounded tired, and a little troubled, and reached over to put a hand on her thigh. "It's the next step up, and there's a ton of competition now—look at all the Bay Area bands who are coming to the end of little piddling contracts that didn't do anything for them, or who haven't been signed at all yet. We want it. A lot. We'll do whatever it takes. Short of selling our souls, that is."

Rennie glanced into the rear-view mirror and smoothly changed lanes. "You may not have that option."

"'Walk like a man, walk like a man, walk like a man, my SUH-uh-uh-UN!'"

Prax and Juha and Chet were harmonizing, with great tunefulness, to the Four Seasons on the car radio an hour later.

"*Sing* like a man, Mr. Valli!" commanded Rennie.

Juha laughed. "Frankie Valli, Last Italian Castrato in Captivity." He looked out at the landscape, green with recent rains; they were past Monterey now, past Carmel, deep into the coastal mountains. "Why didn't we go to Tassajara, Strider? It's so peaceful and spiritual and laid-back. The Airplane were spending a couple of days there before the festival, just Zenning out."

"Yeah, but…way back in the mountains and all, no road, no electricity, so hard to get to. Plus it's all Buddhist and vegetarian. Buddhist is fine, but I'd have had to smuggle in ham sandwiches to stay alive, and I couldn't bring myself to sully the purity of the place for the sake of pork."

Rennie turned the rented blue station wagon off the famously scenic Route 1 and down a county road into the narrow, tree-hung canyon of a small river. She'd leased the car specially for this trip, since her wedding-present Corvette was too small for four people, not to mention the guitars that three of them refused to trust to their own equipment van, plus assorted personal luggage. It was the uncoolest car she'd ever seen, her own *parents* wouldn't have such a dorky car, and she was very much enjoying driving it. Cool was what you made it, not what other people said it was.

"Besides," she continued, watching for signs through the thickening trees, "Mojado Hot Springs may not be a hip Buddhist meditation center like Tassajara, but it is every bit as laid-back and groovy. It's an old Victorian resort village, owned by the woman whose house we're staying at. Owned by her husband's family, actually. If I understood her correctly, back in the reign of King Edward VII, or President Theodore Roosevelt, whomever you prefer to use as a place-time locator, it used to be a private nature spa for Episcopalian nudists. Which is just, I don't know, *weird*... But it's got the same hot-springs water as Tassajara, it's near the ocean, and, best of all, the food hall doesn't sneer at carnivores — the burgers and grilled chicken come highly recommended. And there's electricity. And a lovely tiny village. And the festival is right there. Also we have a really nice house to stay in on the neighboring land, so we don't have to camp out with the huddled masses or even stay at the resort or in the lovely tiny village."

"Are you sure this woman doesn't mind a bunch of crazy hippie musicians crashing in this really nice house of hers?" asked Chet shyly. "She doesn't even know us, only you."

"Well, technically she doesn't know me either. She's a friend of my vile mother-in-law, Marjorie. I've only met her briefly, at one of Marjorie's society bunfights. She called me at the paper the other day and said she'd heard I was going to be at Big Magic and Monterey and did I and any of my friends care to stay with her. Marjorie probably tattled on me, hoping for sympathy. But I bet she *never* thought Romilly would invite us all for a sleepover. What a surprise for her."

"Romilly Ramillies Revels," said Prax dreamily. "Never mind 'Jennifer Juniper', I could write a song about that name..."

"She's *really* Old California. The first Ramillies came to these parts with Sir Francis Drake, and the Revelses, her late husband's family, are one of those founding big-money coastal clans, like the Rindges of Malibu. What is it with all these California R's? Anyway, they've been pals with the Lacings back to the days of the great earthquake. Romilly owns most of the land around Mojado, as well as the resort itself. She's a sculptor, a very famous one, Barbara Hepworth- Henry Moore famous: she does these monolithic pieces in local stone. So she's creative, and she understands the creative mentality. Which is why she asked us to stay. Which is why I can't imagine how the hell my mother-in-law knows her. Marjorie doesn't cotton to genuine artists. They make her nervous, because they're real, and she doesn't understand. But Romilly's a *socialite* sculptor, so I guess that makes all the difference."

Prax suddenly recollected something. "Does she have a daughter our age, maybe three or four years older? You remember—there was a Becca Revels we knew in the Haight. Hung around with the Dead and Quicksilver and the Chrome Panther. Did a lot of acid. She dropped out of sight a couple of years back. Romilly isn't her mother, is she?"

"Not now, Praxie honey, please? It's too upsetting and I don't want to get into it just yet... So," Rennie continued after a strained little pause, "have we heard anything more about who's on the bill for both festivals?"

"Not so much," said Chet. "The lineups seem pretty firmed up by now. I doubt there will be any big surprises the way the fans are chattering about, like Dylan or the Beatles."

"Probably just as well," agreed Rennie. "Nobody wants a riot. It could be exciting enough with the Byrds and the Mamas and the Papas and Buffalo Springfield, some members of which may or may not draw guns on each other onstage. Which I, for one, would pay good money to see."

Juha scoffed. "Oh, now that's just mean—those bands are as good as anything out of the Bay. They're certainly a hell of a lot more commercially successful than we all are."

Rennie waved a dismissive hand. "Yeah, yeah, I know, I dig them too. A lot. But at the moment they're not exactly the happiest of campers, are they, with each

other. And the rest of the L.A. slate is a sackful of
bogus — gold-chain-and-leisure-suit acts that should have
stayed sunk in the primal ooze of the Vegas lounges
they've been dredged out of. Not what I'd call cutting-
edge rocknroll. At least the goddamn Monkees weren't
asked to play."

"You *like* the Monkees," protested Chet. "You've
even said so in print."

"I do, I have, they've got great songs. I even go-go
danced to them, back in the days when I go-go danced
for money. But I know what they are, and I know they
don't belong at something like this, and I'm glad at least
some kind of line's been drawn. The organizers have left
out enough great acts as it is."

Juha nodded knowingly. "Anything hard or dark
or progressive. That's why the *really* heavy L.A. and New
York talent didn't get asked: Love, Owen Danes and
Stoneburner, the Doors, the Mothers of Invention, Chris
Sakerhawk, the Velvet Underground. Just plastic
peacenlove, baby. Paint your face, stick some flowers in
your hair and shut the fuck up about anything
important."

"Yeah, but it's always been like that," countered
Rennie. "This whole thing went to hell as soon Papa John
promised the Monterey officials that none of the festival
profits will go to what they perceive to be wild-eyed
hippie organizations, like the Diggers and the Food
Banketeria and the Mime Troupe and the Delvers.
However much good any of those outfits could do with
the money, and they could do a lot. And what do you
want to bet that there somehow won't *be* any profits,
despite the soundtrack album, the movie and whatever
else is going in the way of dodgy side deals? No action?
Didn't think so."

"But that's how they hooked all of us in the first
place," said Prax, understandably annoyed, and still a

little stung that Rennie had curtly cut her off earlier. "Because they said it *would* be for charity. The Southland slickster weasels told us we'd be helping the community out, then they said Oops, oh no, sorry, can't do it. Really meaning won't do it. By that point it was too late for us all to pull out without looking bad."

"It was worse than that," said Rennie gloomily. "John Phillips is a used-car salesman who didn't so much persuade the burghers of Monterey to let him throw a festival in their town as cogently snake-oil them. He totally suckered Monterey in — even the mayor fell for it, a sweet old granny named Minnie Coyle, how's that for a name of fine bourgeois respectability — just as he suckered the San Francisco bands in."

Chet laughed. "Gotta admire his bloody style, though."

"Oh, I do, I do. I've always admired pirates and highwaymen and robber barons. I just don't want them running my world. And without the rich-hippie clothes and the beads and the beard and the dope and that stupid fur hat, and of course the majorly great songs he's written, Phillips is just That Man Behind the Curtain. Fortunately, people *do* pay attention, and they are well aware he's hardly Oz, the Great and Powerful. Too bad not enough of them realized it sooner."

"So that's why this Big Magic thing was put together."

"You bet," said Rennie, a little distracted, looking for the entrance to the Revels estate among the trees that lined the road. "To counter the evil fu, as perceived, of commercial, soulless Monterey. The Delvers, who are as we all know the Diggers' radical younger siblings, persuaded Romilly to let Big Magic use her land. Then Monterey got so big so fast that it somehow became impossible for the bands to get paid, gosh, imagine that, what a surprise, and they would just have to do it for free and for love. Even though the movie and TV rights were bought by ABC. For two hundred fifty thou. But somehow the bands still have to work free for nothing. For the purity of it all." She laughed suddenly. "I heard Chuck Berry turned Phillips and Adler down flat; said the only charity *he* played for was Chuck Berry. Too bad more of you guys didn't take Charles's line from the start."

Prax sighed. "The starving artists are always the ones who get stuck picking up the tab. But you never know. Maybe some of the right charities will get some decent money out of it, somehow."

"And maybe teensy baby bunnies will fly out of my pink and heart-shaped ass."

"Dill wasn't very happy that we're playing," remarked Chet, peering out the window at the clear bubbling river in its rocky bed. "But we outvoted him. We *want* to be there. In spite of all the politics and bollockses. We figured it was more important to be heard in front of a major audience at Monterey—not just fans, all those record company execs and managers too—than to get paid a few hundred bucks."

"And you were quite right," Rennie told him fondly. "I know that Dill, being your manager, has your best interests at heart, and I'd never gainsay him without good cause, but you guys really, *really* need to play there and I'm so glad you are. This trip's going to be way bigger and more important than anyone thinks."

"And Big Magic? Dill gave us orders that we're not to do an impromptu guest shot as a group, though he said he doesn't mind if we jam as individuals or sit in with other bands."

"And Dill is quite correct: mustn't dilute the impact of your big Monterey debut. But don't be regretting Tassajara, Juha, we'll get all the soaks we want at Mojado. Us and everybody else. Hot springs all over the place. Meditation possibilities up the wazoo. That was one of the reasons why the Delvers went to Romilly when they started looking around for a place they could set up at on such short notice. Plus…her daughter Becca belonged to the Delvers. That's why she decided, in the end, to let them use her land."

Prax glanced warily at Rennie, wondering if she'd get snapped at again, but figured since her friend had spoken it was okay for her to speak too.

"So we do know her. Becca."

Rennie sighed and nodded. "Yeah, we know her. Or we did. I'm not sure that anyone really knows her anymore. Maybe not even her mother." She geared down to negotiate a hill that was suddenly right there in the middle of the road. "Anyway, we're only going to stay at Waterhall, that's the name of the estate, for the Big Magic nights, before we move over to Monterey. Becca lives there now, with her mother, but we probably won't see very much of her."

"Why not?" asked Chet.

"Very sad." Rennie slowed down to a crawl, turning right at a stone gatepost and easing the car onto a gravel road between high hedges, apparently more willing to discuss Becca now that she was on Revels home turf. "She got her brains fried on bad LSD, and she just—was gone. Away with the fairies. Maybe she'll get some of her neurons back one day. So much for the charming hippie fiction that there are no acid casualties."

The others in the car looked sharply at her, so savage had been her tone, but she kept her eyes on the road.

"So—Big Magic is designed to be Monterey counter-programming," said Prax presently, to change the subject again. "Just not on the same nights."

"Exactly. Not even the Power to the People people want to miss hearing the big names playing

Monterey. So Monterey Pop will run Friday through Sunday night. Big Magic, 'the People's Monterey Music Festival' "—Rennie took both hands off the steering wheel to make sarcastic air quotes—"starts Monday afternoon and finishes up Wednesday night. That gives everybody Thursday free, to make the great tribal migration over to Monterey."

"Whatever," said Chet, letting one of his remaining Irishisms loose. "Big Magic's got a very, ah, *eclectic* roster, though."

"Gonna be great!" Rennie crowed jubilantly. "Among numerous others, there's Bosom Serpent, Theodolite, your folkie fellow countryman Finn Hanley, Stoneburner, my old college pals Powderhouse Road, the Screaming Prawns, that performance-art chick Decima Dix, the one who gets naked and covers herself in gold stars, some Beat poets from New York, this crazy writer-folksinger from Carmel who's married to Joan Baez's sister. And on and on. Not to mention our favorite nut jobs Cold Fire. Who weren't invited to play at Monterey—apparently their musical and/or personal vibe isn't peaceandlovey enough."

Prax snorted. "Nor have they been known to ass-kiss any of the festival organizers, neither publicly nor privately."

"Also their singer is borderline psychotic, and maybe not even borderline. But they're the *headliners* at Big Magic..." Juha's voice trailed off wistfully, and Rennie threw him a quick reassuring smile over her shoulder.

"Don't you worry, axeman. Even though you'll be in a middle-of-the-program slot at Monterey and you could have headlined Big Magic yourselves, you're still better off. I promise. Nobody knows for sure how big this Monterey thing is really going to be. But, and you heard it here first, I say it's going to be *huge*, and I also say it's going to be huge for you guys personally. And that's not just hype. 'Cause as you know I never do hype."

"Didn't you say they're bringing a bunch of Brits over too?" said Chet, not concealing his pleasure at Rennie's words.

"Some. Though not the Beatles, not the Stones, not Cream, not the Budgies, not the Kinks, not Donovan. Don and the Stones couldn't get visas — drug problems, of course. Like Ned Raven and half of Bluesnroyals."

Prax nodded. "And the Beatles just weren't into it, and Cream's manager decided this little rustic outdoor gig wasn't the kind of American splash Cream's hyper-super-duper importance deserved. The Kinks apparently had issues with the music union."

"And the Budgies, being disassembled, were right out," added Juha. "Though there's been talk that some Budgies and Fabs are planning to turn up on their own, sub rosa."

"Or sotto voce." Rennie rolled her eyes. "Ned seemed to be pretty sure that Graham Sonnet and Prue Vye would put in an appearance, though, and I'd *really* like to meet them, now that Gray's an ex-Budgie and he and Prunella have their own band. Anyway, all the Beatle teasetalk is just foreplay from the festival publicist, that sweetie Derek Taylor, to get yet more press and attention. And since Derek handled the lovable moptops for a good long while, and is helping to organize this little bash, people are tending to believe him."

"So?" Prax kicked the back of the seat. "Who else? Come on, come on! I didn't bother reading your stories, since there was nothing in them about us."

"If you didn't read them, how do you know there was nothing about you? Well — Basil Potter and Roger Hazlitt are definitely opening Friday night."

Prax hooted joyfully. "Baz and Haz! Oho, you'd better steer clear of *them*, missy! I know you've been

friends for years, but after the review you gave their last
album? Watch that pretty little back of yours."

"They're still my friends," said Rennie
defensively. "I still love them. They still love me."

Juha shook his head, grinning. "Man, if that's the
way you write about someone you love, we'd better be
careful *we* never put out an album you don't like. You
were really rough on them."

"Well, it's the spouting whale that gets the
harpoon. And if the whale spouts badly, you can't expect
me not to mention it. Or not to use it as a harpoon,
either."

"Aye, Queequeg, but wham, right between the
eyes?"

"I wasn't trying to hurt them, I was trying to get
their *attention*… They'd gotten sloppy and lazy on that
album, the one before it too, and I was just pointing that
out. More in sorrow than in anger. 'Sides, they're artists;
they already know. I wasn't telling them anything they
weren't aware of. And I wouldn't be so rough on them if
I didn't love their music so much."

"I hear that they're not happy with their contract
and their label, not to mention their label president," said
Juha. "And who could blame them? Except for the head
of a&r, Elk Bannerman, and he's supposed to be mob
even though he's straighter to deal with than all the rest
of them put together, Rainshadow is a gang of uncool
pirates, and that Pierce Hill is a prize phony. Do you
know, he's started calling himself El Magnifico? And he's
not being ironic, either; he thinks he deserves it. Just
because he's the label founder and president. And he
makes his staff call him that as well. What a jackass. Hey,
I wonder if maybe Baz and Haz are trying to tank
deliberately, so he'll dump them and they'll be free."

"I'd hate to think that of any artist," responded
Rennie with some primness, and pulled up with a

flourish at the end of the long, long driveway, in front of a long, low house. "Well, we're here. Put on your shoes and clean up whatever mess you've made. Don't make me come back there."

Chapter 4

POISED BETWEEN THE RIVAL BEAUTIES of Big Sur and Monterey, the tiny and madly picturesque village of Mojado Hot Springs sits in a leafy valley—a valley that opens on to grasslands sweeping down to cliffs rising sheer out of the Pacific. The coast highway bends briefly inland here, and between the Santa Juana mountains and the ocean, a redwood-spired canyon, with the small, lively Mojado River running through, holds the series of waterfalls and cascades and hot pools that gives the place its fame and its name.

Mojado has been a spa resort since the nineteenth century. The village boasts everything you could ask for in a village of that sort: gingerbread-trimmed hotels; old-fashioned shops lining the two-street business district; a stone church lifting its steeple against a redwood frieze. The resort itself, called, simply, The Springs, consists of a bunch of romantic period wooden structures: a bandstand, a pier jutting out into the lake, two hotels, some enchanting guest cottages and bungalows and gazebos, a pair of dining halls and meeting halls that look like mini-castles — the compleat Victorian trip.

Despite the turn-of-the-century Episcopalian nudists Rennie had uneasily wondered at, Mojado's day of glory, such as it had been, was long past, and the weathered buildings reflected the neglect; but when the hippies started discovering groovy natural things and meditation, not to mention the seductive combination of the two, Mojado, surprised, had found itself rejuvenated, a queen once again among resorts, or at least a duchess.

As had been pointed out, the other rural retreats in the neighborhood sanctimoniously didn't allow things like dope or music or meat or sex or electricity — a pseudo-pious attitude Rennie had no respect for whatsoever. Hey, if you can't keep your precious spiritual purity intact with fleshpot temptations besetting you on every side, then you weren't really ever all that pure to begin with, were you? No, you weren't. And so, allowing all those things and many more, Mojado had happily re-entered the hot-springs mainstream.

Much to the residents' chagrin: they'd gotten used to the unbroken peace and quiet, and even such temporarily increased hubbub as this Big Magic thing deeply annoyed them. But Romilly Ramillies Revels ruled everything between Mount Mojado and the sea, and her word in those parts was law. Her late husband's family had been in possession of that particular chunk of California coast for over two hundred years, and the main house — the original was long gone — bore witness to that dominion: a sprawling old dwelling contoured to the roll of the land.

Romilly had added on a wing or two, tucked into the blanketing stands of cypresses, pines and coast redwoods, and with her sculptor's eye had contrived to not only harmoniously blend it with the old but somehow at the same time make it look completely new and fresh. Behind the house, in a dip of lawn that ran up to the redwood groves, was an extensive sculpture garden full of her work: massive, graceful monoliths in various kinds of native California stone, looking as if they'd grown there, organic shapes of shell and wave and tree.

Most of the Big Magic performers were staying on the actual festival site at The Springs, the resort proper, on the other side of the valley from Romilly's woods. Of course, the best on-site rooms had been reserved for the performers and for the people who could afford them — who were not always the same. Others, already booked into motels up at Monterey and Carmel, or in the inns of Mojado village, would be commuting; but most of the audience here was camping out.

It was a charming place, though the festival accommodations would hardly suffice to shelter the multitudes who were en route — possibly as many as five thousand coming to Big Magic, which would balloon to at least ten times as many on the last night of Monterey. Clusters of small cottages, hidden in the trees and nestled against the hillside, looked as if they'd grown there, as if hobbits had built them. The rest of the resort was thousands of acres of open land and wooded hills, picture-perfect for pitching tents. The village too was prepared to happily receive guests, instead of forming a shield-wall to repel invaders, as some residents had darkly suggested.

Before its moment, Mojado drowsed; and, miles away to the north, Monterey heard the wake-up call, and stirred in uneasy slumber.

Rennie pulled up in the drive, having edged to the shoulder to let a snappy little red Triumph blast by, and got out of the car, drawing in a deep delighted breath of the cool air. While the others hefted the bags and guitar cases, a bit overawed by the big house as well as by the vast mountainy silence, broken only by a stream burbling past a few yards away, Rennie went up the broad stone terrace steps to meet the tall, elegant woman who stood there awaiting them.

"Welcome to Waterhall," the woman said, holding out both hands. "You're Rennie, of course; we've met a time or two. Let me look at you, lovely girl. Marjorie's spoken of you often."

"Mrs. Revels, thank you, how nice to meet you again. Yes, I'm sure she has."

Romilly Ramillies laughed heartily, and her blunt-cut, gray-blond hair swung as she did so.

"It's 'Romilly', dear child, and you do understand where she's coming from."

"I do indeed. She thought she was getting a nice, biddable lass that she could recruit into the Lacing ranks and overawe into robotic Junior League submission. She was dying to go all Pacific Heights Henry Higgins on my little middle-class New York behind, and teach me the fine points of San Francisco high society."

"And you had contempt for that."

"Not at all. It's only those who can't get into society who have contempt for it, as some cleverdick person once said. No, I just thought it was completely irrelevant—to me and to what I wanted. But let's not get into that now," she added, as the others came shyly up the steps to the terrace, lugging the bags and guitars, which they didn't want to leave out overnight in the damp.

As she performed the introductions, watching their hostess greet Prax, Chet and Juha with an artist-to-artist warmth that put them instantly at their ease, Rennie found herself wondering just how Mrs. Ramillies-Revels had managed to fish that little miniconfession out of her, and also thinking that if Marjorie Lacing had been

this woman instead of the woman that she was, how
much easier so many things in both their lives might
have been. And now that she thought of it, for that
matter, how in seven different sorts of hell had Romilly
and Motherdear ever managed to become friends in the
first place? Perhaps she'd find out later. And Becca—
Well, maybe she'd find out about that later too.

Everyone was soon settled in their rooms, in one of the
newer wings that reached deep into the redwoods—
Rennie with Chet, Prax with Juha. The other three
members of Evenor—keyboard player Dainis Hood,
drummer Jack Paris and bassist Bardo (just Bardo)—had
for reasons of their own declined Romilly's kind
invitation, preferring to fend for themselves. Bardo, at
least, planned to camp out; the others were staying in one
of the hotels.

In the car on the way down, the four had
wondered a bit uneasily about how prudish their hostess
might be, and had reluctantly prepared themselves to
share bedrooms girl-girl and boy-boy. But as Romilly
considered their sleeping arrangements to be absolutely
none of her business, it turned out not to be a problem.
She had simply shown them serenely to a wingful of
guestrooms and left them to sort it out. And the rooms
were as lovely as the house that held them: spacious
chambers with big windows both stained-glassed and
crystal-clear, clean-lined furniture, comfortable natural
fibers, wide-planked floors.

Unpacking and showering before dinner, Rennie
put on a long Moroccan caftan and went downstairs to
meet her hostess in a high-raftered living room graced by
a travertine fireplace—another Ramillies creation. No one
else was there yet, Rennie being pathologically early as
usual, and Romilly suggested they go outside to walk for
a while in the sculpture garden.

Occupying a beautifully landscaped twenty acres of the vast Revels estate, overlooking the Pacific and crossed by the tumbling stream that fell over the cliffs to the sea and gave the house its name, the sculpture garden was filled, though not the slightest bit overcrowded, with five decades of Romilly's work: big, even monumental, abstract and representational shapes done in native stone like Sierra Nevada granite or the local coast serpentine. One could walk by, or even through, a massive slab like a triumphal arch made of melted ice cream, modernistic, completely pleasing, and then come slap up against a classical something that looked as if it had been carved by the guy who invented Corinthian columns—and the contrast was perfect and harmonious. Clearly, Romilly believed in mixing her sculptural metaphors.

They discussed the pieces as they strolled through the garden, and Rennie learned much, not just about sculpture; apparently her hostess's philosophy about art, and specifically about *her* art, extended deep into her life. At Rennie's timid request, Romilly, roaring with laughter, detailed her long and oddball friendship with Marjorie Lacing, and Rennie, considerably more at ease, reciprocated with the tale of how she'd ended up a Lacing herself, and how she wasn't one anymore except in name.

As they walked back to the house, Rennie remembered something. "Does your family live here with you? We passed a little red sports car driving out when we were coming in."

"Two of my children do. My youngest, Rebecca. I believe you know her? She lives here now, with me."

Her tone was guarded, as if she was unsure exactly how much Rennie knew. But Rennie merely nodded, and Romilly went on, sounding relieved.

"And my oldest, Simon, lives here too, though he spends most of his time over at the resort, which he runs with the help of his wife and my college-age grandkids. My other two children live in New York. But my goddaughter and her husband are visiting, up from L.A.; they're the ones you saw leaving in the Triumph. You'll meet them at dinner. Brandi Storey and Danny Marron."

Rennie turned to look at her. "I know those names?"

"Probably. Brandi's father runs Bluewater Studios."

"Of course, Brandon Storey. Big successful movie mogul. Brandi's a model, I remember now, and Danny does experimental films and documentaries. He did that one on Beat poets a few years back; I saw it when I was still in college."

Not for an instant was it lost on Romilly that Rennie diplomatically offered no opinion of Danny Marron's cinematic work, and she smiled a small little smile.

"Brandi's very lovely, and, yes, a model—well, of sorts. When she works at all. And Danny's quite—artistic. Unfortunately, he never seems to pick commercially viable topics."

Well, that's putting it mildly... "Is that why he's here? To film Big Magic?"

"Yes, exactly. Brandon was beginning to talk about lowering the cinematic boom. No more money for Danny's experimental stuff, it never paid off critically; and no more money for his 'commercial' movies, they never paid off financially. Always some excuse: bad scripts, worse actors, biased critics, Philistine audiences. Then, when Danny heard about the festival at Monterey—some of his L.A. pals are involved in putting it on—he proposed filming the whole three days as a documentary with music. Videotaping it, rather; a very new process, which he claims he can do a lot more with."

"But I thought that D. A. Pennebaker was—"

Romilly nodded. "That's the problem. Danny couldn't get the access he'd told Brandon he could get because Pennebaker's team had already been given sole filming rights to the music, so when he heard about the plan for Big Magic right here at Mojado he re-ran the pitch. Music from Big Magic, 'color' from Monterey. A cinematic tone poem to the area and the people who come here or live here. In the end, Brandon would do almost anything to keep his daughter happy, so he gave the greenlight."

"And the greenbacks."

The older woman nodded again. "Danny's reasoning was that Big Magic will be full of all sorts of new and happening musical acts that no one's ever seen or imagined, much purer and finer than the sell-out commercial trash appearing at Monterey, and he'll be the one to bring them to the world through his ground-breaking documentary, thus making all their names and his too. Between you and me, I'm thinking not so much. In any case, Brandon went for it. So we'll see."

She looked at Rennie, face suddenly somber. "I expect you're wondering about Becca, and you're much too polite to ask. No, no, it's only natural you'd be curious. You knew her. Come, sit with me. We still have a few minutes before dinner."

She took Rennie's arm and headed them both over to a giant wodge of pink rhyolite, which was both a sculpture and a surprisingly comfortable seat, still warm from the late-afternoon sun.

"Five years ago, Rebecca was very much in love with Danny Marron," she said presently into the deep silence, and Rennie, who had been checking out the far side of the piece, peered around in surprise. "When she was a college senior at USC and Danny was a teaching assistant in the cinema department, they met and fell in love, or at least my daughter did. He got her on acid—he was an early apostle of LSD, which was still legal in those days, and a close friend of Dr. Timothy Leary—then he dumped her to marry Brandi Storey, Becca's roommate and best friend. My daughter was devastated. She moved to New York for a while, to try to get away from it, living with my other two children, her brother Tobias and sister Marietta, but that didn't—work out."

Rennie heard the subtext: Becca was too heavy into the drug scene by then, and Marietta and Tobias couldn't control her.

"Then when everything started up in San Francisco," said Romilly with great precision of tone, "she came home. I bought her a little place on Russian Hill, and she was fine for a while, but pretty soon it deteriorated into a crash pad. Drugs and whores and people shooting up heroin—it was terrible. Then she ran away and lived on the street in the Haight, dropping LSD like aspirin. Thank God she got taken in by the Delvers. At least they made sure she was clean and fed and sheltered, and they let us know where she was. Simon and I were desperately grateful, and gave the group substantial support and funds; Rebecca wasn't the only runaway they helped, and they weren't doing it to get paid. I don't know why she let *them* care for her, and not her own flesh and blood. But she accepted their help where she wouldn't take ours. Maybe it was cleaner help. I don't know. At last we managed to persuade her to come home, and she's been here with us ever since."

"But Brandi—"

"—is my goddaughter, as I said. The Revelses and the Storeys have been friends for many years; Brandon and Geoffrey, my late husband, had known each other since childhood, and the Storeys still have a weekend house in the Carmel Highlands. But the marriage created a certain constraint on both sides, to say the least." Her forced smile was distressing to see. "My other children and Geoff were furious, and so was Brandon, whose wife Sylvia had died when Brandi was thirteen; I was furious too, but I didn't want the families split because of it, and we tried to muddle through. Brandi is a spoiled little brat, and I say so who love her—charming and lovely, but shallow and totally wrapped up in herself. Even so, she's passionately loyal to the people she cares about— and she does truly care about some people. Including Becca, though it's sometimes hard to believe. Still, Brandi wanted very much to marry Danny, and, being a spoiled brat, as I've said, she got her way."

"Does she know—" began Rennie delicately.

"What Danny did to Rebecca? No. I've never told her, and I'm quite sure no one else has either. Brandon might have, hoping to keep her from marrying so very unsuitably"—for the first time, her voice carried a faint but unmistakable echo of Marjorie Lacing, and Rennie grinned privately—"but that would have been a tactic of last resort. And since they did marry, obviously Brandon couldn't bring himself to tell her. Certainly the news wouldn't have come from Danny. If Brandi did know, I don't know what she'd do—she loves Becca like a sister. I'm well aware that the prevailing wisdom is that LSD can't hurt you, that it doesn't lead to harder stuff, and by and large that's true. But speed and coke and heroin didn't do this to her. Acid did. I know what you're thinking," she added, "and are much too kind to say— that my daughter should bear a large part of the blame herself. Or that I should; I could have protected her better. And you're right to think so. But Rebecca doesn't often remember about Danny. Or about other things either. As you'll see. I just wanted to warn you. She's not the Becca you used to know."

At seven, Waterhall's houseguests assembled outside, on a torch-lit flagstone terrace overlooking the sculpture garden and shaded by jacarandas. Romilly introduced everyone to her eldest offspring, Simon, who was in charge of The Springs and thus of Big Magic as well: a slim, dark-haired man of middle height, in his early forties, resembling his mother only in the charm department but according to Romilly the living print of his father. He was affable, very, though a little preoccupied; whether that was due to concern about the festival or concern about his sister, who had remained in her rooms all day, Rennie wasn't sure, but he introduced them in turn to his wife, Chloe, explaining that their two kids had elected to eat at the resort with college friends who had come for the festival, rather than dine with their boring old family.

The Marrons had finally put in a leisurely appearance, returning from wherever they'd driven off to earlier—lunch in Big Sur, as it turned out—and greeted everyone overenthusiastically.

Nobody was impressed in the slightest, and they let their unimpressment show. Danny was a typical Hollywood sleazebag with a leathery, fake-looking tan and carefully styled poodle-curly black hair, his weirdly wide chin and mouth giving him the grin of a hammerhead shark hoping to make new friends. While Brandi was a sharp-nosed reddish-blonde in Rive Gauche faux-hippie clothes, spaniel-friendly and society-condescending at the same time—quite a trick. Rennie disliked them both on sight, intensely, but she was a guest here and they were family so she kept her mouth shut, or else firmly attached to her gin and tonic.

Two more guests were expected momentarily, Romilly explained to the group, so they'd just have drinks out on the terrace until they arrived and then go in to dinner, as it was too cool to eat outdoors. The ice hadn't melted in their glasses before a car pulled up in front of the house and two figures hurried up the terrace steps.

"Marcus!" said Romilly delightedly, turning to look. "Come and give me a kiss, dear boy, it's been much too long."

Rennie paused, stricken, still clutching her g&t, and turned to look, only to have her worst fears confirmed. How many people in this part of California and these social circles were named Marcus, after all? She watched stonily as Marcus Dorner introduced his friend Brent Gilmore to Romilly and to the company at large, and then Romilly led them all inside to the dining room on the other side of the terrace doors.

"Marjorie told me to ring up and say hello, as long as I was going to be in the neighborhood," he said in an apologetic undertone as they sat down at the candle-lit table, taking the place to Rennie's left at Romilly's direction. "And then of course I got invited to dinner. Don't sulk. I couldn't say no."

"Well, strictly speaking, you could have." Rennie picked up her fish fork and knife and attended to some fresh-caught local halibut, ignoring both Prax's mocking grin beside her to the right and Chet's possessive glower across the table. "So, this Brent is the guy you're down here to help out? He seems really nice."

Marcus smiled and passed the rolls. "He's from New Jersey originally. Moved out here to be near family and friends. We were probies together in cop school. We stayed friends through our various postings; then, as I believe I told you, he started to feel burned out in the city and moved down here a couple of years ago to be a deputy sheriff. He's a lot happier."

"Well, who wouldn't be?"

As they moved on to the next course, there was a movement at the dining-room doors, a flash like a fawn in a thicket. Rennie looked up to see a slight girl with tangled chestnut hair and lightly freckled skin, wearing no shoes and a flowered-silk frock, leaning on the doorframe. Rennie opened her mouth to speak, to greet the newcomer by her name, with gladness, but Romilly had turned and was calling the girl in, coaxing her like a swallow to the nest.

"Sweetheart, I'm so happy you decided to join us tonight," she said, smiling lovingly. "What a pretty dress you have on, too—come and say hello to our guests."

Rebecca Revels inched forward along the wall, soberly studying the faces of the guests at the table, one by one, but she didn't greet any of them. When her glance got to Rennie and Prax, though, her face suddenly lighted with joy, and she came forward all in a rush.

"Oh, you're here! You came! I knew you would!" she said happily, hugging them, her eyes moving back and forth between them both, and promptly launched into a torrent of eager speech.

Rennie deliberately turned her gaze to where Danny Marron sat beside his wife, Brandi Storey. Brandi was looking upon Becca with all the caring affection of a sister, anxious that she not stress herself; Danny, on the other hand, was staring intently at his plate. Rennie kept her gaze on him, and pretty soon, feeling her attention like a hot needle pushed between his eyes, he looked up at her. Defiant, guilty, scarlet-faced, ashamed—as well he should be.

But Becca was still standing there, prattling excitedly. Romilly smiled, a little strained.

"Rebecca, sit across the table, over there, darling, we left you a place next to your brother. No, dear, there's no room between Rennie and Prax. You can sit and talk with them after dinner."

Rennie felt Becca shut down instantly, but the girl yielded to her mother's wishes and silently circled the table, to sit across from Prax; Simon gave her a little hug as she sat down, and Chloe cast a concerned glance at her sister-in-law. Rennie threw Romilly a frowning look—what the hell difference did it make, they could easily have squeezed Becca in if that made her happy—but Romilly nodded approvingly, and returned to her conversation with Simon and Brent.

After dinner, everyone withdrew to the sitting room, a warm, cozy space with a glassed-in porch overlooking the stream, filled with comfortable furniture—not 'decorated', just pleasant and obviously well used. Becca, having been denied at table, immediately threaded her arms through those of Prax and Rennie, and steered them toward a sofa before her mother could command otherwise. Rennie glanced swiftly at Romilly, but her hostess just smiled at her encouragingly, and turned aside to talk with her other guests.

"That wasn't so bad," said Rennie gamely, up in her bedroom before retiring. "No, it really wasn't. In spite of Marcus showing up."

She and Prax were conversing through the open door into Prax's room; each bedroom had its own bath, but the two rooms also intercommunicated. Rennie had just gotten out of the glass-walled shower that faced into the redwood grove, and now, wrapped in a big soft bath towel, she was combing out her hair and talking to her friend.

"No, it wasn't so bad at all…and oh, to see Becca again, and to talk to her…" Prax's eyes were bright with unshed tears, sad and happy together.

"She looks healthy," offered Rennie. "Healthi*er*… And she seemed so glad to see us."

"Yes, and did you see how pleased Romilly and Simon were? That Becca knew us and could talk to us?"

"That she even came in to dinner at all. I hope the festival doesn't freak her out too much," said Rennie with sudden concern. "The people, the noise…"

"Romilly wouldn't have let it happen if she thought it would upset her. I'm thinking maybe she's hoping the music will be good for her."

Rennie looked suddenly bleak. "She always loved the music as much as we do. Pity we can't take her over to Monterey with us: she was so tight with the bands in the Haight, before."

Before. Before Danny Marron messed her up on crappy acid and then dumped her and married her best friend and had the gall to keep coming here and reminding her. Though she didn't remember, really, all that often, or at all, maybe, and that might or might not be a mercy. But other people did…

"I doubt Romilly would let us," said Prax sadly. "She'd be too worried that Becca would freak. And maybe she would. But we could get some of the guys over here to see her. Jerry and Pigpen would come for sure, maybe Tansy and Bruno, a few of the others."

"We could ask."

Chet, toweled up after his own shower, water still gleaming on his bare skin, came up behind Rennie and put his arms around her, regarding Prax pointedly, chin resting on the top of Rennie's head.

"Okay, Irish, I get the message," said Prax, laughing, and closed the connecting door.

Big Magic

Chapter 5

Monday morning, June 12

BIG MAGIC'S OPENING DAY. Though the program wouldn't get seriously going until noon, there were already small musical knots strewn across the landscape: people playing, people digging the playing — or digging the players. Most of the musicians had been here for a day or two, like Rennie and her friends, showing up early to enjoy the hot springs and some kickback time before the gig. Already there had been a bit of friction between the factions: the Power to the People hippie-fascist organizers; the Big Magic artists; and the smug Monterey-bound musicians who were here merely to cop some vibes and lord it over the peons. But for the most part the scene was pleasant and calm.

Early risers both, Rennie and Prax came walking

barefoot across the dew-soaked morning grass from Waterhall, shoes in hand and smiles on their faces. They were headed to the resort café, preferring superlatively grilled hamburgers on soft toasted rolls to the nice healthy breakfast gracing Romilly's table.

As they came down the slope, Prax took a deep breath of the sea-cooled air and looked around, and continued their bedtime conversation of the night before.

"It was so nice to see Becca again. Too bad Danny and Brandi were there. Bit of a strain in the room."

Rennie nodded. "I just wish we—could have *done* something for her."

Prax slipped her arm around Rennie's shoulders, squeezed. "Honey, last night? I think maybe we did. She talked. She laughed. She understood. She *remembered*. She sat and chattered away to us nonstop for three hours after dinner. She was like her old self. Even Romilly said so. We were there, and she knew us, and she was happy to see us. That's so much better than it could have been. Maybe that's as good as it can get, with her."

She waved her arm across the landscape and changed the subject. "Look at them out there all biblical and Bedouin-ish—they're settled in for a week at least. I bet some would stay all summer if Romilly would let them."

Rennie allowed the subject to be changed, and looked. "Well, they'll have to clear out on Thursday if they want to make the scene at Monterey, which even the purity Nazis who organized this little here–now blast want to do. Probably a lot of the camping contingent couldn't care less about Monterey and will stay put, but by Wednesday midnight Big Magic is done. Coaches back into pumpkins. Come Thursday morning, everybody except the diehards will be lemming-ing over to Monterey. Including us. Oh, God, Praxie, don't look, quick, let's try to make it to those trees before he sees us."

Too late. A young man was running toward them, waving wildly. He was small, slight, barefoot, with long brown hair and a touchingly eager smile on his extremely pretty face.

"Who's this, then?" asked Prax as they waited for him to come up. "Someone you know? Someone crazy and weird?"

"All those things. His name is Adam Santa Monica. Don't tell me you've never met?" At Prax's bewildered headshake: "Oh, Lord. He's this demented groupie kid who thinks he's the bastard offspring of Elvis Presley and Jacqueline Bouvier. Because they had an affair, you know, El and Jacks, and he was the happy result, but of course he could never be openly acknowledged, since Jackie was going to marry J.F.K. So his mother abandoned him as a newborn, in a shopping bag at the Wilshire Boulevard I. Magnin in L.A.—on one of her frequent trips there, no doubt. That's the usual story, though sometimes it's other places he was abandoned: in a large handbag in the powder room at the Beverly Hills Hotel, in a blanket under a table at the Brown Derby. It changes like that."

"I see."

"No, I don't think you do, my little woodpigeon, not entirely. He *was* abandoned in a shopping bag, the poor kid. Just not by Jackie. So one can understand why he is the way he is. I guess I'm lucky he's not claiming *I'm* his mother... Anyway, I have been happily informed that he was finally made legitimate when Jackie married Elvis after J.F.K. was killed. Of course, since Adam was born in June 1951, El would have had to sire him at, let's see now, age fifteen—precocious but possible—and Jackie, age twenty-three, had just met Jack Kennedy for the first time the month before. I did some research. So it's fairly unlikely that she was eight months preggers by Presley or anyone else at the moment—surely Jack would have noticed. And if she ever does remarry I somehow doubt it will be to Elvis. Still, he *is* the King, and king trumps president. But anything's possible, especially in Tupelo. Or Back Bay Boston. Which are not as unalike as people in both places care to think."

"So, crazy as a bedbug."

"Pretty much. Before you ask, I have *no* idea what his real name or story is. Lately he's been hanging around Chris Sakerhawk, who's about ready to kill him, but there doesn't seem to be any agenda there—he's not claiming Chris as his long-lost bastard half-brother or anything. Anyway, I met Adam backstage at the Avalon a few months ago and made the mistake of being nice to him, which is how I found out all this stuff, and now he won't leave me alone. Why I seem to attract delusional psychotics, I haven't the foggiest. Not you, of course. Don't laugh at him, though," she added.

Prax looked wounded. "I would *never*."

Adam Santa Monica came hurrying up the slope to them, smiling eagerly. "Oh wow, Rennie Stride! Hi, I haven't seen you for weeks, so cool you're here—and Prax McKenna, groovy!"

They took him to the resort's terrace café and fed him, because he had no money and he looked hungry and they felt sorry for him. But charity and patience only extended so far, especially when he started bugging Rennie over the burgers and lemonade.

"I've told you before, Adam, I have *no* pull in Memphis and I absolutely can*not* get you in at Graceland to see Elvis."

"My father," explained Adam proudly to a politely nodding Prax, whose perfect deadpan was an achievement in itself. "My mother, Mrs. Jacqueline Bouvier-Presley, abandoned me in the ladies' dressing room at the I. Magnin in Beverly Hills. She never came out to California, so she thought that would be the best thing to do—no one would recognize her if they saw her leaving me there."

"Good thinking."

"She's smart as well as beautiful, right? No wonder my dad fell in love with her. They were married a year after the assassination, you know, so I'm their legitimate son now."

At last they escaped, Prax pleading a splitting headache and Rennie an emergency trip to the village to buy aspirins for her. Prax made a clean getaway, but Rennie found herself immediately importuned by Adam for a lift into town and back, like a happy floppy retriever puppy longing to go car-car, and she gave in with a better grace than she might have expected.

From the resort, it was a mere five-minute drive into Mojado village. Parking on the more 'main' street of the two small existing ones, Rennie left Adam sitting in the car with his little backpack while she ran into the drugstore, where she noticed Brandi Marron perusing mascara and successfully dodged down another aisle, and he was still there when she came out of the neighboring sporting goods store, suppliers of local campers and hikers, twenty minutes later.

Approaching the station wagon, Rennie watched him covertly for a minute, from under the shady concealment of the soda-fountain shop awning: he was humming happily to himself, checking out the action on the street, and she felt a sudden pang.

How many kids were there like him around the scene? Okay, probably not many others who believed they had the fairytale ancestry of a hidden prince—the secret son of the Queen of Camelot and the King of Rocknroll—but still there were hundreds, thousands, maybe hundreds of thousands, of sad, wounded, innocent souls that nobody cared enough about to try to fix. Or knew how to fix. Or even knew about at all. She herself had never come close to such a place, thank God, but she knew plenty who had — she'd seen one of the luckier ones only last night.

She pulled the car door open and got behind the wheel. "Adam. Here."

'Here' was a shopping bag containing a pair of hemp-and-leather sandals, three heavy-duty cotton t-shirts, a pullover sweater, half a dozen pairs of thick, soft socks, a hooded windbreaker, a red-and-black flannel lumberjack shirt, a waterproof poncho, a bucket rainhat, a pair of sunglasses and, folded inside the jacket pocket, two twenty-dollar bills. And a sleeping bag, extra-thick and warm, which she tossed into the back seat. Everything she could think of, in a hurry, that he might need. It was a lot of stuff, but it hadn't cost that much, and even if it had, still it was money well spent; at least her conscience would be clear. She couldn't do anything for those other kids, or even for Becca, but she could help Adam out a bit…

"It's going to be cold tonight, maybe rainy. You need something on your feet. And on the rest of you. I don't want to hear about you freezing to death sleeping outside, so look around for a dorm tent — the resort put up a bunch for campers who don't have tents of their own. Or find somebody to crash with. And buy yourself something to eat, for God's sake, will you? Don't spend the money on dope, and don't sell the stuff to *buy* dope, either."

He thanked her all the way back to The Springs, putting on the new sandals, exclaiming over the flannel shirt and the shades, happily cramming the things she'd bought him into his backpack, asking if he could keep the shopping bag, faithfully promising he'd buy food, not acid, with the money — those big thick burgers at the café were only fifty cents, even cheaper ones at the soda fountain, he could eat here and for the next two weeks back in town and still maybe buy a little pot, was that okay, if he did that? — and Rennie said Yes of course you're so welcome Adam to everything.

She dropped him off at the terrace where they'd breakfasted earlier. She had a previously scheduled interview, and now she pulled away, intending to drive the few hundred yards down to the resort cottages rather than return with the car to Waterhall and walk all the way back.

When she glanced in the rear-view mirror, she saw Adam, who was sitting again at the little table where they'd breakfasted, the sleeping bag and backpack at his newly sandaled feet, smile and wave with sudden excitement, as if he recognized someone he knew and liked, was pleased and surprised to see there. Rennie tried to follow the sightline into the milling crowd under the trees, but she couldn't tell who, if anyone, the kid had seen. Maybe he was waving to his parents. Hey, it could happen.

But she felt a lot better knowing she had provided for him over the next couple of days, and even a bit beyond. A rock mitzvah, befitting a former Girl Scout. If he showed up at Monterey, she and Praxie would help him out a little more. They could both afford it now, she was happy to note, and, besides, it was a very nice feeling. No wonder the Lacings had gotten into major philanthropy — though, on second thought, that probably hadn't been their reason at all.

Rennie hadn't been lying just to escape Adam. She really did have an interview, or at least an appointment. Baz Potter, half of the British folk superduo Potter and Hazlitt (and widely known as the English Art Garfunkel, to both his and Artie's extreme mutual annoyance), had been staying at a Springs cottage to gather his strength before the main event at Monterey. He hadn't been able to get into the idea of Tassajara any more than Rennie had, but apparently he wasn't yet ready to head over to Monterey, either, where Baz and Haz, as they were known to fans and detractors alike, were opening the festival Friday night.

They and Rennie had been friends from her college days. Basil Potter and Roger Hazlitt, a folksinging duo then going by the name of Grendel's Mother and recently arrived in New York City off a cheap-fare student ship out of Southampton, had been a nightly piece of acoustic set dressing at the Sea Witch, an old-school Macdougal Street coffeehouse in the West Village that Rennie favored when she and her friends drove down to the city on weekends, hanging out in the new hip clubs, or the newly hip old ones.

The Sea Witch was gamely trying to update itself to the Sixties ethos and compete with the cool places down the block and around the corner, like the Kettle of Fish and the Café Wha? and the Village Gate, where young Bobby Dylan and young Phil Ochs and young Peter, Paul and Mary were among the big draws, and which were always packed full of starry-eyed fans like young Rennie Stride.

The British lads—Baz a dark-haired, valley-haunted Welshman, Roger a Viking-fair Highland Scot— had come cheap, being hungry and eager to play, and they weren't as politically protest-y as most of those others, so they became the Sea Witch's house act, and had quickly developed a loyal following.

Rennie'd interviewed them for a Cornell journalism school assignment; they hit it off immediately and had been friends ever since. They'd even affectionately christened her Ace, for Ace Reportorial Goddess. Better than the acronymic Arg, she supposed. Anyway, the tag had stuck, though thankfully only with those two: with the recent exception of 'Strider', and even then but few were granted the liberty, Rennie did not permit nicknames.

And now those boys of hers were folk icons. Baz and Haz—and it was BAZZ-il, not BAY-zil, thank you very much—toured endlessly in both Britain and the States; they had a dozen albums out, and had written some classic songs. Baz's gorgeous tenor—though not as high and pure as Art Garfunkel's, nobody's could be that, and nobody could be more aware of it than Arthur either—combined with Roger's rich baritone, not to mention their lit'ry lyrics heavy on the Romantic poets, had improbably charmed the masses, and their audience crossed all age barriers. So they had become hugely and internationally successful. Which might or might not be a good thing.

Over the hill on the open stage, Big Magic had officially started up at the stroke of noon, with a local tribal shaman chanting to bless the scene, followed by an equally local band called Sycorax—experimental music that sounded like zithers being played with lizard skeletons, and wordless shrieking vocals that could not only shatter glass but etch your initials into it on the way to the ground.

Comfortably distant from the din, Rennie and Baz sat on his cottage's brick-paved terrace, under the shade of a jacaranda just hitting its full purple glory, and surveyed the open valley before them. The area was right on the botanic borderline between northern and southern California: the oaks and redwoods and lush grasses of the former, the eucalyptus and chaparral and coral trees of the latter—a charmed and charming landscape.

"So," said Rennie, sipping iced tea. "You and Pierce Hill work out your little issues yet? You can tell *me*. Off the record, of course. Unless you want it *on* the record. *About* the records. We've really never discussed it, you and I and Roger, and you don't have to tell me now, but maybe it might help."

Basil Potter looked at Rennie and sighed. "You decide, Ace. But off record for now. As to our differences with Pierce—creative, contractual, financial, personal—it wants a bloody U.N. peacekeeping force to sort them out. Northern Ireland will see joyful days sooner than we will."

"Well, I'm not saying you should stay loyal to Pierce, 'cause I think he's an utter scumbag, but he did discover you two and sign you to Rainshadow. And he *is* your record company president."

"Yes, well, there's the rub. Not only did he discover us and sign us," said Baz gloomily, "he holds our publishing rights. *Personally* holds them. He talked us into signing them over to Rainshadow when he signed us up; in fact, that was part of the deal."

"And you idiots fell for it? Why have you never told me this before? Who was your manager? Where was your lawyer? Drunk? Asleep at the wheel?"

"We had no money, as you may perhaps recall? We couldn't afford to hire anyone, so..."

Rennie cast up her eyes to heaven. "Oh, let me guess—so famous altruistic artist-loving Pierce Hill recommended a groovy, kind-hearted entertainment lawyer he knew who wouldn't ask you to pay up front and would only take his ever so modest legal fees once you'd made your first record."

"Right."

"What a prince. You babes in the woods realize he screwed you with your clothes on, don't you? That they both did?"

"We figured that out pretty quickly," said Baz ruefully. "But Pierce has got us over the proverbial barrel. We'll never leave without our songs, and he'll never give them back to us."

"You guys have made many, many truckloads of bucks, even working for Pierce's slave wages. Couldn't you hire someone to break the contract? Or failing that, take *out* a contract? On him?"

Baz set down his empty glass and poured himself a refill. "A tempting idea. But we've tried. To break the contract, I mean. And, technically, we *can* break it. But only if we're willing to lose every song we ever wrote up to now. He's got them locked up tighter than a nun in a chastity belt. He even named the publishing company, with *our* songs, for his little daughter's nickname. Scout Music. It's like some horrible Faustian nightmare. That's one of the reasons he's at Monterey, to keep an eye on us. But also to dump a few of the Rainshadow old guard and to look for his next big score."

"Well, he'll have to queue up right sharpish. Every record company president in the galaxy is going to be there personally, or at least is sending a rep with deal-making powers. RCA, Columbia, Isis, Atlantic, Warner, Sovereign, A&M, Centaur, just for starters. And every big-name manager too, from Albert Grossman on down. They're all after the same thing: fresh meat. Fresh meat that's going to make them a ton of money."

Baz nodded. "I know. But Pierce really means it. He wants to sign as many hip new rockers as he can and drop as many as he can of the allegedly unhip old folkies his label established, like Ushuaia and Rainbow Corner and that Irish chap Finn Hanley. He wants new people. People he can get cheap, people who'll be grateful and humble and won't make waves. And yet he won't let *us* go, we who have got our walking shoes glued to our feet, ready to decamp at a moment's notice. We ask him and ask him, we *beg* him even. He always listens politely, and then he just twirls his mustache and laughs his villain laugh. And that's *not* off the record, Ace; the more people who see what a greedy prick bastard he is, the better, maybe. You might want to warn Prax and Tansy, by the way, make sure they're on their guard—I have no doubt he'll be sniffing after them and their bands."

"I'll do that. But what do *you* want, my dear, both of you?"

"You already know what we want. We quite desperately want to either split up and go our solo separate ways before we kill each other, or else to follow Mr. Dylan's fine example and change our sound and style to something harder and rockier and electric. Hopefully without having to break our necks in a near-fatal motorcycle accident. But I have to say, we'd pull that too if we thought it would work."

"But that still wouldn't stop you from wanting to kill each other."

"Alas, no. It's gone much too far for that. But if we're doing new stuff we might actually be able to stand being around each other. Of course, if we're dead, no problem." He laughed at her exasperated expression. "Well, I never said it was uncomplicated, babe..."

No, he was right about that, it certainly wasn't. When approached by Baz and Haz, Rainshadow, their folkie-purist record company, whose current prosperity was founded largely on Potter and Hazlitt catalogue and whose spiffy new midtown Manhattan offices had been funded entirely by Potter and Hazlitt royalties, had indeed listened attentively to the plea of their stars. And then it had said no way in hell. In fact, in the personal person of Pierce Hill had it said no way in hell.

"And when he said that, what did you say?"

"We said we'll sue to get out."

"And when you said that, what did he say?"

"He said we'll change our sound or break our contract only over his dead body."

Rennie gave a short laugh. "Meaning of course 'Over *your* dead bodies, lads: if we wanted a new sound from you we'd ask for one, and anyway we hear there's plenty of other groups out there already doing that newfangled rock stuff so just stick to what you know and what you can do and what makes us all rich and happy even though you're *not* happy because we don't give a flaming toss whether you are or not as long as you keep coming across with the same old sound and bringing in the same old tons of money.' "

Baz stared at her. "How is it that you know these things? That's *exactly* what he said. You're quite frightening, really. Can you control storms and sway the future?"

"Something like that. No, it's just that I know Pierce Hill, I know his little weasel ways. Everybody thinks he's such a cool dude and a friend to the music and all, but really he's just annoying forty-three-year-old pissant Percy Epps from Rego Park, Queens, finally getting even with everyone who beat him up outside yeshiva school. Hardline, but not hard to figure out. Listen, he discovered you boys in that Yorkshire pub singing for cheese sarnies and ale. And then he got you to America, and you were all lucky and grateful to have found each other. As well you should have been. But the times they have a-changèd: now you're big huge stars and he's used to the filet mignon you put on his table and the fancy Connecticut estate you put his family's behinds into and the fan behinds you put into all the concert seats that he's getting a nice piece of change out of. You deserve so much better, we all know you do; but he's not about to give all that up without a fight."

"He may have to," said Baz grimly. "If we should happen to suddenly find ourselves unable to write songs…"

"Oh, *bad* idea, sweet boy, don't be doing that! He'll just hang on all the harder, like a lobster to the side of the steamer pot, and he'll make your lives even more of a misery than they now are. You owe how many albums to Rainshadow? One? Right. Hold your noses, make the damn record, give it to him and then hightail it out of there and fling some public poo at him as you go, just so everybody knows. I'd be happy to help with the poo-flinging, you know I will. But I don't see what else you can do. It's too bad about your beautiful songs being lost forever, but you'll write more, either both together or each of you on your own."

"If we kill him, will you give us an alibi?" he asked hopefully.

She laughed. "Don't tempt me."

"Well, we may just take the hit. Split up, go our separate ways. In fact" — Baz took a deep breath, pausing for maximum dramatic effect, or to gather his courage, or perhaps merely to make sure that Rennie was giving him her full attention — "we're going to announce it onstage at Monterey Friday night. Well, *I* am announcing it, actually. That's what I wanted to tell you. I wanted you to have the scoop first. Maybe you could get it into the Clarion that night, while we're still onstage, even. What say you?"

Rennie looked and sounded every bit as surprised as she, in fact, was. "Wow, that's…"

"Yes. It is. The public demise of Baz and Haz, in front of a convocation of our peers. Nice and dramatic and satisfying, not to mention something we can't deny or step away from later, at least not without looking very, very stupid. So yah boo sucks to Pierce bloody Hill and all his bleeding works and pomps! It will be deeply worth it. For some very personal reasons."

"More personal than money and being artistically ripped off?"

"How about Roger is sleeping with my wife? That personal enough?"

Yeah, that could do it… "I'm sorry, Baz, I didn't

know."

"No… We aren't exactly proud of it, the three of us. And I haven't been the best of husbands to Pamina. It's my fault, not hers."

"How's that?"

He was distinctly uncomfortable. "I've ignored her a lot. I've been away a lot. I've had other women *really* a lot. And I've—smacked her around a bit. Quite a bit, actually."

The air between them chilled so fast Rennie was surprised that a tiny thunderstorm didn't form over the terrace. "I'm very sorry to hear you say that. And very disappointed in you, my friend."

"I know. It's drugs, it's booze, it's the pressure, it's the biz."

"No excuse."

"No. No, Ace, it isn't."

"Is that why Pamie started balling Roger? To get back at you?"

Baz looked surprised. "No, they seem to be genuinely in love. Which we haven't been, she and I, not for years now. We're just together out of habit, really. Habit and money… Though revenge may have been part of it for both of them. At least maybe at first."

"Do you mind?"

"The revenge or the balling? Well, either or both, less than I thought I would, to tell you the truth."

"But enough to belt her around."

"I hadn't been keeping up my end of the marriage. In fact, I've had several affairs myself—not trampish groupie scruffs, though those too, but women I really cared about. But somehow, when she did the same, it was different. You're married and separated yourself, you know how it is," he added.

"Not like that, I don't, no."

Rennie wanted to be sympathetic, especially

given her own situation, but she found she really couldn't manage. Stephen had never once struck her, not even when he found out she'd started sleeping with other men. And she'd only begun doing so after their separation, after she'd moved out—she'd never have been unfaithful before that, under the same roof as he, sleeping in the same bed with him. And after she'd left him, of course he'd been free to sleep around too. But what he'd do now, how he'd feel, if he found out his dearest cousin was bedding his not-yet-divorced wife, even though he apparently had a new lady of his own…well, that was yet another reason why Rennie and Marcus had to end things.

But Baz was shaking his head. "That was before. I haven't seen enough of her lately to get pissed off enough to—well, anyway, that's why I'm staying here at Mojado. They're together over at Monterey, at least until I get there. Then Pamina will come swanning back to me as if nothing whatsoever was amiss. She's very good at that. And of course I'll take her back as if she'd never even been gone, because *I'm* very good at *that*. But I don't know how long I can keep on doing it; hence the need of breaking up the act. I just can't deal with it anymore, on any level."

Rennie reached out to put a hand on his arm. "Why have you not talked to me about this sooner? We're friends. You can tell me anything. Always."

"I know." He covered her hand with his, squeezed hard. "And we are. Forever. I was too embarrassed, I suppose. I've been a cuckold and a dupe."

"I don't think people still consider themselves cuckolds so much anymore? Not since the days of dear Queen Victoria, anyway."

"If you say so." He looked straight at her, with a kind of sad desperate resolve. "Just a dupe, then, right? But no matter what Pierce Hill or a whole squadron of his flying devil monkey solicitors have to say, this is the last hurrah for Roger and me. After this festival, not only will we be free of our servitude to Pierce, one way or another, but we won't be performing together in public ever again. In fact, I very much doubt if we'll ever even be *seeing* each other again. Friday night's the night."

And so it would be.

After Baz had bidden her an affectionate farewell and gone in for a lie-down, Rennie, sad and troubled, wandered over to the active festival area. A stage of weathered gray wood had been built at the bottom of the valley's natural bowl, a slope covered in lush grass, belts of redwoods framing it on three sides and the sea on the fourth. It was a handsome structure, and Rennie could see Romilly's design fingerprints all over it.

In the wings, watched narrowly by Simon Revels, Danny Marron could already be seen energetically and hyperdramatically shooting the action with the hand-held video camera Romilly had mentioned, his assistant manning a backup 16mm film camera on a tripod. Lots of cheesy and pretentious David Hemmings 'Blow-Up' moves, on his back shooting up, leaning right or left, bent double, over under sideways upside down.

The advantages of the videocorder, as Danny had called it when explaining it at dinner the night before, were obvious: a small, lightweight camera with a mike attached and a cable connecting to a tape recorder that you carried like a shoulder bag on a strap. A modestly cumbersome thing about the size of an attaché case, the recorder pack weighed about ten pounds and worked off a battery; it used half-inch magnetic tape—not light-sensitive—like audio tape, which didn't need to be developed and could be spliced, so that was easy enough. There had never been anything like it before: you could schlep it around all day long, if your shoulder was strong enough, and shoot as you went. She could see why Marron was so into it.

Watching now, Rennie laughed. Danny never seemed able to keep himself out of what he did. All artists were all over their own art, of course, they had to be, that was what made it art; but somehow Marron made his films all about him in a way that completely negated the art, as Romilly had said, and ended up being just tiresome. Since he had lost out on his bid to be the official filmic chronicler of Monterey—Donn Pennebaker having grabbed that out of his hands, which was a blessing all round for the festival and the audience and the entire future history of rock and roll, Penny being a much, *much* better filmmaker—Danny obviously was determined to make the most of his reduced opportunity. As Romilly had also said, this was not-so-young Marron's last chance before his father-in-law cut off the money feed, so obviously he'd be sweating to make it count.

Eager to get her mind off Baz and Roger and Pamie and their manifold and triangular woes, not to mention off Danny Marron, Rennie turned her full attention to the music. After all, she *was* working here…well, sort of. She spent several happy hours listening to the acts now seriously presenting themselves, judiciously critiquing, taking notes for future professional use and personal enjoyment. Her friend Chris Sakerhawk had done an additional early set just to get warmed up for his official slot tomorrow night, backed by some members of the Chrome Panther, and she'd dug that a lot. Right now there was a dynamite Celtic folk band called Bardaun on stage, commanding her admiring attention: wild Irish vocals, fiddle, bombarde—a Breton bagpipe—some cool percussion, Welsh harp notes like a shower of silver arrows. Made you want to dance warrior dances upon the headless bleeding bodies of your enemies. She was not at all surprised to see Chet in the wings, Gibson in hand, getting ready to jump in the instant someone invited him, and he didn't have to wait long.

That evening, after another excellent dinner at Waterhall—though Becca didn't join them, and Romilly was a bit distracted because of it, leaving them directly the meal was over—Prax and Juha and Chet headed back to the festival. Rennie begged off accompanying them, saying that much as she'd love to, she was just too wiped out; she'd been listening to music all day long, from noon onward, and she'd kind of overdosed, so now she needed to recharge for a bit. So they'd all waved bye-bye and split.

  Alone, she contentedly watched TV for a while— her favorite, 'The Avengers', was on—wrote up some notes, phoned Burke Kinney at home to catch him up on events, then walked alone through the dripping nighttime woods up to the High Springs—a pleasant fifteen-minute stroll, the music a distant throbbing that somehow didn't seem intrusive on the quiet landscape.

  A series of three interconnected pools of varying sizes and degrees of heat, hottest at the top end and cooling off as they stepped down the hillside, the High Springs were the private property of the Revels family, like everything else in the valley. Open to the public like the far larger and more accessible Middle and Low Springs, they were located in a narrow, caveish ravine full of prehistoric-looking ferns and other creepy, squashy vegetation. Also boasting a small waterfall that provided a cool shower after one's hot-water soak, the springs were about equidistant from the festival grounds and the Waterhall compound.

  Deep in their dense grove of redwoods, the High Springs were also much less crowded than the lower ones, even in the daytime. Despite the many jokes made about the name, the hippie visitors were just as lazy as anybody else, and few could be bothered to walk the extra uphill half-mile from the campsites; so at this time of night the springs would be completely deserted. Rennie was already topless—lots of women at the festival were, and nobody seemed to mind—and now she slipped out of her cutoffs and sandals, untying her shirt from around her waist. Putting down her towel, she stepped onto the natural flat stones that made a shelving entry into the lowest, least scalding of the pools.

O bliss, o rapture! O rapture, o bliss! Steamy hot perfection, and not a soul here to bother her. She closed her eyes and submerged herself to her chin, sitting on a rock rising up from the clean, graveled pool bottom through the sparkling water, her long hair twisted and pinned up to keep it dry. Man, the Indians were right about the purifying qualities of places like this...

The dominant tribes of the neighborhood, the Esselen and Ohlone, had discovered these pools long ago, as other tribes had found other hot springs, deep in the still-volcanic Sierra and up through Napa and Oregon to the Olympic peninsula, east into Nevada and west to the fringe of the sea, in all the regions through which the great faults ran—where, according to a brand-new geologic theory, giant tectonic earth plates slid past each other far beneath the crust, their friction across a fourteen-mile-wide magma river heating the water and pushing it bubbling to the surface. Knowing that the Indians had used these pools for thousands of years was a comfortable thought, though Rennie reflected that she probably should not be feeling quite so comfortable as she did, sitting right atop the place where the fault moved through—if it shifted now she'd fall straight down to the center of the earth...

She jerked herself awake just as she began to

gently subside into the 80-degree water, like Excalibur beneath the waves. Had she heard something? But no, there was nothing around: just heat, relaxation, the patter of the waterfall cascading onto the well-worn rock — nice, but not worth drowning for. It must have been some kind of hallucination of the ear. Here, tucked away in the ravine, even the festival noise was cut off by the natural baffles of rocks and trees; strain her ears though she might, she could detect not so much as a single note coming from the stage.

Time to haul out, and try for something balmier. Emerging from the waters, a hippie Venus on the half-shell, and, except for a turquoise-chunk necklace she'd bought that afternoon at a crafts stall, every bit as divinely bare, she moved uphill along the stone-lined overflow stream to the middle pool, significantly hotter than the one she'd just left, but not too hot to stay in comfortably for a good soak; the topmost pool, where the water burst from the rockface at scaldingly high temperatures, was far too dangerous for anyone to go in at all. Perching on the stones, dangling her legs in the water, she was startled to see a man preparing to enter the lower pool, where she'd just been.

Black-haired, mustached — even through the wisps of steam rising she could see the flash of white-Irish blue eyes. She smiled at him, and he smiled back, flinging down his towel and shedding his shirt, shoes and trousers. Better and better — even though it was a total breach of etiquette to check somebody out at the springs, overtly or covertly. You were supposed to be above low and lustful thoughts, it was all noble and spiritual and cleansing and pure. Uh-*huh*. Sure it was, kitten.

She slid splashlessly into the pool, sinuous as an otter, and leaned back against the rocks, breasts carefully kept just above the waterline, as he made his way up the little spillway to join her.

"I thought I'd be the only one here," he said, and submerged beside her, right up to his well-defined and just furry enough pecs—Rennie quite liked chest hair, as long as it was unruglike and confined to the thorax, with perhaps a lightly suggestive scattering down below the belt buckle. He had a pleasantly Irish-accented speaking voice, though the inflection was different from Chet Galvin's and utterly different from Ned Raven's East London snap. What *was* it with her and guys with accents?

"Me too. Great minds thinking alike, and all that," replied Rennie, with a smile.

Now she recognized him, though she didn't let him see that she had: the Galway folksinger Finn Hanley, the one that Pierce Hill was planning to dump from Rainshadow's roster. Obviously he hadn't recognized her in return. No reason why he should, of course, though there had been plenty of pictures of her in the papers over the last year, to do with all the murders. But she didn't often cover folk stuff, though she loved it, and she'd never interviewed him, so though he might recognize her name from her utterly unsecret identity as Murder Chick, she was probably safely anonymous otherwise. He was here to play Big Magic, of course; she knew he hadn't been asked to Monterey, so perhaps he was pissed off and vanity-stung. But way more famous people than he also hadn't been asked, so there should be no shame in it.

They sat in companionable silence for many minutes, enjoying the peaceful warmth. Rennie could feel the tension forsaking the back of her neck, her muscles unknotting in the damp heat. After a while, they started chatting about the two festivals, and found they shared a number of musical tastes.

"Are you in the music business at all, by any

chance?" he asked then, and her muscles instantly knotted themselves right back up again.

"I have friends who are," she said, evasively but honestly.

"So you probably know what's really going on here."

"Unfortunately, I do. I think that to many music biz powers-that-be, or powers-that-wannabe, Monterey points the future. And it's a future they intend to have a big, *big* piece of. Because it's going to be rock—not pop, not jazz, not blues, not folk. Different kinds of rock, played by different kinds of bands. Nobody's ever seen anything like it, not even the artists who will make it happen." She shifted in the clear and swirling waters. "This is going to be a feeding frenzy—Big Magic as well as Monterey. And the people who make money off the backs of artists, they can smell the chum in the waters of song, and they'll be doing their predator thing, coming after the bands like hunting orcas after clueless baby seals."

Oops, maybe a bit too much of a knowledgeable and forceful opinion for someone supposedly not in the biz. But he didn't seem to notice, just to be admiringly amused.

"Christ, that's cold. Nice metaphors, though."

"Why, thank you. Cold, perhaps; but I fear only too accurate."

"More's the pity," he acknowledged.

"Still, the musicians are here for the right reasons, at least; they're here for their music. They don't think like that. They just want to play."

"And play we shall!" He eyed her sideways, transparently wanting her to pick up on that 'we'; but Rennie was made of sterner stuff. "Are you going over to Monterey, then, from here?" he asked after a while, defeated.

"Oh yes."

"May I see you there? In the sense of obviously I've already *seen* you, but see you in the sense of perhaps I could take you out for a nice seafood dinner?"

Rennie resolutely kept her glance above the old silver Miraculous Medal on a leather cord at his throat.

"Thank you, I'd like that."

"How will I find you, then? The festival's a big place."

"Oh," said Rennie vaguely. "You know what? *I'll* find *you*."

Chapter 6

Tuesday, June 13

JERRY GARCIA HAD DRIVEN DOWN from Monterey with Grateful Dead keyboardist Ron McKernan, known to all as Pigpen, and a couple of friends to catch a bit of Big Magic, and while the friends headed over to the stage area, Jerry, Pig and Rennie sat on Romilly's terrace drinking tea, nice and hot in the last of the morning chill.

Becca had shown up briefly, moving through the lingering mist, plainly fearful of the seeming strangers, then coming warily up onto the terrace. She'd greeted the two guys shyly though rememberingly, which brought tears to Rennie's eyes. Pig had spoken softly to her in his gruff, stony rumble of a voice, and Jerry even more gently than usual; they'd even sung her favorite Dead song for her, a cappella, and she'd sat rapt, listening.

Then she'd flashed Rennie a fleeting smile and vanished into the depths of her mother's sculpture garden, again the fawn, seeking solitude and shelter. Pigpen, deeply troubled but not wanting anyone to see, stalked abruptly off to join his friends, while Rennie and Jerry both gazed after Becca but said nothing for many moments; when they spoke again, they talked only about the festivals.

"Right off the bat, we—and by 'we' I mean the San Francisco bands—were deeply suspicious. Why wouldn't we be? They're all Los Angeles flashmen running this thing. Joe McDonald told anyone who'd listen that they're just a bunch of sleazebags opposed to everything we stand for, dragging show biz into it, and he was right."

Rennie gazed upon him sympathetically, though also a bit impatiently. "I really think it's about time all you adorable longhaired schmucks realized you *are* in show biz, however much you may like to think you're not. Though maybe this is a hard way to learn it... Listen, they knew they needed you and the rest of our bands. With about two and a half exceptions, and we all know who they are, the L.A. groups on the Monterey bill aren't going to blow anyone's mind, and the ones who *could* weren't invited because the organizers either don't like them, are jealous of them or can't control them. So they're between the hard rock and the harder place. They need you. They can't do it on their own. Whether they like it or not."

"Ralph Gleason went on about it in the Chronicle; he said from the first that it's nothing but a Hollywood-based energy rape of the San Francisco scene." Jerry glanced over at her. "You wrote something along those lines yourself. We should have listened harder to both of you."

"Great suspicious minds think alike. And Ralph

and I are both absolutely right. As usual. Did you *hear* that thing John Phillips wrote for his pal Scott McKenzie? The weasel goes pop... The first time I heard it, I almost threw up everything I'd eaten for the past week." Rennie put on a mock and syrupy falsetto. " 'If you're go-o-o-oing to Saaan Fraaan-cisco/Be sure to we-e-e-a-a-ar some flowers in your hair.' Oh, just shoot the snake oil straight up my bum, why don't you? This from the guy who wrote 'California Dreamin' ' and 'Monday, Monday'!"

"So peace and love take the pipe."

"Quicker than you think, cute hairy man. You guys *know* that, however imperfectly you and the rest of your kind may implement it. Peace is in the contradictions, and love's wherever you can find it."

"And it's down to money yet again."

"Rock is always down to money. It's only the poor snookered audience who doesn't believe it is. You asked all the right questions upfront."

"We thought we did." Garcia shrugged. "We're very familiar with the mechanics of huge outdoor gatherings, as you know, and we wanted to be sure of a lot of things that far more civic-minded persons than us flaky hippies didn't bother to ask about. There were going to be thousands of kids without tickets, without food or places to crash, camping out; how would they be taken care of? Who by? The Diggers? Feeding the hungry's not their bag, though they often do. Their radical cousins the Delvers? They weren't welcome at Monterey from day one; hence Big Magic. There are supposedly charities that will benefit, but nobody knows which or whose, or, if they do, nobody's saying. This TV special, now there's plans to release it as a movie. If that happens, where's the money from *that* going? We haven't even *seen* any deals for the extra stuff, much less signed off on any. Because there's going to be a hell of a lot of bread floating around, no matter what people seem to think. Or want the musicians to think."

"Well, we'll all find out in time. I hope. Maybe it'll all work out." Rennie drank off the last of her tea. "They're already talking about next year, making it a regular fixture like the jazz and folk festivals. Though I somehow don't see this as an annual event."

"I think you've got that right. At least not at Monterey."

"It might not be as bad as it seems?" asked Rennie, after a while.

"I don't think it could be," said Jerry, after a while longer.

When Garcia had gone, heading out to join his friends, Rennie lingered alone on the terrace, reluctant to go anywhere or do anything just yet. After a while she sighed and pulled a weed from the terrace stones, absently tying its flexible fuzzy stem into knots. It was unbearable to think that there might no longer be such a community vibe and ethos in the rockerverse, as she liked to think of it, no more music for the music's sake. She was all for musicians making a comfortable living wage from their art, and often editorialized about it in one or another of her columns. But if the biz got all star- and money-driven, as could so easily happen, that would be exactly what would go down, and everyone would lose. Dollars to doughnuts, though, the record company sharks and the bloated promoters didn't give a damn about that. Not as long as they got theirs.

Reluctantly, she heaved herself to her feet and followed in Garcia's footsteps over to the festival. Best not to think like that; you don't want to anticipate karma, good *or* bad, and besides it was never a good idea to give form and reality to downer thoughts, because you just might make them happen. The universe had enough scary ideas of its own without you helping it out. In the meantime, though, *music* was happening, and time was a-wastin'.

Powderhouse Road were in the middle of their opening set as she approached the stage, and Rennie was delighted to see them. She'd gone to school with them in upstate New York and she had vivid memories of them playing at a couple of frat parties she'd attended as a cute sorority girl. Well, maybe not *memories*, exactly—it had been frat parties, after all—but she'd been there, and so had they.

Once they'd all graduated, they had hung out in New York City together, while Rennie started Columbia journalism grad school and Powderhouse tried to get paying work. She had cooked dinner for them on more occasions than she could count, because she couldn't bear to think of them going to bed hungry—no feasts, just her signature dish of spaghetti and meatballs, cheap, easy and filling—and they would never forget her kindness. They repaid her with some musical occasions none of them would ever forget, either: she recalled them taking her to shindigs at ramshackle coldwater flats, East Village and West; many club nights spent listening to people like the Mamas and the Papas before they *were* the Mamas and the Papas, and the ubiquitous Dylan, and the Young Rascals and the Lovin' Spoonful, and Tom Paxton and Patrick Sky and even the Smothers Brothers (who were affectionately known to their audiences as the Village idiots); after-hours parties with many of those same people wailing away at Dave and Terri van Ronk's crazy pad. Unspeakably hip.

Powderhouse had moved out to San Francisco not long after she had, and they'd happily gotten back in touch—even more happily when they learned she wrote about rock for the Clarion. But that was cynical and unworthy: Buck and Mike and Jeff and Laird and Stevie—like Roger and Basil, they'd always been her friends and always would be.

She listened to them now, though, purely as a critic. God, they sounded great. Their stuff had just gotten tighter and brighter and tougher, and Laird's lead guitar and Mike's lead vocals were as good as any around. When they got offstage, they came bubbling over to tell her they'd just been invited to Monterey to play one of the jamming stages. She was so pleased for them: they really deserved it. In years to come, when they were all hugely famous, their tangents and Rennie's would come together again under grave and terrible circumstances. But just now it was all only beginning, and she was as thrilled as they were.

She happily stuck around straight through the afternoon's performances, delighted with almost everything she heard, took a dinner break at the café with Chet, and was joined by Prax just in time to hear Diego Hidalgo and his band Cold Fire, shaking things up about halfway through the nighttime bill.

Cold Fire, of course, had not been asked to play at Monterey on any stage at all, or even set foot on the fairgrounds in any kind of musicianly capacity, having, as Prax had pointed out in the car on the way down from town, neither the proper commercial credentials nor the proper peaceandlove validation nor the proper humble petitioner status with the festival organizers. Plus being a band who loved to think that every man's hand was raised against them and every woman's hand was down the front of their pants. And none of that was without a certain degree of truth. But she adored their dark and intricate music.

"Run, little hippie bunnies!" Rennie chortled between songs, watching the front rows of the audience nervously flinching as Diego reeled around the stage like a stoned marionette, shaking his long black hair angrily, or invitingly, depending on how you felt about it. At least he still had his clothes on. "Run far and fast! This dark scary forest is no place for you!"

At her side, Prax giggled. "Yes, go, run, be free out on the sunny meadow! It's too upsetting having to actually *think*!"

"What the hell is the matter with us, I wonder? We really don't have a very high opinion of the people we would have to say *are* our people, do we. Let alone what we think about those who are *not* our people...we seem to mock and scorn them all pretty equally."

"That's not new."

"And it'll never be old."

The festival was supposed to pull the plug promptly at one each night, by Romilly's command, though for the closing night, Wednesday, she'd agreed to let it stay up as late as it liked. Walking back to Waterhall after Cold Fire's set, not feeling like waiting till the music shut down, Rennie was recounting the episode with Finn Hanley in the pool, to Prax's peals of laughter, when they were startled to hear what seemed to be the howling of a wolf, alarmingly close at hand.

"No wolves here," said Rennie nervously, trying hard to be positive about it. "Not for ages. Coyote, probably."

Prax laughed with relief. "No, just a naked ape." She pointed ahead, to where a stone Gothic-style bridge, arching across a stream, appeared to be the point of origin of the howling.

The ululations were coming from a very specific source: Diego Hidalgo, newly off the stage and apparently not yet done performing, was standing completely nude on the bridge's near parapet, long hair streaming and arms upflung to heaven, baying at the moon.

Rennie regarded him dispassionately. "Now that's something you don't see every day. Well, actually, with him you do… Great singer, but sometimes I wonder whether he's from L.A. or from Mars."

"Oh he's from Mars," said Prax without hesitation, and grabbed Rennie's hand. "Come on, let's go sit with utopian hermit monks sidesaddle on the Golden Calf. By which I really mean let's get back to Romilly's quick as we can and into bed with our handsome gentleman friends."

Rennie pretended to scout around. "Hey, is Bob here, I thought I felt the moon turn to blood…but there are no kings inside the Gates of Eden, you know."

"Yeah, I'm hip."

They walked on in companionable silence, arm in arm. When they got to the boundary woods between the resort and Romilly's private lands, Rennie paused.

"You know what, honeybun? I think I'm going to have another dip in the pools before I go to bed. Chet's probably not even back yet anyway. But if you see him, tell him I'm on my way, so he doesn't start without me. No conversing with any more nekkid Irish folk musicians, I promise. See you in the morning."

Prax walked away waving, and Rennie went off up the slope through the woods to the High Springs grotto. She could see where this might become addictive; it was great for one's skin, and for bedtime purposes it was better, and better *for* you, than a downer or even hot chocolate—too bad it wasn't readily available in town. She'd already been in once that day: her Powderhouse friends had joined her for a nice long midday soak, and they'd all been relaxed and fizzy as they headed back to the festival.

Nearing the springs now, Rennie touched the choker necklace she'd bought earlier in the evening: beautiful tiger puka shells, strung by a young Hawaiian girl who ran the nicest bead stall in the dealers' circle and who was taking her wares over to Monterey later in the week. On his last visit home, Stephen had brought her a gorgeous strand of pink South Sea pearls, perfect and absolutely enormous, to go with the matching creamy white strand he'd brought her the time before and the iridescent black one the time before that. She was always knocked out by his generosity, of course, and invariably properly grateful. Still, it was nice to buy stuff for herself too—far more modest stuff, sure, but according to her own tastes and out of her own efforts and earnings. That was something she'd learned in the early days of her self-liberation from Lacingworld, a hard lesson and harshly learned, and she hoped she would never forget it.

She didn't have a towel with her this time, but her clothes were cotton, they'd suffice as ad hoc toweling. It wasn't really warm enough to walk back to Romilly's naked, though no one would be offended if she did, or even see her... She began to unbutton her shirt as she approached the pools, looking around, and, for all her denials to Prax, half-hoping to see Finn Hanley again. Maybe this time they could do something more interesting than gently poach themselves and talk about evil music biz fu. But the springs appeared to be deserted tonight, the steam hanging undisturbed in the still air.

No, there was somebody there after all. Seeing the figure floating peacefully in the water at the far end—the very hottest pool, the one where the water was too hot to go in, which was why nobody ever did—she knew at once that it wasn't Finn. Too small and short and scrawny.

Dear God, what's he DOING *in there! He'll boil his skin off! Literally!* She started to run up the slope toward the pool, calling out a frantic warning to the unknown bather, but... *Oh God...oh no...ohGodohGodohGod...*

Adam Santa Monica looked asleep as he bobbed there on his back fully dressed, except that his skin was reddened and soft-looking, scalded from the water's searing temperature. *Which would delay rigor and keep body temperature artificially warm…*then was appalled at herself for thinking it.

But it would; and if rigor was delayed then time of death was debatable. Something killers often counted on to alibi themselves, as she very well knew. And when she got to that point, which took far less time than it takes to tell it, Rennie screamed for help.

Chapter 7

"WATER TEMPERATURE in the pool precludes getting an accurate time of death," said Deputy Sheriff Brent Gilmore, predictably, two hours later.

He'd shown up, with Marcus in tow, barely thirty minutes after Rennie had frantically shouted for aid; they had arrived on the scene so quickly only because they'd both been home and awake at Brent's place down the road, watching an extra-innings baseball game on television, and they'd jumped in their cars and raced up to Mojado. Not so lucky nor yet so local, a couple of stunned and sleepy-looking deputy sheriffs, who'd had to drive all the way down from sheriff headquarters in Monterey, were now blocking off the High Springs with scene-of-crime tape. No problem with gawkers; everybody was either asleep, stoned or listening to the music still going on over the hill.

It was pure luck that some campers had been passing nearby and had heard Rennie yelling. They'd helped her pull Adam out of the pool, and then she'd stayed with the body while they'd run to one of the nearby cottages and found a phone to call the only genuinely local fuzz: the state police, California Highway Patrol, who had a substation in Big Sur and could respond immediately, or as immediately as possible. The CHiPs had arrived on scene nearly as quickly as Brent and Marcus had; the sheriff's contingent—a car with the two deputies followed by a paramedic van—had taken almost an hour on the twists and turns of the foggy coast road. For all that, it hadn't yet gone one in the morning; the festival music could still be heard if they came up out of the ravine.

Now Marcus scowled at Rennie, where she sat on a mossy boulder off to one side, watching the paramedics zip Adam into a body bag and load him on a stretcher, her arms crossed and her hands hugging her shoulders, face expressionless, clothes still damp and palms reddened and tender from pulling Adam out of the water.

"Which I don't have to tell *you* at this late date, missy."

"Which you never *did* have to tell me!" she flared back at him. "And yes, as I said before, I pulled him out. With help. Because I didn't know if he was dead and I thought maybe I could revive him. I was a Girl Scout, I know how to do that kind of thing, so don't look so unflatteringly skeptical. I couldn't just—leave him in there."

Marcus relented. "I know…it probably won't matter anyway that you moved him. That water in the top pool is around 120 degrees, and it can spike up close to 160, the local guys tell me. Which you get second-degree burns in minutes and the water's hot enough to destroy any possibly useful evidence. But maybe forensics can tell from the burns how long he was in the water, and give us a rough time of death. The heat would have affected his blood pressure, too, so if there was a temperature spike, he would have gotten woozy pretty quickly and just passed out. Either way, he was dead long before you got here; you couldn't have done anything, and we most likely wouldn't have learned anything. But I think we'll find that he just drowned."

Rennie bowed her head, resting her chin on her still-folded arms. "Anything under his fingernails? Or did the water do for that too?"

"Most likely. Though he has longish nails, at least, so it's possible the M.E. can still find something."

"He played guitar."

"What?"

"Guitar. Folk guitar. That's why he has long nails. I've heard him play; he wasn't bad."

He let that pass, giving her some space; she looked pretty upset, and he didn't blame her. "We could get lucky," he said presently, in a gentler tone. "He might even have managed to leave a mark on whoever killed him. If anyone did kill him, I mean—if it's not just another stupid stoned-out accident. His having his clothes on could argue either way. What did you say his name was?"

"Adam Santa Monica." She straightened up and breathed a shaky laugh. "Well, that's the name everybody knew him by, the name he used. His real name is probably Jay Goldberg or Tony Moretti or Parkerson 'Binkie' Cabot IV. He wasn't a friend; I just knew him a little from the scene. Prax and I had breakfast with him—yesterday? Yes, yesterday morning. Over at the café at The Springs. We bought him burgers and lemonade and fries. And then I drove him into the village and back."

Brent came over to them from questioning the campers who'd helped Rennie with Adam's body, and nodded to her in sober acknowledgment. "Do you know if he has family, or at least parents? We couldn't find any I.D. in his clothes."

Rennie let out a choke of desperate laughter. "Oh yeah, he told me all about his parents…"

"Elvis? Jackie *Kennedy*?" said Brent when she'd finished, and Marcus looked just as stupefied. "Was he on glue or acid or what?"

"I don't think so much that he was a druggie. Though he was. But he really was crazy."

"How crazy?"

"Ten tenths. Oh, and he had a backpack. Which wasn't here. You might want to look around the festival field for it. But this whole thing is insane."

Brent shook his head. "It may be insane, but for now it's an accident too. Until we get some proof that it's not. We'll try to keep it as quiet as possible, by the way, so as not to spoil either festival. So mum's the word. Good thing it was you who found him, Mrs. Lacing. I hear you know all about it."

Rennie raised her brows, back in control of herself. "*Very* good thing. And it's 'Miss Stride', Deputy Sheriff Gilmore, if you feel you really can't manage 'Rennie' in a professional capacity. And I certainly do know all about it. Wish I didn't."

"So do I," muttered Marcus.

After a bit more questioning, Marcus drove her back to Waterhall. Everyone in the house was sound asleep when she let herself in, even the dogs; she was cold and tired, and unutterably depressed, and she didn't feel up to waking people just to fill them in about Adam. They could find out about it at breakfast like everybody else, and she desperately wanted to get at least a few hours of sleep herself, however troubled.

When the dawnlight began to filter through the trees outside the bedroom windows, Rennie put on her

Moroccan robe, pulled the hood up and stole barefoot out of the house; Chet hadn't stirred when she came shivering into bed, and he didn't move now as she left. Cutting across the sculpture garden in the drenched and chilly grayness, through the morning mist and dense fog, the dawn chorus of unseen birds racketing all around her, astonishingly loud, she impulsively climbed into one of Romilly's giant curving shell sculptures, curling up inside the polished granite like the mollusk that would have inhabited such a shell in real life, and gave herself over to sadness.

Past the punishing headache and the strange sinking dread, like a toothache all over her body, she was trying to discover how she felt about it. Adam Santa Monica had been an annoying little person, but he was basically a good and decent kid, and he certainly hadn't deserved to die like that, murdered or not. Nobody did, though she could probably come up with a few names if she really put her mind to it.

And what *was* it with her finding him, yet another dead body flung in her path like a broken-stemmed flower—how many did this make, six? Eight? Well, who's counting? No wonder Marcus wanted her to stay away from this sort of thing. But she couldn't. It was her job. She couldn't stay away from it however much she might want to. Because it would find her no matter what.

Be at peace, Adam...whoever you are, or were, or will be...

For the past few minutes, she suddenly realized, she'd been hearing a distant undertow of conversation that ran along under the noises of bellowing birds and bubbling stream. It seemed to be coming from the other side of the hedge that the sculpture backed up on, the curvature of the sheltering stone acting like a cupped hand, collecting the sound and channeling it to her ear. Her first instinct was to move away, not to listen, but then she caught a few clear words, and after that a twenty-mule team couldn't have dragged her from the spot.

" — drowned — springs — last night — "

The voices faded in and out like a bad AM radio signal, first muffled by the fog, then oddly amplified by it. Instantly on the job, sadness and headache alike forgotten, Rennie slipped out of the shell and eeled through the sculpture garden, silent on the wet path, following the sound, using the monumental stones for cover, ducking into another of the huge shells whenever she reached one. No shortage there: they lined the hedgerow like monoliths, over a dozen of them in a single line, a mollusk Stonehenge — Romilly must have been on some weird giant snail trip when she carved them. She couldn't see the speakers through the fog, and she didn't recognize their voices: seemed to be men, though it was remotely possible that one could be a woman's voice, a very deep woman's voice.

Suddenly the voices stopped, as if they had heard something. She hadn't moved or made a sound that could have alerted them, so it couldn't be her presence they had become aware of; and after a moment the low talk resumed, as if the radio had been better tuned in — perhaps the speakers had moved closer to her, or the wind was carrying their voices in her direction, for the conversation was now continuous and only too clear.

" — face the light? Yes, that's good, hold that..."

" — dropping you from the label."

"Hardly a surprise."

"Nothing personal, Hanley. For myself, I still love your music. Always will. But that folkie protest stuff is tired and old. You haven't electrically updated the way Dylan did, or even gone psychedelic like Donovan. They both knew what was blowing in the wind. You, not so much. Your sound isn't the sound of the future: if I want to compete over the next few years, which of course I do, I'm going to need some of these acts being heard right here, here and at Monterey. And I need to free up money to sign them now, while I can, before they get out into the public eye and other labels throw more money at them than I've got."

A familiar, Irish-accented voice. "Of course. Nothing personal, as you say. I quite understand."

"Hey, man, it's not just you. We're letting Ania go, Silverwing, Rainbow Corner, Ushuaia, bunch more. With what the label saves on you dinosaur folkies, we can pick up a slew of these cheap little rock kids. Those chicks Tansy and Prax and their bands, Powderhouse Road, that Brit act Lionheart, that crazy black guitarist with the hair."

"And yet the one act that's dying to leave, you keep chained to the studio floor."

In her hiding place Rennie leaned forward, straining her ears, breath caught back with amazement. From the context and the now-recognizable voices, this was, incredibly yet also indisputably, Pierce Hill, president of Rainshadow Records the self-described El Magnifico himself—conversing with Finn Hanley, recently naked Irish folksinger; and the one was apparently firing the other. Well, *that* was trippy…

Someone else was there also, but she couldn't tell who, and what the hell were any of them doing in Romilly Ramillies' sculpture garden at dawn, or any other hour, anyway? But Pierce was talking about her friends now, and her attention zeroed in like a bird dog on a hidden pheasant; maybe she could pick up something to help them…

"Baz and Roger aren't going anywhere for the rest of their natural lives. I've got them and I plan on keeping them."

"Aye, I heard all about it. Pretty clever bastard,

aren't you, latching onto their publishing rights like that. At least you haven't got mine."

Contempt edged Pierce Hill's voice like glass. "No, you were older and smarter and tougher than that, weren't you, Hanley. But they'll stay with me because they don't want to lose their beautiful famous songs. And that suits me fine. They bring in the college sophomore crowd, and the middle-of-the-road crowd, and even the over-forty crowd. Everybody loves them, even if they think it's not cool to admit it. There isn't a college dorm room in the country that doesn't have a Baz and Haz record or two, though they might be hidden in Rolling Stones sleeves because nobody wants to be embarrassed in front of their roommates. Not to mention they pull in a shitload more money than you ever did. Any of you."

"So you won't let those poor buggers change, but you're dumping *me* because I *haven't* changed."

An unexpected cackle. "Funny little world, isn't it? Sad and sorry. Even funnier, I'll have your professional bumping-off—ha, *contract* killing, get it?—recorded for posterity. But you'll find a home at some other label, Finn."

"I don't doubt it for a moment. Basil and Roger mayn't wish to be parted from past hits, right enough, but I'm a bit less sentimental than they are. If I'm gone, I'm suing Rainshadow as I leave, and you, Percy boyo, can kiss me royal and litigious Irish arse. I'm out of here and I'll see you in court. Hope you got all that, camera boy."

And that was when the shots rang out.

Rennie almost fell out of her shell with surprise; then, slipping to the ground, she peered cautiously around to see what she could see. Nobody. They'd probably all hit the dirt hard. Unless somebody had been winged. No, there would be screaming and yelling, at the very least.

But now she had an excuse to dash over, all concerned, oooh was that a shot? *Two* shots?

She came running out of the fog into the rose garden quadrangle, pleased to see she'd been right; they were all just scrambling to their feet, stained with dew and badly rattled, from the lawn where they'd flung themselves. Even Danny Marron, who Rennie now saw was the third man present — and more concerned with his own and his precious video camera's safety than with his companions' — looked shaken up.

'Camera boy', eh? I might have known. And just what were you *shooting, I wonder? What* else, *I mean…*

"I thought — I heard — were those SHOTS?"

Perfect delivery, apparently, as they hastened to reassure her — big strong males all protective of the cute little female fwustered by fwightful noisy scawy shots. Rennie tried not to laugh in their faces, but neither did she feel it necessary to inform them that she knew her way around a gunshop.

Last fall, still freaked from the Fillmore episode and the Avalon Ballroom one that followed, she'd bought a neat little silver .22 and started going to a firing range down in Daly City, to learn how to vent her rage and ventilate an attacker. She'd progressed rapidly, moving on to bigger, cooler weapons with greater stopping power, but she'd gotten bored after a few months and let it slide, though she did carry the current gun in her purse from time to time, utterly unlawfully, on dodgy assignments. Thank the great god Earp she'd never had to use it.

Still, considering how little time she'd spent at the range, she was a natural, an undeniable dead-eye. Even Marcus, who had given her some practical instruction much against his better judgment, had said so. Tansy Belladonna, appalled by the fact that her dear close friend owned and operated firearms, had uneasily rationalized that perhaps it was something Rennie'd learned out of necessity in a former life, the way she also instinctively knew, barely taught, how to ride and fence and do archery, all the lethal skills that came so naturally to her. And Rennie, knowing how Tansy's mind worked, hadn't disabused her of the comforting notion—but dear God, if so, who must she have *been* in that former life, Annie Oakley? A Comanche warrior? Ma Barker? Or just Douglas Fairbanks?

"Was that a *rifle*?" she asked wide-eyed, playing it to the hilt, though clearly they already bought that she'd fled to their reassuring masculinity out of sheer feminine instinct, a frightened doe looking to the mighty stags for protection. Yeah, right. "Who would shoot a gun around here, there are *people*!"

"Me, sometimes," came a woman's voice from the other side of the hedge. Romilly stepped through to join them, looking thoroughly shaken herself. "But not just now. Where did the shots come from?"

Pierce scowled suspiciously. "Hard to tell, it happened so fast. And you are—?"

"Oh, my manners," said Rennie, and hastily introduced Pierce Hill and Finn Hanley to Romilly. Finn, she noted, gave not the slightest indication of ever having met Rennie before, and certainly not naked. Strange, but she wasn't about to pursue it here and now.

Danny stepped self-importantly, and perhaps self-justifyingly, in. "We were just discussing a few things having to do with my film and the festival, Romilly, I hope you don't mind that I brought them over here? We needed some quiet and privacy, and of course they were dying to see your work—"

Rennie privately considered that, in the light of Adam's drowning—which the men obviously already knew about, having mentioned it—Danny might better have gone with some other verb to indicate their eagerness to view her hostess's sculptures, and it was pretty darn nervy of him in any case, godson-in-law though he was. But Romilly seemed pleased and flattered, and offered to show Pierce and Finn around, and they were already deep in artistic discussion as they moved away.

As she headed slowly back to the house, the broadening light making the wet grass sparkle as the fog lifted, Rennie noticed a damp trail of bare footprints on the slate path, which faded before they reached the terrace steps. Somebody from the house, returning after firing the shots? Or somebody who merely wanted people to *think* the shooter was from the house? Had Romilly been barefoot? She couldn't remember.

She startled violently as a ghostly face and form materialized on the other side of the glass terrace door, but relaxed as she realized it was Marcus.

"You scared the hell out of me," she told him reproachfully as he opened the door and came out onto the terrace.

"Ah, if only that were true! I suppose I don't have to ask, but did you hear the shots?"

"Of course I did. I was in the sculpture garden, but they seemed to come from over thisaway, not out thataway. What are you doing here?"

"I'm on my way up to Monterey to join Brent at the cop shop, as you like to call it. I stopped off to tell Romilly about the death at the High Springs, which is after all on her property. Before she found out about it from an unofficial source." He gazed pointedly at her.

"You mean little old unofficial me? Not a chance, flatfoot! I had a bad night, though I don't expect you to understand that, and I needed to get out for some air before breakfast. Didn't talk to a soul. No harm in the world."

Brandi Marron came out onto the terrace then,

sleepy and disheveled in a flame-red Chinese robe and gold slippers. She looked distracted, and Rennie turned to her brightly.

"I say, Brandi, old girl, did you hear shots a few minutes ago?"

Brandi's eyes widened. "Is that what it was? I was in the shower and I heard something loud. It could have been shots. Is anyone hurt?"

"No…but someone could have been. Danny included."

Brandi's eyes widened still further. "*My* Danny?"

She was just getting good and worked up about it when Romilly returned alone, and, seeing them, detoured up the terrace steps, smiling at Rennie, whose gaze immediately went to her hostess's feet. Bare and damp with dew, fresh grass cuttings all over them. Hmm.

"*Nice* men; friends of yours, I gather." Before Rennie could open her mouth to set her straight: "Danny is seeing them off. He's *fine*, Brandi; not to worry. Good morning, Marcus. Has Rennie filled you in on our little incident just now?"

Marcus nodded. "I heard the shots myself, right after you left the house. Sounded like a rifle to me. Who do you think was doing the shooting? And who can get their hands on a weapon around here?"

The mistress of Waterhall shrugged. "Could have been anyone; there's a few other houses down this road. We have rattlesnakes, lots; mountain lions, even some bobcats and bears sometimes, come down from the hills. So everyone's got a long gun, and they all keep them by the door. I can't speak for the neighbors, but on my land we don't shoot to kill, at least not the bears or the wild cats—just to scare them off. The rattlers are another story. But *I* thought it sounded more like rifle shots, too. As for the shotguns and rifles here—anybody could get at them;

that's the idea, emergency access in a hurry."

"Will you call Brent Gilmore, or shall I?" asked Marcus, standing up to leave. "To report it, I mean."

"Oh, I think we won't involve the sheriff's office, don't you?"

"I'm sorry?"

The glance Romilly turned on Marcus was worthy of Marjorie Lacing at her chilliest. "No one was hurt. It was probably just one of the neighbors; I'll speak to them all later. I'd rather not have Becca upset, if you don't mind. It's hard enough on her already, what with all the music from the festival. I thought it might be good for her, but— Anyway, I won't be telling her about that poor dead child in the High Springs, or this either. You understand me, Marcus."

Rennie looked at Marcus expecting to see his all-business cop response to the contrary, but he met Romilly's gaze for long moments, then just nodded, while Rennie, forgotten for the moment, quietly observed.

Huh. I'll find out more later. For now, go with the flow. Except…just one little cotton-pickin' minute here…

How had Pierce or Danny or Finn, whoever had mentioned it, known about Adam? Out in the sculpture garden, before she'd gotten close enough to recognize their voices, one of them had said something about drowning and the springs. If Marcus had been in the house just then, breaking the news about Adam to Romilly, before Romilly came out to them in the garden, how the hell had they known? And just whose bare damp footprints had those been on the slate path?

When Marcus left to drive up to Monterey, Rennie headed to her room, where Chet was still in bed, awake and wondering where she was. She kissed him good morning, pushed him into the shower and, stripping, joined him there. When they were scrubbed and clean and dried, she knocked on the connecting door, and when Prax and Juha came out, she told them all about Adam and the events in the sculpture garden. They were properly shocked and saddened, and curious about the shots, but even more so about the discussion between Finn Hanley and Pierce Hill.

"So Pierce really is getting ready to dump his classic folk acts." Prax wrapped a soft knitted throw around herself and leaned back against Juha, who was lounging on the sofa.

"You knew about it?" asked Rennie.

"There's been talk. Tansy told me the other day; she's good friends with Ushuaia. She said one of the Rainshadow product managers tipped Shai off, in case she maybe wanted to do something. Though I don't know what exactly she *could* do. If El Magnifico wants her off the label, she's off."

Though Rennie and Prax loved her dearly, their friend Tansy Belladonna, co-lead singer of Turnstone, was as flighty as a flock of flamingos, and everyone knew it. But she was also utterly truthful, and quite sound in the rumor-mongering department: if she said Pierce Hill was preparing a label purge, it was so. And the majestic Ushuaia, a respected and well-known folk singer in the tall, stately Odetta/Miriam Makeba mold, a pure-blooded Mapuche Indian from the wilds of Patagonia, was not to be doubted either.

Rennie considered a moment. "If Finn hadn't been standing right there, I'd have thought *he* might be the shooter. Since he's the one about to be dumped by the only label he's ever had."

"Maybe he hired somebody," said Chet. "Though if he did, you'd think he'd have hired a better shot."

"Unless it was a *really* good shot, and the whole idea was just to scare Pierce, not to hurt him. But it all seems so pointless."

"Or so at least we think."

When they went down to breakfast, it was to learn that the mood around the house was not of the best. Becca was having a difficult morning, and Romilly was upstairs with her in her rooms, caring for her, helping the nurse-companion. Polishing off scrambled eggs and toast, Rennie tried to keep her mind off the speculation that maybe Becca was in an unstable mood because she'd just fired off a rifle at the guy who'd dumped her...

But brought down by Adam's death, the four of them couldn't decide if they wanted to clear their bummer moods by distracting themselves at the final afternoon of Big Magic, or by going for a drive down to Big Sur for lunch, or by just going back to bed and dropping something and screwing their brains out. Since the High Springs were barred to them until further notice, even a nice private stress-relieving soak was impossible. In the end, they did all three, but they didn't notably succeed in cheering themselves up.

That night was Big Magic's last hurrah. Finn Hanley gave his featured performance, opening for a carefully chosen bill — those who'd been the biggest festival hits, not more than six acts, each playing pleasingly long sets. He was very good, and very well received, but for various reasons, some of which were a mystery even to her, Rennie took great care not to let him see her in the audience. Though one *very* good reason was that she was there with Chet, and Chet and Marcus were already pissed off enough about each other's presence without either of them thinking she was eyeing yet another musician.

All in all, the death of Adam Santa Monica had caused remarkably few ripples. Fewer than he had in life, even, maybe. The fact that he'd died in the remote High

Springs, where very few festivalgoers had troubled themselves to go, certainly helped; but as word inevitably spread, the casual reaction was all Oh wow, poor kid, what a downer, here have a joint. Not unexpected — but it still saddened Rennie to see it.

It saddened Brent Gilmore for a different, lawman's reason: if very few festivalgoers had been around the scene of the possible crime, then there would be very few people who could help the sheriff's office with their inquiries. In fact, so far it looked as if the only one who could was Rennie Stride. And though she'd been just as helpful as she knew how to be, there really wasn't anything else she could give them.

Despite the general feeling of vague malaise or casual unconcern, Big Magic still wanted to go out with a bang, and did its best to ensure a satisfying ending. The penultimate act was a mind-blowingly good encore set from a very happy Powderhouse Road, and Cold Fire closed things down at midnight. Somehow nobody felt like playing right on through till dawn; it was misty, raining lightly now, and the fact of Adam's death seemed finally to have closed down on them all, like the hand of the mist itself.

Thursday morning, Rennie and Prax and the guys were up early to head north to Carmel, checking into the Highlands Inn when they got there. A lot of the top-level performers were staying there, or else at the equally posh Inn at Otter Point, on the cliffs overlooking Otter Cove and the whole glorious sweep of Monterey Bay. The artists who hadn't made their reputations just yet and who couldn't afford such luxury, or who just thought they'd rather spend their money on essentials like drugs or food and it didn't matter where the hell they slept, were grateful to be lodged in the tourist-quality budget motels just outside Monterey town. At least they had access to beds, or couches, or floors to crash on, which was more than most other festivalgoers could say.

Evenor couldn't afford the Highlands Inn either, but Dill Miller had staked them to it, thinking it would be a good investment to have his protégés in the heart of the offstage action; you never knew who might cross their path. Right place, right time: proximity was often how deals were made, and he very much wanted to be making deals for Evenor before they all went back to San Francisco. Just one would suffice—as long as it was the right one.

Danny Marron had left Waterhall before dawn, like a spy in the night, his Mercedes van packed full of expensive movie-making equipment, intending to meet his two assistants at the Monterey County fairgrounds where the festival was being held. Brandi was planning on following him in the Triumph, after a leisurely breakfast. She'd told Rennie and Prax that she and Danny were spending the festival nights in a house in the Carmel Highlands that her grandfather had owned since the Thirties, hey, maybe she'd see them all at the festival, or they could come over to the house any time to hang out in the sauna or the pool and do some blow, here, she could draw them directions!

They had thanked her, of course, politely and noncommittally. Yeah, right, we'll just see about *that*...

Dressed for rocknrolling in a miniskirted red Betsey Johnson dress and an equally short cream linen coat and her favorite red suede Olofdaughter clogs, Rennie was now packing up the station wagon in the drive. Her passengers were still in the kitchen with Romilly and Brandi, having a last cup of excellent coffee, when Marcus drove slowly in from the lane. Pulling up beside the wagon, he opened his passenger-side window, slid over and watched Rennie for a few silent moments.

She paid no attention, just kept loading the bags

into the cargo section. Slamming the tailgate closed, she turned to face him.

"So. Adam. Accident?"

"That's what we've been telling people. And will continue to do so. Even now that the medical examiner found what he found."

"And what would that be?"

Marcus looked at her for a few silent moments more. "Marks on the deceased's face, throat and shoulders. Marks that conclusively suggest that someone — a rather strong someone — held him under the surface of the water, right down there in the hottest, deepest part of the pool."

She stood very still, staring at him. "Not an accident, then."

"No. Most definitely not an accident. Also some scraped skin under those guitar-playing fingernails you mentioned. Any thoughts as to who the person who owned the skin might be?"

Rennie had regained her composure. "Big old ix-nay on that. But it ain't me, babe. It ain't me you're lookin' for." She slammed the tailgate shut. "Or anybody I know, either."

"So you hope."

She jerked her head in a northerly direction. "Are you heading up to Monterey? Us too."

"See you there, then."

"You bet you will."

"I have something to tell you," said Rennie to Prax fifteen minutes later. "And you won't like it any more than I do..."

They were out in the sculpture garden awaiting a delayed start while the guys rearranged the luggage in the car, squabbling mildly over whose guitar went where; his message delivered, Marcus had gone inside to talk to Romilly, so the two girls were alone. In a few brief sentences Rennie quietly told Prax what Marcus had just had to say, and both of them stared at each other uneasily.

"You're right," said Prax at last, reaching out to pluck a feathery pink wildflower growing out of a natural crack in the sculpture she was perched on. "I *don't* like it any more than you do…" She visibly shook off the mood that had gripped them both. "But what about those shots yesterday? What does our Marcus have to say about those?"

"Strangely, not a lot. Not anything, really. Which leaves *us* to try to sort things out. So — who's feeling cranky and inclined to firearms in the direction of Pierce né Percy right about now? Baz. Roger. Maybe Pamina Potter. I'd say Finn Hanley, but he was right there. Hell, let's say Finn anyway. Possible hostiles over at Big Magic? Or even at Monterey? Jealous fellow artist? Enemy fellow record company exec? Pissed-off girlfriend or boyfriend? Adoring fan? Hating fan?"

Prax shook her head; a ladybug had crawled from the flower onto her hand, and she tipped it gently into a neighboring honeysuckle vine before she spoke.

"No idea. But that's where the real danger always is, isn't it: the flipped-out loser you never see coming, the one who pops out of hyperspace with a gun in his hand and a killer trip in his squirmy little brain. Well, there were three possibles out here in the garden: let's run it down like they do on 'Dragnet'. Bullets at Dawn: who might have it in for Finn?"

Rennie welcomed the flip tone; anything graver or gentler, and she would have lost control of this morning's fragile self.

"Off-hand? Nobody I can think of. Who on earth would be out gunning for Danny?"

"Besides   outraged   friends   of   the   American

cinema? Well, Romilly's not extra-fond of him, obviously, despite his wedlock with her goddaughter. For what he did to Becca, and who could blame her."

"I don't think she'd *shoot* at him, do you? Besides, she's had any number of better chances for years and years."

"Revenge? Best served cold?"

"Not her style. She'd be more likely to push him over a cliff in broad daylight or blow his brains out in Times Square at high noon. Or drown him in the hot springs." A sudden silence, like a caught breath. "Yes. Well. But why would she try to pop him, if indeed that's what she was trying for and not just to put the fear of lead in him, in front of two other people she knew were there—and whom she might have hit—and one she didn't?"

"You sure about that? That she didn't know you were there, I mean."

"When I hide, I am *hidden*," said Rennie with dignity.

"No doubt, but don't forget, Romilly made those statues herself, she knows every little nook and cranny where somebody could squirrel themselves out of sight. And sights. And yet still hear everything there is to be heard. She also knows every little vale and dell from which she could get off two shots with nobody seeing."

"Other people know all that too," Rennie pointed out, with some reluctance.

"You're thinking Becca? Sure, she has the best cause of anybody to shoot at Danny. But—forgive my lack of charity—half the time she doesn't know who *she* is, let alone anybody else. Apart from the three hours you and I spent with her after dinner, and when Jerry and Pig came over, we don't even know she knows anyone's here at all."

"Well, we have only Romilly's word for that. But

don't forget cute little Brandi, either. She's been coming here all her life to visit her godmama."

"She adores widdle Dannykins, or so we're always being told by Romilly and by herself. And whyever would she want to shoot Finn or Pierce? Oh, wait, I know—Brandon Storey himself, trying to make his daughter a merry widow!"

Rennie spluttered with laughter. "Yeah, I can just see him, crawling round the plantings in his thousand-dollar suit."

"Well, that's the whole backstage list." Prax slid down off the sculpture. "There's the Waterhall groundskeepers, and the house help, and I know you can't rule anyone out but I'm pretty much thinking no for them? And Simon Revels went home to his wife and kids in the garden wing at a reasonable hour, so he and they are possibles too, but extremely unlikely ones. If it was someone who snuck over from the festival to put the frighteners on, we might never find out who it is. Or who they were after. If they *were* after someone."

"Stan Hirsh!"

"Why would he be after—"

"No, no, he's got that crime reporter head buzz going. Maybe now's the time to get him to use it. I could ask him to make a few calls, find out some stuff about Danny, Brandi and her father. Romilly and the Revels clan too, come to it."

"You think they're mixed up in any of this?"

"Well, I have no idea, do I. That's what I want him to find out."

"Is he over at the resort? We didn't see him the whole time we were here, now I think of it."

"No, Burke told him to go straight to Monterey from the city, not to bother coming to Big Magic since I was already on the scene. He got there yesterday; he's staying at the Highlands Inn, same's us. Let's go call him before we head on up there ourselves. He can spend the morning talking to people in L.A. and then meet up with us this afternoon. Preferably at the bar."

"If we're talking crime — don't forget Adam."

"I haven't forgotten," said Rennie soberly.

The Revels house had emptied fairly rapidly, though of course Romilly had invited everyone to stay on as long as they liked — as she pointed out, it wasn't much of a drive to Monterey, they could easily commute. Rennie had gotten the feeling she had very much enjoyed the company of a houseful of young people and didn't want to be left alone, and she sympathized, but not to the point of staying. She needed answers, and she had a feeling they were more likely to be found at Monterey than here.

They didn't see their hostess again — they'd already bidden her thank you and goodbye at the breakfast table — but as Rennie turned the station wagon out of the drive at last and headed down the lane leading to the road through the Mojado Valley and thence back to the coastal highway, she glimpsed a figure standing at a window, upstairs in the main house. She waved her hand slowly as the car went past, and thought, though she couldn't be sure, that Becca Revels waved back.

Monterey Pop

Chapter 8

Thursday, June 15

PERCHED ON A HILL above the Pacific in Carmel, a short drive from Monterey proper, the Highlands Inn is a lovely old hotel dating from the early 1900s, tucked in a sheltering grove of pine and cypress trees right off famously scenic old Route 1. As Rennie had mentioned, quite a lot of the top-of-the-bill festival musicians were staying here, or at least the ones whom the festival organizers, and the hotel manager, deemed worthy.

Thanks to Dill Miller and the Clarion, Rennie and Prax were pleased to find that they had separate but connecting rooms on the ocean side, while Juha and Chet were in one room across the hall. In the interests of work, the girls had decided not to bunk with the boyfriends: Rennie needed her privacy to interview and write, and

Prax needed her pre-performance rest. The guys had grumbled a bit, but they were performing too and needed rest likewise, and at least they had a room, and a bed apiece, so they didn't complain overmuch. The owners of far more famous names than theirs were already sleeping three to a bed, or even on the floors, in plain and fancy hostelries for twenty miles around, and were grateful to have as much as that. Besides, if anyone needed or wanted anyone else, for any reason or no reason, they had only to cross the hall.

The other members of Evenor were stashed on the far side of the hotel, down the hall from where Stan Hirsh and Clarion staff photographer Vince Bays were sharing a double double-bedded room — though Stan had already warned him that if his girlfriend Marishka turned up as promised, Vince would have to be prepared to let her share the room. As Rennie had told Ned Raven, nobody really believed Marishka existed anyway, despite the large silver-framed photograph prominently displayed on Stan's nightstand; but to humor him they all dutifully nodded and smiled whenever he mentioned her.

Feeling lucky and important to be billeted in such a nifty hostelry, bedded down in rooms right next to those of major festival stars — some of whom they'd both bedded down right next to considerably closer than that — Rennie and Prax wasted no time unpacking and doing a joint out on their balcony overlooking the ocean, solemnly agreeing that this was certainly the life and there were way worse jobs they could have and they were deeply grateful to the gods of rocknroll for giving this to them. Then they went across the hall to fetch Chet and Juha, dragged them down to the car and drove over to the Monterey County state fairgrounds to check out the festival site.

The morning chill had burned off by now, and it had turned into a perfect June day, the air cool for early summer but the sun warm and strong. As she drove into the fairgrounds, Rennie saw at a glance that the scene was already happening. Happy heads and sunny freaks as far as the eye could see. Music, tinkling-twangling-drumming-clapping, sparkled in the air like oxygen. The festival field and parking-lot campground, with blue plumes of incense rising all over like smoke signals to summon the tribes, were dotted with tents as bright and colorful as magic mushrooms. It wasn't just the festivalgoers who had already pitched canvas but merchants selling colorful and enticing wares — clothing and jewelry, bells and leather goods, a whole stall full of nothing but feather masks, all manner of food and drink. A caravan stop on the Silk Road must have looked very like this, with colorfully clad travelers and smiling purveyors alike, all milling around. Over by the gated entrance, a giant Buddha statue benevolently observed, while the field perimeter was lined with tents and wooden buildings where musicians could play and sample the latest amps and guitars pushed by hopeful manufacturers.

As soon as Rennie parked the car in a privileged section, proudly displaying her press sticker — the coveted and newly acquired official press plates were home on her Corvette — Juha and Chet lit out for the guitarmakers' displays, while the girls headed for the backstage area, to check in and get passes that would enable them to go wherever they liked — performer's cred in Prax's case, press in Rennie's. Not that anyone was making a fuss over such things, but it was always good to be valid, and the badges made them feel pleasantly official.

Musicians were all over the place, as ubiquitous as the colorful Hawaiian orchids that would later be carefully set on all the seats: Bay Area faces as familiar as their own; almost as well-known ones from L.A.; illustrious London and New York countenances known chiefly from photographs in music magazines. Rennie saw Brian Jones pass by, as if in a force-field bubble, no one approaching closer than six feet or so. She'd already encountered him in the hotel lobby; he was a brief and former flame, and they were still on excellent terms. He'd kissed her and talked earnestly about how he felt Mick and Keith were pushing him out of the Stones, which had really been his band to begin with. He hadn't looked so good, she thought privately; he seemed even more worn and weary now, as he shambled through the crowd, festively clad though he was in satins and laces and fuzzy old marabou, with a hand-embroidered shirt—a Rennie Stride original—underneath all the groovy King's Road tat.

In fact, Rennie Stride originals were everywhere, making the original Rennie Stride very happy. Janis Joplin wandered past, wearing a fur-trimmed velvet cape that Rennie fondly recalled sewing—one of her best pieces. She had liked it almost too much to sell, but if she kept every piece she liked she'd have to turn her whole flat into a closet and she'd never have any extra money. So she'd ruthlessly consigned it to the little shop on Haight Street that always took her stuff, and she'd been thrilled to hear that Janis had bought it out of the window the very next day, for a price that had paid Rennie's rent for three whole months.

They stopped to chat, and before parting company Janis took off a string of cherry amber beads and looped them affectionately around Rennie's neck, pressing a half-empty bottle of Southern Comfort and a kiss on her at the same time. Some things never change.

But there were giants in the earth and upon it. Record honchos trod the ground like colossi: Goddard

Lieberson and Clive Davis of Columbia, Freddy Bellasca of Centaur, Mo Ostin of Warner Brothers, Sovereign's Leeds Sheffield, Jerry Moss of A&M, Jerry Wexler of Atlantic, Pierce Hill his own nasty little self—lords of the music jungle. There was even a special "dress circle" for them to inhabit, a snooty Valhalla where the tickets were a hundred and fifty bucks a shot and all income went to charity. And again, the word "non-profit" raised its battered, bleeding head, gasped and was still. *Benefit of the doubt*, Rennie silently reminded herself…

It was almost sensory overload, though in an utterly benign mode: try as she might, Rennie could detect no trace of paranoia or freakout, at least not among the civilians. At the stage end of the arena area, it was a different story: they were still actually *building* the stage, for one thing—it wouldn't be finished until a mere hour or two before the concerts began the next evening, but even there nobody seemed overly panicked or concerned—and the sound and light guys hadn't finished their work either.

In the little alley that served as a backstage, a greenroom had been set up in an old quonset hut, its well-laden buffet tables available for anyone among performers, press or the otherwise privileged who felt hungry or thirsty at any time whatsoever. Not just stale sandwiches, dry and curling up at the edges, either: the sign above the door read "Hunt Club," and that wasn't far off the mark—platters of seafood, steak, burgers, fried chicken, cold cuts, fancy salads, munchies for the pot-affected, all manner of things to drink, alcoholic, non-alcoholic and even healthful.

The noshers had the organizers to thank for such largesse. Lou Adler and John Phillips had remarked—publicly and loudly, to make sure they got the credit—that creative artists deserved the best and almost never got it, so insofar as was within their power, the perks for performers at this festival would be top of the line: the best food and drink and dope, the nicest hotels, first-class air travel, even personal cars and drivers to ferry them around Monterey. A noble thought; but Rennie couldn't help but wonder if perhaps, just possibly, the artists might not have preferred simple cold hard cash, the creative person's *real* reward, and she wondered again at the almost arrogant assumptions on display here. Where, oh, *where* did people get these nutty romantic notions about what artists needed, or wanted?

Still, nobody could say that the people running this show weren't pulling their weight, and more: Man Behind the Curtain John Phillips, magisterial in brocade tunic and fur shako, was marching around like a hippie hussar; his wife, Michelle, delicately pretty and strong as steel lacework, was working as hard as he was; Cass Elliott was answering phones; many other people Rennie knew — publicists, record company brass, stagehands — were all doing whatever they could to bear a hand with whatever might be needed to make the festival happen.

As she passed an amp manufacturer's tent, Rennie's ear, ever alert, was caught by amazing guitar music coming from within, and she peered inside to see what was going on. In front of a new model cabinet, she caught a glimpse of a wild head of frizzy dark hair and another, smooth and blond, on a higher level. Oooh, that Hendrix cat from Seattle and Turk Wayland of Lionheart, the two guitarists Ned Raven had, well, raved about: she recognized Turk from his pictures on Lionheart album jackets, and everybody at the festival had already heard plenty of buzz about Jimi. The jam that was now coming off the amp they were sharing was incredible, and she sat down for a bit to listen, as about twenty others had also done, and also to admire the manly beauty on display. What an ad it would make: the lad from London and the spade from Seattle plugged in together, gold and onyx, two gorgeous soul brothers united in guitar genius. No racism, just music and magic. Though she very much doubted that the amp company was hip enough to go for anything of the sort.

Out of the corner of one eye, she noticed Tansy Belladonna prowling like a hunting tigress on the other side of the tent, casually moving in for the kill, though she couldn't tell from here which of the hunky and hapless gazelles was her intended prey. Maybe both: her friends loved Tansy, but they put nothing past her in the sex department. Bimbo Baggins, as Prax liked to call her... Rennie shook her head, laughing, and left the tent, running into some people from New York she'd been wanting to meet, and again, joyfully, her Powderhouse Road friends, just arrived from Mojado.

"We're on tonight, come and see us! It's only a little barn stage, but it's still freakin' Monterey," said Laird Burkhart, Powderhouse's lead guitarist and Rennie's closest friend among them, swinging her off her feet in a ferociously happy hug.

"Wouldn't miss it."

Buck Lai, the drummer, grinned at her as Laird set her down. "Did you know we've been ticketed by the Big Magic purity police? Yes, we have! They pulled us right over and wrote us up and screamed bloody murder when they found out we'd be playing here. Said we were sellouts and dirty pros and pathetic dupes of the fascist music state. We never even knew there was one."

"They called you *professionals*, dear boy; take it as a compliment. Those people are out of their gourds. But when are you on? We'll all come over to hear."

Leaving the Powderhouse boys and walking on, digging the joyful tribal vibe, tickled to see all the heads, Rennie saw Baz Potter moving like an Elf-lord through the crowd, his wife Pamina clinging to his arm, the fans parting before them, all but bowing and curtseying as they passed. Baz and Rennie exchanged appropriate greetings, and also a look fraught with meaning, which Pamina either didn't register or chose to ignore, though she smiled at Rennie, whom she'd known for years, and hugged her with her usual sunny cheer.

"Well, Bazzer-me-lad," said Rennie after a bit of silence that was equally fraught, "all set to open this thing up tomorrow night like a bag of chips?"

"Crisps, darling, *crisps*. How many times do I have to tell you, we're British? But yes, we're ready. Roger and I just finished making out the set list."

"Still going to spring your little announcement?" murmured Rennie, as Pamina, her attention caught by something bright and shiny, wandered away to a nearby stall to look at beads.

Baz sobered instantly. "Oh yes. I can't wait to see Pierce's head explode when he hears it. Roger and I have it all worked out."

Rennie studied her fingernails. "Strange—that's not what I heard from Roger when I talked to him on the phone yesterday. He never mentioned anything of the sort, just bitched about Pierce and everything same as ever. You haven't told him what you're planning to do, have you? No, you haven't, or Pamina either. No, no, don't lie to me again or I'll have to hit you."

She felt guilty to see Baz's face fall. "You're not going to tell him, Ace? Or Pamie?"

"Well, that depends."

"On what?"

"Oh God give me strength! On why you're keeping this colossally important big honking thing a secret from your musical partner and your wife in the first place! Tell. Now."

Baz looked off into the middle distance, and Rennie didn't know what he saw there: the past, the future? It must not have been particularly pleasant, though, because he came back into his face with a sigh.

"Because, with the best intentions in the world, they'd discourage me. They'd try to stop me. Even though all three of us know it has to be done, for everybody's health and sanity. Baz and Haz have to get away from Rainshadow. Roger and Pamina and I have to get away from each other. And all three of us — all four of us," he amended, looking at her, "also know deep in our hearts that this is the only way it can happen, and that things will be much better for everyone afterwards. Somebody has to be the one to do the amputation, and I've decided it's going to be me."

He turned to face her, full on out of dark Welsh eyes, and Rennie sighed; he didn't actually fall on his knees and beseech her not to spill the ever-so-sensitive beans, but they both took it as read. Asked and answered: she'd keep his secret as a faithful friend, but she was by no means happy about it, and she just wanted to make sure he knew that.

Baz did, and hugged her. "Thanks, Ace. You know I love you…"

"Yes, well. Sometimes I wonder why I bother to love you back."

He was undaunted. "Never mind. You're the only one who knows what I'm going to do. And say. Besides me, that is."

"Not Pierce?"

"Christ, him least of all! No, the whole point is to surprise him. Maybe he'll stroke out or have a coronary when he hears me announce we're history. But it isn't Pierce who's involved the most deeply. It's Roger and Pamina and myself. Our lives, our work. For a while I thought, we both thought, that if we could change our music — move on, the way Dylan did, the way the Beatles are doing — that maybe Baz and Haz could stay together. Maybe then it wouldn't make such a difference — our differences. But it's not going to happen. I finally saw that. And I have to be the one to cut it clean. So that there's no going back, you know."

He smiled at her then, and for an instant he looked exactly like the thin, hungry, intense young artist from the rugged Black Mountains border country whom she'd met years ago in a dank club in Greenwich Village. And Rennie found that her eyes were unaccountably stinging…

"So? Still want the hot scoop? As I said, you could write the story up tonight, have your editor hold it overnight and have it popping out tomorrow evening in—what do you journo types call it—yes, the bulldog edition. Your bosses will love it, and your illustrious reputation will only be burnished all the more. Deal?"

She smiled back unwillingly, watching Pamina heading back toward them from the bead stall, several new and pretty strands around her neck.

"Deal. Much against my better judgment, though. Just so you know that. And after? Once you're free of the label?"

"After—well, we'll let that take care of itself. It's still not certain if we're breaking up forever, though the situation with Pamie would seem to say we are. But at the very least, after tomorrow night I can say with utter certainty that there will no longer be a Potter and Hazlitt as we now know it."

Rennie found herself suddenly desolated to hear him say it; he noticed, and reached forward to grasp her shoulder.

"It's okay, Ace. It will all be fine. You'll see."

"Oh God, Baz. I hope so."

Bidding farewell to the Potters, who hugged her and gave her the double-cheek Eurokiss before parting company, Rennie wandered toward the stage, which was still being constructed at one end of a big open arena-like space, now being filled with rows and rows of folding chairs. The state fairground was the venue for many fairs and livestock exhibitions throughout the year, and this corral-like enclosure was where the cattle were judged and the rodeos took place. Very appropriate.

Suddenly she was overcome with a flood of excitement and anticipation that pushed aside all her professional critical detachment and blasé posing like a logjam in a river. This was going to be *amazing*. Most of the artists she loved best in the world, playing the music she loved best, in a beautiful festival setting, some dear friends of hers too—nothing like it had ever been before. *And I get to be part of it. How incredible is that! I'm here to write about it, and I'm getting* paid *for it. I just hope it all comes off as well as we're hoping...but why shouldn't it?*

She had arranged to meet Stan Hirsh backstage, her fellow Clarioneer. She didn't know him all that well yet, but what she knew, she liked. A couple of years older than she was, though looking less than his age, Stan had been a reporter on various mid-size Midwest papers, as Rennie'd told Ned Raven, but had felt himself in a rut, and considered the new field of rock journalism his ticket to the big time. He loved the music as much as she did, so the gig was a natural.

Compared to his Wyoming cattle-town past, though, out there on the dusty, dun plains of bovine boredom, almost anything would seem like the big time, she guessed. But she thought he was a fine writer and a smart, groovy guy, and she *really* liked the feeling of not being the new kid at the Clarion anymore. This was going to be a good and productive weekend for him, work-wise; she'd introduce him to people, show him some of the major ropes—though not of course so many ropes as to endanger her supremacy. But fortunately he seemed not only to like her and to respect her writing but to be a little bit in awe of her, and she fully intended to encourage all those feelings. Especially the awe.

"Casper? I'm sure it's a fine place to be if that's the kind of place you like to be in. But me, I couldn't *wait* to leave. On any plane, train, bus, car, Schwinn bike, Shetland pony or Conestoga wagon that would let me aboard. As for the local paper, I think the cows did more reading in that town than the people did."

Rennie and Stan were lounging comfortably in some empty seats in the 'dress circle', the roofed and raised arcade that extended out like open arms from either side of the stage. They were drinking lemonade they'd scored from the greenroom, and he was giving her a brief rundown on his professional life before San Francisco. With precision, clarity and a fair degree of bitterness.

"My journalistic colleagues, if I can call them that, weren't a patch on the people at the Clarion. Just to give you the tiniest of examples of their quality, they fixated on my given name, Stanley, admittedly not the hippest, and called me all sorts of less than delightful nicknames, with what passed for wit in those parts: Steamer, Stingo, Stinger, Stringer, Stinker. They did that sort of thing to everybody, but they knew I really hated it, so they did it to me more. Once I'd managed to get the hell out, I swore no one was ever going to call me anything but Stan, ever again. So 'Stanley' is right out, in case you were thinking of trying."

"I wouldn't dream of it," Rennie assured him earnestly. "So then, what did you find out about the allegedly storied Storey-Marrons?"

He passed her a small steno notebook. "Not a lot. To recap the highlights: Brandi is a slut and a cokehead and a Hollywood hanger-on running with the most shallow and stupidly mindless crowd going, but she adores her father and worships her husband to the point of unbalance. Danny is indeed the scrounging hustler that he appears to be; though devoted to his wife, he does on occasion pimp her out for his art, and she doesn't seem to mind. Whether he would feel such keen devotion for her were she not her father's daughter, I cannot say. And the great Brandon Storey, who's an old-fashioned tyrant, himself has a few, mmm, dubious incidents in his very colorfully checkered movie-mogul past. So colorful and so checkered that it practically strobes, in fact."

"Anything homicidal?"

Stan gave her a look. "Doubtful. Were you hoping?"

"I'm hoping for anything that can tell me who killed that inoffensive little kid Adam Santa Monica. You weren't there. You didn't see him. It was—it was not very nice."

This from the girl who'd found two pretty much headless bodies lying in a welter of gore on her own living room carpet, back last year. But though that event had been horrible and shocking, seeing Adam floating in the pool, and then after, when she'd desperately pulled him out to try and revive him, and when Brent and Marcus had wrapped him in a blanket to try again for the resuscitation they all knew was already far, far too late— somehow that had been different. Perhaps because the violence of the earlier deaths had in some fashion distanced her from the fact, made it all seem unreal and theatrical; while Adam had merely looked asleep and helpless and young. Or maybe it was because she'd had a soft spot for Adam and hadn't much liked the two earlier victims. But no question, his death had struck Rennie harder than she had expected.

"I'm going to find the bastard who did that to him," she said aloud, and Stan looked at her, startled at her tone. "And then…"

He waited politely, but she didn't finish the thought.

After Stan had excused himself, eager to go scope out the festival, Rennie stayed where she was and skimmed through the notebook, grinning at some of the pithier comments; then, since she didn't have anywhere she had to be, she decided to drive over to the Inn at Otter Point, to talk to Roger Hazlitt. Without giving away Baz's plan, she wanted to see if she could find out how Roger felt about it all. Maybe there was still a way out of it—a way that didn't involve what Baz was intending...

As Baz had mentioned, Roger had been staying at Otter Point with Pamina Potter, happily and adulterously ensconced in an oceanfront room, where Rennie'd spoken to them yesterday, until Pamie had moved dutifully over to the Highlands Inn last night, to join her lawful spouse. What an act: to judge by how lovingly cozy and maritally together the Potters had looked an hour ago strolling around the fairgrounds, you'd never have thought there was anything amiss. Though of course that bright shiny conjugal air was strictly for public consumption. But how Rennie was going to pick her way across this personal and professional minefield, with Roger, she had not the slightest idea.

So now the two were sitting by a big picture window overlooking the wildly beautiful Otter Cove, drinks at their elbows, in a cozy room all done up like a English library, with *real* books that actually looked read, where lesser hostelries would have had shams in matching bindings bought by the yard—Potemkin library. Outside, it had gotten cooler as the sun crossed the yardarm behind shrouds of cloud, and they were both glad of the fire in the serpentine-stone hearth.

Rennie took a sip of her drink and studied her companion. They weren't the closest of friends, not like her and Praxie, or even her and Tansy, but they were long and steady ones: they'd known each other, what, four years? Five? Since her junior year at college, anyway. Roger hadn't changed much; he was still the same blond, lean, sardonic Scot she'd met when they were a bit younger and a lot greener. Though the neatly shaped Van Dyck beard, raising the ante on Baz's well-groomed 'stache, was new.

It was odd that they'd never gotten the least bit romantic, she and Roger, or for that matter she and Baz; the two Brits were funny and smart and literate, very attractive to, and attracted by, the ladies, and had groovy accents, and that would certainly have been plenty enough reason to date them. But somehow it had never happened, and then Stephen Lacing had entered Rennie's personal picture, and he had been jealous even of friendship.

There's no way in hell to do this diplomatically, is there. So what say we just get right the hell into it...

"You think this is a good and wise thing?" she asked all at once, with that unpreambled abruptness possible only to those between whom there is long friendship or familial attachment. "You and Pamie?"

"I didn't make it happen, Ace," he said quietly, looking up at her out of troubled hazel eyes. "You've talked to Basil, haven't you? Then you know the score. Pamina's a flake, but she's a lovable flake, and she's hardly the idiot he treats her as. She graduated from Cambridge, after all."

"So she did."

"She's not the punching bag he also treats her as, either."

"He told me about that. There's no excuse, of course. But is there an excuse for this?"

"I can't answer that," he said simply. "It's how we feel. Is that an excuse or a reason? Or merely a fact?

Anyway, she and I would love nothing more than to be together publicly, right out there in front of the world and his wife. But we can't. They can't break up the marriage until Basil and I break up the act. And as far as I can see, because of the Pierce thing and the songs, that's just not going to happen anytime soon. Maybe not ever. At least not without a huge public brawl and a ton of money being involved. So we're stuck for the foreseeable future. Impasse."

Rennie hid her surprise, and her guilty knowledge, behind her drink. Baz had been telling the truth, then: Roger was utterly innocent and ignorant of his partner's plan to announce the Potter and Hazlitt breakup from the stage tomorrow night. No, that just *couldn't* be possible! Surely he knew! Should she casually lead into it, and see what happened? Or—maybe he thought *she* didn't know, and didn't want to blow the gaff. Well, was she a reporter for nothing? There were certainly any number of ways to get it out of him…or she could just believe Baz when he told her Roger didn't know. Yeah, right.

But Roger was still talking. "Pamina and I—we didn't plan on this. For whatever reasons of his own, Basil kept pushing us both away, so we turned to each other, just to comfort and cheer ourselves—strictly friends, no sex, nothing more intended. But then we fell in love, and that was it. Basil wasn't in love with her anymore, and she wasn't in love with him. Who were we hurting? If she left him right now and came with me, the public reaction wouldn't be good, but it might be less toxic all round just to bite the bullet and get it the hell over with."

"Well, if you do go public, that could also force Rainshadow to let you do what you want and split up, cut you loose from the label and go your separate ways. You might become a sort of moral liability."

"We thought of that—all three of us did, actually. But it's just not on. We're talking Pierce bloody Hill here. 'Moral' isn't a word that conveys any actual meaning to what it pleases him to call his mind. He knows all about the situation, and he doesn't give a toss. It's in his own selfish interest to keep things as they are. I think he even enjoys making us suffer; in fact, I know he does. Of us all, going public would be roughest on Pamie. I mean, we're not the Beatles, but the fans would absolutely savage her. And I'm not about to let that happen."

"Of course you're not." Rennie reached over and squeezed his hand, and he smiled back at her, obviously relieved.

"I'm so glad to be able to talk to you like this, Ace—or do I have to call you Strider now, isn't that what I hear?"

She laughed. "Ace is fine—there aren't many people who can call me that. It's nice to have that kind of connection to the past."

They sat in silence for a while, then Roger shifted in the chair. "What about that young lad who died over at Mojado two nights ago? We didn't see that much about it, just your story in the Clarion. Jenny on the spot, as usual."

Rennie looked suddenly wary. "There's not much more than what you've heard: he drowned in the hot springs, probably stoned. Sad. I was the one who found him, actually," she added with a certain reluctance.

"Did you now! Well, I certainly don't remember seeing *that* in the paper..." Catching the warning flash from her eyes: "No, no, not going to say it. But I don't have to, do I... So, do you know anything more?"

"Not really." She wasn't about to tell him what she did know, what she'd been told, what she'd surmised for herself: the broken fingernails, the scratches and bruises, the way Adam Santa Monica had fought for his life before the waters closed over his head and spilled scalding into his lungs.

But before she left, she couldn't resist trying once more to winkle the big announcement out of him, if indeed it was even there to be winkled.

"Must run like a hare. Can I give you a lift over to the fairgrounds? No? But—dear man, are you two really truly up for tomorrow night? What a moment for you: you're opening this whole amazing thing. Setting it up for everybody else. A chance to lay it all out."

"It certainly is," said Roger, smiling broadly as he said it, so no, there it was: either Roger Hazlitt really was as ignorant and innocent of Baz Potter's intent as Baz Potter claimed, or else he was a much, *much* better actor than Rennie'd thought. "And we really are up for it. You know, once we're onstage, we're perfectly fine, Basil and I. All the other stuff goes right away. It's just us and the music."

She smiled back, and leaned to kiss his cheek and give him a big hug, both of which he happily returned, not without obvious relief.

"I do know. And so does everybody else."

Chapter 9

WHEN RENNIE GOT BACK to the Highlands Inn, the first thing she beheld was Marcus Dorner sitting in the lounge facing the door, looking both patient and expectant. She stopped dead, casting up her eyes to heaven in exaggerated exasperation, then strode purposefully over. Prax, who was perched on the big velvet couch beside him looking much too comfortable, beamed up at her friend but said no word.

Rennie pitched her voice to be heard in Carmel village, hoping against hope to embarrass him, though she knew only too well from past encounters, both professional and personal, that Detective Inspector Marcus Lacing Dorner, SFPD, was just about embarrass-proof.

"I have had an *incredibly* rotten few days, and I *really* thought Monterey was going to help me get *away* from all that, and now I find *you* lurking here waiting for me like a big old *spider*. What a downer. Dorner downer."

"I'm only here to help out Brent, as I told you,"

said Marcus mildly. "Just advising. I have no lawful authority whatsoever. And I went to Romilly's only because Marjorie ordered me to. She'll be expecting to hear all about it. Believe me, I know better than to cross dear sweet Auntie M, so I wanted to make damn sure I have a few Romilly stories to tell her when I get back to town."

"Gosh! Auntie M!" said Rennie appreciatively.

Marcus laughed unwillingly. "Well, dear sweet Cousin M, to be accurate. You know what a stickler she is for proper family nomenclature. You should have heard my mother when I was a wee harmless lad, on the subject of how to best negotiate Cousindear By Marriage Once Removed, as I think I may safely call her."

"Not removed anywhere near far enough, I'm sure. But negotiating Marjorie is a lesson we all come to learn, sooner or later."

"Some of us obviously being quicker studies than others. But I'll be hanging out around here over the weekend to see what I can pick up."

"Don't you mean *who* you can pick up?"

Marcus considered. "No, I don't think I do. It may come as a bit of a surprise to you, but there are those of us who are actually here to *work*."

"That's so bogus," said Prax matter-of-factly, after Marcus, nodding to them both, had left. "He's here because he's in love with you."

"*WHAT?*"

"Oh, he knows *you're* not in love with *him*. He just wants to be around you—he's hoping on the one hand not to frighten you away and on the other to get you to fall in love with him back. Tricky, that."

"Hope—what a pathetic, embarrassing little emotion it is, to be sure. Never going to happen, you know—what he wants."

"Difficult on so very many levels," Prax went on,

as if Rennie hadn't spoken. "But most particularly on the level of (a), you're still married to his cousin, whom you're both extremely fond of, and (b), you *have* been letting him sleep with you."

"Well, yeah, a little, but—"

Prax shook her head. "Sometimes, for a smart chick, you can be *so* stupid… What, you thought balling him on a regular basis wouldn't give him the idea that maybe you *like* him, that maybe he actually stands a *chance* with you once you and Stephen finally get around to the divorce?"

"I *never* thought he'd think that was a possibility," said Rennie with some heat. "I just figured—the first time, it was sort of an accident…"

Prax leaned back, laughing immoderately, and took another toke off the joint she'd just started.

"An *accidental fuck*? How does that happen, I wonder? Is it like rear-ending a car on a hill? You just crashed into him while you were trying to park and found your, uh, bumpers locked together, so you both figured since you were halfway there already, why not just go ahead and get off? Pray continue, I'm all ears."

"You know perfectly well how those things happen. Everybody knows." Rennie had gone a little blushy, and a lot defensive. "You're having a nice evening at your apartment, home-cooked dinner, joint or two, bottle of good wine, nobody has any agenda more than that. Just two friends together, well, okay, in-laws, you're saying goodnight at the front door and then all of a sudden you're naked on the floor with a guy on top of you and you're having some pretty darn fine sex, better than you ever had with your husband except the time he raped you—"

Prax rolled her eyes. "Stephen didn't rape you. You told me all about it. Anyway, that's not accidental sex, what you've just described. That's a sex accident that was waiting to happen. And not so much an accident, either. At least not for Marcus."

She pinned the joint with a fancy new amethyst-studded silver roach clip she'd bought at a craft tent, and looked at Rennie soberly.

"I understand, I really do. If it were me, I wouldn't kick him out of bed either. Except to do him on the floor. But I'm telling you, it's way more than just a casual thing for him. He really cares about you. If you don't see him as anything more than something cute and groovy to go to bed with occasionally, knock it off. Though I say so about someone who helped arrest me for two murders I absolutely did not commit, and no one would think the less of me if I held it against him for the rest of our natural lives, Marcus is much too nice a guy for you to mess over. There are plenty of other cats around you can use for that."

"You're right. You're so right. You always are." Rennie brooded, then brightened. "There's always that offer I got from Finn Hanley in the springs at Mojado the other night. Of course, we had no clothes on at the time, so perhaps that might have colored our mutual perceptions. But he did ask me to go out to eat with him when we were here."

"Sure he didn't just say eat him?"

There was one more bit of business Rennie had to attend to that afternoon: before he took his leave, Marcus had passed along a word from Brent Gilmore, an all too official word that summoned Rennie to Monterey police headquarters to explain a few more things. He'd be there too, her cousin-in-law told her; so before she could get really comfortable and abandon herself totally to rock and roll, Rennie left the inn for the second time that day and drove into Monterey town to get it the hell over with.

At the stationhouse on Madison Street, she was ushered with slow and friendly courtesy—*man, people down in this neck of the woods are just the* nicest! *Must be the civilizing influence of so much gorgeous scenery*—into an empty office, where the purchases she'd made for Adam Santa Monica, most of them unused, all of them looking forlorn, were laid out on a side table with all his other small possessions. The sight caught her by surprise, to say the least, and she sat down hard, staring at them bleakly and blankly.

A few minutes later, Brent came in with Marcus and a tall, red-haired, square-faced man, who reached out to shake her hand as she stood up.

"Mrs. Lacing? Miss Stride, sorry. Audie Devlin," he said in a voice as solid as his grasp, as forthright as his face. "Detective Inspector Devlin, Monterey Police Department," he added, in case she'd missed it, and gestured her to take her seat again before he took his. "We're asking you and a few other people to come here to talk because it's a long drive down to Mojado, and most of the people we need to talk to, like you, have come up here for the festival anyway."

"I see."

"Our jurisdictions are often complicated: us, of course, as PD of record for the city; sheriff's department for the county"—Devlin nodded in the direction of Brent Gilmore—"and state police, if a crime occurs on state property like the fairgrounds or state land. We share cases, offices and facilities all the time. But as far as we're concerned, the sheriff's office has full control on the murder of the Santa Monica kid."

"Positively Solomonic," said Rennie lightly, and got a two-second stare in return. Ohhhhkay, obviously not a Bible scholar or a fan of sarcasm… "Officially on the record homicide, then? Can I say so in print?"

"Yes," said Brent. "Yes, you can."

Devlin didn't elaborate, just glanced at the folder on the desk. "Adam Santa Monica, that's the victim's name, isn't it?"

"It is as far as I know," said Rennie evenly. "You *did* read my original statement, Inspector? The one I gave Deputy Sheriff Gilmore here, since it's officially a sheriff's department case?"

"Oh yes," said Audie Devlin. "I read it. But it can't hurt going over it. I'd like to hear it again from you. If you don't mind."

"And if I do mind?" Though she smiled when she said it. "But I don't. Not a bit. Ask away."

With Brent and Marcus looking on, Devlin led Rennie through it all over again: how she knew Adam from the scene, how she'd met him at Big Magic, how she'd found him floating in the High Springs. He didn't ask her anything about Romilly or Becca Revels, or the Marrons, or the shots fired at Waterhall the morning after the murder, and Brent and Marcus gave no indication that perhaps something along those lines needed to be asked.

"I bought him all that, yes," she said, when Brent asked her to identify the items and confirm that she had purchased them herself, as her credit-card receipt was still in the shopping bag that had been crammed into Adam's backpack. "We drove into Mojado village together on Monday. I had to get some things at the drugstore, and the sporting goods shop was right next door. It was going to be chilly that night, and he had nothing but what he was wearing and whatever he had in that little backpack, he didn't even have shoes on. So I bought him the clothes and the sleeping bag and gave him forty dollars so he could eat for a couple of weeks. If the money's not there, maybe he spent it on drugs, even though I told him not to. Even though he promised he wouldn't."

Her voice quivered a little on that last, and she flushed, sensing a certain quality in the men's silence.

"I felt *sorry* for him, *okay*? He looked so hungry and so cold. He was just a kid." She made a move of revulsion. "Keep the stuff, I don't want it back. If it's not evidence, give it to the Goodwill or a church or someplace. Obviously it's never been worn. There must be someone who can use it."

Devlin nodded, his dark eyes unexpectedly sympathetic. "I'll do that... Did you see him with anyone that day? Anyone else but you and Miss McKenna, I mean."

Rennie was in control of herself again. "No. Wait—no, not *with* anyone. But when I dropped him off at the festival café after we drove back from the village, I did notice him looking *at* someone in the crowd. Someone he looked happy to see."

"I suppose it's too much to ask who?" said Marcus pointedly, from where he lounged on the other side of the table. Instantly the vibe in the office was like something out of a Roadrunner cartoon, and both Brent and Devlin paid keen, if somewhat bemused, attention to the new dynamic.

"One may certainly *ask*."

"Your much-self-vaunted powers of observation didn't happen to come into play just then, did they?" he piano-catapulted at her. "As they so often have been known to do at even such minimal provocation?"

"Couldn't! Tell! I was just the teensiest bit preoccupied," Rennie Acme-anvil-dropped right back. "I had troubles of my own, and besides I was driving away to go talk to Baz Potter. I only glimpsed him—Adam—in the rear-view mirror. Could have been anyone. Gosh, if only I'd known it was going to be so very goddamned important to the fuzz later on, I'm sure I'd have paid a whole lot more attention. How careless of me."

"We have to ask these things, as you very well know. There's no need to get shirty about it." Marcus made no mention of how deeply touched he had been by Rennie's charity to the late young Mr. Santa Monica: he knew she would only smack him.

"Where'd you find all his stuff, may I ask?" said Rennie after a while. "I didn't notice it at the crime scene."

"Wasn't there," said Brent, eager to shift things to safer footing. "He'd been crashing in a tent with some kids he knew from the Haight, and they were a little concerned that he'd left his stuff there and never showed up again after Monday night. They came over yesterday when they saw us asking questions, and brought us the backpack and the rest of his things."

"You don't find that a little suspicious? That they were suspicious of his absence at all, I mean. Hippies that actually went to the Law for help, stop the presses! Didn't they see the story on the news or in the papers and connect the dots?"

"Not really," said Devlin. "They hardly had access to media, camped out there in the fields like that. Besides, aren't all you hippies supposed to be looking out for each other all the time?"

Rennie looked at him levelly. "Not being a hippie, Inspector, I wouldn't really know."

That seemed to shut things down right there. After another ten minutes' light questioning, mostly about Big Magic and the Monterey festival itself — which Devlin was quite looking forward to, being a big Jefferson Airplane fan, who'd have thought, and very impressed to hear that Rennie knew them — the little group broke up. Devlin had paperwork to fill out, or so he said, and Marcus and Brent walked out with Rennie.

"Nice guy," she offered when they got outside again, and for all her annoyance, she really meant it.

"For a detective?" said Marcus innocently.

"No, just for a guy. Have you worked with him often, Brent?"

"Audie? Sure, lots. The Monterey city PD, and the sheriff's office, which is county, and the state police and the highway patrol too — we each have our own turf, as Audie said, but we also cooperate on anything that needs cooperating on. There's not a lot of wrongdoing to go round: we don't get all that much crime in these parts. Domestic disputes, stolen cars, break-ins at empty vacation homes, teen vandalism, traffic stuff. Every now and then there's a firearms violation; lots of people carry around here, legally and not. Lately we've had our eye on some pot growers way back in the hills — strictly domestic. Nothing like that big Charlemagne operation you two busted up. Very smart work, Miss Str — Rennie. I read about it — that took a lot of guts. Believe me, I'm not complaining that things are so quiet," he added. "It makes a nice change from San Francisco. Best thing I ever did, moving here."

Impulsively, Rennie gave him a hug, which he first hesitantly accepted, surprised, then, after a moment, returned.

"I'm glad."

Once Rennie had stopped preening herself over the compliment Brent had paid her for the Charlemagne bust, and once Marcus had stopped squashing her down for it, he cadged a ride with her back to the Highlands Inn, where he'd left his car, and promptly vanished once they got there, which suited Rennie fine. Fighting the crowds now thick on the ground as festival participants and observers alike milled about — it was already like the world's biggest press party, and it was only going to get worse — she made it upstairs to her room just in time to dive through the door and grab the ringing phone.

" — No, not much new. Dead in the hot springs, as found," she said into the receiver, having listened awhile. "Poor kid. What? No, as I wrote in the first piece, he was stoned out of his mind and passed out in the water and didn't wake up even when he started to drown. At least that's what the cops have been saying publicly. — Well, hell, I don't buy it either! Because now they're saying privately that someone held him down in the pool until he *did* drown. Marks on his face and neck and shoulders. And they finally gave me permission to say he was murdered. But I can't say how, yet. — Yes, yes, I know, burying my lead, cardinal journalistic sin even in a phone conversation. But I won't when I write it up. Now that I'm actually allowed to."

She gestured to Stan Hirsh, who had appeared in the open doorway and was standing there politely until she got off the phone, to come in and join her.

"Gotta go, Stan's here. I'll tell you everything as soon as I know anything more and we'll phone in another story tonight."

Stan indicated the phone as she hung up. "Burke?"

She nodded. "Returning my call. He wanted to know about the latest in the Adam Santa Monica case. Which is, basically, nothing. I was just over at police-cum-sheriff headquarters, ID'ing the clothes I bought Adam at Big Magic, but that was pretty much it. We still can't say anything about the bruises and marks on him."

"Damn."

"I so agree. We *can* say it's now officially a homicide, but not why they think it is. Still, grateful for small favors, right? Anyway, Burke says you and I should do some more scouting around, write a follow-up piece tonight, call it in and share the byline tomorrow. I mean, only if you want to, of course. Very nice to be here working with you, by the way," she added. "I forgot to say so when we talked earlier."

Stan flushed with pleasure at the offer and the compliment both. "Thank you. Nice to be working with you too. And thank you again—you don't have to do that, you know. About the byline."

"I know I don't. I want to. And more to the point, Burke wants to. We are but minions, you and I, his little journalistic cat's-paws, and we must do his mighty bidding."

"So what else can I do to help?" he asked, after they had relocated, with Prax now in tow, downstairs again, in the main lounge, where a wood-burning fireplace even bigger than the one at Otter Point blazed away. They wanted to be in the middle of things, checking out the new arrivals, but they also wanted to restore themselves, since, as Rennie had noted earlier, it was still a long and empty road to dinner. To that end, drinks had been ordered, and serious hits were being made on the upscale hot hors d'oeuvres passed around by jacketed waiters: pastry puffs filled with Chinese roast pork in sweet barbecue sauce; pigs in blankets; boiled shrimp; Swedish meatballs; the ubiquitous rumaki.

Prax took one of the latter, eyed it dubiously. "Do people really eat these things? I see them all over the place, at press parties, but I don't believe I've ever seen anyone, however hungry, actually consuming any. And so many of us go to press parties just so we *can* eat. What, in fact, is it? Is it really as alien and unfoodly as it, come to think of it, seems? Does anyone actually know?"

Stan grinned. "Sure. Roo-MAHK-ee. Bacon-wrapped chicken livers and water chestnuts, marinated in gingered soy sauce and brown sugar and broiled to perfection. See, bacon can make anything taste good, even liver! Hawaiian in origin, I'm told. From one of those newly discovered food groups we hear so much about: fat, salt, chocolate, bacon. Delicious and nutritious." He downed one rumaki in one bite. "So? Again? Help? How?"

"Maybe check out Danny Marron some more? Follow him around, see what he films, who he talks to?" Rennie crammed some more pork puffs into her mouth; the hot dog and ear of corn she'd grabbed from a fairground stall earlier that afternoon had worn off long ago. "God, these things are good... Yeah, what you found out, very helpful. Romilly told me some stuff, but I'm sure there's a ton more dirt we haven't even heard yet. And anything else you can find out about Danny and Brandi, together and separately. You mentioned she's a cokehead, but I didn't see any signs of her using while we were at Waterhall. Which doesn't mean she's not; she simply might not have wanted to be seen snortin' up a blizzard right under her godmother's nose. Also, Romilly said that Brandi is deeply devoted to Becca, who was her college roomie at USC. In spite of the fact that she stole away the man Becca was in love with and married him. I'd like to find out a little more about that, if I can, and it would have been rude to have pressed Romilly for it. Hurtful, too."

"Romilly Ramillies' daughter was in love with that piece of garbage Marron?" Stan whistled softly to himself. "I've actually seen some of his films. *Those* are several hours of my life I won't be getting back."

"That bad?"

"Well...technically he's brilliant, no question. But there's nothing there to actually be brilliant *about*. Plot, character development, narrative flow, setup and payoff, continuity, dénouement: for Danny Marron, these are all things that happen to other people and other people's movies. He seems to think his cinematic *fleurs de verité* deserve the run of the filmic garden. More like big boring old weeds."

"Total jerk, then."

Stan nodded. "I'd say so. Oh, and there was some chatter about how Marron needed the exclusive documentary rights to Monterey to hand his father-in-law or else, but—"

"But Donn Pennebaker got there first. We know. He was hand-picked by the festival board members, because of that Dylan documentary he just came out with. Donny, not Danny."

" 'Don't Look Back'," said Prax approvingly. She had only been half-listening, until Dylan's name caught her attention. "Great, great piece of work. Marron couldn't have done anything like it in a million years, not if Bob held the camera for him himself."

"So, envious. Maybe even killer envious?"

Rennie looked at Stan, considering. "You're thinking since Danny only got rights to the B-list Mojado, maybe he'd be feeling deprived and homicidal? That's creative, but I doubt it. If he was that pissed off, you'd expect him to poison Pennebaker and crew at the greenroom buffet table, and then nobly volunteer his own services. Instead, he was one of the unlovely trio that got shot at, down at Romilly's place. Which, by the way, Marcus apparently still hasn't told his pal Deputy Dawg about; neither has he shared with Devlin the Monterey PD detective. But what would Danny's motive be for killing Adam?"

"No. Freakin'. Idea." Firmness and annoyance were in Prax's voice in equal parts. "Now can we pleeeeease stop obsessing about it? We're here to have fun, and work our tails off, and enjoy everybody else working *their* tails off. Let's concentrate on that, shall we?"

"We can't do much about it anyway," said Rennie with resignation. "In fact, we can't do anything about it. So okay. And Dill Miller is taking us all out to dinner on Cannery Row, so we'd best go change into something groovy. Praxie, you go first, I'll be along in a minute. I brought fancy clothes in my big suitcase, just take what you want. Not your concert dress, of course. We're saving that."

Watching Prax walk away, Rennie touched Stan's arm. "She's so nervous she's about to throw up, but she'll never let us see it. It's finally their big chance, hers and Juha's, and Bruno's and Tansy's, all of them. You know how hard they've worked. I'd hate like hell to see them cheated of their moment because of the murder or Marron's stupidity or anything like that."

"Me too. I really do want to see it happen for them all."

"And while it's happening, let's you and me see what we can find out, all the same. We can write everything up after dinner, before it gets too noisy and party-ish around here, and then call it in to Burke's office. I brought my trusty college-vintage Olivetti with me, so we don't have to rely on my eldritch scrawl, which, believe me, neither of us wants to. What, you're surprised I travel with a portable typewriter? Tool of the trade. Just as much as the guys' axes."

Stan glanced curiously at her as they headed upstairs themselves. "May I ask a question?"

She gestured expansively. "Anyone may ask me anything. Anything at all at any time in any place."

"Why did you get into all this to begin with? Surely not just to meet musicians!"

Rennie smiled and patted his arm. "Couldn't care less about meeting musicians. I got into it because I wanted to meet the music."

While they were all in their respective rooms changing into respectable restaurant clothes—Chet and Juha as well—Rennie suddenly remembered something she'd promised. So before any dinner was consumed, a two-car convoy headed over to the fairgrounds to catch Powderhouse Road.

Powderhouse had just begun their set on the jamming stage that had been set up in one of the fairground barns, and they sounded amazing. The dinner-bound couldn't stay until the end, so Rennie contented herself with blowing kisses to Laird and Buck over the heads of the sizable audience—who were, she was pleased to see, really digging the sound. Turning away after four songs, unable to delay dinner any longer and too hungry to want to, they ran into Bruno Harvey, the leader of Turnstone, who was now solidly hooked up with Tansy Belladonna—at least as solidly as any man *could* hook up with Tansy—and asked him along too. But he politely declined, saying he and Tanze and the rest of Turnstone were going out to eat with members of Quicksilver, and they promised to get together sometime over the weekend, before Turnstone performed on Saturday.

"And that's all very—*comment il faire*...? Why can I no longer remember French?" lamented Stan, as they headed toward the cars.

"Because the French brain cells die before the ones that let you recall every single TV ad jingle you ever heard from the age of four and a half onwards. I can still sing the Castro Convertible song. Though that might be just a New York metro-area thing. Oh, and it's *comme il faut*, the phrase you're rummaging your cortex for."

"How do you know that?"

"Obviously not all *my* French brain cells are dead yet. Shall I now sing you the Castro Convertible song?"

"Some other time."

Dill's moss-green Benz leading off, they headed over to Cannery Row: Rennie, Prax, Juha, Bardo and Chet in the blue Chevy station wagon, Stan in the Benz with Dill, Dainis Hood, Jack Paris and a writer from New

York. She'd introduced herself at the inn's front desk and begged a lift to the fairgrounds, and they'd invited her to go with them to hear Powderhouse and have dinner.

Belinda Melbourne, just their age, was a tall, brown-haired, brown-eyed New Yorker who wrote about rock for various underground newspapers. Her mainstream gig was for Lord Fitzroy's new Manhattan tabloid outlet, the rather grandiosely named New York Torch-Ledger, and, as fellow Fitzian hot young properties, she and Rennie had had numerous fine phone conversations over the past year, though they hadn't met face to face until now.

In the cars, the talk was mainly about the festival, and their respective publications and editors and rivals, but once they were all settled at the table and dinner was on, the topic gradually changed to what had happened at Big Magic.

Rennie shook her head regretfully in answer to Belinda's artful questions. Of course, she was now at liberty to speak and write about the fact that Adam's death was indeed murder — now that Marcus, Brent and Devlin had given permission, and wouldn't take her out behind the barn and tan her hide if she did, or, much worse, cut her off from future access. But with her cagey journalistic instincts, she thought she'd keep it all to herself just a bit longer. Certainly she wasn't giving it away before her story breaking the murder news ran in the bulldog edition, a few hours from now.

"All I can say," she primly concluded, "is that it's been treated out of the box as a sad accident: many people have affirmed that Adam Santa Monica was deeply under the influence of illicit substances before deciding to take a dip in the hot springs, and it's presumed that he so succumbed and drowned. That's all. Really."

"And he was really Elvis's bastard son with Jackie

Kennedy?"

"That? Not so much."

Belinda grinned and snapped her fingers. "Dang! I *knew* it was too good to be true."

Stan said, not looking at anyone, "I heard a rumor that El's posse, tiring of either Adam's lies or Adam's truth, whichever you prefer, and in either case not wanting the Big Guy to be bothered anymore by this little twit, sent Vegas goons or the Memphis Mafia to off him."

Rennie's mouth quirked before she could stop it. "I'd laugh, but it doesn't seem appropriate. It's much more likely that he went into the springs stoned, became all woozy and drowned, just as my detective cousin-in-law's friend Deputy Sheriff Brent Gilmore announced to the press. Besides, I don't know what all these parvenu journos think they can find out that we already haven't. It's *our* people, *our* turf and *our* story. If I catch any of them horning in on it, I'll beat them up like cookie batter. And you know I can."

That was self-protection as well as annoyance. The wave of journalists that had crashed onto the shores of Mojado, stirred up by Adam's death, had now sloshed over to Monterey in search of whatever story they could get, annoying not only Rennie and Stan but the rest of the local reportorial talent. In the absence of fresh, real news, and in the presence of the organizers' mandate that nobody should tell the press a damn thing about the drowning lest the spirit of the festival be somehow dampened and besides it had happened thirty miles away anyway and had nothing whatever to do with Monterey, a spin was now being put on Adam's death at Mojado to distance it even further from events here.

So far it seemed to be working, too, thought Rennie bitterly. People in San Francisco probably knew more about Adam Santa Monica than the hordes of festivalgoers did. Indeed, most of them didn't seem to know about it at all—at least the ones who hadn't been at Big Magic, and even those... Just wouldn't do to bring people down, now, would it. Bummer for Adam, but hey, God forbid it should keep the fans from having a happy, trippy weekend.

In the meantime, Rennie just wanted to keep journalistic rivals off her tail. If there was anything to be discovered, or indeed revealed, then Murder Chick, along with her faithful Indian scout Stingo, absolutely was going to be the only one doing the discovering and the revealing. Besides, historically, she never did share very well with the other kids.

Chapter 10

IT WAS JUST AS MR. JAMES JOYCE HAD SAID, Rennie would think much, much later, when everything was finally over: Here Comes Everybody. Just as he'd put it in that big fat murky impenetrable book of his. By the time the festival, or even the evening, was over, there would probably be ample fodder with which Mr. James Joyce could stuff an even bigger fatter murkier more impenetrable book…

As soon as they got back from dinner, she and Stan had dashed up to her room, where they dashed off the follow-up story breaking the newest news about Adam, and also managed a short sidebar on pre-festival festivities, with quotes they'd collected that afternoon from Country Joe McDonald and a Byrd or two and some of the Brits and the ever-gracious Michelle Phillips. Rennie had typed up clean copies, or relatively so, phoned in both pieces to Burke's office, and now they were caught up workwise. So they were feeling industrious, virtuous and quite pleased with themselves.

Another scoop for Murder Chick and Stingo!

Therefore they also felt that they were now free to amuse themselves without guilt. So, down in the lobby yet again, Prax beside her, Stan and Belinda in two flanking armchairs, Rennie had been watching a continuous torrent of people she knew, or at least knew *of*, parade by her where she sat by the fireplace like a bear on a flat rock by a salmon river, thoughtfully eyeing the big or little fishies headed upstream, or upstairs.

The New York, London and L.A. contingents of writers, musicians, publicists and label execs, just off their shuttle planes from San Francisco International or out of the cars they'd driven up or down in, had been checking in all evening and heading straight for the bar. Not necessarily in that order. But the joint was jumping: in the space of half an hour, Rennie had encountered Francie Nolting, a talented photographer based in New York and West Hollywood whom she'd known for a year or so; Hacker Bennett, given name Henry, a Jewish-Afro'd, wild-eyed Princetonian who wrote for the East Village Khaos and other underground rags; Sledger Cairns, the only female lead guitarist in rock—the only good one, anyway, and she was very, very good indeed; Punkins Parker, London seamstress to the stars, with whom Rennie had an intense and professional discussion about clothes and exchanged a promise for a mutual fashion show before the festival was over; even Rennie's ex-bedmate Owen Danes, leader of Stoneburner, who'd driven up from L.A. and had just swung by to greet her affectionately.

Out of nowhere, Tansy Belladonna came running up and nearly tackled her. "You're *here*! You're both *here*! When did you *get* here? Why didn't I see you sooner, *where* have you been *hiding*?"

She kissed Prax and Rennie, hugging them extravagantly, her long, tousled yellow hair thrashing like a wheatfield in a windstorm, and then threw herself with equal fervor on Stan and Belinda, who looked amused and alarmed respectively.

"And I know *you* two, Rennie's told me all about *you*, Stan, and I saw *your* stuff all the time, Belinda, when I was living in New York for a while. Where have you guys *been*? Have you seen Bruno? Rennie, did you bring me something nice to *wear*? Can I get a *drink*? Or something to *eat*? Where are you guys *sleeping*? Have you heard about—"

Prax got up and put an arm around Tansy, and they went off together to find the rest of their bands and talk musical shop, leaving the journalists alone. Then, before Rennie could draw breath to explain the natural phenomenon that was Tansy to the two who'd just met her for the first time, an even more natural phenomenon, the first Baron Holywoode, in the flesh, Oliver Fingal Flaherty Fitzroy, came sailing in to crown it all, pleased with himself for the surprise of his presence—pleased even more with the little ripple of recognition that accompanied him—and after suitable greetings insisted on standing Rennie, Belinda and Stan, as his loyal employees, to yet more drinks.

"Only a flying visit, punters," he told them in his clipped Cambridge accent. "Just so I can say I was here. My driver's outside with the car, and I'm straight on to the city, to drop in at the Clarion, late though it be, before I lay me down to sleep this night upon the nice crisp sheets and *luxe* mattresses of the Fairmont... I've never gone from L.A. to Frisco except by plane, and I'll probably never have another chance, so I thought I'd take advantage of the opportunity. Especially since I'm not doing the driving—all I have to do is look out the windows. Quite a pretty little jaunt it's been."

"We don't call it Frisco. Ever," Rennie informed him severely. "S.F. is acceptable, but that's it. If you're heading up to town, though, please could you take our stories with you? We phoned them in to Burke's office an hour ago, but I'd feel safer knowing a typescript went too, and the way your chauffeur drives it'll be there before the Linotype can say 'etaoin shrdlu'."

"Truly? Truly? Not Frisco? Ever?" Fitz, in his impeccably tailored Savile Row suit and equally impeccable Beatle haircut, gazed at her intently, as if he were a member of the Inquisition and she were Galileo swearing that the earth went around the sun. "Astonishing. Very well, if you say so. And you would make your boss your lowly messenger? Just kidding — I'd be quite happy to sherpa your stories. Are they good? Of course they are. I shall read them en route, since it will be too dark by then to admire the scenery. They had better be good. Now, tell me how things are with Burke. I was so sorry to hear about his wife's accident; I sent flowers to the hospital."

As Stan and Rennie assured him that the stories were indeed good, rife with homicide and music, and that Jeannie Kinney's broken ankle, result of a Telegraph Hill tangle with an Afghan hound's leash, was on the mend, and gave him other bits of Clarion and rockworld gossip, Fitz's hard blue eyes never left his young talent's faces. He was well pleased with what he saw: Hirsh was proving the promise of the reputation that had preceded him, there was good report of Melbourne at the Torch-Ledger, and of course Strider, that clever, clever thing, was teacher's pet, head girl, chief scorer of the freshman team at Fitzrovia United. Whatever was going on here, she'd be the first to know, and he'd be the first to have it. That was, after all, why he'd hired her.

After Fitz, their stories safely ensconced in his handmade Asprey briefcase, had gone, blowing across the room like a rogue meteorite and leaving a satisfying trail of craters in his wake, Rennie sat on, glad to be alone for a bit. Stan and Belinda had disappeared, not together, and she was happy to just sit and observe the traffic. Also too tired and lazy to get up and move. She'd been chatting up the passers-by she knew and liked, nodding civilly to the ones she didn't, and occasionally getting up to hug and kiss the ones she really cared about.

There had been very few of those last: the Chronicle's Ralph J. Gleason, dean of San Francisco music critics, in tweed jacket and tie, ever-present pipe in hand, uproariously having one for the road with Fitz — only milk for Gleason, who was a diabetic; a few Airplanes and Dead; several publicity people Rennie dealt with regularly, including Jacinta O'Malley, who had been her favored flack contact at the giant PR firm of Rogers Cowan, and who had quit last year to start her own boutique agency; her actress friend Quinnie St. Clears, who'd gone to Mill Valley High School with Prax. Then…

"It *can't* be! Can it?"

Staring at her in equal disbelief was someone she'd known longer than anyone in her life except her parents and her two sisters and her grandparents. And what on earth *he* could be doing here…

"*RENNIE*? Rennie Stride? Is that really you?"

She leaped up and ran over to him, hugging him hard, and Gerry Langhans hugged her back even harder.

"I don't *believe* it!" She held him off to stare at his smiling face, then squealed and hugged him again.

"Believe it, babe!"

"What on earth are you *doing* here?" they asked simultaneously.

Gerry laughed and shook his head. "I'll go first! I already know what *you're* doing here, you being the queen of San Francisco rock writers and all."

"Why do people insist on making me their queen?" asked Rennie, throwing her arms out in blind appeal. "I have never longed to wear a crown; nay, not even a tiara. Though I have indeed worn one. But no matter! Let my people cheer me!"

"Too modest you are by half. Those nuns we both suffered under as tots taught you much too well. As to what *I'm* doing here—you do remember I've been working at Rainshadow Records for the past year, running their East Coast a&r department? Yes, well, Pierce Hill ordered me out here from New York to help him scout the festival."

"Uh-*huh*. So 'artists & repertoire' really means you're one of the major buyers at the cattle auction."

"Well, that's a hell of a way to put it, but yes, very true, I am. And by all accounts, it looks as if there's going to be quite a herd of talented little dogies in the corral for me to get the Rainshadow brand on."

"Charming." She linked her arm through his. "Come and have a joint in my room, it's way too noisy and smoky down here."

When they were ensconced in chaises on the balcony, Rennie took a long toke on a joint Gerry'd just rolled—best Michoacan—took a long pull on one of the beers from Chet's supply, looked out at the moonlit ocean view and sighed contentedly.

"This is—not bad. Not bad at all. As I said to Prax earlier, how brilliant of us to choose this line of work, since it pays a bunch of money and really isn't anything in the *slightest* degree like actual work... Here's to us, then!" They ceremoniously clinked beer bottles. "So, how's the fair JoAnn? I haven't seen her since your wedding, you guys don't get out here much. At all, really."

"She's great, she's working at Epic Records, having a fine time. She sends love and says to tell you that you made a terrific best man."

Rennie laughed. "And you were so kind to ask

me! But really, who else *would* you have asked? We've known each other since we were in our prams. Before that, even, our moms having been best buds since they themselves were rug rats."

He grinned back and nodded, newly lengthy brown hair moving as he did so. "Friends from in utero, you and I. My mother claims I started bouncing around inside whenever your mom showed up with *you* inside. Even then we knew. And then of course we did share that parochial school education from the stormtroopers of the Vatican until we were twelve."

"Ah, the ties that bind! No, I mean *really* bind. The hand that holds the ruler swats the world. Of such experiences are mighty life chains forged."

"Chains is the word, all right."

They finished the joint and started another, reminiscing with great peals of laughter, so that people passing in the garden below would look up at the sound and smile. Gerry was the brother she'd never had, and she was another sister to him. He had four brothers and three sisters, so one more made no difference, but at least with her there was none of the usual sibling fraughtness. There'd been other sorts of drama over the years, sure, but not that. And certainly nothing romantic. They'd known each other far too well for far too long.

"Sooooo," said Rennie luxuriously. "Just who *does* the creature Pierce, or Percy, as I always prefer to think of him, have his eye on in the vicious bidding war for talent that is really what this festival is all about?"

"Man, you really *are* a journalist, aren't you! So young, so cynical, such a credit to your trade… Well, it's no secret. We're after the same talent the other execs and managers are after. They don't understand the music at all, the suits don't, most of them; but I and the other company freaks like me do, and they trust our judgment calls. And let me tell you, we know a hot property when we hear one. We're all hoping that, being hip and funky freaks working for powerful corporations, we might present a more sympathetic face to the musicians than the suits will; and, dangling such rich, bright and shiny bait as might lure them away from the small, poor labels some of them are now with, we'll be able to hook and reel them in like prize marlins."

"First dogies, now game fish. Charming images. Though all too accurate. So who do you think will bag the biggest fishies?"

Gerry shrugged. "Hard to say. We'd *really* love to get Lionheart, but I don't think we will. Reprise has Hendrix sewn up already, I believe, though I'm sure they don't have a clue as to what to do with him. I know for a fact that Albert Grossman wants to add Janis to his ever-burgeoning collection. Greedy bastard: he's already managing Dylan, Mike Bloomfield, Odetta, and Peter, Paul and Mary, just for starters. But he thinks Janis's blues thing will be a no-brainer, have vast appeal to a wider audience."

"He's probably right. He usually is. Though Janis herself doesn't strike me as exactly middle-of-the-road. But Big Brother's been signed for awhile to Mainstream; they recorded some songs, well, more like demo tapes, and they plan on releasing an album if the band does well here."

"Piffle. If it even happens, it'll be no promotion, no publicity, crappy jacket art. You'll see. No, Big Al will pry them loose, and I bet you a steak dinner at the Palm that their next five albums will be on Columbia—full-on major production values, big-name producer, every studio luxury CBS money can buy. But I don't see the current band configuration enduring, not for the long haul, anyway."

Rennie looked startled. "You mean Grossman would dump the musicians and just cherry-pick her to put in front of a new backup group? I don't think she'd go for that! At least, I'd hope she wouldn't. Okay, they're not the smoothest band around, but they do just fine behind her. They're organic and groovy and I can't imagine her without them, or vice versa. I'd like to think she'd be loyal. They've all stuck together through such a lot, and they're so cute. Especially that Sam Andrew. Great hair."

"You do go for the hair almost as much as the music, don't you? And why the hell not? Well, since the band is just about unknown outside the Bay Area, nobody out there is attached to any of them — sorry if that sounds brutal, but there it is. Janis is the one who's going to be the star. In fact, most of the label big boys think the band is a mangy mob of druggies who drag her down and couldn't play their way out of a badly rolled joint. The word is she'll never be the star she deserves to be until she cuts herself loose and gets something behind her that can not only measure up but push her along. Big Brother's not like the Airplane, where everyone's a master, or even the Dead, where most of them are. And I'm telling you — so far off the record that it's on a whole *other* record — that Janis has long ago privately come to a conclusion not altogether unlike it. Though she'll never admit it publicly. But your pal Sam might make the cut."

Seeing her troubled look: "It's just show biz, babe. They'll be fine. And if not, well… Come on, let's go back downstairs. We can talk about murder, if you'd rather — I hear you're up to your old tricks again. Tell me all about it."

She gave him the look that only someone who's known you since the womb can give you.

"I *don't* think so!"

"Oh please! You know you want to."

"I know. And I do. Just — not yet."

With the luck of dodgy karma, or bad serendipity, the first people they ran into were Pierce Hill and Danny Marron, who seemed to be having a cozy confab in a corner, and who both imperiously waved Gerry and Rennie over as soon as they saw them.

For my sins, sighed Rennie to herself, *which are, no doubt, grave and manifold, not to mention manifest, otherwise why would I be punished so very harshly...* But she trudged along after Gerry, resigned to a few more minutes of record-biz purgatory. It was getting late, she was really tired, she wouldn't hang around long...

It took her all of three and a half seconds to realize that Pierce was deep in his cups, and not amusingly or even attractively so but meanly and bitchily. Rennie perked up at once. *Well, this might be worth sticking around for...* As if to justify his existence, or perhaps merely to look good in front of Pierce and the rest of the movers and shakers, Danny was frantically shooting the lobby action, which if anything had only intensified since Rennie and Gerry had gone upstairs forty minutes ago for their quiet time.

Across the lounge, Graham Sonnet, looking like no one but himself—perennially rumpled in a gorgeously cut Italian shirt and trousers and jacket and tie, his shaggy brown hair and bright blue eyes unmistakable even at forty paces—was standing conversing cheerfully with his wife Prunella Vye, their old friend and label president Leeds Sheffield, and Leeds's rock-critic girlfriend Carson Duquette.

Rennie perked up even more: she knew Carson very well, and Leeds a little—maybe she could scrounge an introduction to the Sonnets through them. What with Graham—founder of the now-disbanded Budgies, the greatest group that had ever been on land or sea—and Prue—queen of the charts in her own right before their marriage—having recently formed their own band, it was only natural that Rennie should covet entrée to the Sonnet presence. And she was by no means the only one who wanted in, since almost every pair of eyes in direct sightline were fixed on Gray and Prue, covertly or overtly: the royal family of Great Rock Britain, more illustrious than either Beatles or Stones.

The eyes that weren't on the Sonnets were on Brian Jones, only Stone to so far show, and, as it would turn out, the only Stone who would come rolling into Monterey at all. He was sitting enthroned in a leather armchair far from the fireplace, looking bemused, perhaps at his monosyllabic companion, the blond lobotozoid Nico from the Velvet Underground, who was in close and constant attendance. And sprinkled around the lobby and bar and public rooms, like sparkling raisins in a dense and delicious cake, were all manner of strange and wondrous creatures: freaks, millionaires, hippies, artists, freakish millionaire hippie artists, starving artists, even cranky journalists.

But Pierce Hill had already climbed atop his pet hobbyhorse, and now he was riding it hell for leather, with a heavy hand on the whip and a heavier on the tumbler of Scotch. And he was loud enough and crude enough that some of the nearby, and even far removed, notables were casting pained and irritated glances his way. It was nothing he hadn't said many times before, in public or in private, but in this company, at this venue, it suddenly seemed extra-offensive. And the notables, greater and lesser alike, were quite right to be offended. Which didn't stop Pierce's boorish bellowings for one heartbeat.

Well, just because a jackass brays doesn't mean you have to listen to it. Though this particular jackass was braying so loudly that it was hard not to. Rennie gave in and listened a bit. All things end, and so would this. In the meantime…

"Artists! They all think they're so great and talented and sexy, but they barely know how to tie their own fucking *shoes*. That's why we have to do it *for* them, *and* feed them, *and* wipe their fucking noses, *and* clean their fucking bottoms, *and* babysit them when they OD and all the rest of it. It's an accident that they manage to get off any art at all, and then no sooner have they done it than they want to fucking *change* it. They're always whining about their fucking *art*, or their fucking *craft*, pissing and moaning about *growing* as artists when they *should* be thinking about where the next fucking hit single's coming from. Give me a dead artist over a live one any day of the week! You can handle a dead one so much easier."

By some cosmic, or karmic, fluke of timing, the way it often happens in a convivial crowd, the drunk and raving words, and the last two sentences particularly, were pronounced with perfect clarity into a suddenly hushed airspace. The Sonnets glanced over, decided they'd heard quite enough, thank you ever so, and with native British dignity excused themselves to go upstairs. A number of others followed, or moved decisively away into one of the other lounges or restaurants. Pierce didn't even notice.

"Death now, death's the best way of controlling an artist's creative output," he railed sottishly on. "Jus' makes sense. If'n artist's dead, he can't change 'smusic on you, meaning of course on *me*, and his backlist's not just gold but a gold mine. Diamon' mine. Stays a diamon' mine, too."

His diction deteriorating with every installment of Chivas that slid down his throat, Pierce pointed erratically at Danny Marron, now prudently filming on the other side of the lounge. He was using the new videocamera equipment that Romilly had spoken of, though Rennie had no idea what difference it really made. Maybe if you were deeply into it, which she wasn't; but it was new and some people always thought new was better.

"Looka him. No, looka! See? Little pathetic man making a little pathetic movie. He can't film the acts here 'cause somebody else got the rights first. So he's just pissing around filming whatever he can. Now, now, now think how much innerest a big important rock death would give his little pissy boring footage. Never mind Pennebakererer, Penisbaker, whatever the fuck, Marron would be the big dog forever if he could shoot something like that. Even something like that little rent boy, died over at the other place. Pity he couldn't have gotten that down on film. But he never will."

Gerry Langhans couldn't take any more; he stepped forward and spoke into his boss's ear for quite a few moments. Pierce laughed raucously.

"You a diplomat all of a sudden, Langhans, you think I better shut up? You think I'm saying a buncha shit I shouldn't? Hell, everybody here is thinking 'zactly what I'm saying, they just don't have the balls to say it out loud, much less act on it. You don't seriously think we *take* these kids seriously? Expect any of them to be on the charts in five years, or even alive? 'Course we don't! And we don't care, either!"

His squinty pig-eyes had lighted on Rennie. "Hey, Rennie Stride, you pretty thing, come over here and sit on my dick, always wanted to get into those hot little panties of yours. No? Your loss. But, but, now *you're* a rough tough journalist, babe, murders an' all, don't you really think the same 's me, same 's I do, 'bout all these little pishers? You 'member those little assholes got murdered at the Fillmore, at your apartment? Just stupid smack slobs, stupid pothead acid freak druggies—well, the sooner they all off themselves the better! Just 's long as they make a few records and make me a ton of money first. After that I don't give a good goddamn. Jus' business. 'S all I'm sayin'. Jus' my 'pinion."

"If I wanted your opinion, Percy," said Rennie evenly, "I'd just read your entrails... So it's just all about the money, then, is it?"

She was trying very hard to restrain her right arm from conveying her right fist to Pierce Hill's nose, accurately and painfully, and dodged his grabbing hands as he lunged for her breasts, missed and fell back, cursing and laughing.

She looked at him with scorn and disgust, spoke to be heard across the room, enunciating every word.

"You slobbering, drunken pile of ripe rhinoceros poo. Try to touch me again and I'll rip your arm out of its socket and pound you to death with it. Unless someone else beats me to it."

Then: *'Rent boy'? Are we talking about* Adam? *What do you know that I don't, Epps? And how do you know it?*

She glanced across the room, to where Rainshadow Records' second in command, Elkanah Bannerman, was watching his boss's display with a face like thunder. Elk was a short, balding, bull-necked, New York Jewish-Italian ex-garmento king; he did not suffer fools, gladly or indeed at all, and as Juha had mentioned, there were some pretty solid rumors that he was mobbed up. He'd bought into Rainshadow five years ago, to please his rock-mad teenage kids; and as Juha had also said, mob or not, he was the only honorable person at the whole entire label. Well, apart from Gerry.

But Elk was old-school, from a very old school indeed: you did not act like a drunken jackass in public; you did not insult women; you did not conduct yourself in such a manner as to displeasingly discredit or embarrass your organization—or your lieutenants— before colleagues and rivals. And just now Elk did not look pleased with Pierce Hill, no, he did not look pleased at all.

Pierce was oblivious. "Damn right it's jus' all about the money! Bands — poor little hippie sheep that have lost their way, blah blah blah, never knew it in the first place, and now we're gonna do some major shearing. Oh, they'll get a few bags of wool for themselves, but the labels are the ones who'll be wearing cashmere, not the musicians. Jus' looka me, my label. My label Rain. Good old Rainy. Rainshadowrainyrain. I'm cleaning out the old and feeble sheep, yes I am, gonna bring in some big macho rams and some pretty little lambs. But I'll still be the shepherd. Fleece 'em all! You'll see. You'll all see."

He tried to get up, couldn't get his legs under him and sprawled back into the chair, laughing like a hyena, and any artist still left in the room turned away.

Gerry Langhans wasn't on the same page, or even in the same book, as his boss; in fact, he was looking utterly disgusted, and he went over to talk to Sledger Cairns before she went off like a grenade. Daughter of the great blues-guitar legend, mountain man Galt Cairns, who had taught his offspring everything she knew, the orange-haired Sledger — Veronica Lee, as her driver's license declared her — had heard Pierce Hill's entire diatribe, and instead of turning her back on him like a lady she was now glaring at him like a laser.

In fact, she looked about ready to stuff a mattress with his shredded connective tissue. Good thing there weren't any weapons handy — she'd never waste a good liquor bottle, not even an empty one, on cracking his skull. Though from what Rennie knew of Sledger, for whom the word 'volatile' was merely a jumping-off place, the absence of ordnance wouldn't stop her for long. Failing everything else, she could always smother him with her tits — the finest rack in rock and roll, by many votes and many cup sizes. But it looked as if Gerry had gotten her calmed down and moved out of firing range before the furniture had a chance to take wing.

More revolted by Pierce's vomitous little speech than she could say, or could trust herself to say, Rennie looked around to see if he was right. He certainly seemed to be, she realized with a sinking heart: the battle lines were already drawn, as clear and defined as the Continental Divide. Musicians and writers and label or p.r. freaks on one side; on the other, men in costly suits and frightening morocco-leather tans, who reminded her of her father-in-law and his cronies. The first were happily all about the music; the second were utterly uncomprehending of what was really happening here, concerned chiefly about getting the hell away from the festival and its headachey music and drug-besotted children to go play golf like successful grownup powerbrokers on the tempting greens of nearby Pebble Beach, if they could finagle themselves a tee time. No real understanding of the scene, little if any love for the sound. Just business as usual.

Oh, there were civilized and sophisticated and knowledgeable exceptions, as everyone knew: Clive Davis, Leeds Sheffield, the urbane Ahmet Ertegun, universally known as Omelet. But for the most part, Pierce seemed to have nailed it, speaking for his fellow moguls, and that made Rennie sad. Did it really *have* to be like that, she wondered, thinking back to her conversation with Garcia on Romilly's terrace. No common ground between, say, the clean grace and artistry of a Turk Wayland or a Graham Sonnet and that sodden oaf across the room smeared all over the sofa? Was there no way to reconcile hipness and business, to the greatest good of all? Until artists ran their own labels for themselves, art for artists' sake, maybe not.

And maybe not even then, she thought in all honesty, as she trudged upstairs to a shower and bed, suddenly unspeakably weary and hoping she'd be over it by tomorrow morning. Perhaps the artists would be easily and immediately corrupted, and turn out to be just as vile as the current crop of masters; maybe they'd simply be unable to adjust to business-as-usual and would go down in flames trying to do business as *un*usual. Artists already knew they couldn't trust the labels to do right by them: it was to be dearly hoped and devoutly wished that they could trust themselves.

But she wasn't so sure. Because however well she knew music, and by now she knew it very well indeed, by now Rennie knew musicians even better.

Chapter 11

Friday morning, June 16

THE OPENING DAY of the Monterey Pop Festival dawned as cool and grayish as the day before: mid-coastal low ocean cloud moving inland to veil the sun. It would lift later, burning off as it always did. But the morning vibe couldn't have been brighter.

Rennie, well rested and geared up to face the day and feeling much more cheerful about everything, was having an early breakfast at the inn, with Marcus and Brent, who'd come over from town, where they were crashing for the festival nights with a local artist friend. And up until that very instant she'd been enjoying herself. Brent had even off-handedly inquired if Rennie could introduce him to Prax, on whom apparently he had a tiny long-distance crush, and Rennie had been entertaining the idea with pleasure. But now he had just ruined all that, and she stared helplessly at him, then at Marcus. *No help THERE…*

"So you're telling me—" she began clearly and carefully.

Brent kept his eyes on her face. "I'm telling you that the bullets that were fired at Waterhall came from a single-shot rifle owned by Romilly Ramillies, who is, as I needn't remind you, godmother to Brandi Storey Marron and mother to Becca the acid casualty."

"What rifle?"

"Oh, give it up, Rennie!" Marcus twitched so violently in his seat that he upset his coffee cup, luckily empty. "Nice try—I particularly admire the wide-eyed note of injured innocence, you do it very well—but I've already told him that Romilly asked us both not to mention the gun incident."

"Oh. Well, then. What else does the ballistics department tell you, Deputy Sheriff Gilmore?"

"Not one little damn thing. The gun had been wiped and we never found any bullet casings."

Rennie attended to her plate again: no sense letting good poached eggs and corned beef hash get cold, she could certainly eat and think at the same time, even in such company. Especially in such company.

"I see. That would seem to argue *against* it being Romilly, no? I mean, it's her rifle, her fingerprints would be *expected* to be all over it, she wouldn't *need* to wipe it. If she's guilty, it would just make her look more so if she did. Wipe it, I mean."

"Well, no, she wouldn't need to. But Brandi or Becca would."

Rennie snorted. "Yeah, if you think either of them could hold it together long enough to get off two shots— which they'd have had to load separately, that rifle was a single-shot Ruger, bolt-action, very nice—that came pretty darn close to hitting someone. Which I, personally, do not think that they could."

She put down her knife and fork and pushed back from the table. "Maybe it *was* just one of Romilly's neighbors shooting at a rattlesnake, the way she said. They do have a lot of them around there—snakes. Could have been a local with really bad aim."

"I live not far from her place myself," said Brent patiently. "I know all about the snakes. And when people in my neighborhood shoot at rattlers, we generally use shotguns. On account of the snake being, you know, a few feet away from you? Because what you want in that situation is a reptile blown to snakeskin smithereens by two barrels of shot. Meaning that no right-thinking country dweller would try to kill a rattler with a single-shot rifle that throws a quarter mile. Trust me. They just wouldn't."

"Be that as it may, there were upwards of twenty people at Waterhall and environs that morning, as far as I know. Apart from the fired-upon trio, of course." Rennie ticked off on her fingers. "The four of us: me, Prax, Chet, Juha. Romilly, Becca and Simon Revels. Simon's wife, Chloe, and three college-age or teenage kids. Danny and Brandi Storey Marron. Becca's in-house nurse-companion. The cook, the maid, the driver, the groundskeepers and the houseman. If it wasn't one of us, then who?"

"So—by process of elimination—you think that it was Romilly who did the shooting," Marcus said, not looking at her, "and that's the reason she asked us to keep it quiet. Not likely it was Becca or Simon or the other family members, though if it was, then Romilly could be covering for them. Couldn't be Danny or Brandi, since Danny was one of those being shot at, and, by our mutual observation, yours and mine, Brandi was asleep until just after the shots were fired. Wasn't any of you guys, unless you're holding out on me. Extremely doubtful it was one of the staff. That leaves Romilly. Or someone not from the house. So who do you think?"

Rennie gave Marcus a long cool look. "Me? I have no idea. Not who did the shooting, or why anyone would shoot at Finn Hanley and Pierce Hill and Danny Marron, or why Mrs. Revels would command our silence. Does it matter?"

"It might." Brent shrugged. "Or not. It just struck me odd—once I finally heard about it, no thanks to the two of you—that she bothered to ask you to keep quiet about it at all."

"Yes," said Rennie before Marcus could get there first. "Yes, we thought it was a little odd too."

When Rennie went upstairs again, there was another message from Burke waiting for her, and she returned his call at once.

"That was smart work giving Fitz your stories last night," he remarked, warm amusement in his voice. "Only you would make Oliver Fitzroy, first Baron Holywoode, into your own personal long-distance chauffeur-driven messenger boy…oh, I'm only kidding, it tickled him no end. We had a nice breakfast just now, he and I; he read the stuff in the car on the way up, and he said to tell you he's very pleased. Anyway, the color piece is in today's editions—good job, both of you—but I wanted to hold off on the other in case you had revises."

"Fitz didn't seem annoyed to be pressed into service carrying dispatches," said Rennie, feeling a little guilty. Still, if she'd offended his lordship by being presumptuous, surely he would have said so on the spot, and he'd certainly seemed amenable to her request… "He insisted on driving up—well, being driven—all the way from L.A. Said he'd probably never get another chance to see the coast properly and as long as he had a chauffeur at his disposal, why not."

"That's our boy!"

Rennie lowered her voice, though the door was shut and she was alone in the room.

"And you do remember that the big secret Baz and Haz story I called in all unbeknownst to anyone but you and me isn't to run until tonight's bulldog? Baz is making his little announcement from the stage, so we don't want to anticipate it. But we do want to have it in print before anyone else. Preferably while they're still onstage. Synchronicity. That's the ticket."

"Yeah, I got that… I must say Jeannie and I are very disappointed to hear about the break-up. We both really like Potter and Hazlitt. However uncool it may be to admit it."

"Well, don't you two give up on that just yet. According to them both, separately, there may be more music yet to come, separately. And you know, I still wouldn't even count them out together. I somehow don't think Baz is going to find it as easy to part ways with Roger as he claims. Not that he thinks it's going to be easy. Anyway, must run. Time to get over to the fairgrounds."

"Have fun, did I say that?"

"I'll do my best."

Even without no performance scheduled to happen until that evening, backstage was cheerful chaos, raised to a high degree by the level of the component parts.

In the Hunt Club, the talk was all of Pierce Hill's flamingly spectacular freakout the night before. Nobody who'd been there could believe it had actually happened, and nobody who hadn't been there could believe it hadn't happened. But no one was surprised, least of all Rennie, whom Belinda Melbourne had gleefully filled in on their drive from the hotel to the fairgrounds. What did stagger her was the reported reaction of Gerry Langhans.

"He. Actually. PUNCHED. Pierce." Rennie shook her head in admiration and wonder. "And I *missed* it! Man, I'm so jealous I can't see straight. Do you know how many people have longed to do a lot less than that, and never did? Me included? Oh, that Aloysius Gerard! I'm going to give him a big old hug, and perhaps arrange for a medal. Maybe the Nobel Peace Prize—nobody else really deserves it this year. Let's hope the rest of the festival isn't quite so warlike."

Belinda nodded. "I hear that the Monterey police chief, guy name of Frank Marinello, called out his entire forty-six man force. Forty-six fuzz against forty thousand heads, freaks and other such exotic fauna. Brave fellas in that thin blue line. Outnumbered a thousand to one. Sounds like some ancient classical battle. Thermopylae! Where are the Spartans when we really need 'em?"

"Didn't we hear he hired like a hundred or so reinforcements from the surrounding towns—off-duty cops and deputy sheriffs?" asked Stan, laughing at the image. "And even alerted the National Guard encampment, 650 soldiers at Fort Ord, just up the road."

"Too true," agreed Rennie, rolling her eyes. "Brent Gilmore told me all about it, being one of the hires himself. I also heard that Marinello ordered that all officers should patrol the festival grounds in full uniform, including guns and nightsticks. Funny thing, though: since a few hours in, yesterday afternoon, an awful lot of them suddenly had flowers tucked somewhere about their authoritarian persons—flowers given them by longhaired barefoot braless hippie beauties. I didn't notice too many of the coppers refusing."

"All in the interests of keeping the peace."

"Getting a piece, more likely. But it's all totally copacetic. No hassles on either side. Marinello seems like a cool enough dude. Let's hope everything stays that way."

"Have you talked to the detectives again, Rennie?" asked Belinda.

"No, and I'm beginning to think there's really nothing else there to talk to them about. Nothing new about Adam, anyway, except that Pierce Hill in his cups last night called him a rent boy. Which means what I think it means, right?"

"Right, and one then must inevitably wonder just how Pierce knew that," mused Stan. "Or was it merely a bow drawn at a venture?"

Rennie grinned. "*And* the lad can quote Scripture to serve his own purposes! No wonder that Wyoming heifer heaven ran you out of town. But yes, it does raise an interesting question. And makes for a possible motive, maybe, even."

Well, it did. There was no proof, of course, not the slightest whisper, that Adam and Pierce had even known each other, much less had *that* sort of relationship. But maybe it wasn't Pierce himself...maybe he'd just been tossing out a reference to someone else. Such things did of course occur in rock, of course, just as they did in every other field of endeavor—stockbrokering, academia, theater, high-seas piracy, the Catholic Church, whatever. And basically, no one in the rock scene cared if you wanted to bugger *sheep*, for heaven's sake—as long as the sheep was over the age of consent and had a good time too.

It was just that nobody ever talked about it out loud for public consumption; rock was a manly business, and the men in it were manly men, or wanted to appear so, at least. The desired body count of desired bodies was measured in chicks, not cats. Plus the fans didn't want to know: if they resented their idols being married or even in committed relationships, and they did—John Lennon had had to keep his wife Cynthia and their son Julian a secret for years, and he wasn't the only one—they certainly didn't want to hear that others of their crush objects were into, as it were, guys.

It didn't seem to carry the same freight with chicks. Everyone in rock knew that Janis Joplin, for instance, was just as likely to fly the friendly thighs of Trans Girl Airlines as she was to share her fuselage with a guy. But again the fans were kept ignorant, despite the fact that Janis wasn't anywhere near as discreet about her lady friends as, say, Prax McKenna was. Once more, it was nobody's damn business, and nobody in the biz particularly cared. Not as long as the music kept on playing.

Still, assuming that Pierce was right about Adam, how did he know? And as to how that might make a motive for murder…well, that was still something to be figured out. And if it was there at all to be figured, even the tiniest littlest bit, Rennie intended that she herself should be the one to do the figuring.

The little conclave broke up after a while: it was still early, but there was shopping to be done, and dope to be done, and musical decisions to be made—not necessarily in that order. Rennie wandered off by herself, taking mental notes for the next color story that Burke might require of her. She had given much thought to her first official public appearance at this historic occasion, and in spite of the weather she was wearing a sparkly gold crocheted vest over a white see-through cotton poet shirt over bare tits, and patchworked velvet hiphugger bellbottoms with a pair of handpainted leather clogs. Ordinarily she wouldn't have dressed so formally, but considering the people who were here, and what *they* were wearing, she felt the need to compete, or at least measure up. Besides, it was fun to flaunt your nipples in public; even Joan Baez was doing it lately.

By now the festival was in full spate, though not a lick of official Monterey music had yet been heard. Adler and Phillips had given way under the press of sheer numbers and public opinion, and everyone who showed up at the gate was now being let in for free. They couldn't all fit in the arena, of course, that held only about seven thousand or so; but the fairgrounds were spacious, and the hordes comfortably dispersed themselves over the many tree-shaded acres.

Or maybe, thought Rennie cynically, such benevolence was meant purely for show rather than as good will, and had been planned that way from the first, Adlips, as she liked to think of them, knowing full well that the walls would never prevail against the rising tide of hungry freaks and music fans, and only wanting to get the hipness credit for the free admissions. She wouldn't put anything past them.

But it made for a happy bunch of people. Of course, the drugs did a lot toward making them happy too…

Music had already begun in various places around the fairgrounds — the main stage was *still* being worked on, but, again, no one seemed terribly concerned; though maybe the drugs were responsible for that as well. Everything was harmoniously building toward the moment that evening when Potter and Hazlitt would take the stage to open the First International Monterey Pop Festival up for business.

Rennie pushed her way through the crowd, scanning for anyone she knew. From a distance she saw Roger Hazlitt's blond head above the crowd. He was looking annoyed and concerned, and she headed over.

"What is it?" she asked as she came up to him.

He was scowling, though not at her. "I can't find Basil. We have to do a bit of rehearsing — as you see, the stage still isn't ready, and probably nobody will even get to do a sound check. So a brief bout of rehearsal will have to suffice—just to go over the set list, if nothing else—and there's a very small window of opportunity. He knows this."

"Anyone out there looking for him?" Rennie fell into step beside him as they began to quarter the backstage area.

"Sure, roadies and all sorts. We're thinking he got seriously stoned and just zonked out somewhere, but we can't be having with that. After all, he's bloody well half of this damn act."

Rennie looked uncomfortable, but said nothing, and Roger didn't notice. *Well, he'll find out soon enough, like the rest of us, and maybe Baz will still give him the tip beforehand…maybe.*

On their sweep, they ran into Danny Marron, who offered to accompany them, shooting this morning with yet another impressive-looking camera. No one from Pennebaker's team tried to stop him, which was one small mercy—because pretty soon there wouldn't be much mercy around, not anywhere, and not for a long time to come.

Twenty minutes later, Danny still shooting, they found Baz Potter. He was lying beneath and behind the flap of a canvas-fronted display table in a tent Rennie recognized immediately as belonging to the young Hawaiian bead stringer from whom both she and Pamie had bought necklaces. A strand of agate beads lay broken and scattered around him, and the metal strings of his beloved stage Martin—smashed beyond repair—were cutting deeply and redly into the flesh of his throat, the broken-off custom headpiece, with the distinctive P&H monogram inlaid in mother-of-pearl, having been used as a fulcrum to twist the strings tight.

Chapter 12

GARROTED, YES, AND VERY, VERY DEAD. Standing in the tent doorway, Rennie could see how deeply the thin steel strings had bitten into Baz's neck, breaking the skin, cutting through the soft tissue and the arteries, the great puddle of blood beneath him, the way his dark hair fell forward across his unnaturally pale cheek. At least his eyes were decently shut; she didn't think she could have borne seeing them open and sightless and dull, their familiar intelligent gleam put out like a candle. She stood there numbly, pressing her hands to her mouth.

Oh, Baz…

She ruthlessly suppressed tears and the onrushing tsunami of grief, forced herself into reporter mode. *I can't cry, I CAN'T, I must remember how this is, I must see everything, it's my JOB, it's the only way I can help him now…*

The late Basil Potter was wearing the same clothes he'd had on yesterday afternoon, when they'd talked not a dozen yards from this very stall: a white cotton embroidered Egyptian shirt, satin trousers and suede ankleboots, with the addition of a denim jacket, presumably against last night's chill. Besides the guitar strings, he had been bound and gagged with macramé and strands of beads and several tie-dyed scarves. *Tie-died, one could say...dear GOD what the hell is wrong with me...*

Without what could have been called a conscious thought, Rennie automatically moved into a blocking position, protecting Baz's fallen form, to keep anyone from getting to him, at least until the cops showed up. It seemed a thing for a friend to do. It hadn't hit her yet, she knew, not even the tiniest bit, but when it did... Belinda Melbourne, who'd been with them, had vanished, presumably to fetch the police, and Rennie felt suddenly very alone and very light-headed. Shock. Maybe she should drop a Valium or something...

She was aware of movement all around, though carefully not too close to Baz: even Danny Marron, camera vulture, realized he had to back off. But hey, that was what big old zoom lenses were for, right?

Before anyone realized what was happening, a smallish, strawberry-blond whirlwind rushed in and collapsed over the body: Pamina Potter, crying hysterically and stoned out of her mind, kneeling beside Baz and keening like a banshee. Stan Hirsh and Prax came up behind her, looking dumbfounded, and stood beside Rennie as they helplessly watched Pamina's meltdown. Which looked, they had to say, utterly genuine. And it probably was: just because the Potters' marriage had tanked didn't mean they didn't still care about each other.

"I did it, I confess to it, oh Baz my darling I am so sorry, I didn't want him to go on, I didn't want him playing electrically, betraying his roots like Dylan, selling out everything he stood for!"

Rennie and Stan exchanged glances. Yeah, right. *Undoubtedly* it had been something like that. Rennie bent forward and put her arms around Pamina, pulling her gently up and away from Baz. She noticed as she did so that the English girl's hands were a little sore-looking and reddened, and not with her husband's blood — though her velvet minidress now was smeared with it, and her legs where she'd knelt in the grass.

"Come with me, sweetness," she heard herself saying. "There's nothing for you here. Come on now, Pamie, come away. We'll take care of him."

Pamina allowed herself to be led outside, Danny filming all the time; still hysterical, Pamie never noticed, and Rennie, shaken to her soul, didn't think to tell Marron to knock it off. They were standing uncertainly outside the tent when the law showed up at a run, led by Belinda, and immediately began taping off the area as a crime scene.

Well, Baz got his wish, Rennie heard herself thinking somewhere way far away, in the huge hollow airless silence that pressed close around her, tightening and tightening like the counterhoop rimming a drumhead.

He wanted to be out of Potter and Hazlitt by today, and, by God, he was. In fact, about ten hours ahead of schedule…

"Nobody actually believes her," said a distracted Brent Gilmore. "But she was screaming so loudly that she'd killed him that they probably heard her in Santa Cruz. I had to get her out of there, if only to shut her the hell up. *You* don't believe her, do you?" he asked suddenly, looking up at Rennie.

Rennie, deep in shock but also both curious and dubious, like a good journalist, had tagged along unchallenged as Brent, with Marcus's help, shepherded

Pamina away from the bead tent to a backstage office, which opened on the main Hunt Club space and had been hastily vacated by horrified festival staff, so the cops could question her in privacy. Danny Marron and his camera had been firmly barred from the premises; Rennie didn't know where he'd gone. Just now she had been staring blankly at Pamie, until Brent's question had forced her to focus outward again.

"Me? God, no, of course not, she's just off her head. And who can blame her? Listen, I know you have to get back out there: do you want me and Prax to stay with her until you can get a policewoman up here?"

Brent looked relieved. "I'll leave one of the officers with you. Thank you, Miss Stride" — formal in the public face of duty — "And I know I don't need to say it, but —"

"Then don't. You'll just insult me."

"What didn't he need to say that would insult you?" asked Prax as soon as he was out of earshot.

"That I can't use anything Pamie might confidingly tell me in her newly widowed hysterics. Use in a journalistic context, that is."

Prax looked outraged. "That little piece of garbage! How dare he suggest you might —"

"Easy there, rosebud. He's probably right." Rennie looked at Pamina, who had curled up in the only comfortable chair in the small, cluttered space and now was rocking back and forth, crooning brokenly to herself. "All we can do for her is be here. I don't envy Belinda, having to tell her the way she did."

On her way to fetch the police, Belinda Melbourne had run into Pamina, and, not wanting her to come unprepared across the tent and her husband's body, had broken the news to her, with such results as they'd all seen.

"Better her than me... Do you really not think

Pamie killed him?"

"Anything's possible." Rennie shifted in her chair. "If she did, though, she sure as hell didn't kill him because he was betraying his noble and acoustic folk roots."

But Prax had caught the undertone. "You know something, don't you? We all heard rumors that he'd been beating up on her—is that it?"

Rennie didn't say anything for a while. "If it is— whatever 'it' is—we'll find out. One way or another."

Suddenly the keening stopped: Pamina was looking straight at Rennie, her red-blond hair tumbled and tossed, eyes dark and enormous in a ghost-pale face.

"You knew. You knew, didn't you? He said you knew. You always knew everything, he said."

Feeling oddly guilty, Rennie tried to brush it off. "Knew what, Pamie?"

"He told you. I know he told you. It's okay. He didn't think I knew it, but I did. What he was going to do tonight."

Rennie didn't take her steady gaze off Pamie, but out of the corner of her eye she could see the motion as the cop straightened in his seat over by the window and began to take notes. Hell. Still, there seemed to be no stopping it…

"What was that, then?"

And then Pamina Potter pronounced the murder motive, loud and clear for all to hear. And, to Rennie at least, it came as no surprise.

"He *told* you that?" Brent Gilmore stared at her, and Marcus stared even harder and colder. "That he was going to announce the break-up of the act actually onstage tonight? And that Hazlitt didn't know a thing about it?"

Half an hour later, the two had returned,

accompanied by a policewoman and another young deputy, and Pamie had been unprotestingly and limply — having taken Rennie up on the secret proffer of a nice gentle downer — turned over to them, put in a squad car with great considerateness and driven off to the stationhouse. Prax had gone off to look for Potter and Hazlitt's manager, a personable young Englishman named Rick Henries, to advise him of events. Pamie would be needing a lawyer, probably immediately, and nobody here had any concealed about their persons, exactly: what musician would bring a lawyer to a music festival? What lawyer would even attend one? Though, come to think of it, since everyone had come armed for deal-making, there probably were at least a few shysters lurking about who might be commandeered into service, if only for the moment.

For a brief instant Rennie had considered phoning Kingston Bryant, the Lacing family lawyer, an imposing, white-maned legal deity who had defended Prax last year in the two murder cases where she'd been wrongfully accused. Or at the very least, her old college friend Berry Rosenbaum, now one of King's junior partners. Still being a Lacing, if only in name, Rennie retained both the right and the resources to call upon King's services. And Pamie was, after all, Mrs. Basil Potter, wife of half of the greatest folk act in Britain — not to mention her unofficial affiliation with the other half of the greatest folk act in Britain. King loved high-profile cases, and Pamina could certainly afford to pay his high-profile fees.

But she decided against it almost immediately. Stephen would utterly freak if he found out she was involved in yet another murder. Two murders. Two *more* murders. She'd put him through enough over the past year; and she didn't want to give Ling-ling Delphine de la Fontange any more cause to think badly of her.

Brent repeated his question, a bit more sharply this time, and Rennie flushed before answering.

"Well...yes. Yes, he did. I guess Pamie knew after all, and maybe Roger too. But he made me promise not to say anything."

"Sure, to his partner and his wife and his record label people! Not to not say anything to *us*. Us cops. Do you realize how many motives this gives how many people?" Brent ran a hand through his hair. "Now the state police are involved too, because the fairgrounds are state property. So it's officially them and the MPD, with our help, on the Potter murder, which is huge, and us by our lonesomes on the Santa Monica kid's murder, it being—sorry, Rennie—suddenly considerably less huge. And if it turns out the two killings are related, which I frankly cannot imagine they aren't, and if they find out you were sitting on a possible motive for one of them ever since Monday at Mojado..."

His silence was more eloquent than speech. Rennie felt sorry for him, and a touch nervous for herself—yes, she could have said, and she probably *should* have said—but she couldn't come up with anything more to help him, and as she stared across at Marcus, she saw that he didn't have anything either. In fact, he looked pretty annoyed with her, as well he might.

So, torn between sticking to the rules and sticking to her job and sticking to her friends and sticking to the chance of finding something out, Rennie decided to just remain right where she was, for now, taking further copious notes for the bare-bones story she had already called in to the paper, and see what happened when word got out of Baz's death. Should be impressive... And when she heard herself thinking that, she was disgusted with herself, just as Marcus was disgusted with her: Baz was her friend, she should be upset, she should be comforting Pamina and Roger, and oh by the way where *was* Roger? He hadn't come here with Pamie, or gone with her to the cop house either; in fact, he seemed to have vanished after the discovery of Baz's body, and she wondered briefly what, if anything, that might mean. Belinda had gone back to the hotel, considerably shaken up; she might be writing up a story of her own, but Fitz wouldn't let hers beat Rennie's — Murder Chick being the crime flagship, after all, of his newspaper fleet.

By now the Phillipses and Lou Adler had been told of Baz's death, and the guy who was in charge of security, and about a dozen more of the festival brass. They were all sitting around a table at the other end of the Hunt Club, staring numbly at one another; some of the women were weeping. Marcus, sent over to them by Brent, gave them as many details as he could; in shock, nobody had any questions for him, and he rose to leave. As he did, conversation burst like an overstressed dam behind him: oh my God what will we do, what about tonight, who'll open, can we move some acts around.

Rennie gazed upon them with loathing not unmixed with empathy. Not one of them had yet offered so much as one sorrowing syllable about Baz: why was he dead, who had killed him, how were Pamie and Roger, *where* were Pamie and Roger. Sure, they had the festival to think of, and they would do whatever they could not to spoil the trip for all those thousands of people, at least to not spoil it any more than they had to, but still. Rennie felt as if she were going to be sick, and she fled outside again...

Feeling better, she balked at returning to the fraughtness of the Hunt Club and festival office; wandering aimlessly, she found herself being drawn against her will over to the bead tent, scene of the crime. After her first phone call to Burke, giving the bare details of the story, she'd sent Vince Bays, the Clarion photographer, to get whatever pictures he could—no matter how she personally felt, the murder of Basil Potter was still a big giant news story and she was the ranking Clarion reporter on the scene. Burke Kinney and Garrett Larkin would expect her to remember that, and to have photos to go with her and Stan's assorted stories. But she didn't have to be there when those photos were taken...

They were just getting ready to move Baz out of the tent and into an ambulance from the coroner's office. Prax, who had come with Rennie to pay respects, couldn't stand it, and broke and fled weeping, but Rennie felt she had to stay, to witness and report as was her duty; and also to see her old friend safely taken away. It was a million times worse than finding two dead bodies in her flat last year: even though she had known those victims and it had been a real shock, Baz had been a real friend, for years and years; they had history...

Beside her, Roger Hazlitt stood like a statue, face as bleak and granitic as his native Scottish mountains. So this was where he'd been all this time—keeping vigil over his partner. Rennie wondered fleetingly why he hadn't gone with Pamina, then he turned to her, and she knew why.

"Did you know? What he was going to do tonight onstage?"

She was so startled that she stepped back a pace, but his tone had not been accusatory, and he read confirmation in her face.

"He told me not to say anything," she heard herself stammering yet again, and knew as she said it that maybe she should have tried to find a way to tell him, somehow, *something*; and that Roger might never forgive her for not having done so, that he might even think that if she had, Baz might still be alive; that he might even be right to think so. "I'm so, *so* sorry, Roger... How did you know?"

"Pamie told me. I don't know how she found out." He ran a hand over his face, spoke wonderingly, dazedly. "He was going to break up the *act*. He never even told me what he was going to do; did he think I wouldn't go along with him, or would try to stop him? Hell, I'd have been *thrilled* to help him smash Baz & Haz to bits in public, he knew that; I thought he knew that..."

He stared at the shrouding canvas of the tent concealing what lay within, as if he could burn it away with eyefire.

"And now he's dead. He's dead, and we're still on the label. Which is what Pierce bloody goddamn sodding buggering Hill wanted all along. He even said so last night, at the hotel. And now this morning Basil is dead, and the sound is never going to change, and Pierce doesn't have to deal with Basil ever again. Perfect motive. So why haven't they arrested *him*?"

Or you, *my friend: you've got a pretty solid motive or two there yourself—stop Baz breaking up the act and going public with all the embarrassing drama, or punish him for it, and there's always that little matter of you and Pamina...*

She laid a hand on his arm, and felt his sudden tensing, but then he covered her fingers with his own, a strong, firm musician's grasp.

"It takes a bit more than that to hook someone up for murder, my dear," she said quietly. "Believe me, I know."

"They took Pamie away quick enough."

"She's not under arrest. It was more for her protection than anything else. And now they're going to take him away too. Look. Here they come."

They unconsciously drew themselves up, straightening their shoulders like an honor guard, and stood by in hopeless silence, holding hands, two uncomforted children, as the tent flap opened and the stretcher with Baz's body was carried past them.

"I'm going with him," said Roger abruptly, as they watched the ambulance doors open to receive Baz's shrouded form. "Will you look after Pamie?"

She nodded, still holding his hand, her other hand pressed to her mouth. "Prax went to find Rick Henries. If she needs a lawyer—Pamie, I mean—I can probably fix her up with one. The one who got Prax off last year, in fact. Not that Pamie's going to be charged…"

Roger hugged her hard. "You've always been a good friend. To all three of us. Thanks, Ace."

Rennie watched as he climbed into the van, the requisite cop already sitting inside on a jump seat, and then the doors closed on Potter and Hazlitt, together for perhaps the last time.

It occurred to Rennie then that she had never, in the course of their long friendship, heard Roger Hazlitt call his musical partner by the diminutive 'Baz.' No, it had always been 'Basil', and she had never wondered at it: the formality, or the rivalry, or whatever it had been. Perhaps it had come from their first friendship, or maybe Roger used it as a means of annoyance, or just because he was a man who set great store by dignity and found nicknames beneath him. Or maybe Baz had liked his full name being used, and had never bothered to tell her, or to protest at her using the nickname.

Now she would never know, and suddenly it troubled her deeply, though, from her experiences over the past year, she knew exactly why. Displacement: that's what you did in the face of a sudden shock—you put the huge, soul-shaking enormity of it off on something else, something innocuous, because if you didn't, you would go mad. You might anyway, of course, but at least you delayed the possibility.

If I'm such a good goddamned friend—oh, Baz—how could *I let this happen?*

Rennie stood there in the sun, alone, for a long time. The utter normalcy of the crowds passing at a little distance, just on the other side of the second row of tents, rattled her considerably: how could they be so happy and uncaring when Baz had been murdered! But she couldn't blame them for their obliviousness—so discreet had the cops been that most of them didn't yet know that the great Basil Potter was dead, and all concerned, from Papa John Phillips on down, had agreed that the masses should remain ignorant, as far and as long as that was possible. The news was bound to get out, and sooner rather than later; but until then the fewer who knew about it, the better.

All the same, like pressing on an aching tooth, Rennie couldn't help lingering at the place. The little bead stall—there was a handmade sign above the tent flap, To Bead Or Not to Bead, she hadn't noticed that before—was now roped off with scene-of-the-crime tape, and a state trooper stood guard. But he knew who Rennie was: he'd seen her with Basil Potter's wife earlier and with Roger Hazlitt just now, and knew she was approved by Brent Gilmore and Audie Devlin, so he nodded to let her duck under the tape.

She had no intention whatsoever of going back inside the empty tent, that just wasn't possible; but as she looked around, she noticed that the young Hawaiian bead-stall owner had been allowed to remove her stock, and was standing now behind the tent, uncertain, trays of her wares stacked on the grass.

Rennie approached, carefully. "Hello? Are you okay?"

The dark-haired, honey-skinned girl looked up, and Rennie could see that she'd been crying. "Oh—aloha. Hi. I remember you. You were at Big Magic. You bought those tiger puka shells and the ocean jasper beads. And you were here this morning when they found him.

You're a friend of—of his."

"Yes. Rennie Stride. And you're—?"

"Keala Lopaka. I came over from Maui just to be at Big Magic and here. I only wanted to sell some beads and hear the music and make enough money to get back home with."

She gestured helplessly at the trays: heaps of intricate strands of shells, stones, colored pearls and coral, the bright colors and sparkling facets shouting in the sun. To her shame, Rennie instantly, and reflexively, coveted everything there.

In the midst of death we are in life, or at least in shopping mode...but I don't think Baz would mind...

"Do you know how he might have gotten into the tent?" she asked gently, but now in, inevitably, also reporter mode.

Keala shook her head. "The dealer tents are locked at night. It's just canvas, and a canvas dropcloth front from the table, but there's a steel framework that can take a padlock, and all my stuff goes in a big metal trunk, a lockbox, underneath. It's my own tent, I bought it second-hand in San Francisco just for the two festivals. At Big Magic, I slept under the table myself, but here I was crashing over on the football field with some people I met. Maybe if I hadn't—if I'd been here in the tent, it might not have—"

If you had been there, you might very well be in the morgue right now, right next to Baz... But Rennie didn't say that, and let the girl talk, as she obviously needed to.

"I've been here on the fairgrounds since Wednesday, and there wasn't a bit of *pilikia*—I mean, trouble. Now"—she gestured around again, once more on the verge of tears—"I don't know what to do. I don't know anybody. The cops told me I can't go back in there. They did enough letting me take the trays out, they said. How can I sell anything? And if I don't sell anything I can't get back home…"

Rennie put an arm around her. "Listen. I know a few people here. And now you know me. I bet I can get you set up in a new tent. A better tent. To make it up to you. Would that be okay? We can let the cop watch your stuff for now. It'll be safe here. They'll let you have the tent back when they're finished examining it. I promise. So why don't we go and see what we can do? Just for now. We can talk. Shall we talk?"

Two hours later, after petitioning a shocked and sympathetic Michelle Phillips, Rennie saw with satisfaction all the beadware spread out for sale in a brand-new tent over next to the barn that held the jamming stage, a much better location indeed. And already it was happening: word was beginning to get around, and suddenly lots and lots of people—some sincerely freaked out, some merely curious—wanted to buy Keala Lopaka's handiwork.

"They're all fucking ghouls," Rennie observed aloud, bitterly, to Prax and Tansy, who had just come up to join her. "They just want to walk by the tent and see where it happened, then come over here and buy her beads as some kind of gruesome souvenir. And I'm a ghoul too, 'cause I basically pumped her for information and it's my own dear friend who's dead and I can't even cry about it. But she didn't know anything; she wasn't even there last night. At least the poor girl won't have to go back to Maui flat broke. Come on, let's buy some stuff ourselves, help her out, if that doesn't make us all ghouls…"

She turned to move to the stall as customers cleared away, but Prax grabbed her arm.

"What? What is it?"

Prax was visibly vibrating with excitement. "I don't mean to disrespect Baz, you know I loved him, but... We just talked to John and Lou. They moved us up in the lineup. We're going on tonight, after Johnny Rivers and before the Animals."

"And *we've* been moved to Saturday night," added Tansy. "Between Paul Butterfield's band and some chick from New York called Laura Nyro, whoever she may be."

In spite of her care and sorrow, Rennie's tired face lighted up to match her friends'. "Doesn't matter! You two are going to wipe the floor with everybody on either side of you. Baz would want it that way. And I'm dressing you both for it. I brought a bunch of stuff with me. Let's go back to the hotel and see what's there. I have to call my editor again, anyway. But just let me at those necklaces first. I need to buy something. You know. For a memorial. Something to remember with. I'm allowed."

Friday night

Potter & Hazlitt (canceled)
The Association
The Paupers
Lou Rawls
Beverly
Johnny Rivers
Evenor (rescheduled from Saturday)
Eric Burdon & The Animals
Simon & Garfunkel

Chapter 13

"SOFT, *SOFT* LINEUP," said Rennie confidently to the assembled members of Evenor, running her eyes down the list of the evening's performers. "Soft as an old down pillow. Soft as a little fluffy kitten. Soft as cotton candy in the rain. Soft as — well, some more very soft things."

It was about six by now. They were all in the Hunt Club, where the band was trying to force-feed themselves from the lavish buffet. Tansy had vanished, saying she had to go meet someone, somewhere, for something or other, but promised she'd be back before Evenor went on. Rennie had commanded them to eat, saying they needed to take on ballast before they went onstage, and they were doing their best to obey. Nobody had forgotten Baz, how could they, but they now had a performance to give, unexpectedly soon, and it had to be prepared for.

"You'd think they'd have scheduled some major stuff to kick off with, right?" Rennie continued. "Blow people out of their seats straight out of the gate. But no."

"I heard the reasoning was the organizers wanted to save the heavy stuff for later," said Chet. "They figured people wouldn't really have their heads into it the first night. There'd still be people showing up, and they'd have bigger crowds on Saturday and Sunday, so why waste the headline bands."

"Which makes a certain kind of sense, to certain kinds of people," suggested Juha.

Rennie nodded. "It just feels as if something big and important should be happening tonight, though, and, judging strictly by the lineup on paper, it isn't there. Which means that you, my darlings, will not only *be* that big and happening important thing but you will totally knock everyone's little cotton socks off. They won't be expecting you, and man, are *they* going to be surprised."

Prax smiled, a little uncertainly. "Dill told us that the big boys running things tried to move acts around as fast as they could, once Baz — happened. Oh, and then the Beach Boys bailed out of Saturday night's show. Supposedly they were too freaked to go on, not because of Baz but because of some dispute over billing. Or because Carl Wilson is scared of being busted for draft evasion. Or because they're just afraid they'll be shown up as the pointless dinosaurs they are. Or maybe it *was* because of Baz, and they were afraid they'd be targets too, for some weird goddamn reason. Or because Brian Wilson is out of his freaking mind."

"Any and all of those things."

Bardo, Evenor's inscrutable bass player, scoffed gently and reached for a sandwich. "We shan't miss 'em, shall we. No, we shan't."

"The murder's still being kept pretty quiet," added drummer Jack Paris. "Nobody's even planning any kind of announcement from the stage. So as not to bum anybody out. Yeah, right. By now the fans know about it, most of them anyway. But I think it seems unreal to them."

"It seems pretty unreal to me too," said Rennie, "and I actually saw it. Saw him. But that won't last, so let's make the most of it."

She saw their surprise at her seeming off-handedness, or lack of respect, and she swept the group with a hard and haunted gaze.

"Yes, Baz was my friend. Yes, I knew him a long time, longer than I've known any of you. Yes, he's dead. Yes, I'm devastated that he's dead. I don't know what I'm going to do about it, once I actually have time to feel it and think it. But me being all freaked out and weepy right now isn't going to help him. I'll do that on my own time and in private; that's my business and his. What *will* help him is me doing what I can to find out who killed him. And I'll do *that* on my own time too... Now, you guys are alive, and tonight is your night. You have to get up there in front of everybody and play. I don't want you thinking of anything but that. And neither would Baz. He was an artist. He'd want to see you behaving like artists too. That's how you can show respect."

She felt the change in them, and gave them a small encouraging smile. "Yessir, that's my babies... Okay, then. Here's how the lineup goes. Potter and Hazlitt—yes, well. So now the Association opens it up, lame-o, boring, lounge-lizard pseuds. You guys should have been first on."

"We're a mostly unknown band outside the Bay Area, and the Association has charted nationally," Juha pointed out nervously. He was still a little shaken by how Rennie had rallied the troops; man, she was stone scary when she got going like that. She must have been one of Genghis Khan's generals in a former life. Or a battlefield correspondent in the Civil War. Or a Bronze Age warrior queen: he could see her in a fur bikini, with copper breastplates and a big old honking sword. *Some*body lethal, anyway.

The warrior queen glanced up briefly, then away again. "See how much I do not care? Yes, that much. Then something Canadian, calling itself the Paupers— man, a name like that, that's just *asking* for it. But maybe they'll surprise us. They're another of Albert Grossman's quid pro quos—the deal was they had to be on the bill or King Al wasn't gonna let the Blues Project play, and *everybody* wanted *them*. Although he still couldn't, or wouldn't, produce Dylan."

"And Albert, as we all know, is the giant gorilla, so here they are, musical paupers or not." Chet reached for another piece of fried chicken; he was the only one, apparently, whose appetite was unaffected by either Baz's murder or the upcoming performance—scarcely anyone else could manage more than a mouthful or two. Well, grief did strange things—they all knew that from first-hand experience. Or maybe he just wanted to be particularly well ballasted.

Rennie waved dismissive fingers. "Never mind. Moving right along, Lou Rawls—he's spent too much time in Vegas, but he gets to take up time and space here because he was once, after all, Lou Rawls and he did Lou Rawls's stuff. And also he's Lou Adler's pet act. Then this folksinging Beverly person, Paul Simon's pet; then Johnny Rivers, another Adler once-great. What the hell are all these barnacles doing here, hogging slots that could have gone to real musicians with something to say and something to play? Then you. Evenor! For the honor and glory of San Francisco. After you, Eric Burdon and the Animals—well, they'll be good, so there's that. Though not as good as you're going to be. And Simon and Garfunkel to close it out on a lovely soft note."

"That was supposed to be a bookend thing," Dainis Hood, Evenor keyboard player, pointed out. "The two premier folk duos of the U.K. and the U.S.—Baz and

Haz to open, Paul and Artie to close."

"Didn't quite work out that way, though, did it." Rennie flipped her notebook shut and took the last grilled cheeseburger off the platter, biting into it and then practically inhaling it; she hadn't had any appetite at all, but she also hadn't realized how much she needed fuel. Grief did *that* to you too.

"But mark my words," she added—and if she'd intoned 'Thou shalt see me at Philippi' her voice could not have held a more prophetic ring—"Evenor is going to be the hard diamond center to all that fluff. And Evenor is going to *shine*. Now you guys finish eating and go get cleaned up and dressed. Praxie, don't forget your stage shoes. We'll be waiting for you out front."

Before Rennie, rejoined by Tansy, who'd been off to one side with Bruno and the other members of Turnstone while Rennie was giving Evenor the cheerleader pitch— could leave the Hunt Club, Marcus showed up again with Brent Gilmore, annoyingly, and the deputy sheriff had a lot more questions about Mr. and Mrs. Basil Potter, for Rennie and Tansy both.

So Rennie heard the first four acts at Monterey from backstage, and they all went pretty much as she had expected. Her smile turned more and more smug and sharp-edged as each act spun on and off again, doing nothing to really rouse the crowd; but eventually Brent was done with his questions and she and Tansy were free to go.

They dashed out front and found their seats next to Belinda and Stan and Bruno just as Johnny Rivers was opening the lackluster set Rennie had predicted. Well, yes, okay, it *was* the Monterey *POP* Festival, not the Monterey Balls-Against-the-Walls Flat-Out Full-On Rocknroll Whamfest. So maybe lightweights had a place here, after all; and, in fairness, nobody so far had been

utterly unlistenable and there had even been a few
modestly pleasant moments. But the world was about to
change. Rennie twitched in her seat, hardly able to sit
still, and Tansy, beside her, was scarcely less excited.

By the time Evenor made it to the stage, Rennie
could sense that the audience was longing to have its
mind blown, hungry and impatient for something
dynamite, something *real*. And as Prax and Chet and the
rest came out onstage, she could also see that Evenor was
ready, willing and able to oblige.

Tansy and Rennie grabbed each other's hands
and sat up straight as Prax surged to the front edge of the
stage like a hurricane tide, ripping the mike from its
stand, stamping her right heel to kick off the beat.
Bardo's bass started a long bubbling run that brontosaur-
stomped up the middle of everybody's chest, drummer
Jack Paris, back with them after a brief fill-in stint by his
cousin Zane, snapped out a crisp and irresistible line on
the snare and the toms, and Juha's Gibson began to fly.

Rennie had personally wardrobed Prax for this
all-important appearance, wanting her to make a visual
impression like a cleanly landed punch. She had
succeeded brilliantly: the lead singer of Evenor was up
there now in front of all the moguls and musicians and
fans, sparkling and flashing in the spotlight in a Rennie
Stride outfit custom-designed for her: a rose-colored
panne velvet microskirted dress embroidered with
arcane symbols in crystal beadwork. Peace signs, Norse
runes, an ankh, a Virgo glyph, an Om symbol, a
spectacular peacock feather covering the entire back of
the dress — it had taken Rennie three weeks to do the
beading.

And the stage shoes hadn't been forgotten: little
velvet tap shoes dyed to match the dress. The boys were
by no means shabby either: resplendent in buckskin, tie-
dye, Mexican peasant jackets, embroidered workshirts of

Rennie's own making. She had put her foot down in no uncertain terms about Army-Navy surplus, meaning of course *no* Army-Navy surplus; and, a little cowed, they had obeyed.

They opened with 'Jam Today', the best song from the first album, did a solid set of six, their full half-hour allotment, then, daringly, pushed a little, closing with 'Severe Clear', the hot new single from the second album, for an encore; nobody tried to cut them off. Rennie noticed a delighted Pennebaker and his crew filming from several angles, and smiled with satisfaction — her darlings were going to look *great* in the movie. Evenor was airborne and alight — you couldn't really call them phoenixes, because technically they were being born, not reborn, but something along that line, anyway, trailing clouds of glory — and the crowd was reeling. Watching proudly, tears in her eyes, Rennie saw Prax recognize her moment and grab it with both hands. She was the first honest thing that the Monterey audience had seen, and turning in her seat, Rennie watched them fall in love with her for it.

After that, it was all a little anticlimactic, at least for Rennie. Eric Burdon and the Animals had a great night, and were a brilliant follow-up to Evenor; there was even a terrific electric violin solo on their cover of the Stones' 'Paint It Black', but they failed to still the echo of Evenor in the audience's mind.

Then Simon and Garfunkel came on as the closers, the intended bookends for Baz and Haz. They were pleasant and charming as always, and just a bit too smooth, also as always, but Rennie and everybody else already knew that Prax McKenna would be the musical memory forever seared into the collective consciousness from Monterey Friday night. Still, Paul and Artie encored with an undeclared memorial song for Basil Potter: a lovely piece of Gregorian chant, Art's voice silver-pure as air and water, Paul's as warm and golden as the sun.

After the last clear note had faded away, Rennie and
Tansy went backstage to find their friends. They'd
deliberately delayed, knowing that Evenor would be
inundated directly following their set, and that it would
be better to wait till things had calmed down a bit. It
didn't look particularly calm even yet: the band was still
surrounded by shoals of well-wishers, including a couple
of reporters and a couple more predatory record
company execs, all being expertly held at bay by their
manager Dill Miller and the Avalon Ballroom's Chet
Helms, a good buddy of bass player Bardo's who was
scheduled as Saturday's emcee. But Prax blazed up
joyfully when she saw the two of them come battling
through the mob at last.

    Rennie and Tansy both hugged her, and she
hugged back even harder. They didn't have to speak;
they all knew what had gone down here tonight, and
they knew it was going to happen again tomorrow for
Tansy.

    After the excitement had died down somewhat,
they left the festival grounds to go eat in the hotel's
fanciest restaurant, to break in Rennie's new expense
account. They were joined by Stan Hirsh, whom they
hadn't seen since Evenor's appearance, and Belinda
Melbourne, who had been taken into their full confidence
and had been with them most of the day, since she'd
been there when they'd discovered Baz's body and had
of necessity to be sworn to secrecy.

    All of them were famished, and the journalists in
the group were anxious to discuss the grim events of the
morning — which Rennie, being the pro that she was, had
managed to get into that evening's Clarion bulldog
edition, yet another scoop, if not the one intended. But
Prax was bubbling over like a fountain of diamonds, and

they let her run down, not wanting to spoil her joy, until at last her head drooped toward the table, a spent and happy flower.

"Praxedes. *Eat,*" said Rennie, and Prax stared at her plate as if she'd never seen food before and didn't know what to do with it, then fell on it with the table manners of a starving leopard, suddenly desperate to restoke the energy the performance had burned away.

Dill Miller cast Rennie a sober glance. "What's the latest word on Baz?" he asked quietly. "We haven't heard anything since this afternoon."

"The Monterey PD says Pamina Potter is cleared," said Rennie, with a certain moroseness, though not for Pamie's innocence. "She's been sleeping with Roger Hazlitt for the past year, so that made for an interestingly possible motive for both of them, singly or together. Roger told the cops he and Baz were on the outs because of her as well as for professional reasons, and Pamie finally admitted she only confessed to cover for Roger, since he didn't have an alibi for last night."

Chet snorted. "Silly bint."

"I quite agree. But he did say he just walked around Monterey and went to dinner alone and then back to the Otter Point Inn and to bed. Where he said he looked around for Pamie, but she wasn't there."

"Not much of an alibi," observed Stan. "Hard to prove."

"Or disprove—well, probably someone noticed him somewhere and can vouch for his whereabouts."

"Where has Pamie been all day today?" asked Belinda. "I hope she isn't alone?"

"She and Roger are holed up together in their suite at Otter Point. With a deputy sheriff outside their door. Protection as much as surveillance," added Stan. "Better safe."

Rennie nodded. "Exactly. They should be

together, and I doubt they want to go out in public anyway. Hopefully the cops now don't think the double motive implicates Roger. The way I know Pamie did."

Prax woke up from stuffing herself into a food coma and stared at them. "Pamie thought *Roger killed Baz*?"

"She didn't know where he was last night, so obviously she feared the worse." Rennie rolled her eyes. "So she immediately made up that ridiculous tarradiddle about how she'd killed Baz herself to save him from musical blasphemy. Which nobody bought for an instant. But *she* didn't have an alibi for last night either."

Prax had the grace to look embarrassed. "She certainly does, and I told the cops so, when they asked me all those questions this morning. I don't know why they didn't tell you. She was sleeping with me at the Highlands Inn."

"Oh. Complicated?"

"Not really."

"And you both—"

"—got up at nine and took Pamie's car and driver and had breakfast at a little coffee shop in Carmel. We got to the festival site ten minutes after the body was found. As you, being there, will recall. We saw Baz lying in the tent and you standing over him like an on-duty Valkyrie, all ready to haul him off to Valhalla. All you needed was the winged helmet and steel bra and nice pointy spear. Pamie instantly flipped out, as you, again being there, will again recall."

"And last night?"

"Nothing, of course. She only likes boys."

"Yes, but you bat in both leagues."

Prax dismissed this with the sound usually represented by *Phbbbtth*. "She just wanted to sleep next to somebody. Sleep. Some body. Just not to be alone. Baz was mad at her, and Roger wasn't around. We talked for hours and just zonked out."

"I see. Well, that's pretty iron-clad, as an alibi for Pamie anyway. You say you told Detective Devlin? And Brent?"

"I did. They took it pretty well, considering."

"Considering Brent's got a bitty wee crush on you."

"Why am I not surprised?" said Stan, smiling at Prax, who just looked embarrassed. "Everybody falls for her. But they think Pamie was merely being noble? Or just hysterical? Surely she can't have been a *serious* suspect."

Prax, shaking her head and finishing off her steak: "No. She never was. In fact, Sheriff Brent told me she wasn't."

Rennie was oddly annoyed. "And what else did Sheriff Brent tell you, pray? That he didn't tell me, I mean."

"It's more like what *we* didn't tell *him*. Or you either." Prax twiddled her rings to cover her reluctance. "Your good friend Gerry Langhans," she said at last. "After you went up to bed last night, he had that huge screaming fight with his boss, the imperforate-anus'ed Pierce Hill. When he decked him. And then he quit. Which you did hear about. What you *didn't* hear about was that, in fact, he threatened to kill him."

"Well, surely you can see why we didn't want to mention that," Juha pointed out, returning to the topic.

They had been turfed out—very respectfully, considering the impressive size of the dinner bill and the even more impressive size of Rennie's tip—from the hotel restaurant, because it needed to close, and now they were all hanging out in the fireplace lounge again, Evenor still effervescent from their triumph, accepting congratulations both genuine and grudged from everyone who walked by. Gray Sonnet said they were terrific! Brian Jones too! Eric Burdon thought they had been amazing! Prue Vye had drawn Prax aside for a long private chat! How the heck were they going to *stand* it?

Dill Miller had herded them all there, like a border collie with a flock of unusually ungovernable sheep; commanding them to stay, he had gone off to do manager stuff. Evenor was just thrilled that apparently there were a good few opportunities for him to do such stuff. Maybe something groovy would come out of it all for them; there seemed no reason why it shouldn't.

Now Rennie stared at Evenor's lead guitarist with exasperation. "What part of 'This is a murder investigation and we have to tell everything we know' do you people not understand?"

"We weren't the only ones who saw Langhans go off on Hill after you left," Juha pointed out defensively. "The whole room did. And I don't think everyone kept their mouths shut. So obviously the police know all about it. Not to mention the rant Hill was on *before* you left, which I'm quite sure you haven't forgotten. But Langhans is your friend, and—"

"And that's precisely why you *should* have told me about the threat. And the police. Yes, Gerry is my friend, but that's no excuse. If I'd been there, and seen it, I would have been the one telling Brent and Devlin myself."

"It didn't seem relevant," said Chet with a certain mulishness to his tone.

Rennie cast up her eyes to heaven. "Holy Mother of God! Pierce Hill says for the whole world to hear that the only good artist is a dead artist, and it's a well-known fact that he's feuding with Basil Potter, and then that same Basil Potter turns up horribly dead not twelve hours later? After Pierce Hill is punched out and threatened with death by his own employee? Am I the only one who thinks this is just too coincidental for words?"

"Trout in the milk time again?" murmured Prax, and Rennie swung round on her with fire in her eyes. Before she could speak, Stan smoothly intervened.

"I think we all need to cool out. We're all upset, and flipping out behind this isn't going to help anyone. Rennie, you and I should go upstairs and call Burke and then write everything down. Or up. Or hand it over to that crime guy, what's his name, Ken Karper. Besides," he added, "Danny Marron told me he stayed with Pierce into the wee hours of the morning, to make sure he wouldn't do anything else stupid."

"*Danny* told you that, did he?" said Rennie flatly. "And you believe him?"

"Well, yeah. Because there are no truths outside the Gates of Eden."

Prax rolled her eyes in turn. "Will you lay off with the Dylan? When are you people going to start quoting Evenor?"

"When the truth is found to be lies," said Rennie promptly. "Or can't we quote the Airplane either?"

"Or the other way round," said Chet.

When the lies are found to be truth? I'm not holding my breath, Irish! Though—I wonder if you're not on to something there...

"God grant it may be so," said Rennie presently, without getting struck by lightning on the spot.

Nothing having been settled, the boys went off to spend some time at the hotel bar; after a few drinks, Chet went upstairs with a pretty brunette, and Rennie wasn't even distressed to see it. *On the contrary; right, good, fine, that'll keep you out of my hair and I maybe can actually do some thinking...*

Prax poked her in the ribs, with sympathy. "How are you *really* doing, cupcake? You may put up a nice plausible front for the guys, and the cops, and the rest of the world, but you can't fool me. Adam was bad enough, but now Baz—I know it hurts. It's okay. You can tell me."

Instantly contrite, Rennie ruffled her friend's blond hair. "I don't mean to fool you. I don't *want* to fool you. I wouldn't even think of trying. But I don't want to spoil this for you guys, either. You do know how good you all were, don't you?"

"Oh, I think we do," said Prax complacently, but Rennie could tell she was thrilled beyond words; they hadn't just been good, they'd been world-class outtasight incredible, and they all knew it. "Besides, you couldn't spoil it for us even if you wanted to, which of course you never would. I think Baz would say as much himself."

Rennie looked suddenly bleak and sorrowful. "I wish—I just wish he'd seen you play."

Prax smiled, and patted her friend's shoulder. "Me too. But you know, honey, I think he did. I really think he did."

Chapter 14

Saturday morning, June 17

RENNIE AWOKE feeling as if someone had been beating her with a tire iron all night long. And the dreams, Holy Mother of God, the *dreams*! She lay back and pulled the light summer duvet up to her chin, shaking all over and very glad she was alone in the bed. She remembered everything, and wished to hell she didn't.

Baz had come to her in the night, as she had known he would, sitting on the sofa across the room, smiling at her the way he always did. He'd come to say goodbye, of course: he was dressed in his favorite shirt and pants and boots, his hair ruffled, his beloved Martin dreadnought magically whole and unhurt again—of course it would be—slung across his back. He looked young and happy, relaxed and ready for his road trip.

The best and longest road trip of all. She couldn't remember exactly what he had said to her, or what she had said back to him, but the feeling of the dream was one of love and warmth and peace and great tenderness. God, she was going to miss him; but she knew too that he would never be really gone. *Not as long as his music is with us...*

Through the connecting door she heard Prax pottering about—oh, dear, scratch that, *messing* about, apparently moving furniture or something, singing softly to herself.

Well, she had every right to sing. Evenor had done brilliantly, and the first thing Rennie had to do this morning was write some more about it. There had been feverish writing yesterday and last night, of course, and tremendous phonings to Burke, and then it had all hit her like a ton of wet sand across the back of her neck; she'd collapsed on her bed, not even a pill needed to shut down, had gone out like the proverbial light and not moved again until morning. No, shower first. *Then* she'd call Burke again, *then* writing. After that, something to eat and over to the police station with Stan to see what fresh hell might have come to pass. Then back here to pick up Miss McKenna for lunch and go over to the fairgrounds.

Miss McKenna, who had come in as soon as she heard Rennie shut off the shower, approved the schedule.

"But what will *you* do all morning?" asked Rennie, pulling on a favorite pair of denim bells and a new embroidered Romanian peasant shirt she'd bought at a festival stall. She didn't think Baz would mind: she didn't have anything suitably funereal with her, and she had a feeling that even the Widow Potter wasn't going to be wearing weeds this morning. Or any morning. "Unless you want to come with?"

"No—actually, I thought I'd go over to Otter Point with Rick Henries, he said he'd give me a lift, and see if Pamie needs anything? I know she's with Roger, but I bet they're both totally freaked out and could use some help or at least some company, and Rick maybe too. As their manager he's going to have a lot to take care of, and he might be glad of a hand. Since we're done playing, I've got the time… At least they didn't sleep here last night, Pamie and Roger. Well, they couldn't have anyway, could they, Baz's room is all cordoned off. Plus how creepy and dishonorable would that have been?"

Rennie shuddered. "I'm sure they never even dreamed of it. And that's a great idea, to go hang with them. I was going to do that later myself. But now Stan and I can poke around on our own. And I can write you guys up without you peering over my shoulder to make sure I write only good things."

"Well, that's a given, isn't it?" Prax laughed and dodged the pillow Rennie threw at her. "Seriously—you just write. Whatever you want to write. About us, or Baz, or anyone else."

"I'll do that, then."

"And write something for Baz," said Prax, suddenly somber again. "Not for the paper. Something just for you and him. Write him a letter. Before you forget what it was like."

"I won't forget," said Rennie with matching somberness. "Ever. But I *will* write it."

But before she did anything else once Prax had left for Rick's room, Rennie called Burke. It was early, but he was already at the office, gloating over yesterday's lead story, which had appeared in the bulldog edition and had scooped every other paper in the world—the first published news of Basil Potter's murder—and the extensively revised story, now a sidebar but still an exclusive, about the planned breakup of Baz & Haz.

"God, honey, I am so very sorry," he began, though he'd offered his honest condolences yesterday as well. "I know he was your good friend, and for you to see what happened to him, in such a horrible way—"

"Yes. Thank you. Yes." She took a deep, ragged breath. "Are you going to send Ken Karper down here? On account of it being a crime story and all?"

She felt rather than heard Burke's surprise: Ken Karper was the Clarion's top crime reporter, and over the past year he had been more than happy to take anything Rennie had sent his way, beginning with the Fillmore murders. But Burke was surprised for a different reason.

"Well, truth be told, he's already on his way. Should be there in an hour. Nothing to do with you, or the confidence I have in you; it's no slur on your professionalism, so don't get all bent out of shape. I knew this would be hard for you to deal with, so I talked to the news editor and we decided to send Ken along. I'd have let Stan take it on, but he's not ready for something like this yet by himself. Besides, it's not as if you and Ken haven't worked together before. It'll be easier on everybody: he can handle the crime, you stick to the music. That's not a problem for you, is it?"

"No problem at all. Thank you." Rennie's voice was calm and even, and that should have been a tipoff."Yes, thanks. I really do think that might be best."

She replaced the phone in its cradle and stared out the window at the glass-smooth sea, well pleased, in a grim and Fate-ful kind of way.

Because now I can go find things out on my own, and not have to be all journalistically objective and even-handed. Because now I can come down like the wolf on the fold, like the hammer of Thor, like the wrath of the Navajo thunder-gods, on whoever did this to my friend. And God help anybody who tries to tell me I can't...

The first person upon whose head she longed to bring down that hammer was of course Pierce Hill. But she set aside her fury and started to write — first things first — and an hour later she'd produced a glowing story on last night's show apart from the murder, a rave review pinned around Evenor but not neglecting the other bands who'd played, plus an exquisite sidebar tribute to Baz that had come pouring out all unlooked for — a lament for a much-loved friend as well as a salute to a great artist. Later on, she'd write her own personal letter, as Praxie had suggested, but this piece was for public consumption, intended to make people realize the extent of their loss. Which, in her opinion, they really, really needed to do: Potter and Hazlitt, like Dylan, like Baez, like the Budgies and the Beatles and the Stones, had been iconic of their class and kind, and deserved a good epitaph as much as Baz did himself.

It was a good, exhausting, solid morning's work, and once she'd called it in to the Clarion she started to feel a little better, to the point of actually being hungry. So she headed downstairs looking for a late breakfast; what she found in a corner of the sunlit dining room was Rainshadow's president, fake gravity and smarmy bogus sorrow seeping from his every pore, like ooze from a toxic dump, talking to a small knot of reporters and TV cameras about Baz Potter.

It was a good thing she hadn't had breakfast yet, because it would all have come hurtling up right there. *How fucking DARE he! That evil slimy crapweasel! He knows damn well what Baz wanted to do...*would *have done, if he'd had the chance...*

Pierce Hill's gaze drifted over to Rennie where she stood stock-still in the doorway, radiating revulsion in his direction like a malevolent little pulsar. He faltered a bit, so palpable was the flaming blast of hate — if it had been solid, it would have knocked him to the ground and flattened him flatter than a beer can under the wheels of a semi — but he recovered smoothly and went right on.

"And there's the girl who actually discovered the body, an old and dear friend of his and mine, Miss Rennie Stride of the San Francisco Clarion," he announced, smirking as the reporters' heads swiveled as one to Rennie and then they all went running over.

She cut them off with a brisk 'No comment,' and when that didn't work, with a snarled 'Back *OFF!*', which did.

Pierce was watching her, the smirk still on his face. "It's for the best, Rennie," he said in a mocking tone of faux condolence. "To the most merciful thinking. You know it, I know it, Pamina and Roger know it. If I were a believing man, I'd say Baz knows it too."

Rennie moved very close to Pierce, within reaching distance of his throat, though she didn't touch him, noting as she did so the lovely purple and green bruise on the left side of his jaw — *nice work, Gerry!* — and as he got a closer look at her eyes, he shrank back in the chair as far as he could get.

"I'll tell you what's for the best, you little cockroach," she said softly. "If somebody should be caring enough to send you to join him. Finish what Gerry Langhans so very well started."

"Is that a threat?" Pierce tried to smile scornfully, but his lips weren't working along those lines just now.

"A threat? Oh, no. More like a prophecy," she said, still in the same soft voice. "The Egyptians sent dogs and horses and slaves along with their dead. A rock star accompanied into the afterlife by his label president — makes sense to me."

"You'd be the prime suspect," he blustered, but his voice was shaking. How had he never noticed what terrifying eyes she had? People had seen eyes like that behind a dueling pistol on a misty meadow at dawn. The last thing they ever saw.

"Would I?" Rennie smiled, and that was even worse. "Oh, I doubt that, Percy. I doubt that very much indeed. But if it pleases you to think so, hey, knock yourself out. Before someone knocks yourself off."

She patted his cheek twice, turned and left.

When Ken Karper pulled up in the Highlands Inn driveway, Rennie was sitting on her balcony finishing up room service breakfast—somehow she hadn't wanted to stick around in the dining room—and watching the traffic come and go, and as soon as she saw the car she went down to meet him at the reception desk. He greeted her warmly—why not, she was responsible for sending some primo stuff his way over the past year or so, no reason to think that streak wasn't about to continue, which wasn't nearly as heartless as it sounded, and besides, he liked her a lot personally—and she brought him upstairs to fill him in on developments.

He was deeply sympathetic about Basil Potter, suitably suspicious about Adam Santa Monica, and laughed until he cried at the Pierce Hill-Gerry Langhans episode. Rennie watched him making notes: Ken was in his mid-thirties, shrewd and savvy, a family man, a baseball nut, a fine writer—and a real newspaperman, the kind that Stan Hirsh hoped he himself would be one day when he grew up.

Which reminded her: Stan had been informed he'd have to share his room with Ken, even though he was already sharing with Vince Bays, the Clarion photographer—Ken had foresightedly brought his own foldaway camp bed, since the hotel had long ago run out of rooms, beds and cots, and most of those under its roof were by now sleeping tripled and quadrupled and quintupled up, like something out of Chaucer. People were even sleeping on floors or sofas or in two facing armchairs lashed together. For a brief moment, Rennie and Prax, hogging two whole spacious rooms with beds and couches and balcony lounges just for themselves, had felt a bit selfish; but that hadn't lasted long.

With a start she realized Ken had stopped writing and was watching her with a faint smile. "Sorry? Did I miss something?"

He laughed. "No, *I'm* sorry—I was just thinking about what Burke said to me about you last year, before we worked together on the Fillmore murders."

"Something about what a ruthless and talented journalist I am?" asked Rennie hopefully.

The smile broadened. "Definitely along those lines." But what Burke had actually said, Ken declined to share. "How do you want to work this, then? I got the feeling from Burke that you'd prefer to stay away from the reportage, because of your—well, because Basil Potter was your friend."

"That's right, I would. I do. So?"

"So—I stopped off at the Monterey PD before I got here, and I talked to your Inspector Devlin." He began to draw little flourishes in his notebook. "They have preliminary findings from the M.E.'s office. If you haven't heard yet—do you want to hear?"

"He's not 'my' Inspector Devlin. And no, I don't want to hear. But I have to. Just tell me quickly. And don't dress it up with sympathy, either."

He took her at her word. "Strangulation with the guitar wires. No surprises; it was just as it appeared. His trachea was severed, also the carotid artery and vagus nerve. He would have passed out almost instantly; he wouldn't have suffered very much at all. I'm so sorry," he added reflexively, then flinched.

"If one more person says to me how very sorry

they are," said Rennie conversationally, "I'm going to kick their face out the back of their head. I don't mean to be ungrateful, I know it's all people can really offer. But I just don't want to hear it anymore."

"I understand," said Ken, and he really did. "Well, how *do* you want to handle things? If you'd rather not deal with any of the — story aspects of the story."

Rennie laughed shortly. "Treating it as a story is pretty much the only damn way I *can* deal with it. But again, I don't want to write it myself. Anything I find out, you can have. So in that sense a team effort."

"And in all other senses?"

"I don't think that really concerns you," she said presently, and not in a snotty way but in a way that conveyed this was simply the way it was, the way it was going to be. "Or Burke, either."

"Yes, that's what we thought you'd say." Karper seemed unruffled. "So you, or you and Stan, will do the digging that needs to be done?"

"And then you get to do the heavy lifting. But you can dig too, you know. And don't forget Adam Santa Monica, either."

Ken's eyes sparked. "Do you think the cases are connected?"

"I have no evidence that says so. But I just have a feeling they are. I don't know how or why. We'll talk more about that later; I have some stuff about Adam that didn't go into the story I did, stuff I haven't passed on to Burke yet."

"Why am I not surprised?"

When Ken, eager to get started, left a half hour later, Rennie sat on for a while. Presently she went over to the desk and picked up the long strand of beads that lay there: the memorial beads she'd bought from Keala Lopaka. Keala had wanted to give them to her, as *mahalo* for the *kokua* — thanks for the help — with the new tent and location. But Rennie had insisted on paying; it felt right. They were lovely beads, dark-red faceted antique garnets, glowing like tiny bonfires of deep memory.

In Queen Victoria's time, she reflected, toying with the necklace, bereaved ladies wore full mourning attire—unrelieved matte black, jet jewelry, long black veils—for a year and a day; then second mourning, which allowed for trimmed and figured fabrics, but still black, and a shorter veil, maybe even pearls. Then, in carefully prescribed stages, they would gradually introduce the half-colors of half-mourning back into their wardrobes—gray, purple, lilac, white, violet, this dark garnet color.

She laughed suddenly, picturing Pamina Potter working her way through the stages of mourning dress. Yeah, that wasn't going to happen; probably the best Baz could hope for was a black minidress at the funeral. If there was one. But she herself would wear these beads, maybe not right away, but oh yes, she would wear them; and when she did, she'd think of Baz.

But there was a lot that needed doing first.

Saturday afternoon

Canned Heat
Big Brother & The Holding Company
Country Joe & The Fish
Al Kooper
The Paul Butterfield Blues Band
Quicksilver Messenger Service
The Steve Miller Blues Band
The Electric Flag with Mike Bloomfield

Chapter 15

"CAN'T TURN MY BACK ON YOU for a *minute*, can I?" Rennie demanded. "Much less take you anywhere. And now I suppose you want me to help you avoid the shackles and striped suit. Not to mention the ball and chain. And I don't mean Janis's song, either."

Gerry Langhans had the grace to look embarrassed. "It's not that bad, is it?"

"I don't know. Why don't you tell me? In fact, why *didn't* you tell me?"

They were in Gerry's room at the Highlands Inn. Rennie had come pounding on his door after her little confrontation with Pierce Hill and her talk with Ken Karper, and she was still loaded for bear. Gerry might be a teddy bear, but just now she was almost as angry with him as she was with Pierce.

He sighed. "I didn't really have a chance, did I. Besides, you were there for most of the row yourself. After you left, Pierce made professional as well as personal threats. Basically, his position was if Haz or Baz happened to get themselves dead, they couldn't change the sound and the catalogue would be gold forever."

"I know *that*! He's said it before, and, no doubt, he will be saying it again. I just figured he was stoned, or maybe drunk—though that was by far the worst I'd ever seen or heard from him. I'm surprised Sledger Cairns didn't go for his throat. Gray and Prue Sonnet had to leave the room, and so did Leeds Sheffield. And it would not surprise me in the slightest if Elk Bannerman's mob buddies, the ones which of course we all know he hasn't got, pay Pierce a little visit before we're all much older. Not that I approve of mob violence, you understand. Or Mob violence either."

"I do understand," said Gerry soothingly. "So then you think that Pierce is the one who killed Baz?"

Rennie sighed. "Much as I desperately long to believe it, it doesn't seem likely. Too obvious. I'd put money on Art Garfunkel before I'd back Pierce Hill. So what happened?"

"Cops and I had a little chat. You know the one, I'm sure." Gerry shrugged. "I admitted everything. Heck, I'm proud of it. I only wish I'd hit him harder."

"I like to think that's my influence at work," said Rennie, shaking her head, but her eyes danced with approval. "What then?"

Gerry laughed. "Not much. They talked to me, or at me, for a couple of hours and then let me go. They said they could still charge me with battery and assault, depending on how things went." He looked pleased. "I almost hope they do: it would go a long way toward giving me serious cred with the bands; musicians're always getting arrested for something. A bust like that would prove the pigs are as down on me as much as on them."

"No, don't," said Rennie. "Don't call them pigs. Some of them are, sure, but most of them really aren't. I used to think that, too, until I got to know a few, and saw how they work. So no gratuitous pig-calling, please. At least not unless it's warranted."

"As you wish, Rennie, of course," he said, surprised at her sudden seriousness. "What'll you do now?"

"I'm goin' back out before the rain starts a-fallin'," she quoted irresistibly, and also appositely. "There are some things I have to take care of. And nothing really interests me on the afternoon's bill but Big Brother, Country Joe and Quicksilver. So I'll take advantage while I can. And I'll speak to the cops for you. You just stay here and stay out of trouble, will you? Can you do that for me? Yes? There's a good lad!"

Rennie headed over to her room to change yet again — it was fun to put on different clothes every few hours, and besides, it was good advertising for her rock-seamstress sideline. She'd save the lace-tablecloth pantsuit for tonight, if it didn't rain; hopefully Janis hadn't brought hers, so Rennie wouldn't look like a copycat. Besides, she'd made her own first.

Despite her orders, she knew Gerry wouldn't stay in his room for long, but at least maybe she'd made him think, and what he'd said had made *her* think. And what it made her think was that she needed to have another talk with Detective Devlin and Deputy Sheriff Gilmore.

Opening the door of her room, she came to a sharp braking halt as her gaze took in a huddled form sitting by the balcony windows. Heart hammering, she unfroze in her tracks when she realized it was Romilly Ramillies. *Whoa! Kind of a replay of last year, when I came home and found Marjorie infesting my apartment. But Romilly is a much nicer surprise than Motherdear, to find lurking in your room…*

"The door was standing open," said Romilly, apologetically. "I didn't know where else to look for you, and I didn't want to go away and leave the room unlocked."

"Open? Really? Well, that's not good."

Rennie gave the bedroom and bathroom a worried onceover. Nothing seemed missing, though if an illicit search had taken place, she couldn't have sworn to it: as a rule any room Rennie Stride was present in for more than ten minutes looked as if it had been tossed by a more than usually untidy burglar. *Must have been Praxie, or the maid…no, this probably is the way I left it…God, I'm a slob…*

"I'm so sorry," said Romilly, and she sounded as if she really meant it. "I heard about your friend, what happened to him. Is there anything I can do to help?"

Somehow the conventional expression of sympathy came acceptably from Romilly; at any rate, Rennie didn't punch her face out the back of her head, as previously threatened.

"No. No, not really. Oh, wait, you *could* tell me why you're here lurking in wait for me? —I'm sorry, that was really rude. How can I help you?" she added, yanking a change of outfit from the closet, a minidress of her own design: black with tiny white flowers, the cuffs, collar and hem edged in eyelet lace. Suitable for a confab with the Law: made her look like a sweet and innocent English schoolgirl. Well, perhaps that was a stretch. But it could be taken as a kind of mourning attire for Baz; anyway, it was the only black she had with her, and it suited her mood.

"No apologies necessary; I truly understand." Romilly looked away. "Well, I came to confess, in fact."

Oh dear God is there no END to the stupidity… "Confess to what, may I ask?"

"I'm the one who fired the shots in the sculpture garden."

"Did you now! And to what purpose and intent?"

"I was trying to kill Danny. For what he did to Becca."

Rennie sat down, pulled on white tights and low-heeled black leather Mary-Janes, and regarded Romilly for a long moment.

"No," she said at last. "I don't buy it. You've had any number of chances at him, and at least five years in which to take them."

"I tell you I did." But she wouldn't look the younger woman in the eyes.

Rennie heaved a dramatic sigh. "Fine! I was on my way to talk to the cops anyway, so why don't you come with, and you can tell them all about it. And then *I'll* tell them that you're lying like a rug, thinking to nobly cover for Becca like a good mother. Because you are, aren't you? Or at least you're trying to?"

All the iron went out of Romilly's stance, and she dropped her head, but not before Rennie had seen tears come to her eyes. When she looked up again at Rennie, there was a faint smile on her face.

"I understand why Marjorie is afraid of you—oh yes, she is! But I've tried and tried to make it otherwise, and it *can* only be Becca."

"Rubbish," said Rennie, so positively that Romilly stared at her with surprised, dawning hope. "Those guns were right there; anyone could have gotten at them. Anyone who knows the house. Anyone who snuck in from the festival, even. I could have gotten at them myself if I'd wanted to."

"Which means—anyone."

Rennie gently touched the older woman's arm. "I refuse to believe it was Becca. We know her and we love her. And we know it's not in her nature."

"Oh, who knows what her nature has become?" Romilly's cry was heartfelt and bitter. "Sometimes it's as if she's a total stranger, not my own dear daughter anymore, and other times she seems the same sweet girl she always was. I don't know what it will be like for her down the road, and when I'm gone…"

"Not for years and years." Rennie gathered Romilly's hands in both of hers. "And not to worry: when you're not here to take care of her, her brothers and sister will. Her family. Maybe by then she'll be back to herself, even. You don't know. You *can't* know. Nobody can."

"No—I suppose not." She smiled gamely. "You're pretty smart for a youngster."

"Damn straight! And I'm only going to get smarter as I go on… Now, let's go." Rennie gently lifted Romilly to her feet, and felt the older woman's weariness for the first time, as Romilly leaned on her.

"Where are we going?"

"You said you wanted to confess, didn't you? Well, we're going to go talk to someone I think can get through to you."

"So that's what Mrs. Revels tells me. And I thought you ought best hear it."

Rennie glanced at Romilly, sitting across from her in Brent's office at the stationhouse, then back at Marcus, who had been listening to Rennie's discourse with a look of remarkable neutrality. Now, though, he and Rennie exchanged freighted glances, and Rennie cast her eyes up to the ceiling. Which meant: they were both agreed that this was utterly bogus, but it was left to Marcus to be the one to sock it to Romilly Ramillies Revels. Which was why Rennie had come to him—the one without any lawful jurisdiction in this matter—and not to Brent or Audie Devlin.

And Marcus did not disappoint: he took a bracing tone, probably the only kind the would-be confessor would have responded to.

"Romilly—we know this is not true. You'll only hurt Becca if you're lying about this thinking to protect her. We already knew the bullets came from your rifle. No one was hurt, you have the proper permits, the gun was fired on private property. You asked us to keep quiet about it, but I must tell you now that I didn't. I told Brent and Detective Devlin"—he ignored the surprise on Rennie's face—"and we decided that it didn't merit being considered a police matter. I'd like to keep it that way. Frankly, so would the sheriff's office."

"But if it *was* Becca—"

Marcus shook his head. "I don't think it was. I'm with Rennie on this one. And it wasn't you, either."

"Then who?"

"I don't know yet." He kept his gaze away from Rennie, who had noticed that he very carefully did not mention that the rifle had been wiped clean of fingerprints, and he noticed that she had noticed.

Ooooh, he does *know who it was! And I bet so do Brent and Devlin. But he's not saying, because he hasn't pieced the rest of it together yet.*

She straightened in her seat, didn't look at anyone, tried to keep her sudden excitement under wraps. *And, you know, I think maybe I know too...*

After Romilly had gone, considerably lighter of aspect and spirits, Rennie hung around for the police discussion that had moved down the hall to Audie Devlin's office. She wasn't entirely sure why the cops were cutting her so much slack, letting her sit in on some, at least, of their sessions when no other reporter was allowed. It was a bit irregular, even though most police departments had close relationships with local journalists; the arrangement often benefited them both. But this whole thing was irregular anyway, well out of normal police parameters, and she very much doubted it was just because they put so much faith and trust in Murder Chick's observations.

Still, she wasn't about to argue: Ken Karper had been there earlier, and as the two of them had already discussed, he would be pursuing more orthodox avenues of journalistic inquiry. Though she was willing to bet it wouldn't take him very far; in the meantime, she'd grab what she could get and do with it what she could.

"*Could* Pierce Hill have killed Basil Potter?" Brent Gilmore seemed baffled as he repeated Marcus's question. "Yes, I suppose he could have. But what's his motive?"

"It's a more or less open secret how overextended Pierce is financially — I mean his personal finances; the record company itself is sound," said Rennie reluctantly, when no one else spoke up. Though why she was reluctant to rat Pierce out she could *not* imagine, except that it opened the door to all sorts of speculation about Baz and Haz...

Audie Devlin nodded, as if he'd expected to hear exactly that. "And a timely murder of half his marquee act could bring in some nice change from the insurance company. Double indemnity at least. Plus the act would now be manageable if half of it was dead, and also newly profitable, since death always raises public interest. At least its — what do you call it? — its backlist would be profitable."

"Yes, I'm thinking that very much," she said. "Among other things."

"And those would be?"

"If Baz is dead, which he is, his half of the song rights stays with Rainshadow — and the songs would continue to be profitable forever. It's also unlikely that Roger Hazlitt, or Pamina as Baz's presumptive heir, would gear up to engage in a big old court fight at this point when nobody bothered to do so — or at least felt they *could* do so — when Baz was still...alive."

Brent heard the hesitation. "I'm sorry, Rennie. I know how difficult this is for you. Potter was your friend."

And still is. So nothing's getting said by me that's going to hurt him…and I know I said I'd punch out anyone saying how sorry they are, but punching out a deputy sheriff is just such *a bad idea…*

"Yes. Thank you. Okay, not Pierce himself, maybe, but if someone murders Baz at Pierce's behest, or to curry favor with him…"

"Someone like your friend Gerry Langhans, you mean? Last seen at the Highlands Inn punching Hill's lights out and threatening to kill him?"

"Well, I had to say it, didn't I! You guys were thinking it so hard and loud that his name was making Braille patterns on your foreheads."

"We *were* thinking that," said Devlin abruptly. "But it makes no sense for him to go off on Hill in public like that, to physically assault him, and actually quit the label, then to do Hill a favor by killing Potter a few hours later. Besides, we understand he was hired by another record company within thirty seconds after he decked Hill and quit Rainshadow. So he wouldn't be wanting to do Hill any favors even more."

"He's not a suspect?" Rennie felt relief like a great wave washing over her.

"Nope. Not unless something else turns up. So you can tell your friend he's off the hook."

"And of course there's Roger Hazlitt himself," said Marcus, and Rennie tightened up all over again like a little spring. "He might have been pissed off that Potter was going to unilaterally break up the act without even consulting him. So he kills Potter to—break it up first, permanently? No, that makes no sense. And since it's Hazlitt who's sleeping with Potter's wife, not the other way round, the jealousy motive makes no real sense either. She'd hardly be wooed into permanence if she knew her boyfriend killed her husband, and we're already agreed she wasn't in on it and wouldn't be pleased by it. So no go there."

Rennie felt relief so sharp it melted her knees; she'd been certain of that, but it was nice to hear it officially confirmed.

"Have you talked to Pierce?"

"Of course," said Brent. "And we've talked to Langhans again, too. But you already knew that. That's why you're really here, isn't it?"

"Not entirely."

And then she told them why she *was* really there, and then she left, leaving them staring after her.

"Who *is* this person?" asked Audie Devlin, with heartfelt bewilderment, after a few moments of stunned silence.

Marcus ran a hand through his hair and sighed. "Sometimes I have no idea."

Rennie didn't plan on spending a lot of time with music that day. As she'd told anyone who would listen, the bulk of the Saturday afternoon lineup didn't interest her: too much of it was the kind of non-black blues that set her teeth on edge, however much it might be applauded among the ranks of the terminally hip. For herself, personally, she needed a bit of tweakishness to really get into the blues: British bluesers, like Mayall and Clapton, almost always did it for her, and blues-rockers both American and English, but the rest was more problematic.

And she might be a professional music journalist, but she didn't have to like *everything* she heard, oh no she didn't, and white-boy blues was one of those things she just didn't feel like liking. The real, genuine stuff was fine and fantastic, of course, that went without saying — Delta,

Chicago, Memphis, blues from Harlem and blues from Detroit, the Kings B.B. and Albert. But this? Not so much. It did not move her; did not stir her heart, mind, soul or crotch the way rock did.

Anyway, Stan could cover the afternoon's blues parade, if there was anything there that merited comment, and indeed some of the artists came highly recommended. But there was other stuff that she absolutely didn't want to miss, and she arrived back at the festival field just in time to catch it.

When Big Brother and the Holding Company came ambling out onstage, Rennie was right up front and smiling to see them, glad she could forget her troubles for half an hour, glad they could make her. So shaggy-dog they were, those boys, and so endearing: she loved their music, rough and unpolished though it was, at least by comparison to the work of the Airplane and Quicksilver and the Dead.

And Janis, of course, was dazzling.

For her big day, she was dressed in a simple top and jeans and all her bead necklaces, having decided against her "peace dress", an A-line mini with peace symbols printed all over it that many chicks from the East Village to the Haight were sporting. But it didn't matter what she had on, because what came out of her mouth made everything and everyone else utterly irrelevant. Like Prax last night before her, she got right up in the audience's face and she grabbed them by the ears and she shook them until their gonads rattled.

The fans weren't the only ones to get off. What Janis herself got off was astounding. She just opened up her throat and her heart and her soul, and let it all come flooding out like sunlight. Everything was terrific, but Rennie was especially pleased to hear among them one of her favorite Big Brother songs: their amazing double-time hard-rockin' version of the old folkie standard 'The

Cuckoo', with the long singing guitar line that always took the top of her head off. In a good way, of course.

And then she did 'Ball and Chain', and there wasn't a sound to be heard on the fairground. Just her.

Rennie, who over the past year and a half had heard her fair share of amazing Joplin performances, each of them better than the last, was not the only witness who thought this was perhaps her greatest ever—even Janis herself wasn't sure at first, but was quickly reassured on that count. And yet it had not been captured on film, by Pennebaker or anyone else, because the inexperienced Big Brother had taken their even more inexperienced manager's advice and refused to sign the movie release.

"Do you *believe* it!" demanded Prax, when she returned from backstage to sit with Rennie half an hour later. "That may possibly be the single best thing anybody ever saw in the whole history of rock and roll, and nobody got it on film. Because their manager advised them against it. Dill would *never* have allowed them not to sign the release."

Rennie shook her head. "Where's Albert Grossman—or even Danny Marron—when you really need him?"

"Well, all may not be lost. Janis just went weeping to John Phillips once she realized it may have been the finest performance she'll ever give in her life and there's no filmic record of it, and he and Adler agreed to give them another shot on Sunday night. Only half a set, and maybe it won't be as magical, but it's still something and at least it'll get filmed this time."

"Why can't they dump one of those feckless pet-lamb acts instead?" groused Laird Burkhart of Powderhouse, who was sitting with them. "The Group with No Name? Spare me! Or the Butterfield rerun we're getting tonight? You can't tell me anyone could seriously want to hear either of them over Big Brother."

"It's all a power trip," said Rennie wearily. "It was never anything but that from the first. No matter how much everybody pretended it wasn't. If it's turning into something else along the way, that's no credit to anything but the music itself. Or maybe it's just autohype."

Following Janis was probably the one band who could have, Country Joe and The Fish. Joe McDonald — Janis's boyfriend on and off, when she was interested in boys — stoned on STP, his handsome face oddly solemn in war paint, or antiwar paint, led the band through intricate and trippy changes: a hypnotic set. When Al Kooper and the Butterfields and Steve Miller and Mike Bloomfield and the Electric Flag began the procession of blues, though, she took her leave in no uncertain terms.

Instead, she headed to the other side of the festival field, to see what she could see. As she'd discovered, much to her surprise, it really was an actual, active fairground, used not just for summer music fests — the Jazz Festival had been held there since 1958, the Folk Festival too — but all year long, for things like the big Monterey County Fair and other events in the annual cycle of a rural California farming community. So it had barns and corrals and open-sided roofed sheds for the displaying of animals and farm equipment and suchlike; she'd even been told that the arena where the audience was currently grooving on musicians was normally a show ring for cattle and horses and even rodeo stuff.

On the roof of one barn set among trees a few hundred yards away, a bunch of kids were clinging to the shingles, apparently planning on staying up there to watch the music from a nice vantage point above the heads of the crowd. Also because they were stoned out of their minds, happily giggling away on pot.

She smiled to see them, then noticed a young

deputy sheriff, honestly afraid they'd hurt themselves, trying to gently coax them back to the ground. They all stood up obediently, as if to slide or scramble back down the way they'd gotten up there in the first place, and then, to the great amusement or shock of everyone watching, they all gracefully swan-dived off the roof and landed on their feet. Rennie could hear one of them earnestly assuring the horrified deputy that Hey, man, it's cool, that was the quickest way down. Couldn't argue with that. Besides, they were all so loose-jointed from being stoned that nobody would have gotten hurt anyway.

She turned away, still smiling, and found herself right up against Danny Marron, who was standing next to her filming the kids as they were leaping balletically from the roof.

"Well, haven't seen *you* around for a while," she said, recovering from her surprise. "Got any more bodies on film lately? No? Just the one? Maybe someone else can oblige you by dying dramatically in suspicious circumstances."

"Why do you hate me?" he asked simply. "You don't even know me."

Rennie was taken aback, but not for long. "I don't really *need* to know you, do I. I just have to look at Becca Revels."

"I didn't know you were a friend of Rebecca." But his eyes had gone all shifty, and he found something of great interest in the housing of his camera.

"Oh yes, I'm a friend of Rebecca, all right. We knew her from the Haight, Prax and I. That night at Romilly's, when she came down to dinner, that was the first we'd seen her in a couple of years. And we didn't love seeing what we saw."

He had regained some of his bluster. "Romilly told you I was to blame for the way Becca is, didn't she.

ot going to take it away from her. Brandi loves her
godmother, and she loves Becca like a sister."

"Yes, so people keep telling me. But you know,
I'm just not seeing it. Borgia sister, maybe. Stealing the
man she loved. Not that there's much here worth
stealing."

Danny put out a conciliatory hand; Rennie leaned
quickly away, not wanting him to touch her. "Look,
you're upset over your friend being murdered. I was
there, I helped you find him, and now you're taking it
out on me. I understand that, and I don't blame you,
Rennie, I really don't. But the situation is a lot more
complicated. I'm just hoping that maybe we can get past
it and be friends."

"*Friends?*"

"Why not? Brandi told me she invited you over to
the house in Carmel Highlands—listen, why don't you
come for brunch and a swim tomorrow, you and Prax?
Bring the rest of Evenor if they want. It's just boring Ravi
Shankar all afternoon, so Brandi and I are staying in. We
can all get to know each other; we didn't really have time
at Waterhall. Maybe even help each other out
professionally: I've always wanted to make little short
films of bands doing one song at a time, with really far-
out creative visuals. I talked to Bill Graham yesterday,
and he said he'd be interested in running something like
that along with the light shows at the Fillmore when the
bands played. Evenor could be the first, if you'd put in a
good word for me. What do you say? Will you at least
talk to Prax about it?"

The charm he exerted during the course of this
speech was positively blinding. But Rennie was proof
against it; indeed, one of her very first j-school lessons
had been Don't let them charm you, because every
chance they get, they will try, and if they succeed, you

are forever doomed and might as well give up journalism and go be a plumber or a lawyer or something.

"I'll mention it," she said at last, wondering why he was so eager to make nice now when he had been fairly indifferent about getting to know her and Prax before. Even her standing as a Clarion reporter and her access to and influence on Prax, now a bona fide festival star, didn't seem to warrant this new interest. "We'll think about it."

"That's all I'm asking," he said, smiling.

Rennie watched him walk away, filming as he went. *No…that's* not *all you're asking, not by a long shot. So just what the holy hell* was *that all about? And just what did you do with that film you shot of Baz dead, you slimy shark? Is it safely tucked away in Audie Devlin's evidence locker? Or is it somewhere else? Maybe I'll come for that swim after all. Just to find out. I owe it to Baz — and maybe to Becca as well.*

Saturday night

Moby Grape
Hugh Masekela with Big Black
The Byrds
The Paul Butterfield Blues Band
          (reprise, filling in for the Beach Boys)
Turnstone
Laura Nyro
Jefferson Airplane
Otis Redding
          with Booker T. & the MGs

Chapter 16

THERE WAS A CERTAIN GATHERING MOMENTUM to the festival now, almost a sense of excited runaway inevitability, like a big rig just about to run out of control down a one-in-four grade, its tires hydroplaning, on the point of going airborne. Rennie was still a little sorry that she still had to be there listening to music, even though she loved it and it made her so happy, when really she wanted to be going around asking questions. What would be the bigger story, after all, when everybody came out of this on Monday: how well the Byrds had played Saturday night or who had killed Basil Potter? And who would be the reporter to be remembered for reporting it?

After the typically warm afternoon, it was a typically chilly mid-coast California evening, the feel and scent of rain on the air drifting in from the sea, which made people nervous for tomorrow—nobody wanted a washout. Besides, the change in the weather seemed to affect the bands, and not in a good way. There had been complaints from neighboring areas, places like ritzy Pacific Grove, that the music was carrying only too well on the prevailing winds, and the atmospheric changes, though subtle, were felt by the artists. The canary in the mine shaft had been Quicksilver Messenger Service earlier that afternoon, the lone hard-rock oasis in the middle of the blues marathon: a fine-sounding but ultimately disappointing set, especially for Rennie, who was a huge fan and had expected a blow-out, and who thought John Cipollina was the most underrated guitarist in San Francisco rock.

The first act on tonight's schedule was another Bay Area classic and Rennie favorite, Moby Grape. And again, for some strange and unaccountable reason — meteorological, pharmacological, or just plain karma- ological — it just wasn't happening. Unable to get it together for the most important performance of their life as a band so far, the Grape finally left the stage in disgust because they weren't allowed to jam; Rennie heard later they'd gone sulking back to the city and promptly gotten themselves stoned and busted. Well, whatever works.

At least the stage crew had settled into an efficient groove: movin', movin', movin', keep those dogies movin'! On, off, stage cleared, next act. Which happened to be South African 'jazz' trumpeter Hugh Masekela, a spotlight hog who bogarted everything for a pointless eternity, which was in actuality only an hour but still twice as long as everyone else had been allowed to play. Though everybody just loved his conga drummer, Big Black, who was not only black and big, as billed, but deeply talented to boot — no word on Masekela's reaction to the ovation he got, as opposed to the booing Hugh himself had received.

The Byrds jingle-jangled, seething with not-so- hidden tensions. Rennie, who loved them — in her critical opinion, nobody but the Byrds should be allowed to cover Dylan songs—had been looking forward majorly to their set, and though they'd set-listed a few of her favorites, the vibes of personal dissension curdled the music like sour milk. And the kicker was, everyone should have expected it. It all came to a head when David Crosby grabbed the mike for a loopy rant about JFK's assassination and the Warren Commission and Lee Harvey Oswald and the drug STP. Leader Jim McGuinn looked about ready to assassinate *him*, but the band played on and lurched through and broke up almost as soon as they got off the stage.

Which almost didn't matter, because Crosby had been on his way out for months. For one thing, he was planning on sitting in with the Buffalo Springfield on Sunday night, which would do little to further endear him to his fellow Byrds, and Stephen Stills, another Byrd about to take flight, had been secretly playing with the Springfield for a few weeks now, preparing to replace Neil Young, who had just quit *that* group. Oh, the unending cycle of giddy incestuousness that was L.A. rock! But it didn't matter even less, because by this time next year Crosby, Stills and Graham Nash from the Hollies would have a whole new band all their own, and Neil would join them later. It wouldn't be a peaceful band, oh no, not with those souls, not a bed of roses; but not a bed of thorns either. At least not all the time. And the music would be a glory and a joy.

Stepping in for the Beach Boys, who were widely rumored to have tanked the match because they were afraid they would be out-hipped by all these new acts— and in Rennie's professional opinion they were quite right to fear so, and they would never again command the coolness factor, such as it was, that they had once possessed—Paul Butterfield and his band played the exact same set that they had played that afternoon. Hey, wasn't the blues supposed to be all about the

improvisation and the surprise and the free-wheeling?
Someone had apparently forgotten to tell these guys —
Butterfield was roundly booed for pompous fake-osity,
as Masekela had been, and both of them richly deserved
it.

"*Rough* room!" said Belinda Melbourne, looking
around the hooting arena with amusement.

Rennie, who was sitting next to her, with Prax on
her other side, laughed shortly and brushed some spilled
pot crumbs off her lace-tablecloth bellbottoms.

"They're big boys. They can handle it. And if not,
then they shouldn't be here. In fact, they shouldn't have
been here anyway. It was only because the Beach Boys
chickened out that Butterfield got a second set. Most
undeserved, especially when the other acts aren't even
being allowed to jam. Adlips could have divided that
empty slot between the Grape, the Byrds and the
Airplane, and it would have been brilliant. Or given it to
Big Brother to make up for this afternoon. But no. Stupid
stupidheads."

She straightened in her seat: Turnstone was just
now visible in the wings, getting ready to come onstage.
The little group of friends — Rennie, Prax, the members of
Evenor and Powderhouse, Dill Miller, Stan, Belinda —
was anxious for them; for Tansy especially, because how
on earth could *any* chick singer follow what Janis had
done that afternoon, even though there were hours and
hours in between to help people forget, which they had
not. But Tanze had seemed confident and cheerful as
they'd helped her dress backstage, and Rennie and Prax
had kissed her good luck and went out front to watch
and cheer, just as Tansy and Rennie had done for Evenor
the night before.

Now they watched lynx-eyed as Turnstone took
the stage. The band looked happy and excited, this boded
well. Bruno was adorable, thought Rennie fondly, and

the other guys seemed totally up for it. Then Tansy Belladonna spun to the center of the stage. Like Prax last night, she was dressed in a new outfit that was a gift for luck and love from Rennie: a feather-and-fur-trimmed suede halter and microskirt, both in a soft spring green. With her streaming butter-colored hair flying upon her shoulders and bare tanned back, and the crown of flowers she wore atop it, she looked like a minor Olympian goddess, the sort of tousled dryad who would be the bride of a river god.

Having to top the apparently untoppable performance Big Brother had turned in was no picnic, and Turnstone knew it. So did the audience, who was sitting with its arms stonily folded and an 'Okay, what've *you* got?' look on its collective face. Turnstone just smiled to itself, and opened with the knockout 'Shores of Ever After.'

Listening to the crowd reaction to Tansy's crystalline yet powerful soprano and Bruno Harvey's grounding baritone, sitting in the second row behind Owen Danes and Janis herself, Rennie looked up at Tansy amazed and delighted, and as Bruno took off on a singing, and stinging, lead-guitar solo, Tansy looked down and winked at her friend, blowing her a kiss. The wink told Rennie, See, I knew I would get here eventually, and so did you know it, and the kiss told her, You helped me more than you can ever possibly imagine, and no, *not* just with clothes, and you're here with me now, and it's all happening, and thank you for being my friend.

And Rennie blew a kiss back, and smiled.

Some poor hapless soul unenviably had to follow Turnstone, and it fell to a caramel-voiced New Yorker called Laura Nyro. She was hopelessly out of her depth, and her performance did not go well, not just because she

had to go on after the unexpected supernova that was
Tansy Belladonna and couldn't measure up but because,
like so many others here, she really shouldn't have been
there in the first place, and she knew it. She wasn't booed
off, as she thought she had been, and as festival legend
would claim for many years thereafter; but neither was
she the recipient of a standing ovation, or indeed any
kind of ovation. Sympathetically enveloping her as she
fled the stage, Michelle Phillips shepherded her out back
to a limo, proffering a beer and a joint for comfort, and
Rennie heard later that they drove around Monterey
until Laura calmed down.

Poor kid. Hard enough to get people to
pronounce her name correctly—rhymed with 'zero',
apparently, not 'pyro', and Rennie would bet good
money she hadn't been born with it—but had nobody
thought to clue her in to the kind of vibe that would be
going down here? She'd shown up in a cocktail gown
with a harpist and two dancing-girl backup singers, for
God's sake, how badly advised was *that*? Being as she
was one of Lou Adler's personal festival picks, you'd
think he'd at least have tipped her off to the freakin'
dress code... But she had a decent voice, and *great* songs;
it wouldn't be the last anyone would hear of her.

The night was wrapping itself up now, chuffing
along like a great sleek psychedelic steam engine that
had finally found its groove. Jefferson Airplane, Rennie's
favorite band in the world, came on with no time to
warm up, and, criminally, were allowed no encore,
though in her professional judgment they turned in one
of the finest performances she'd ever heard from them,
and she'd heard pretty much all of them to date. In front
of the dancing, bubbling colors of the light show, Grace
looked lovely, in a flowing, brown-embroidered white
caftan soon to be seen on the cover of Life magazine, and
Marty had never been in finer voice or brighter spirits—

for Rennie's money, he had one of the three best male lead voices in all of rock; while Paul and Spencer were strong and steady as ever, sturdy wheelhorses giving heft and impetus to the flying chariot, and Jack and Jorma were on fire.

They did a knockout forty-minute set, eight of their very best songs, most of which happened to be among Rennie's favorites, and they did them to utter perfection, which in anyone's book was pretty darn perfect indeed. But they weren't permitted to stretch their rightful moment: before ears had stopped ringing or hands had stopped clapping or the standing ovation had seated itself again, the hovering stage crews, mindful of the newly imposed and rapidly approaching midnight curfew, had swooped in to clear the decks for the evening's closer — Otis Redding, backed by Booker T. and the MGs — and the Airplane was denied a walk-off home run that would have blown the roof off the place. If there had been a roof.

Rennie was disgusted as she watched them file offstage, still charged up. Oh, right, that gasbag Hugh Masekela could hog twice his allotted time and bore everybody into stupefaction, but the best rock band in America couldn't be spared six extra minutes for a richly deserved encore! Typical L.A. envy: nobody wanted yet another Bay Area band upstaging the Los Angeles acts even more. Well, too late for that...the San Franciscans were clearly wiping the floor with the Southlanders, which was as it should be.

By now, the wings and backstage environs were crowded: probably a hundred people all standing watching. Once Turnstone had come off, Rennie'd gone back to congratulate Tansy and the guys, and had listened to the Airplane from there. After that she'd gotten a little fidgety, but when Otis Redding came on she couldn't *not* stay to listen, at least a bit. Redding was a musician with a huge rep on the black circuit, and this was the first time he was playing for this kind of hip white audience — a make-or-break moment for sure.

There had been some bad feeling about the lack of black musicians on the bill; artists, organizers and fans alike had complained about it up front. It worked both ways, though: a number of black performers *had* been asked, but for various reasons they'd turned the invitation down — schedule conflicts (Dionne Warwick; the Fairmont Hotel wouldn't let her out of her supper-club gig that night), or they didn't want to play for free (Chuck Berry, Bo Diddley; and in fairness, some white acts also declined for the very same reason), or they didn't feel they'd get the respect they felt they deserved, or indeed did deserve, from a bunch of predominantly white hippie music fans under age twenty-five.

So ignoring Otis was not the way to cover the full Monterey story. And once she'd heard what he and his band were doing, Rennie was knocked out. She had, in the course of her critical duties, seen plenty of r&b and soul and variations thereof, but this was something as different and as innovative in its own way as the Airplane and the Dead were in theirs — something dizzying, something amazing. It was weird: so far, the unknown acts, or at least an outsize percentage of them, had performed triumphantly and transcendently, and the bands who'd come in with a rep and a track history had been disappointing and disappointed. Well, maybe that would change before things wrapped up tomorrow night.

After watching for a while, though, the antsiness took over, and Rennie needed to move. Letting Stan Hirsh bat reportorial cleanup again, she quit the backstage area and wandered out into the fairgrounds, with no particular place to go. Her ear was suddenly caught by faint music coming from way far over on the other side of the field, from the barn building with the tiny stage tucked away inside, where Powderhouse Road had played on Thursday evening. People, including some very big names indeed, had been continuously jamming there all day long, as well as in the manufacturers' tents, whenever there was no music on the main stage and sometimes even when there was, and some were prepared to go on jamming as long as they were allowed.

But what had attracted her attention just now was a very different kind of sound, and she headed over to go find out. As she went inside, she peered past the small admiring throng and was surprised to see the British band Lionheart. They weren't due to go on till the following night, but obviously they had been unable to resist playing just a little, maybe to take the edge off their nervousness or warm up their chops. What they were playing now, though, sounded like nothing she had ever heard them play before, like nothing she had ever heard anyone else play either.

It seemed to be English morris dance music, which Rennie knew and particularly loved, but the band had slowed it and set it to a march tempo. Turk Wayland began it on banjo, a sparkling tune, eerie, minor, with Jay-Jay Olvera on a hand drum, and then Rardi Lombardi took up the melody on a surprisingly ominous-sounding accordion. Somewhere Shane Sheehan had found a tuba, of all things, and was playing the bass line; Jay-Jay kept up the simple, steady march beat while Niles Clay soberly clashed a tambourine and Mick Rouse filled in the gaps on twelve-string. But it was Turk who was leading off now, as he had led in. Well-played banjos usually sounded like at least two instruments anyway, but he made this one sound like a quartet. The march went on and on, catching them all into it with a grave delight, then one by one the instruments fell away until it was just drum and banjo, then just banjo, then silence.

That was apparently their last, as they gave over the stage to whoever wanted to follow them, returning the borrowed instruments and scattering into the night through the awestruck crowd. Two hours later, Rennie heard the tune still echoing in her head. She'd done a couple of quick, intense backstage interviews in the meantime: the Airplane—fun, since they'd done well and were rightly pleased with themselves, despite the bum's-rush lack of encore; and Jim McGuinn—not fun, understandably, since the Byrds' leader was still breathing fire and slaughter against his impetuous bandmate Crosby, trickster god of rock and roll. Now she drove from the Festival grounds to the Otter Point Inn, to meet whoever was there to be met, and maybe get herself some dinner while she was about it.

Coming into the bar area with Prax, whom she'd found loitering in the lobby, Rennie immediately noticed Tansy over across the room. She was sipping wine and leaning against the side of a very tall guy with thick straight blond collar-length hair, whom Rennie immediately recognized, with a start, as Turk Wayland of Lionheart, last seen two hours ago playing banjo in a barn.

And Tansy was very much, ah, *with* him, if Rennie was any judge. Oh dear. Bimbo Baggins strikes again. Poor Bruno. Well, they didn't have an exclusive relationship, Bruno and Tanze, so the cute Brit was fair game. And he didn't appear to be exactly objecting to Tansy's annexing him, so there it was. Quick work, though, even for Tanze.

Tansy turned and saw them, and beamed. "Rennie, Prax, come over here and meet Turk!"

In years to come, Rennie Stride would often be heard to say that she recalled no particular feeling of fate in the air at this meeting—no sparks on shaking hands, no eyes meeting across a crowded greenroom on an enchanted evening. Though she did remember thinking that Turk Wayland was a quite incredibly handsome man and a quite incredibly gifted musician and, if pressed, she might even have 'fessed up to something along the lines of *My goodness but he's striking I could go for that myself if I happened to be looking which thank you so much I am NOT because I'm totally messed up already with Stephen and Marcus and Chet and Ned and Owen though not them so much anymore and musicians are nothing but trouble anyway and if he's attracted to Tansy fond as I am of her he's obviously stupider than he looks…*

Rennie had been a Lionheart fan from their first folk-heavy album for the tiny Glisten label, but with their fifth, released in England two months ago, a miracle seemed to have happened. For several years now, Lionheart had been putting itself through major musical changes, cycling from solid folk-rock through tough blues-rock into hard rock, but the most recent stage of this evolution had brought them to something that could only be described as art. Art on a whole other level. Art with balls. And brains. And soul. And really good lyrics. And great, great music.

Acid strikes again… We saw it change the Beatles, and Dylan, and the Stones, and we're going to be seeing it change a lot more people, I have a feeling, artists and audiences alike…we watched it all happen, we saw it go from 'I wanna hold your hand' to 'Newspaper taxis appear on the shore'…don't let's make a big old honking deal of it, but don't let's play it down either…

But when taxed with it, Turk Wayland smilingly disallowed the influence of LSD. Sure, they'd all tried it, he said easily, but it wasn't anything they were going to make a habit of and probably the most serious effect it had had on them was on their stage clothes. He was looking quite comfortable at the moment, having doffed a brown leather jacket to stand up in a white shirt and black jeans and brown Frye boots—Rennie's all-time favorite outfit to see on hunky guys, or any guys, and if she could have made it a law to make all men dress like that, all the time, she would have.

"We're just a bunch of English malcontents," he added cheerfully. "Well, in the case of Jay-Jay, our drummer, an American malcontent. But we found him in London so he counts for Brit."

They discussed mutual friends—Ned Raven and Brian Jones chief among them—and moved on to other topics. Then Rennie: "That piece you were playing over on the barn stage earlier? What *was* that? I think it was one of the most amazing things I ever heard."

Turk smiled shyly. "Oh, just a little something I picked up in the north of England. I lived there for a while when I was a lad, and whenever I could, I played for this local morris side. Morris dance music is—oh, you know it—well, then, this particular outfit was into doing morris tunes with, ah, unusual instrumentation. Brass, banjo, hurdy-gurdy, concertina. We were just playing it here for fun."

"It sounded like—like a march to Atlantis."

"Then that's what we'll call it." He smiled again. "We've never recorded it, so we never bothered giving it a name. Maybe now we will. Both, I mean."

He got into some guitar shoptalk with Owen Danes of Stoneburner, who was standing in the next little conversation pod over, almost as tall and blond and talented as Turk himself, and who immediately included Rennie—who had counted Owen as one of her semi-regulars, but not even semi these days, really, just sometimes when she was in L.A.—in their conversation. She was checking out the crowd, only half-listening, then:

"Perry the Winkle? *You* played with Perry the *Winkle!*"

Turk turned courteously to her. "Yes…that was the first band I ever played the States with. I was just telling Owen here. It wasn't much, just a sort of early-Beatles-ripoff rock skiffle outfit. We were quite dreadful, really. I was nineteen, the others weren't much older, and we hardly knew what we were doing. Why do you ask?"

"Well, because I saw you play once in upstate New York."

He burst out laughing. "You're joking! What, one of our dozen gigs on our only American tour ever in the whole two months that we were an actual touring band? How old were you, twelve?"

"Flatterer! Sixteen, actually." Rennie's face was alight with amusement and memory. "You played at Ithaca College when I was a freshman—first year, I started early—at Cornell. The Winter Carnival, to be precise. You were very cute, by the way. And a very good guitar player. You must have been. I remembered you, didn't I?"

Well, a name like Perry the Winkle, you weren't likely to forget. They had been a bunch of young, badly dressed Brits, and they were all uniformly dreadful, the one exception being their lead guitarist, who though he was dressed as badly as the rest was quite astonishingly good even in such a horrible context: a tall blond who also did a lot of the singing—though she could tell he was just finding his feet in a band and his voice as a musician, not to mention the right hip length for his hair.

Given the little ways of rock and roll, she had thought she might hear of him again down the road, but had then considered that there were an awful lot of cute, good English guitarists out there and not much room for a whole lot more. No, he'd probably go the same way as many another, and good as he was there just hadn't seemed to be reason enough to write him up for the college newspaper so she'd never bothered to ask his name.

But she didn't tell him that, only said reflectively, "How things do come around. Did you ever hear of Powderhouse Road?"

"Not until I heard them play Thursday evening on that little stage where we were tonight. They're very, very good."

"Three of them were friends of mine at Cornell, and the other two went to Ithaca. They're the ones who invited me over to see you Winkles. They figured if a bunch of goofy-looking Brits could get a band together and pull chicks the way you lads were pulling them, they could too. And so they did."

Turk grinned reminiscently. "We were just off the student-fare plane from Gatwick, the first time most of us had ever been to the States, or on a plane at all, and we were so green the cows could have eaten us. We had managed to score some jobs playing colleges, don't ask me how, and we drove this ratty van from New York to San Francisco. We didn't have much money—well, no money, really—so we all slept in the van with our equipment, on the mattresses we used to protect the amps, or, when we were really flush, we'd rent one room in some fleabag motel, just so we could all take showers. We prided ourselves on being slaves to the blues, but our shameful secret desire was to make huge top-of-the-pops singles like the Zombies or the Cyrkle, call ourselves the Trapezoyds or something. We were positively dying to sell out. But, alas, no one was buying," Turk added, laughing at his younger self. "So Perry the Winkle died the death it deserved."

"Just as well. Lionheart is much better suited to your talents."

"I've never been accused of being an inspiration before," he said, still smiling. "It's a rather strange feeling, I find. A shock to the system."

They talked a bit more, but Rennie could see that
Tansy was showing signs of wanting to whisk her
conquest off and have her way with him, and Turk was
showing signs of wanting to be whisked, so she left them
to it.

"Tanze really puts the 'strum' back in 'strumpet',
doesn't she?" she remarked to Prax, gazing after them.

Prax grinned. "She sure does love her them there
axemen. Bruno, Garcia, Orlando Pallant, Cipollina,
George Harrison. I'm surprised she didn't try to grab that
Hendrix cat too, even though Janis already has her eye on
him. Bruno was here a little earlier. He took one look and
had to leave. Poor guy. She'll be rolling back to him in—
if it's not just a one-nighter with Wayland, weekender at
most—a month. Six weeks at the outside."

Not thirty seconds later, after Prax had gone to
talk to Juha, who'd just shown up, someone came up
behind Rennie, tugged on her hair, spoke in her ear.

"Remember me? The pool at Mojado? I have
clothes on now, so you might not."

She turned, already smiling. "How could I forget?
I was the naked chick in the turquoise necklace. In case
you're getting me mixed up with some other naked
chick. We had a lovely chat about Yeats and some less
lovely discussion about the music biz. You asked me to
have dinner with you. With our clothes on, presumably."

Finn Hanley grinned. "How could I forget? I so
seldom have really good chats about Yeats these days,
especially with beautiful naked women…no, it's true, I
don't. Still, if I'd known you were a journalist I would
never have—"

"Somebody ratted me out, did they? Well, you
mustn't scare easily, because here you are. And I bet even
if you'd known my profession? Sure you would have."

"Sure, now, I would have… Where are you
staying? Highlands Inn? Too far. Now *my* room is right

down the hall. I know I promised you dinner, but we could have room service instead."

And by 'room' and 'service' we really mean...well, we all know what we really mean. What was I just saying about musicians being nothing but trouble?

Apart from football and not asking for directions, Rennie hated only two things about men: pencil pricks and back hair. Since she'd already vetted Finn Hanley on both counts at the Mojado springs, she didn't have to leap screaming out of bed when he came out of the bathroom, a white towel wrapped rather iconically around his hips.

"Ah, the Jesus look."

"I get that a lot, I do. Well, you'll be worshipping the water I walk on soon enough."

Rennie reached out for the towel. "That depends on what kind of miracles you can perform."

Afterwards, they shared a joint and some wine, then Finn ordered room service, which arrived at the door in a surprisingly short time, which was good, because they were unsurprisingly hungry. Rennie hadn't even finished the rant against record-company presidents she'd been in the middle of, and she continued as they ate.

"Pierce Hill of Rainshadow, Jake Holland of Isis, Freddy Bellasca of Centaur," she enumerated, as she bit into an excellent chicken salad sandwich on home-baked bread. "People like Leeds Sheffield and Ahmet Ertegun are one thing—classy, smart, musically and socially savvy—but man, *those* three are real pieces of work. I think the only question is who should be eaten first if we're all adrift in a lifeboat on the iceberg-strewn North Atlantic."

Finn laughed. "Now there's a topic for debate! Deft and compelling arguments could be made on all sides. More milk? No, here, have it all; unlike most Irish people I take lemon with me tay. A poncy habit I picked up in London. From folksingers."

She looked aside at him as she swilled down the icy beverage—sometimes really cold milk was the only thing that could quench your thirst—and decided to go for it.

"Did you know Basil Potter?"

"I did, and I never liked him, God forgive me."

"Why is that?" She wasn't about to let on, at least not just yet, that she'd been a friend of Baz's for years and years; still less that she'd overheard the conversation in Romilly's sculpture garden, which had had as much to do with Baz as with Finn himself, and oddly, the Irishman still made no mention of the fact that she'd shown up there following the rifle shots. Hardly possible he'd forgotten, or didn't recognize her...

"No reason, except a kind of sibling rivalry, us both being on Rainshadow and all. But I hear he beat up on his pretty lady, and there's no excusing that."

"Not reason enough to get a man murdered, though."

"I wonder would you still say that if you were the one being beat up on."

"I wouldn't say anything at all," said Rennie evenly. "I'd beat up back. Harder."

"I do believe you would."

They both felt warm and sleepy after the sandwiches—tryptophans kicking in, carb fatigue just like after Thanksgiving dinner, and besides, it had been a long day—and setting the plates and glasses aside, brushing the crumbs off the sheets, they snuggled back down again.

Some time later, Rennie woke, startled and disoriented and cold, to a strong, wet wind pouring into the room through the open casement. She looked over to the neighboring pillow: Finn was asleep beside her, apparently unaware of the damp and chill. Perhaps it reminded him of Ireland. The covers were down around his waist, so that his skin was cool to the touch; shivering, she dashed over and closed the window — it had begun to rain lightly, more like billows of mist, and the bare wood floor was slick and cold with water. As she did so, she heard the hollow boom of the surf on the rocks a hundred feet below, sounding very close, and she could taste the salt spray — the tide must be all the way in. Then she hurried back to bed, dove into the warmth and pulled the bedclothes up around their ears.

"Thoughtful," said Finn, as she cuddled closer.

"My middle name. No, that's a lie, my middle name's Catherine. But I didn't mean to wake you."

"Not to worry. I'm sure we can find something to occupy ourselves. I just wanted a breath of fresh air, and left the window open too wide. Sorry."

"Where's your medal?" she asked drowsily, remembering the Miraculous Medal she'd noted him wearing in the pool at Mojado.

Finn looked sheepish. "Ah, that. Well, if you must know, I don't like the Blessed Virgin Mary, Mother of God, to see me having casual sex. Or any kind of sex, for that matter. It's stupid, but there it is. And especially sex with a nice Catholic girl I don't even know. So I took it off. Old habits, no pun intended, die hard."

"Half nice Catholic girl. Other half Episcopalian, presumably equally nice. Though I don't sing in either choir, haven't for years."

"Both halves very nice indeed."

When they were warm again, Finn nuzzled her hair. "I was just thinking, morbidly enough, whatever happened about that poor lad they found dead in the pool over to Big Magic? I never heard any more of him than that."

"I'm not sure," said Rennie evasively. "I think Baz

Potter being murdered kind of trumped him."

"Sad and strange, if oddly symmetrical: two deaths, two festivals."

"Coincidence. Just odds playing out."

"Odds? Potter was *murdered*, lass, as you just now said."

"There's odds in homicide too."

"You sound as if you know a wee bit about it."

Rennie shot him a sharp glance, but he seemed honestly non-referential to her history, just a general observation.

"Maybe you do too," she said presently. "Seeing as you were shot at the other day, over at Mojado."

"Ah. I wondered when that would be coming back to haunt me." He didn't sound haunted, particularly, or even embarrassed. "You've probably heard all about Pierce Hill's master plan by now: to cut the folk acts that got Rainshadow started and to repopulate the label with young rockers."

"I believe I've heard something of the sort. But you didn't have to pretend we'd never met, you know, when I came running out of the fog. Care to explain yourself?"

"I was too gobsmacked," he confessed. "First the shots, then you. It just seemed easier to pretend I'd never seen you before."

"You don't think you were the one being shot at, do you?"

"No idea. I'd not put anything past Pierce, though… Still, it could have been just a little leaden, ha, reinforcement of his main theme: 'You're out, Hanley. And take *that* as you leave.'"

"At least you're not out the way Basil Potter is out…"

"I didn't *dis*like them, you understand, Baz and Roger," said Finn contritely. "I just thought they were a bit lightweight. And when they started trying to do the rock thing—besmirching the purity of folk music by electrifying it up—I went off them, and so did a lot of people."

"Baz was an old friend of mine from New York," said Rennie, a tiny, glassy edge of warning now in her voice. "Roger too...and I think Dylan kinda settled that whole going-electric thing two summers ago at the Newport Folk Festival. Lord, I wish I'd been there! But I was married by then and had been hauled off to San Francisco by the hair, kicking and screaming, so I missed it. *And* missed the Beatles at Shea Stadium. Two of the very few things I'll never forgive my husband for. Still, Pierce has seen the future, and it goes by many names, all of them new and unknown. As you know to your cost."

"Well, I do wish you'd told me sooner, my dear; I surely didn't mean to insult your friend. I'm sorry, truly I am. And you needn't worry about me. I'll find a home on some other label run by a worthier sort. As for Pierce, he's already gone public with his group lust."

"Not to mention his noxious attitudes—were you there the other night, over at the Highlands Inn? Sledger Cairns had to be physically restrained from going for him."

Finn was laughing. "I was, and I would have paid good dosh to see her dismember him in public. And I also noticed that a&r guy Gerry Langhans, a very decent bloke, quitting on Pierce right in front of God and everybody. After flattening him with the most gorgeous right cross I ever saw. A very exciting evening all round."

"Gerry wasn't out of work long: Freddy Bellasca of Centaur hired him on the spot. I would have tried to stop it if I'd been there. The job offer, not the punch. I'm all for punches when they're as richly deserved as that one. Sorry I missed it. But I consider Bellasca another music-biz pigdog, from the same mutant litter as Percy."

"It was a thing of beauty, that punch, and, dare I say, a joy forever. But as far as scumbag label presidents go, old Freddy's not so bad. Not as bad as Pierce, at least. I hear that he's hot to sign Lionheart."

"Isn't everybody? They're amazing. And we haven't even seen them play here for real yet. Even my friend Ned Raven is seething with jealousy of Turk Wayland, and they've been friends for years."

"Ah, that Neddy's a rare good lad—we've cracked a bottle or two, or two hundred, in our time. Cracked some of them over each other's heads, even."

"Festive. And fraternal."

Rennie listened, with as much attentiveness as her renewed sleepiness allowed, while Hanley ranted on about record labels and how unfair Pierce was being to him. Well, at least he'd come up with an explanation, however unsatisfactory, for his non-acknowledgment of her that morning at Waterhall.

And I'm still wondering if those shots were meant for you, minstrel boy. And if they were, were they meant to hit or to miss?

They must have slept a bit more, because Rennie woke drowsy and peered at the clock; later than she had thought. Finn was returning to bed, from the direction of the bathroom.

"Oh my God, did I do that? I'm so sorry!" Rennie had just noticed a few scratches on Finn's neck and shoulders, raw-looking scrapes, and touched them gently. "I guess I don't know my own strength—or the last time I cut my fingernails."

"A little bit, yes, my dear. Though it felt just fine while you were doing it... They just now came up all welted and hurting, I was only putting some cold water on. But more from the rough stuff last night, is all."

"Really? Sorry I missed it."

But the sex they'd had, though pleasant, hadn't

been all *that* rough, and she wondered a little as they
geared up again. Scratches: as in being on the receiving
end of Adam Santa Monica's fingernails? Finn knew
about the High Springs, of course; that was where she'd
met him. But what on earth would be his motive? And
she would have noticed the scratches before now;
wouldn't she?

She found her attention diverted from murder
speculation by Finn's voice in her ear. He had a nice line
of erotic chat before and during, she had to admit; big on
the arousing running commentary. True, he was Irish:
maybe good sex talk was just something they did
especially well over there; Chet certainly did.
Fuckblarney. Though now that she thought of it, 'good
sex' and 'Irish' were words that didn't often occur in
close conjunction, at least not in the public perception. Or
maybe they expended themselves in talk and had
nothing left for action.

But this guy—well, perhaps he'd had enough
rough stuff, and wanted something kinder and gentler
just now, however disappointing she herself might find
it. Rennie didn't care for sex where anyone got hit or
hurt, but she did like it fast and forceful on both sides,
and this had been neither.

"Actually, if you really must know," said Finn in
a confessional voice, "the only rough stuff last night was
me falling over trying to move some amps."

Rennie snorted laughter. "That's what roadies are
for!"

"They were all stoned and out of it. It seemed
easier and safer to do it myself. So wrong, I was."

"Well, aren't *you* the manly man."

"Didn't I just prove that now? Miracles to order.
Multiple orgasms to order, at least. You American lasses
are quite the thing; Irish and British girls are hard put to
it to come even once. I've only ever fucked two who

could. You're so relaxed and into it."

"La, sir, what a sweet-talker you are! So, you're saying American girls are sluts? Orgasmic, but sluts. Hmm. Much more likely you're just fucking the wrong people. Pity your line in miracles doesn't run to raising the sexually inert."

"Or the actually inert. Poor Baz, indeed."

She wasn't about to get into her friendship with the late Mr. Potter, not more than she already had; she wasn't quite sure why. Just said, a little fliply, a little defensively, "If life gives you lemons — "

"Make lemonade?"

Rennie pulled him down again. "Squirt them in your enemies' eyes."

Eventually they both fell asleep, and if there were dreams, neither of them remembered.

There had been real rain in the night, eventually, a grass-soaking rain riding in on a west wind; then it had cleared out in time for a watery dawn under gray clouds. Down on the beach, resolutely unclothed sun-saluters were marching under a god's-eye flag and chanting morning mantras to the beat of tambourines, trying desperately to Zen themselves warm past the shivery chill, when suddenly they were struck into silence, and stood uncertainly on the sands like a naked hippie version of the graveyard scene in "Our Town."

With good reason. At the foot of the cliffs in scenic, boulder-strewn Otter Cove, below the seaward windows of the Inn at Otter Point, Pierce Hill's broken body was lying across a high flat rock, just out of reach of the tide.

Chapter 17

Sunday morning, June 18

THE SOUND OF TWO VOICES, one professional folk tenor, one amateur mezzo-soprano, came out of the morning fog on the fairgrounds, and Prax collapsed onto Stan's shoulder, laughing fit to burst. His girlfriend, the lovely, blond and extremely unmythical Marishka, who'd finally turned up late last night, listened in puzzled amusement.

" 'Who was the first to conquer space? It's in-con-tro-VERT-ible! That the first to conquer living space was a Cas-tro Convertible!' " The singers split into quite surprisingly tuneful harmony lines, then swerved back into enthusiastic unison for the big finish. "'Who conquers space with fine design? And saves you money all the time? Who's *tops* in *the* convertible liiiiine? CAS-tro Con-VERT-ibles!'"

Rennie and Finn Hanley staggered up, clinging to each other's shoulders, happy and fizzing. They'd gotten up early, and had been roving around the festival grounds, seeing what there was to be seen: sleeping fans, meditating fans, toking fans, tripping fans, all bundled up, such of them as actually had the wherewithal to do the bundling—like blankets and spare clothes—against the rainy and chilly morning.

"We're so hungry, it's too early for music, let's go find some food."

Leaving the fairgrounds, they ran slap into Tansy Belladonna and Turk Wayland, and promptly invited them along. They all crammed into Rennie's station wagon and headed to an old-style roadside diner not far from the field. Apparently half the festivalgoers had had the same idea, but the diner knew its business and turned over tables so fast that they had to wait only ten minutes before they sat down.

Rennie glanced curiously at Turk, who was sitting across from her, looking a little wary of all the new faces. Not to mention a tad bit cramped in the booth's confines: no wonder, he was huge, had to be at least six-three and two hundred pounds; the U-shaped corner booth was big and curved, but it hadn't been designed with him in mind. He was wearing the same clothes he'd had on last night at the auxiliary stage and the Highlands bar; both he and Tansy looked pleased with themselves, so presumably things had gone well.

After ordering, they happily discussed the festival and the performances, particularly those of the performers who were present. Finn held court for a while, a little too practiced for comfort, and besides, he hadn't even performed at Monterey, only Big Magic; but he wisely sensed the vibe and backed off to let the younger artists have the floor. Prax and Tansy confided about their hungry days in San Francisco, which were only very recently, and still not entirely, behind them, but Turk was an actual star, at least in England, and they shyly deferred to him. Not a huge star, not as big a star as he was going to be tomorrow, or a month, or a year, from now, but a star nonetheless. Yet he'd had his own hungry times and problems.

Over waffles and sausage, he disarmingly told the table the story of how, his parents having disowned him for becoming a rock and roller, he'd humbled his pride and asked them to buy the band some decent stage clothes for their first big important gig. When they refused, still thinking he'd come crawling home if they only starved him long enough, his sister, who'd just started a career as a model and was pissing off the parents on her own account, had given him the money, and bass player Shane Sheehan's sister Norah had altered and refitted and remade whatever needed it.

Rennie, sipping her hot cocoa and laughing with the rest, was thinking that obviously Lionheart didn't have to rely on their sisters for clothes help any more, though she was also thinking how she would love to get her hands on their wardrobes. No offense to Norah Sheehan, but man, the dramatic clobber Rennie could whip up for Turk *alone* made her thimble finger itch: gold-threaded brocade tunics, doublets in soft studded leather, velvet Cossack shirts—he was so tall and well-built, he could carry off anything, his hair was great but it needed to get longer, a beard would look *terrific*...

With a start she came back to the table. Finn had been openly drinking a more potent brand of orange juice than the rest of them, giving the bottomless glasses of o.j. a bit of a legless kick from the contents of the flask he'd brought with him. Now he was getting into a pissing contest with Turk, or at least trying to, perhaps feeling threatened—the old stag and the young buck.

Oh, for God's sake! If you're going to challenge

someone to a pissing contest, it helps to have a cock that's set for distance…

For his part, Turk was apparently infuriating the Irishman still further by politely declining to respond to the increasingly toxic anti-Brit sentiments, and at last he tossed enough money on the table to cover all their breakfasts — the only sign of temper he'd permitted himself — stood up, smiled at Rennie, Prax, Marishka and Stan, and left with Tansy clinging to his arm.

Finn quieted down at once, and the flask ran out soon after. As if that had been some sort of signal, the conversation turned to the murders, with Rennie listening more than she spoke.

Prax, finishing off her blueberry pancakes, was speculating on the Mojado death, with one eye on Rennie in case she said too much, or not enough.

"I've been thinking: wouldn't whoever killed Adam Santa Monica have like second-degree burns, or at least very red and sore skin, on their hands and arms, from holding him down in the hottest pool, the way Marcus Dorner says happened, which now we can finally talk about? Unless they used a stick or something."

"You'd think," agreed Stan. "So who's wearing long sleeves?"

"Pretty much everybody. It's mostly been too chilly to dress really light."

Rennie said nothing, but ever since Tuesday she had been paying secret and particular attention to what people were wearing on their hands and arms. An exercise doomed to disappointment: quite a few people were flaunting red henna patterns, attractive but unhelpful, while others had fancy lace fingerless gloves on, or those medieval sleeves that come down all pointy over the backs of your hands. While among the honestly forearm-bared, plenty of sufferers were sporting bad sunburns, or poison ivy, or allergic reactions to eating abalone or rolling in grass, or scrapes and redness from moving equipment or raising tents or other sorts of friction. No help there.

Just then Marcus came into the diner, looking around with clear purpose on his face. Seeing Rennie with the others, he came over and pulled up a chair to the end of the table, and told them about Pierce Hill.

"Not *quite* out of reach of the tide," said Marcus, as he and Rennie were scrambling over the rocks in Otter Cove fifteen minutes later, headed to where Audie Devlin and Brent Gilmore were organizing the crime scene, if crime it was. "It was high just after midnight last night, as it will be again a few hours from now, and his clothes were damp with sea water. But only underneath."

"Therefore—therefore what?"

"Therefore he hit that rock as the tide was on the ebb, and landed in standing water. Any sooner, the tide would have been fully in and he'd have gone into a couple feet of slack water, or been washed away altogether. Much later and he'd have been completely dry. I say hit the rock, as in fallen—or been pushed, we found some dubious marks in the grass—from the top of the cliff, but possibly someone could have whacked him on the beach and *then* placed him on top of the rock, to make it look like an accident, that he'd really fallen off the cliff on his own, while the surf would have taken care of any incriminating footprints. There's not much sand to leave prints in, anyway. In any case, say around three or four for time of death, until forensics can bring in something closer."

"I knew that," said Rennie half-heartedly. "About the tide thing, I mean."

She did, too—she even remembered how, when she'd gotten up to close the window of Finn Hanley's room, she'd heard the surf crashing below, and had thought the tide must be all the way in, right up to the foot of the cliff—but she hadn't bothered to think it out until Marcus had mentioned it. At least the body had already been taken away, so she was spared—or deprived of, she wasn't sure which—the sight of Pierce Hill as dead as a doornail.

"Any chance he could have despairingly and suicidally flung himself from the windows of his room?" she asked hopefully. "I'm assuming they looked out on an ocean view."

"Interesting theory, but no. His room faced the other side. The trajectory for him to have self-launched and landed where he did would have required him being shot out of a cannon and around two corners. He'd have had to clear the lawn before he even got near the cliff edge: it's a hundred feet wide, with a terrace, on that side of the hotel. So no, he was on that lawn, at some point, and became airborne from there."

"Well, it was just a thought." She looked up involuntarily at the cliff towering above her, seeing in her mind's eye the flailing figure descending from above to hit the rocks, and—even though it was Pierce Hill and she *totally* thought he'd had it coming to him, in spades— she shivered a little, and hurried on after Marcus.

"Any bright ideas?" asked Brent as they came up to him. Audie Devlin was busy directing his men in a thorough search of the beach area for anything they could find, but apparently they were having no luck, so far at least.

She glanced up sharply, but Deputy Gilmore wasn't being sarcastic. He smiled at her apologetically, as if he knew he'd sounded damn rude, and hastened to explain himself.

"Marcus says you often see stuff other people don't, that you can put things together like nobody's business."

"I like anagrams and crossword puzzles," she said, a little stiffly. "Perhaps that's what Inspector Dorner means."

"Well, if you can anagram this, figuratively speaking, we'd all be grateful. Did you know him?"

"I did, and fairly well too. His name is Pierce Hill, as you're already aware. Real name Percy Epps. The president of Rainshadow Records."

And the nemesis of several — one fewer, now, of course — people I could mention but won't... So she didn't.

As Rennie drove slowly back to the festival grounds, leaving Marcus to assist the police presence on the beach, she turned things over even more slowly in her mind. Okay, now this was getting scary. First Adam Santa Monica, then Baz Potter, now Pierce Hill. Only Baz and Pierce had any connection or mutual motive that she knew of, and they couldn't have killed each other, though each of them could have killed Adam, though for what reason she could not possibly imagine. And Pierce might still be an accident — unlikely though it seemed — but the other two were officially homicides and were being investigated as such, had been for days now.

It had gotten misty again after the night's rain, but it seemed that further precipitation would hold off through Ravi Shankar's concert this afternoon. His appearance was the only thing slated on the main stage all day, and since she wasn't a fan she intended to profit by using the time to snoop around for clues.

"Don't you want to go hear Ravi?" Prax asked when they encountered each other again near a leatherwork stall, where she was buying a headband for Juha and a stash pouch for herself.

"Not I, by God! I'm probably the only person here not deeply enamored of and captivated by interminable sitar yowling. Yes, yes, I know, total Philistine, incapable of appreciating fabulous Indian classical music, don't care. It bores me silly and it makes my teeth hurt and I don't give a damn who knows it. I may be a music critic, which of course I am, and I may love music to pieces, which of course I do, but I don't love every last single little thing and I do not have to. And I don't love this. So, no thank you, Stan can report on it and I will put my afternoon to better use. But. I was down on the beach just now at the crime scene with the coppers, and you need to hear about it."

She filled Prax in, briefly and concisely, and was gratified to see that her friend was suitably shocked.

"And they're thinking murdered, not just accidentally fell over the cliff in a stoned haze or something? But why? I mean, I can *imagine* why, nobody liked Pierce, but—"

"But Baz is dead," said Rennie, as if by way of explanation. "He's dead, and now Pierce is dead too. And Roger isn't. Could it be our boy's done something rash? Fond as I am of him… And if he did, I want to find out about it before the Monterey PD does."

Prax glanced down at her fingernails. "How *are* Pamie and Roger?"

"I haven't forgotten about them, you know," said Rennie a bit defensively. "They're still in seclusion; they've kind of lost their taste for music, as you might imagine. Rick Henries and the roadies are taking care of them; Roger told me they're going to bring Baz back to England as soon as the cops will let them and they can get the clearances and make the arrangements. You'll want to see them yourself before they go."

"I do, and I will. Well, if you change your mind about Ravi, Tansy and Turk and Juha and I will save you a seat."

"Whatever."

"What's going on?" Prax looked at her friend

closely. "You had a good time with Finn last night, didn't you?"

"So I hear."

She grinned at Rennie's doubtful tone. "It's just sex, babe… How many guys have you been with by now?

Rennie mentally added up. "Oh, I don't know, eight, ten, maybe. Is that a lot? Over a year and a half? Marcus and Chet and Ned and Owen being regulars of varying degrees of regularity, though Owen and Ned not so much anymore. And Stephen, of course, who somehow doesn't really seem to count. In the fucklist, I mean; he's sort of got tenure, so I don't include him in the tally. The other ones were just one-nighters, two-nighters at the most."

"Training fucks. They don't count either. Besides, nobody's counting anyway, certainly not me. If you see something you want, and it wants you back, why not? Don't worry, though," Prax added comfortably. "He's out there."

"Who is?"

"The one who's going to make your toes curl and your knees buckle. The one to whom you will do the same."

"Oh, you know, that knee-buckling and toe-curling thing? So overrated."

"Well, we'll just see what you have to say about that when it actually happens. I'd hold out for the click if I were you."

"The *click*."

"Yeah… You know how it is. You see something really really nice, and there's nothing to keep you from having it, and so you do, but somehow it doesn't click with you, however nice it may be. Doesn't have to be a guy. Could be a pair of shoes or an apartment or a car. Could be anything. And then there's something else, maybe it's not as superficially fabulous or maybe it's even more so, but it *does* click, you can actually feel the moment when it does. And so you know it's the right thing for you. You know you don't have to settle. Not that you really settle for the other, but you don't actively claim it the way you do when there's a click, it doesn't feel right and fated in the same way."

Rennie raised an eyebrow. " 'Fated'? We're not back on that karma kick again, are we?"

"You bet we are, sugarplum, so listen up," said Prax imperturbably. "Now *you*: you haven't clicked yet on a guy. Stephen is lovely, Marcus is lovely, Chet Owen Ned, lovely lovely lovely; you have relationships with them, not just relations. All the other guys you've been with? Just pleasant guys and pleasant fucks. It's all practice; none of it goes to waste. Aren't you a lot better at sex now than you were with Stephen? Sure you are! You know what to do now to make it great for both of you, whoever the guy is. And when there's love added to the mix, and that'll happen, it will be like nothing else on earth. You aren't in love with any of these guys. You weren't in love with Stephen either, as we've discussed at mind-numbingly wearying length. None of them is your forever choice, or even your just-for-now choice. They don't click for you. Whatever else they may do for you, and I hope it's a lot otherwise what's the point, they don't click."

"An interesting theory," said Rennie, sounding not the least bit interested.

Prax grinned. "You'll thank me later, I promise. And when he does come along—Click Boy?—I'll be sure to remind you."

"And if he does, feel free to point the finger of I-told-you-so at me for all time. Now can I please go do some detective stuff? And I don't mean Marcus, either."

They hugged, and Rennie continued her aimless

prowl. She didn't really know what the hell she was looking for, just killing time until she came across something, or could pop in at the Monterey stationhouse without being a pest. Orchids were everywhere, as they'd been all weekend: underfoot, onstage, scattered like flowery snow across the lawns and folding chairs. The festival organizers had ordered a hundred thousand flown in from Hawaii, and to most people it seemed like a groovy idea, but the lovely crushed blossoms saddened and angered her. No money to pay the artists who were playing their hearts out to give everyone a good time, oh no so sorry, but money enough to buy thousands upon thousands of exotic blooms—beautiful, fragile flowers that can't stand up to rough handling and only get stepped on in the end. Oooh, what a metaphor! She shook her head and kept walking.

In front of the main stage, she came across Brandi Storey Marron talking to some other Hollywood types. Trippy enough for anybody, and after the morning's earlier events, much too trippy for Rennie, and she turned, hoping to sneak away. But Brandi, seeing her, broke off her conversation and beckoned Rennie over.

"Have you found out anything yet? About the— you know?"

Rennie felt a perverse flare of annoyance. "About the *murders*, you mean?" Heads turned; she didn't care. "No, I haven't. Not yet, anyway. And there's been another death this morning, did you know? Yes. Pierce Hill. Found dead on the beach at Otter Point. Fell over the cliff. Oopsie, then. But he might not have fallen, if you get my drift and I'm sure that you do."

Sensation among the surrounding festivalgoers; apparently the news about Pierce was not yet common knowledge. The name puzzled Brandi for a moment; at least her blank, pretty face screwed itself up as if it did.

"Oh, right, that record company guy Danny was

talking to."

"He was?" asked Rennie, trying not to sound excited. "When was that?"

But Brandi couldn't remember. When they were all at Romilly's house the morning of the shots, she thought. Or maybe it had been here at the festival, after that English guy had been killed, that Baz, was that his name?

As the whispery little-girl voice went irritatingly on, Rennie found herself contemplating Brandi's slender forearms. They were henna'd very prettily, contrasting nicely with her ankle-length Mexican wedding dress. But were they, under the henna, perhaps rather pinker than they should be? As she reached up for a bottle of water from a case on the edge of the stage, she contrived to stumble and fall hard against Brandi, catching at the henna'd arms, hoping for a hiss of pain as burned skin was roughly grabbed.

But nothing. So she apologized, and went on her way.

Chapter 18

IN THE SITUATION ROOM at the Monterey stationhouse, Brent Gilmore set down his coffee cup, smoothed out a list written on yellow legal pad paper and read aloud.

"Just working it on down, then… Killer of Adam Santa Monica. Romilly Ramillies Revels, not impossible. Rebecca Revels, same. Simon Revels, same. Simon's wife and kids, extremely unlikely. Brandi Storey Marron, not likely. Daniel Marron, ditto. Staff at Waterhall: no. The rest of the houseguests at Waterhall: Rennie Stride, Prax McKenna, Juha Vasso, Cathal Galvin, cool name, known as Chet. No, no, no and no."

Marcus Dorner stretched in his chair and reached for his own cup of coffee, turning over the first page of his own yellow pad.

"Killer of Basil Potter. Pamina Potter, no. Well, possible. Roger Hazlitt, very possible. Danny Marron, doubtful. Pierce Hill, possible, but unlikely. The manager, Rick Henries, ditto. Plus except for the manager, they've all got fairly decent alibis. No joy there."

Audie Devlin consulted his own notes; he'd already had two cups of coffee, and he was trying to cut down. "Moving right along: killer of Pierce Hill. Roger Hazlitt, again highly possible. Pamina Potter, also a strong possible for this one; it wouldn't have taken much strength, and he wouldn't have felt threatened by her. Plus both she and Hazlitt are staying at the Otter Point Inn. Miss Stride and the rest of her Round Table, no, though I *am* tempted where she's concerned. Gerry Langhans…"

Brent and Marcus looked up. "Are you really thinking—" asked Brent.

"I have to think it. That's what they pay me the fair-to-middling bucks for. So—Gerry Langhans, what's his story?"

"Aloysius Gerard Langhans. Fine old-school Catholic name. I can see why he goes by Gerry." Marcus riffled a stack of papers. "Twenty-three, lives in Brooklyn Heights, wife JoAnn Haldenway, married in college. Very skilled and respected a&r guy recently employed by Rainshadow Records, the late Baz Potter's longtime label, run by the equally late Pierce Hill. Not to mention a close friend since birth of our Miss Stride. Literally since birth. Once they hit—and I use that verb deliberately—the first grade in Our Lady Star of the Sea, Park Slope, Brooklyn, at five years old apiece, they've been partners in crime, as someone might say. Though that someone would not be me."

Brent rolled his eyes. "Her spies are everywhere."

"Oh, he's just here at Monterey to scout acts." Marcus sounded as sure as he, in fact, was. "But, as we know, he *was* seen leaving Pierce Hill in the bar of the Highlands Inn Thursday night, after a loud public quarrel during which they came to blows. At least Langhans did; got in that beaut of a punch on Hill before he was pulled off by two men and a waiter. Hill just fell onto a couch laughing, bleeding profusely from the nose."

"Interesting." Devlin leaned back. "Refresh my memory."

Brent turned over some papers. "According to several people, Hill was drunk and out of control, and richly deserved what he got from Langhans. He'd been screaming about how all artists were morons, excuse me, *fucking* morons, and record companies were destined by God to bleed them dry. When he started raving about how the only good artist is a dead artist, because then they could be controlled, most of the musicians left the room in disgust. As did Miss Stride. Langhans stayed with his boss. Hill ranted some more, then Langhans went over to him and told him to shut his trap or Langhans would, yes, kill him. If that's what it took to shut him up. Witnesses are unanimous on the threat and the language used."

"So?"

"Hill *wouldn't* shut up, so that's when Langhans decked him and quit Rainshadow Records then and there. Before the echoes of the punch had faded away our boy Gerry was hired, equally then and there, by Freddy Bellasca, the president of Centaur Records. Langhans, I am reliably told, instantly advised Bellasca to sign the band Lionheart immediately, sight unseen and sound unheard, and to try to snag Turnstone and Evenor as well."

"Which would have infuriated Hill," said Marcus, "since Rennie told me he specifically wanted those acts himself and was angling to get them; hence the dumping of Finn Hanley and the other old folkies, as Pamina Potter, Roger Hazlitt and Prax McKenna also told us."

Devlin drummed his fingers again on the pad. "Yeah, but that doesn't mean Langhans *killed* Hill. Hill was drunk as a skunk and as crabby as a sackful of lobsters—it's more likely to have gone the other way. Besides, Langhans had already quit Rainshadow, so apart from a deeply satisfying farewell wallop, which he'd already gotten in, why bother? Unless Hill tried something and Langhans popped him first, maybe even in self-defense. —What about this Bellasca guy, who hired Langhans? Right on the spot like that, suggests some history, doesn't it? Personal rivalry. Corporate competition."

"Same possible motives. He was seen with Hill too, but I don't think any of it means anything. Executives of at least six other record companies were all seen with Hill at various times, and nobody seems to have had a good word to say to him. Or about him."

"Well, we'd better talk to them all again anyway. Especially Langhans." Brent leaned back in his chair, ran a hand over his face, suddenly unspeakably weary at the prospect. But it had to be done; that's what they were there for.

"There were a bunch more people present Thursday night who were noticeably pissed off at Hill's little rant," said Devlin. "His second in command, a possibly mobbed-up guy from New York named Elkanah Bannerman; a girl guitarist called Sledger Cairns, real name Veronica Lee Cairns; couple more that Hill really offended. But enough for any of them to murder him? Doubt it."

"Elk Bannerman," said Marcus reflectively. "You like him for killing Hill? Or even Potter?"

"Maybe. I got a report in last night about him. Bannerman only invested in Rainshadow five years ago, but he invested a *lot*. He might have killed Hill to protect his investment and the company's prestige. Hill was going to dump a lot of older, artier, more expensive acts, and sign up all this new, cheaper talent. If he could get it.

That might not have been in Bannerman's best interests. Yeah, I could see him killing Hill, easy. If he is really is mob, and I hasten to add that nobody knows for sure, it wouldn't be the first time he'd offed someone, and he probably doesn't have any of his people out here, so a hands-on job for him."

"Why would Bannerman have wanted Potter dead?"

"Same reason as Hill. Protect the Potter and Hazlitt catalogue and publishing rights, at all costs. And the added plus: if Hill's dead, Bannerman's in control at the label."

Their meticulous sorting of pertinent details was interrupted by Rennie herself. At sight of her, Marcus leaned back in his chair, teetering it on two legs, and put his hands behind his head.

"Ah. You again."

"No, dear, someone completely different."

The other two glanced up at their tone, which had sounded exasperated and sharp and out of proportion, but Rennie went on in a voice that seemed to suggest she had serious things to talk about.

"You're just lucky Ken Karper is covering this officially for the Clarion. Otherwise—"

"Otherwise we'd have to deal with you a lot more than we are. Yes, I can see that. I'm sure we're grateful for small favors."

Rennie was a little puzzled herself at the note of— oh, *right*, he must have found out she'd spent the night with Finn Hanley, and he was pissed off. Well, too bad. He was going to hear all about it. The relevant bits, anyway. And some other stuff besides.

"Speaking of favors, I have a few things to tell you gentlemen," she began, and she didn't look at Marcus at all.

Rennie didn't leave until they tossed her out on her ear, with dire instructions that though they were extremely grateful for what she had just told them, she was not to come back until they'd had a chance to consider and possibly act on it, because however helpful she might be, they weren't giving her anything more just yet, and that included anything that could be passed along to Ken Karper.

She was neither fazed nor unamused at being tossed; indeed, she conceded that they had a very valid point. But it wasn't going to stop her. And maybe they were right; obviously they weren't sharing as much with her as they *could* be sharing, however much she had been good enough to share with them. They were cops; they didn't have to. But she knew she had given them quite a lot to think about. Besides, she still had the whole afternoon to fossick around. Something else would surely turn up…

Getting into her car, she accidentally caught her long silver Moroccan earring on her hair, painfully. Swearing, she untangled the dangle from the relevant strands, unhooked it from her lobe, then dropped it on the car floor, where she found she couldn't reach it. Swearing some more, she got out and into the rear of the car, groping under the front seat for the errant ornament. What the hell, had it bounced like a tennis ball, where *was* it? And how filthy was it under there anyway, did the rental company never clean these wrecks?

Her scrabbling fingers closed on the earring, successfully, but they also grazed something else, something kicked way back under and lodged against the seat stanchion, and she tugged it out to see what it might be.

It was a small pouch of worn brown leather, about the size of a wallet; in typical hippie style, it laced round the edges and was tooled to within an inch of its life. Not hers; certainly nothing she'd seen Prax or Chet or Juha use, and no one else had been in the car. Presumably it wasn't the property of a previous renter; messy as it was under the seat, anyone cleaning up would surely have found it and removed it.

And then it hit her. No one else had been in the car? Not true. This had to belong to Adam Santa Monica. He must have dropped it when he'd been in the car for the little drive to and from Mojado village, the first day of Big Magic; it had obviously slipped out of his backpack, probably when he'd stuffed the things Rennie had bought him into it, and he'd never even known it was missing. And then he'd been killed the very next night, and no one knew about it, not even her. Not until now.

Rennie stared at it as if it had been a snake, or a sapphire. Of course, it still might belong to someone who'd rented the station wagon before her. In any case, it was absolutely no business of hers. A right-minded, civically correct person would nobly deliver it straight into the hands of the police, the steps of whose building were twenty feet away, without even glancing at what might be within.

Well, that's obviously not me, she thought cheerfully, and opened the leather flap.

"I found this in my car," she announced to Danny Marron. His face went gray and slack as he beheld what she showed him, and hers hardened to see her fears confirmed. "I should have gone straight to the cops with it. But I came to you first."

He tried to bluster out of it. "And why would you do that, Miss Stride? Why would you think I know anything about it?"

Rennie's expression went colder still. "Oh, I guess, maybe, just possibly, because of what's inside?"

On discovering the pouch's contents, she had

driven straight to the Carmel Highlands house where Danny and Brandi were staying: her famous grandfather's place, he who had been the founder of Bluewater Studios, back in the titanic days when Louis Mayer and the Warner boys had walked the earth. Brandi had given her directions when they were at Waterhall, and both she and Danny had told her to be sure to stop by. She'd taken a chance that she'd find anyone home; but she had a feeling they would be — Ravi Shankar wasn't the Marrons' cup of *ghee* any more than he was hers. Besides, he'd invited her for Sunday brunch and a dip in the pool, and it had just gone noon and she wanted to confront him as soon as possible.

Danny had opened the front door, surprised and pleased to see her, and then she had wordlessly held up the little brown leather pouch, like a sort of passport, and the pleasure had rapidly vanished. When he said nothing in response to her challenge as to the pouch's contents, she shouldered past him and walked into the spacious living room; Brandi didn't seem to be around. Maybe she was out by the pool, or still asleep. It was better without her here; at this point, her presence would only unnecessarily complicate things.

Without a word, Rennie sat down on the enormous sectional sofa, drew out several items from the pouch, and laid them down like a trumping hand of cards upon the coffee table.

A hand Danny Marron couldn't hope to beat: a California driver's license in the name of Adam Bouvier Presley — and how in hell *that* had been managed, Rennie had no idea — with a recent photo of the owner on it, looking pathetically young; a half-finished letter, in sprawling, childish handwriting, to a woman whose husband he was apparently having an affair with; and a battered snapshot of Adam himself with that woman's husband. A very identifiable photo indeed.

And Danny Marron looked from those items to Rennie's face, and back to the items, and began to cry.

The tears didn't last long. They seemed genuine enough—though whether they were for Adam or for Danny himself, Rennie couldn't tell. But he was looking at her now with a professionally tragic expression that somehow, all at once, turned genuinely despairing, and for Rennie, at least, gave what he said next the stamp of truth.

"Yes. I had an affair with him. With Adam. I didn't tell the cops because I knew they'd suspect me of killing him."

"Did you?"

"No! I swear it! I didn't kill him and I don't know who did. It was stupid of me to get involved with him at all. It wasn't really much: it started as a drunk blowjob at a party last year, at a big place in Beverly Hills belonging to a friend of Brandon's. Adam was the gardener's assistant there. A couple of encounters after that—all right, all right, more than a few! A lot more... He bought drugs for us too, for Brandi and me, so we didn't have to risk scoring. But if it became public knowledge it could be death to my marriage as well as my career. Please, Rennie—"

Rennie was not exactly fighting to keep her disgust from showing on her face. What a despicable piece of garbage this waste of protoplasm was, to be sure. *First Becca, now Adam... But at least Becca is still alive. Though some might dispute it...*

"Not to mention death to the bankrolling you get from daddy-in-law. Yes, yes, I know all about Brandon Storey and Bluewater Studios and you. Also not to mention a little conversation I overheard in Romilly Revels' sculpture garden, between Pierce Hill and Finn Hanley and, oh, right, one other guy. Conversation for three plus eavesdropper, accompanied by rifle shots. Surely you remember."

"It wasn't me."

"*WHAT THE HELL IS WRONG WITH YOU?* I was *there*, Marron, I *heard* you! I *saw* you! I talked to you later! Romilly talked to you!"

He buried his face in his hands. "Oh God, I don't know what I'm saying, this is a nightmare. You're right, of course, you're right. You were there. What did you hear?"

"I heard Pierce telling Finn he was going to cut him loose, and it sounded as if he had something rather more permanent in mind than just a verbal pinkslip. And he said you'd be filming it."

"No, no, Pierce was only going to *fire* him on camera, not kill him." Danny's face had a gleam in it now. Of what? Triumph? Relief? Strange. But why? She was missing something here. And when he spoke again, his voice was calmer and steadier than it had been, almost light.

"Rennie, I swear I didn't kill Adam. Or Baz either. You have to believe me."

"I do? Why would that be?"

He spread his hands. "Please. You must. I would never have hurt Adam. Yes, we were having a—a thing. I even moved him to San Francisco six months ago, so we didn't have to worry about my wife finding out. It was never serious, how could it be. But he wanted more. He wanted, if you can believe this, my help to get hold of his birth parents."

"That would be Mr. and Mrs. Elvis and Jacqueline Presley, I take it. Who got married a year after the assassination and thus legitimized their firstborn."

He looked relieved. "Oh, so you know about all his delusional crap. Well, yes, of course. I felt for him, very deeply, but he could be a tiresome little beast. He was threatening to go to my wife and her father if I didn't help him out. He said with my Hollywood connections, getting hold of Elvis would be trivial. Right, like I was going to blow my life for *him*…"

"Even though *his* life had been blowing *you*?"

"It was stupid, I know."

"It was statutory rape, you maggot, the kid was barely sixteen!" She looked at him with total contempt overspreading her features. "It was you, wasn't it, that he saw at Big Magic? That first morning? I saw him waving to someone he seemed very glad to see."

But Danny only looked bewildered. "No, it can't have been. I didn't see him at the festival at all, not since the Friday night before, at the High Springs. We agreed it would be too dangerous, trying to hook up again while I was staying at Waterhall. We thought we could get together safely once we were all at Monterey. I had arranged for a room for him at one of those motels on the road outside town, and of course Brandi and I would stay here. It seemed safe enough."

And though Rennie pressed him like the toad beneath the harrow, he clung grimly to his story.

"Well, you have to tell the cops," she said at last. "Because they *will* find out, and sooner rather than later—since I'm going to tell them if you won't—and then it'll only be worse for you. If you're as innocent as you say, best to go to them now and get it over with. Come on. I'll drive you."

Danny looked up at her hopefully. "Can we keep it from Brandon?"

So, apparently his wife or even the cops weren't his chief concern, it was the great Brandon Storey and his deep studio pockets. Rennie didn't even try to keep the disgust out of her voice.

"I don't see how, but maybe if you can prove you had nothing to do with the murders, help them out, they might be able to cut you some slack."

"He was getting more and more demented and insistent about the Elvis thing," said Marron with unseemly eagerness. "He'd started demanding that I make a documentary about him and his alleged father, or else he'd spill the beans about the affair, and the drugs, to Brandon. I was at my wits' end."

God knows that's not all that far to go—and, gosh, doesn't blackmail make for a pretty darn big old murder motive? But Rennie said only, "What else have you got?"

He looked suddenly, unbecomingly, cagey, like a ferret with a big secret. "I might have some footage. It could help."

"Would that be the stuff you were shooting on the fairgrounds in defiance of Mr. Pennebaker's Monterey monopoly?"

Danny raised his hands and tried a sheepish grin; Rennie wasn't buying. "Nobody was looking. You saw; you were with me while I was filming. I didn't notice any documentary police around to bust me for it. Besides, you know Brandon got me permission to shoot anything not musical. And you also know I didn't kill Basil Potter or Pierce Hill, either."

"I know nothing of the sort. As far as I'm aware, you could have killed all three of them." She looked at him for a moment. "You say Brandi and her father didn't know about your affair with Adam. Who *did* know? Who knew and was in a position to do something about it? Something fatal."

He stared uncertainly back. "You're not suggesting Romilly? She didn't know, and why would she want to kill Adam anyway?"

"To punish you for what you did to her family, if she thought you cared about him. Which—obviously—you didn't."

Danny folded his arms on the table and buried his

face on them. "I did, you know. I really did. Maybe I was a coward about showing it—okay, I *was* a coward! But I did care. It wasn't just me using him, you know."

"No, I'm guessing he used you rather a lot too, and who could blame him. Money and drugs: you could keep him in style when you wanted to, or when you remembered about him. I hear he lived in a nice pad on Stanyan Street near Golden Gate Park. We all figured he was just house-sitting. It was much too nice an address for him to be able to afford on his own. Not when he couldn't afford hamburgers. Or shoes."

"I keep the apartment to use when I come to San Francisco. Brandi doesn't know about it, and I'm hardly ever there anyway, so it worked for me too, to have someone staying there looking after it." He looked up defiantly. "At least I gave him a nice place to live, so he didn't have to sleep on the streets or in some horrible crash pad."

"What a humanitarian. That's still no excuse. You're the grown-up. Or you should have been."

Rennie gathered Adam's possessions from the table, put them in her shoulderbag and stood up, a bit of Genghis Khan's general about her once again.

"And now, I swear to God, you're going to be, if I have to drag you there roped up like a hogtied calf. Which you'd probably like. So let's go. We have a date with the fuzz. At least you do."

Audie Devlin shook his head. "What a bastard. Marron, not Adam. Poor kid is abandoned like a bag of trash, grows up the hard way, this scumbucket seduces him and then tosses him away in turn. I hate it."

"Are you going to bust Marron?"

Brent Gilmore shook his head in turn. "I know it seems like good stuff, but we really have nothing, Rennie. We couldn't even get him on statutory rape charges, since the alleged victim is dead. All we have is a dubious diary written by an obvious nutcase, an unaddressed letter and a picture snapped in a beach parking lot. But we're not *telling* him we have nothing, just in case. Let him go on thinking we know something. And we'll hang on to the stuff, also just in case."

"You examined him, I take it. No signs of a recent struggle?"

"If you mean burns or scrapes on his arms from holding the kid down in the pool, no. I'm sorry for it, too. I'd love to be able to nail this creep on something."

They were in the Monterey stationhouse, where Rennie had brought Danny Marron to confess about his relationship with Adam Santa Monica and to explain why he'd previously lied to the police about it. Brent wasn't pleased, to say the least, but after some questioning he'd seen there wasn't any more there—or if there was, that he wasn't going to get it just now—and he'd let Marron go, albeit with a stern cautioning. Danny had been so relieved to get away that he'd phoned his wife to come pick him up, and had then scampered out the door to wait for her outside in the fresh air. Though how he was going to explain his presence at the cop shop to begin with, Rennie couldn't imagine. But that was his problem, and possibly Brandi's as well.

"He was making nervous noises about how he had footage that could maybe help you guys out," said Rennie after a while.

"Yeah, the film he shot when you guys were looking for Baz Potter on Friday morning. It's probably nothing much. Though it might make a nice convenient record of how the body was disposed when it was first discovered. We should have asked for it sooner."

Audie Devlin shrugged in agreement. "I doubt there'll be anything useful there. Which is why we didn't ask."

"Anyway, he's going home now to get it and bring it over," said Brent. "We have somebody following him, of course, just to be on the safe side, in case he decides to bolt for the border. When he does come back with it, we may let you see it. Well, she's earned it," he added, seeing Devlin's eyes narrow. "She did get us the connection between Adam Santa Monica and Danny Marron."

"I wonder if he's really got anything after all, though, Marron," remarked Marcus. "He seemed to give up the film pretty easily. Besides, by the time he got together with Rennie and Roger Hazlitt to go look for the missing Mr. Potter, according to the medical examiner Baz had been dead for hours—since the middle of the night. So we shouldn't be hoping to score any firsthand, accidentally captured footage of the murder, say, with the murderer ready for his, or her, closeup, if you know what I mean."

"That's probably true," said Rennie. "But you never can tell, there might be something we can use. He did actually shoot Pierce firing Finn, at Waterhall, or at least giving him notice, right before being shot at. We could try to—"

"See?" said Marcus, appealing to the two other men. "What have I been telling you? You can't give her an inch. Already it's 'we'."

Audie Devlin fixed Rennie with a stern gaze. "Miss Stride, we're not ungrateful for your help. But you must understand—"

"Oh, I understand all right. I really do." She got up to leave. "I just hope *you* guys understand as much as I do. I'll be back," she added. "Don't start the movie without me."

Sunday afternoon

Ravi Shankar
    with *Alla Rakha and Kamala*

Chapter 19

IT WAS SO BIZARRE, Rennie considered. Here was Ravi Shankar, about to start blissfully playing away, while Danny Marron was fetching footage for the cops and possibly facing charges on the killing of Adam Santa Monica — despite the official doubt, she herself hadn't yet given up hope on that score — and police were still poking around the foot of the cliffs below Otter Point Inn for more clues to Pierce Hill's murder. No doubt it was just all part of the great cosmic game plan. Well, *her* cosmic game plan was to get the hell out of Dodge for the afternoon, until Marron came back to the stationhouse with the film — or at least out of earshot.

As she'd told Prax earlier, Rennie wasn't a sitar fan at the best of times, and she wasn't a fan even more since she'd heard that Shankar had spoken scornfully of Brian Jones, being all snobby and patronizing about Brian's sitar experimentation on 'Paint It Black' and other Stones songs. So what? Brian wasn't a serious devotee, and never claimed to be — he just liked the sound, and nobody had a world monopoly on sitar music. He admired Ravi, sure, but he didn't suck up like so many did (looking at *you*, George Harrison), and it was just plain mean for Shankar to deride him publicly, as Rennie had been informed, telling people that the world-famous Rolling Stone, who had a fine musicianly sensibility, could barely manage to pick out a simple sitar riff, like a kid with a cigar-box banjo. Pretentious bugger.

Maybe she was still freaked out about Pierce and the whole thing with Danny Marron and finding Adam's wallet, maybe that was why she was in such a bad mood. Though she really did loathe Indian music.

Anyway, she wasn't staying to listen to the sitar-a-palooza that was scheduled to clog up the entire afternoon. Instead, she was going to try to find *some* kind of clue to *some*thing before Danny Marron held his command stationhouse screening. It didn't matter what. As long as it made some contribution however small to the sum total of their knowledge about the murders, which was at the moment rather dauntingly and regrettably small indeed. For someone already being called Murder Chick, and not just behind her back, she wasn't playing to her best here. But even Ken Karper was getting a lean and hungry look, and he was a crime pro; he hadn't been able to turn up much new either, and to Rennie's way of thinking they were both overdue for a break.

She walked over to the seating area to recount recent developments to Prax, Juha, Tansy and Turk Wayland, who were all afire to hear Shankar play and still couldn't understand why Rennie wasn't, and so they didn't pay as much attention to what she had to tell them as they would have otherwise. The arena was packed, and only because Juha had gone early and saved seats did they have any at all; the outlying grassy areas of the fairground were thick with bodies, and yet again there were people who'd scaled the roofs of the barns and outbuildings in the hopes of a good view.

Not that there would be much to look at: on the stage, someone had laid down a small colorful prayer rug for the Indian musicians to sit upon as they played and set out some lighted incense sticks in a little brass vase — to make them feel more at home, presumably. There were three of them, the star and two sidemen, one a woman, all clothed in immaculate white, just now stepping onto the stage to warm waves of applause.

Shankar smiled upon the multitude as he began to tune up. "Let us all pray that I can give you a good performance and that it doesn't rain." More applause, incense, flung orchids. "I love all of you, and I am so very grateful for your love of me."

Rennie rolled her eyes so hard she thought she caught a glimpse of her own spine. What the hell was the matter with her? Most musicians thought this guy was a combination music god/holy man, pure and free of the world's concerns; and though Rennie willingly granted the maestro-ship — despite the fact that friends who were genuinely knowledgeable about North Indian classical music didn't think Shankar was anywhere near all that — even so, she could only see him as a self-important phony who made pretentious music that gave her the pip. Maybe Prax was right. Maybe she was just a Philistine after all and a poor excuse for a music critic. Still, Shankar *was* the only artist to insist on being paid for his performance, thirty-five hundred bucks, how material-world was *that*...oooh, beware of Maya!

But the sitar whining and migraine-inducing tabla drumming had begun. Well, thanks to the elephant god Ganesh, Remover of Obstacles, for small favors: at least Shankar would keep everybody in one place for the next four hours — probably passed out cold with boredom — and maybe she could get something accomplished, if only Ganesh would remove a few obstacles for *her* right about now. *Om Ganesh, Om Ganesh, Om Ganesh…get me out of here NOW please, if I have to listen to another note I'm going to rip my ears off…*

Slipping out the row of seats to the aisle, trying not to trip over people too stoned to move their feet, or too stoned to remember they even *had* feet—seeing as she did so Jimi Hendrix nodding in awe, Mike Bloomfield rapt on the side of the stage—she shook her head, and fled as if pursuing Nazgûl rode behind her.

Out in the grounds, Rennie ran into Freddy Bellasca, who looked very pleased to be run into. They weren't friends, but because he was going out with Rennie's photographer friend from New York, Francie Nolting—secretly, of course, him being irretrievably married to a bitchy Frenchwoman named Nicole—they often found themselves in the same places on the scene. Of course, as the youngish, hippish president of a very hip record label, he was a source, and, as a younger, hipper reporter with a rising name, she was a resource. Which cynical dynamic they both understood very well.

"Rennie, how nice to see you! Are you enjoying yourself as much as I am?"

"Hard to say," Rennie replied, with perfect truth. "I take it you're having a nice fat profitable time of it?"

"I hope to. Ultimately. I'm sure you heard from your pal Gerry Langhans that I came to see Lionheart, of course. I mean to buy out their tiny little label Glisten's roster and catalogue for Centaur, and I thought since I was coming here anyway, I'd check out the best part of what I'll buying. Which is of course them."

"I believe Congress passed one of their tiresome little amendments about that, a while back. Outlawing slavery, I mean. You won't actually *own* those boys, Frederick."

Freddy laughed. "For my purposes I will, babe. They've been stuck on Glisten for, what, five albums now? And we've all seen how they've ramped up from a pleasant folk-rock outfit to major-league blues-rock. They're ready for the next stage, like a rocket, and I plan on giving them the boost."

"Have you ever actually heard them play, Freddy? Or have you just heard *about* them?"

"I have, my dear, in England, and on the basis of that alone I must say I'm staggered. All we've seen them do so far here is a half-hour jam on the side stage last night. Morris music, forsooth. Though the other stuff they did was hot as a pistol. We haven't seen them perform for real yet. Just you wait till tonight."

Rennie, unregenerately reporterish, was already taking mental notes; she could do a nice, nasty story on the acquisition of Lionheart and the grabbiness of Freddy...

"Oh, I'm waiting, all right. Only, just one little thing: I had breakfast with Turk Wayland this morning — and Prax and Tansy and Finn Hanley and Stan Hirsh — and Turk told me that Lionheart's Glisten deal was in fact done with the release of the new album. *Fin.* The End. *Finito. Das Ende.* Th-th-th-that's all, folks! The band itself won't be included in the label package. Only their backlist. So I have a feeling, just a feeling, I say, that you're going to have more trouble with Turk Wayland than you think you will. Don't try to engage him in a battle of wits, Fredders. You're only half armed."

Freddy looked annoyed; how dare she rain on his parade! Even though it hadn't even started yet. Surely she could see he was the drum major and the parade marshal and the whole marching band alike and would direct the line of march as he damn well pleased?

"Yes, *yes*, very *true*, I know all *about* it. But I plan on negotiating a new deal, tie them up for five more albums if I can get them. They're going to be superstars, you know they are—especially that lead guitarist and lead singer, what's their names, Turk and Miles."

"Niles."

"Who cares! They're going to make me a very rich man. A very much richer man. After I close the deal, I'm going to re-release the current album in the U.S. I know it's big already among the heads and the Lit. majors, but it deserves way more than their usual modest-except-in-Britain sales. Which I'm going to get them. With a nice fat expensive publicity campaign, of course—would you be interested in doing a story, by any chance?—and a big promo push. Glisten could never afford to promote them the way they deserve. And I'll be doing all this helped out by the professional savvy of my new East Coast head of a&r, yes, none other than your good friend Gerry Langhans. Lovely little fight he had with Pierce the other night in the bar, I was there for it. Most impressive. Pierce always was an idiot. Though I'm quite sure Gerry had nothing to do with pushing him over that cliff this morning. Well, almost sure. So: Lionheart, backlist, new album, the rest of Glisten too. Watch and see how it's done, pretty lady."

"Can't wait," said Rennie politely. "*You* watch and see you don't end up like Percy."

And made her departure before Freddy stopped gasping for air.

"That might be enough to get Adam Santa Monica murdered, don't you think?" asked Stan Hirsh. "The blackmail possibility? Since obviously Marron knew about it. Generally, if not specifically."

"I *do* think," agreed Rennie. "As far as that goes, since Pennebaker has the official monopoly, only the secret influence and major money infusions of Brandon Storey to the festival, uh, charities got Danny permission to shoot around at all. Though I don't know how he thought he'd be able to do anything with his footage."

"Why's that?" asked Ken Karper promptly.

"Well, as I said, Pennebaker has the film rights. So though Danny is able to shoot anything at Monterey but the music, he's still not going to be able to sell it or make any kind of profit off it. A music festival film without music? Not gonna happen! So all he's really got is Big Magic, and up against Monterey I just don't think that'll be enough. How do I know this, you wonder? Well, easy-peasy: I asked Brandi, and she was happy to tell me. Made her dad look good. Powerful, too. But if the Big Magic film doesn't come out a profitable success, Danny is finished at Bluewater and all over the rest of Hollywood too, and he knows it."

Having wearied of the Shankar-a-thon, Stan, Marishka, Ken Karper and Belinda Melbourne had withdrawn to the Hunt Club, waiting for the music to finish and scoring some lunch in the meantime. Rennie had been hailed cheerfully on her drop-in appearance — Fearless Leader back among her people — and had quickly filled them in on how she'd spent her post-breakfast morning.

"Even Pennebaker isn't gonna have all the bands on film," said Stan. "As we all know, Big Brother's manager advised them not to sign the release, so he's probably their *ex*-manager by now. And the Dead, mavericks to the end, refused to sign from the get-go. Couple other bands too, I think. So they won't be in Penny's film, but neither will they be starring in 'Dial Mojado for Murder', or whatever the hell Danny's little masterpiece is going to be called."

"I wonder —" began Ken Karper, and they all turned to him, politely and expectantly; he was the crime expert, after all. "I was just wondering if Marron actively tried to get something on film more, let's say, exciting than just footage of happy festival freaks."

"Something like?"

"Something like murder, of course."

Now *that* was a thought, and he wasn't the first to have it. Rennie sat back, considering. "It wouldn't surprise me, and the cops were wondering along those lines too. But I don't think so. If there had been a plan to murder Baz, Danny wouldn't have had a part in it. He's too much of a coward. On the other hand, there could very well be something else on film. Something *else* else; something apart from the stuff he claims he's turning in to the fuzz. Something Danny doesn't want us or anyone else to see."

"Such as?"

"No idea. But don't forget, he did seem to know where to find Baz on Friday morning. We were all wandering around the field, and he kept steering us in the direction of the bead tent. Which is where we found — found Baz."

Marishka spoke for the first time. "Is there any chance this connects to the murder over at Big Magic? That little groupie boy?"

Rennie looked at her approvingly, but it was Ken who spoke. "Now *that* wouldn't surprise *me*. Not after what we found out about Marron and the kid."

"Thanks to meeee!" crowed Rennie.

Ken bowed to her extravagantly. "I expect at first Danny tried buying Adam Santa Monica off with cash and presents and the nice apartment you speak of and perks like introductions to movie star society — though he was unable to deliver Elvis and Jackie, of course. But then the kid, who you say had been scoring drugs for Danny and Brandi so they didn't have to run the risk — coke and speed, you were right about that, Stan — started seriously threatening to blackmail him. We see that by the letter that Rennie found."

"So you think Marron plans to murder the kid at Monterey and make it look like an accident? And get it — somehow — on film?" Stan looked disgusted, as indeed he was. "I don't really know the guy, of course, but it seems to me that he couldn't kill a bug. Lacks the stones."

Belinda nodded, equally revolted, but pursuing it all the same. "Or kill him at Big Magic. People aren't as interested in that festival as in Monterey, obviously, so Marron realizes a murder could add major dramatic interest to his documentary. Something that the Pennebaker team couldn't get hold of. And he plans to get as much of it on film as he can. Without incriminating himself or indeed the murderer, of course."

Rennie ran a hand through her hair. "But Adam ruined Danny's plans by turning up dead at Mojado. Unless of course Danny really did kill him. But for purposes of argument, let's say not, just for the moment. Probably furious with the unknown killer for stealing his thunder, or at least his victim, Danny must now rethink. And find a new subject."

"Why would he pick Baz, though?" asked Prax. "They had no personal history or animosity."

"No, but Danny did film Finn Hanley's little chat with Pierce Hill at Waterhall, and he got that whole rant of Pierce's in the lounge on videotape too. So as a result his new target is Baz Potter. Big famous star, annoying Brit, much more dramatic and headline-worthy than some nonentity groupie kid. He's already safe from blackmail, since Adam's dead, so he can concentrate on something bigger."

Stan nodded. "Also it would get him in good forever with Pierce, if he were to get rid of Baz. True, he couldn't capture the actual murder on camera, but film was rolling when Baz failed to turn up: intrepid filmmaker Danny Marron, following the hunt for the missing star, shooting as he goes, gets the first few moments of the body's being discovered. Not to mention his money shot: the big dramatic scene when newly bereaved Pamina Potter first beholds the body of her slain spouse, and is led off in hysterics with blood all over her clothes."

Ken Karper, who'd been listening intently to all of them, leaned back in his chair.

"Bit obvious. But yes, interesting that he didn't waste time searching the grounds like everybody else."

Rennie raised her eyebrows and nodded. "Isn't it though! He directed people to go all over, but, apart from what could be construed as a strategic detour, he headed pretty much straight to the tent area with us tagging along as witnesses. Where we found Baz in the bead tent."

"And that *is* all on film," said Ken, making more notes. "Absent the actual murder, of course—though you mark my words, one of these not too distant days there *will* be a rock murder, and it *will* be caught on film, and the band involved will probably release it as a commercially successful movie. So Marron's footage is lacking the murder but very much including Mrs. Potter's hysterical, ever so dramatic confession. A woman who, as she tearfully confessed to us—none of whom were totally astonished to hear it—had been bonking her husband's artistic partner and friend for the past year."

Rennie looked uncomfortable. "Hey, these are friends of mine you're maligning here…"

"I'm sorry," said Ken gently. "But we have to line this out. You don't need to be here, if you'd prefer not to stay. You've given me more than enough to go on."

"No, I'm fine, really. Anyway, I should be getting back to the stationhouse to catch the showing of Danny Marron's epic masterpiece."

But she wasn't fine. And though nobody had mentioned her, neither had Rennie forgotten Becca

Revels: would she have killed Adam to avenge herself on her faithless lover, the man who'd freaked her out on acid, wedded her best friend and pushed her over the edge into madness? If she could have even thought as logically as that? Or would Romilly have killed him, to avenge herself on Pierce Hill, who got her daughter into drugs in the first place?

Still, Rennie chose not to bring up those particular questions at this particular time and in this particular company. Later, if she had to. But not now. Not yet.

It was just rough 16-millimeter footage, newly developed, unedited, unspliced. Nothing out of the ordinary, Rennie thought, disappointed, as they all watched. Half the Monterey police force seemed crowded into the situation room, plus representatives from the sheriff and state police, to cover all jurisdictions and not leave anyone out.

She stole a sidewise glance at Marcus. He didn't look particularly impressed, and indeed there was little to be impressed with: just arty, soft-focus shots of the Monterey crowd; giggly interviews with stoned teenagers, mostly pretty girls with long hair and big floppy hats and no tops on, or even prettier long-haired boys.

Now the footage was from Friday morning, and the vibe in the room changed perceptibly: everyone sitting up, leaning forward, intent. Rennie saw herself and Roger Hazlitt talking, then going off together in search of the missing Baz. Then their arrival at the bead stall. Then Baz, dead: long, almost pornographic shots from every angle, until Rennie stepped between Baz and the camera and took up her protective stance.

There wasn't much after that: just the cops arriving with Belinda, and then Pamie Potter bursting in, with Prax behind her. A few more sequences from outside, the body being loaded into the ambulance, Rennie standing honor guard with Roger Hazlitt, both of them looking stricken; and that was it.

The lights came on, and most of the police personnel who had been present in the room filed out. At last it was just Devlin, Brent, Marcus and Rennie. And of course Danny Marron.

Nobody said anything for a while. Then Devlin muttered something about Thanks for letting us see this, and we have to hang onto it for a while, and Danny said Fine sure whatever take your time. Marcus was scowling, and Brent was scribbling furiously on a pad, but neither of them had anything to contribute.

Finally Rennie stood up to leave, and, from the doorway, framed the question she'd been wanting to ask Danny Marron for days. He was sitting back in his chair, looking far too pleased with himself, as if he'd done something really clever. Well, *that* look needed to be wiped off his face, and she was just the one to do it...

"Oh, just one tiny small thing," she said artlessly. "When I heard the three of you talking in Romilly's sculpture garden, the morning after Adam was killed...someone said something about 'drowned — last night — hot springs.' But that was *before* Marcus came over to tell Romilly what had happened. The only people at Waterhall who actually knew about Adam at that actual moment were me — and the killer."

People speak idly of the blood draining from the face, of someone turning as pale as a ghost, as white as a sheet: Rennie had never had the opportunity to observe the phenomenon before, but she was seeing it now, in Danny Marron's suddenly ashen countenance. And by the equally sudden keen alertness in the detectives' faces, she knew they were seeing it too.

She pressed the point home. "It wasn't Finn, because the voice didn't have an accent. It wasn't Pierce, because I recognized his voice. That would leave just one person, wouldn't it? I wonder if I could put a name to that person, gosh, now, who could it be?"

Unexpectedly and quite spectacularly, Marron broke. "All right, all right, it was me! I said that to the others."

Devlin never even looked up from his notes. "And you said it to them because…? How was it that you knew?"

"Because I killed Adam! I killed him myself! Are you happy? I killed him!" He sank into the chair by the desk, put his hands over his face. "It was me, okay? But it's not okay. It'll never be okay again."

"What do you think?" asked Marcus.

Devlin slapped both hands on the desk and looked across the room through the one-way interrogation room window, where Danny Marron was now weepingly recounting his story of killing Adam to Brent and another sheriff's officer.

"Well, it's certainly a nice big fat dramatic confession. He had motive and opportunity. He's staying at his wife's godmother's house, he knows the kid will be at the festival because he told him to come. He arranges for the kid to meet him that night at the springs, those upper ones where nobody ever goes."

Rennie put her hand up "Me. I went there."

"So you did. And Finn Hanley. But that was all the traffic. That pool was almost always deserted, and it's isolated, too, so anything going on there stays private. So after things get quiet—Mrs. Revels goes to bed, her daughter's asleep, so's the nurse, the rest of you are all over at the festival—Marron slips out of the house and goes up to the springs. Like he said, the kid was going to blow the whistle on him with his wife and father-in-law. Marron couldn't let that happen. So the kid gets drowned, and Marron thinks he's safe. Then Miss Stride here finds the kid's little wallet with the picture and the letter and confronts Marron with it."

"Adam," said Rennie. "His name was Adam. Not 'the kid'."

Devlin looked at her blankly; but Marcus nodded, understanding. "Of course. Adam. Sorry."

"What happens now?" she asked, watching the sobbing heap that was Danny Marron. *I don't buy it...it's way too easy, way too convenient...*

"Oh, the usual thing. We'll let him call a lawyer. Put him in a cell till he can be arraigned. Inform his wife he's here. At least we've got him for something now."

"Do we really, though?" asked Rennie after a while.

Marcus groaned. "Oh, what, you don't think so? Rennie, he confessed!"

"I know. But I still think you've got the wrong person."

Confession or no, they had underestimated Danny Marron, and badly underestimated his wife. Brandi showed up half an hour later with two local lawyer friends—local in the geographical sense, since they were both neighbors of the Storeys in Carmel Highlands, but hardly local otherwise, as they had both argued before the Supreme Court. Courts. California *and* United States.

In a remarkably few minutes, led expertly down subtle legal byways by his attorneys, Danny had recanted his entire confession and was sprung, much to the fury and disgust of everyone. Everyone but Rennie.

"I'm sorry," said Devlin flatly, after the jubilant Storey-Marron contingent had left the stationhouse, rejoicing. "We couldn't hold him. There's no hard evidence, he recanted the confession, his wife alibi'd him and the lawyers are really, really good. Not just local ambulance chasers. As you saw."

"But he knows who killed Baz!" snarled Rennie, who'd been allowed to stay and had followed the questioning from the other side of the one-way glass. "You *know* he does! That makes him just as guilty, the little cocksucker."

"That's enough, Miss Stride," said Devlin warningly.

"Sorry, Inspector. I didn't mean to insult people who suck cock. After all, I do it myself," she added, irresistibly, just for the fun of seeing Marcus put his hand over his eyes. "Still—"she bubbled up again, a fount of optimism—"not to worry. We'll get him back."

"No, Miss Stride, *we* will get him back. Contrary to what you might think, you're really not a member of this force."

Rennie smiled, and stood up to leave. "Well of *course* I'm not!"

Because if I were, then I couldn't do what I'm now going to do, could I? No. I couldn't. And I know that at least two of you noticed what I noticed. So let's just see how this plays out, shall we?

Chapter 20

CARMEL HIGHLANDS IS A LOVELY, RURAL AREA, inhabited by seriously rich people, or seriously funky people, or seriously committed people who have lived there all their lives and their parents and grandparents before them. Sometimes the people are all three of those at once. Joan Baez had a place in the woods on the side of a hill, where Bob Dylan often stayed with her in those increasingly rare moments when they were an actual living-together normal young couple, not the Peace Queen and the Joker King of Folk-Rock. So did the inventor of a new kind of pencil eraser, and a few movie stars, and as Brandi had mentioned, George Gershwin, who had often come to visit the Storey family at this very place.

The white stone house was old and gracious, nestled above the landward side of the highway, on a curving cliff overlooking the sea. Rennie waited until the TR-4 had pulled into the drive sweep by the front steps and the Marrons had gone inside. They had let themselves in; there didn't appear to be anyone else at home, no servants or guests. Odd, but she'd take it and be grateful.

She had tailed them from the stationhouse in Monterey; she'd been waiting and watching in her station wagon, parked a bit down the block, and they'd passed her without a second glance, heading west out of the town center, tooling along in the little red Triumph with Brandi at the wheel. She let them get to the intersection, then quietly pulled out and swung into traffic several cars behind them and followed them all the way here. It was the only place they could be going, so she hadn't been afraid of losing them; besides, you could see the red car a mile away, and the station wagon was notoriously nondescript—they'd never notice such a bourgeois heap. Probably not even if they front-ended it.

She gave them a few minutes, then brazenly walked up to the front door and let herself in; it wasn't locked—in fact, it stood ajar a few inches. No one in the huge living room, no one in the library or dining room—encouraging, if a bit surprising. She went silently upstairs, to find Brandi already largely out of it on a king-size bed in the sun-flooded master suite, a bottle of pills open and spilled on the satin coverlet. Rennie went over to take a look: Nembutal. She'd probably started making inroads on those before she even picked up Danny at the stationhouse, and she'd likely be zonked for hours. But where *was* Danny?

Again guessing, she went back downstairs. He must have a studio or something, somewhere in the house, or maybe out back. She wasn't worried about him destroying the evidence; his ego was far too vast for that. No, he'd hidden it here, and now he was retrieving it, to hide it again, more safely—where?

And again the answer came to her with stunning clarity and force, as if her mind had become some kind of

Magic Eight-Ball: he was going to drive back down to Waterhall with it, right now; that was why he'd left the car out front and the door open, for a quick getaway. Nobody would be looking for the footage at Romilly Ramillies' place. Was that why Brandi had knocked herself out, or had he done that for her? Either way, he didn't want her to know where he'd gone and what he'd done, what he planned on doing.

But would he leave the incriminating material at Waterhall? Rennie rather thought not; that was just a stopgap cache until he could get it safely down to L.A. Once there, it would no doubt be smuggled into the vast, dim archives of Bluewater Studios, arcanely labeled, one among hundreds of thousands—impossible for anyone except him to find, until he thought it was safe to rediscover it.

She took up a position by the front door, where a decorative miniature cannon sat atop a polished marble table flanked by two upholstered chairs. Seating herself in the high-backed chair nearest the door, she put one arm on the chair arm and draped the other over the brass cannon, and waited.

It didn't take long for him to come up from the basement. He was carrying a large round black film can with a white paper label, rather like a wheel of cheese, and he didn't see her at first, so still was she sitting and so dim the corner where she sat.

"Pity this cannon isn't loaded. It would solve so many problems."

Her voice in the silence of the house was unexpected and alarming, and she was pleased to see him jump two feet aside. But he never relinquished his grip on the round can.

"What the hell are *you* doing here? How did you get in?"

"Doesn't matter. Give me the tape, Danny. It's the

real one, isn't it. Yes, and we both know what's on it."

He continued to stare at her—this can't be happening! Not now! Not *her*!—the way Scrooge stared at Marley's ghost. "But why are you *here*?"

"Oh please! I think we're past all the innocent astonishment, aren't we? I just had a feeling you might not want to turn over the footage. The *right* footage, I mean. I'll take that now, thank you ever so much. This is the one that really matters, isn't it? Yes, I thought it might be. Clever of you to hide the little tape box in a big old film can. All the better to squirrel it away among millions of others in the Bluewater vaults. Which *is* what you were planning. I say it yet again: God, it's so boring to be right all the time!"

He hugged the metal container protectively, close to his chest. "Please, Rennie. I'll give you money, as much as you could ever want. Just let me go."

"Oh, you know, I don't think so. I married a Lacing, remember. I already have as much money as I could ever want…"

"You wouldn't even have to lie, not really. You could just forget you ever saw me here—"

The image of Baz's face, alive, laughing, appeared before Rennie's sight. "*Forget*? Not if I swam all night in the Lethe!"

"In the what?" He looked utterly blank, then slyly cunning. "How did you figure it out?"

"Not hard, once I remembered. Romilly told me you were videotaping most of the festivals, not filming it. Cool new technique, really different in look from what Pennebaker's doing, a chance for you to do some radically creative stuff. The footage you gave the cops was 16-millimeter film. Which I did indeed see you using on numerous occasions. Including Friday morning, when you pretty much led us straight to Baz dead in the tent."

She nodded at the container he clutched. "But *that*

is videotape inside the film can. Which I also saw you using, Thursday night at the inn. That fancy new portapack video camera you brought up from L.A. Camera and recorder and all. Tape that doesn't need to be developed."

A certain silence twangled between them as they regarded each other like fencers, blades engaged, waiting for the next move—thrust, parry or riposte. No sound came from upstairs, where Brandi remained unconscious; perhaps she should be checked on, when the standoff was over…

"You gave the cops the 16-millimeter reel," she continued, in a pleasant conversational tone, "which had our whole hunt for Baz on it. Made you look helpful and sorrowful for our loss. Nice dramatic stuff, too: Pamina rushing in, me pulling her off the body, all of us leaving the tent. Plus Baz himself."

She jerked her chin at the film can. "But you held that back. Because it's the actual murder, isn't it. On videotape. You shot this while Baz was being killed, and you were just now on your way down to Waterhall to hide it."

"What if I am? No one's going to believe you, you know." Suddenly he shifted the can to his left arm—the tape rattling inside, as if in confirmation of its guilty presence, or to make sure Rennie knew it was there and wanted her to rescue it—and with his right he grabbed a poker from the nearby fireplace, advanced threateningly. "Maybe no one's even going to hear about it."

Rennie sighed with apparent boredom, though she was alight with inner fury to hear her guess confirmed.

"*Not* gonna help you…"

She flipped open her fringed black leather bag and slid her right hand inside it, keeping whatever she was holding out of Danny's sight, and smiled.

"Oh, the things you see when you haven't got your gun!" She mock-startled, looking down at the bag. "Oops, sorry, wrong again..."

"Gun?" Danny paled a little, took a step back. "You have a gun in there? You're not seriously going to shoot me?"

"If I have to? Seriously. But I'm a very good shot. I promise I won't kill you. Just hurt you where it will hurt the most." She looked fondly down at the bag sheathing her hand, jiggled it a bit. "It's only a small gun. Sweet little Beretta. I learned how to shoot after the Fillmore murders. I have Clovis Franjo to thank for that; how ironic, right? And once I got so darn good at shooting, I thought long and hard, as a peace-loving person, about whether or not I could actually pull the trigger on a living thing."

His fingers crept up again to take a firmer grasp of the poker. "And what did you decide?"

"Oh, I decided I couldn't shoot an animal." She smiled at the look of relief on his face. "But I decided I *could* shoot a person. No problem. Especially one who murdered a friend of mine. So. Give me the tape. Now."

"Give her the damn tape, Marron. Don't make her ask again, she's getting really cranky. I can tell by her voice."

Marcus was standing quietly in the doorway. He was accompanied by Brent, and the guns in their hands, professionally and two-handedly aimed, were a lot bigger than the one nobody could see in Rennie's bag.

She showed no surprise whatsoever. "Took you two long enough."

"Well, you seemed to have it under control. Besides, we couldn't have left right after you did; Devlin would have smelled a rat for sure. Now take your hand off the gun, Rennie, and we'll all just pretend it was never here."

"*I'll* swear it was here!" shouted Danny wildly. "I'll say she broke in and threatened to shoot me and my wife! You're not even a cop here, Dorner! You're *way* out of your jurisdiction."

"And just who do you think will believe you if we all say you're lying?" Brent's tone was reasonable in the extreme. "He may be a rent-a-cop for the weekend, but I'm a duly appointed deputy sheriff of Monterey County, and he's my authorized backup. So, no. That's not how this is going down. Put the can on the table, drop the poker and put your hands behind your back. We're doing this strictly by the book. And you, missy, put that gun that isn't even here somewhere we can't even see it."

Rennie batted her eyelashes. "Oh, officer, can't you let me off just this once? No? Hmph. Besides, what gun? There's a good reason you can't see it, you know. Because I don't have one."

She displayed the bag's open mouth, its insides innocent of weaponry. "I never said I *had* a gun. I just said I'd have no problem shooting someone and boasted of my prowess in marksmanship. Danny drew his own conclusions. Man, people really need to pay more attention to words."

"Good thing we paid attention to yours — at least the ones you said this morning," said Brent, now busy with the handcuffs. "Smart work remembering he'd been shooting on tape with a — videocorder, did you call it? As opposed to a regular old film camera. And tipping us off to it."

"Oh, you'd have noticed eventually," said Rennie handsomely. "And it was still a shot in the dark: he was using the video camera on Thursday night, at the hotel. If he did have footage of the murder, which I thought he might, I didn't think he had time to switch to the movie camera he was using Friday morning. So whatever he had filmed between the relevant hours, it was likely to be on the video camera, not the 16-mm. one; and when he showed up this morning with film, I knew it couldn't be the right stuff."

"We'd probably have noticed sooner or later, true. But by then, he might have had the tape hidden where we'd never have found it. You did good for a rookie."

Marcus laughed. "A *rookie*?"

In the end, Danny Marron came along quietly. Upstairs, Brandi never stirred.

"Do you really want to watch this?" Audie Devlin looked at Rennie with genuine concern as he opened the film can and removed the small square black plastic box that held the reel of half-inch tape. "It might be better if you didn't. If what's on here is what you think is on here…"

"You mean Baz's murder?" said Rennie flatly and coldly. "I'm a reporter. It's my job. I *have* to watch."

And I'm his friend…it's my job to watch even more…

When they ran the videotape for an even larger audience than before, on equipment borrowed from a local TV station, which was delighted to help out in exchange for a news scoop, it turned out that Devlin had been right; it might have been better if she hadn't watched. There was Pierce Hill, accompanying Baz Potter with his guitar, both of them walking past the deserted merchant tents on the festival fairgrounds, in darkness, nobody else around but Marron, skulking invisibly alongside behind the camera. The two men were talking, and though the camera's attached mike was too far away to capture words, it appeared to be an amicable discussion. Until they came up to the bead tent…

In the darkened room, Rennie, watching stonily, did not once look away, though Marcus and Brent kept throwing anxious glances toward her, concerned. It was all there, and she watched it all: Pierce Hill had indeed killed Baz Potter, and Danny Marron had filmed it.

And when they had watched it, Danny Marron smiled with fatuous satisfaction from where he sat under guard.

"Some of my best camera work—really hard to get any shot at all in that kind of light." He seemed to sense their revulsion, if not actually understand it. "It's—cinema," he said wonderingly. "Visual art. It's realer than real. We're not bound by ordinary conventions, things like facts. We have a higher calling, a calling to truth. Why shouldn't I shoot it? You wouldn't have this as evidence if I hadn't, right? Right?"

"How did you know to go with them when they left the hotel?" asked Devlin, in a voice that gave no hint of his feelings on the matter.

"I didn't," said Danny eagerly. "But Pierce knew Baz was going to announce the breakup of Potter and Hazlitt from the stage, opening night. And he knew he could never let that happen."

Rennie stirred. "Wait a minute, Baz himself told me Pierce didn't know. Even Pamie and Roger didn't know, or so I thought. It was all Baz's idea and he hadn't told anybody. Except me, of course."

Danny shook his head. "Baz couldn't resist telling him. It was late Thursday night; you'd gone upstairs by then, I saw you leave. Langhans had punched Pierce out, the excitement was over and the crowd had mostly left. Anyway, they saw each other in the lobby, Pierce and Baz, and they'd both been seriously drinking. Potter was being a pain in the ass: he wanted to bring his guitar over to the fairgrounds and leave it in that room under the stage, so he wouldn't have to schlep it in the morning, but nobody would drive him. Also he just wanted so badly to stick it to Pierce. He couldn't keep his mouth shut about what his plans for Friday night were. So he told Pierce right there that he was breaking up the act, onstage, publicly, and he didn't give a damn about the legalities or anything else, not even the precious backlist."

"And that was when Pierce decided he had to kill him," suggested Devlin.

"Of course! It was the only way. You can understand that."

"Certainly I can understand *that*," said Rennie in a low, cold snarl of a voice that made all the law enforcement in the room give her a quick, sharp look. "But how did Pierce get Baz to come along for a walk through the fairgrounds in the middle of the night?"

"Told him he'd drive him over so he could dump the guitar. Then he said he was reconsidering giving him the song rights back. In direct response to what Baz had told him about breaking up the act. Said they could talk about it: that if that was the choice, he'd really much rather have Baz and Roger stay together, and if giving back the songs was so important to them, then that was fine."

"And Baz believed it," said Brent.

Danny nodded. "Wanted to, desperately. It was a total lie, of course. Anyway, Potter went upstairs to fetch his damn guitar and they drove over to the festival. I followed them in my own car, they never saw me. Then they headed over to the stage, through the merchant tents, where it was dark and empty. And I was right there with them."

"And then you let Pierce Hill kill Basil Potter," murmured Marcus, as casually as if he were saying And then you let Pierce Hill make a sandwich.

Danny pushed back a little in his chair, looked pleadingly all round.

"I didn't 'let' him! What kind of monster do you think I am? He just *did* it! He killed him right there, by the bead tent. He grabbed the guitar away from Baz, clobbered him with it, broke the guitar neck and—used it. As you saw. It all happened so fast. If I'd tried to stop him, he'd have killed me too. And then he rolled the body inside the counter front, under the canvas. Nobody saw; that area was deserted once the merchants shut up shop, and all the kids were over on the other side of the field, sacked out."

"Why the hell did Hill let you film it?" asked a Monterey PD higher-up, who'd been watching with the others.

"I told you, he didn't know I was there! When I saw them leave the hotel together, I thought there would absolutely be something worth shooting. And I had just put a brand-new reel in the recorder, a full twenty minutes of tape. By the time he was—finished, as soon as he rolled Potter's body into the tent, I was out of there. I was scared to death of what he might do to me if he caught me. Anyway, I got away to where there were people and lights, where the kids were camping, and I sort of lost myself among them, until I was sure he was gone and I was safe. The next afternoon, after I'd hidden the tape at the house, I approached him at the hotel and we cut a deal."

"What deal would that be?"

"I'd hold on to the tape as security, and Pierce would bankroll my films if Brandon cut me off." He saw the looks on their faces. "I had to take care of myself! Surely you see that!"

"What we see is that it makes you an accessory to second-degree murder," said Devlin after a while, and Danny looked honestly bewildered, plainly thinking *But I helped you!* How can you possibly turn around and *arrest* me! Devlin continued, in a calm, conversational voice, "You were there during the committing of the crime, witnessing it, doing nothing to stop it, so you're just as guilty as if you'd strangled Mr. Potter yourself. Plus extortion, and withholding evidence in a capital case, and that's just for starters."

"Is that bad? It can't be as bad as what Pierce did! I didn't even touch Baz Potter!"

Devlin smiled for the first time that afternoon, and it was not a nice smile at all.

"Under the law? Every bit as bad. For you, in my book? A whole hot hell of a lot worse. Because Pierce Hill is dead. And you're not."

After a sobbing Danny Marron had been led away by Audie, Brent and one of the state police detectives, representing the troika of law enforcement entities that had jurisdiction over the various cases, Marcus sat on, watching Rennie, who wasn't looking at anything in particular. At least not anything in the room.

"Pretty pleased with yourself, aren't you?" he said after a long, long silence.

She startled, then rallied. "Well, pssh! Who wouldn't be?" He continued to watch her, and presently she sighed. "Well, only for a given value of 'pleased'. I'm desperately pleased that Baz's murderer has been nailed, that Ken's going to write a bang-up story about it, that Pamie and Roger will get some closure. Rough justice, maybe, but better than nothing. Pleased too that you've got the killer of the big-ticket murder of the year, on tape, no less. With bows on."

"But?"

"But my friend is still dead. And his killer's been murdered himself, and you're not anywhere *near* solving *that*. And you also have a confession, albeit recanted, in the other murder, the little-ticket one, as you so charmingly put it."

Marcus frowned. "So your problem is — ?"

"Not sure. It makes perfect sense, of course, that Danny kills Adam. Adam was going to blow everything sky-high about himself and Danny; even if Danny didn't know that until I showed him the letter, he must have had an idea there was a real danger. Him moving pre-emptively to make sure that never happened—it does make sense," she said again. "A sick, weird, horrible kind of sense."

"And he's so vain he doesn't mind confessing to it," remarked Brent, who'd returned from helping to deposit Danny Marron in a holding cell. "The same vanity that made him tape the murder in the first place."

"Or some kind of mutual assurance society," said Marcus, nodding. "They'd each have had some control over the other because of it. Some marker they could call in whenever they wanted: Danny because he had taped the murder, Pierce because he could finger the person who taped it."

Rennie sat forward abruptly, as if galvanized by some short, sharp shock. "You don't think *Danny* murdered Pierce, do you? To get himself out of that very situation?"

Their expressions told her that this had occurred to them long ago. But then they were professionals; they probably saw all possible motives all at once, in a flash of blinding light, then had to sort them out.

"It doesn't take much to push someone over a cliff," said Brent after a while. "But he needed Pierce alive, to bankroll future celluloid epics. Or big groundbreaking videotape breakthroughs."

"True." Rennie brooded for a while. "Well, obviously someone else *didn't* need Pierce alive. Or didn't *want* him alive."

"No shortage of people who felt like that," said Marcus.

"And we're running out of time to figure out who, though you hardly need me to tell you that. This thing is over tonight. By tomorrow morning everyone will be either gone or going. I don't want to see two killers walk out with them."

"Neither do we, Miss Stride," said Brent. He stood up, suddenly looking all law and oddly impressive. "Neither do we."

True to her word, Rennie turned every last little detail over to Ken Karper, who had arrived at the stationhouse like an eager terrier who'd been told there were rats, rats to be dealt with! He went over Marron's statement in the little office to which Brent had shown Rennie and Marcus, devouring it happily, making copious notes. At last he sat up and looked at Rennie, with gratitude, delight and utter sympathy at war upon his face.

"Rennie—"

I know…I know…don't say it, in the name of God and all angels pleeease don't say it…

"He didn't lie," she said, answering the unasked. "He said he hadn't killed Baz. And technically that's true. He didn't. Not himself. But he watched someone else do it, and he filmed it. But now the killer's dead, and he's an accessory, according to his own evidence. As Devlin said, he's every bit as guilty as Hill was."

"That was really smart work, noticing the videotape camera… I do so love seeing criminals hoist with their own petard."

"Show-off. We all know you're a Shakespeare fan." Rennie, who'd been cold and sad and numb up to then, now was trying to control a sudden blast of white-hot fury such as she had never known. *He killed Baz! That fucking bastard…why didn't I beat the crap out of him when I had the chance? Why didn't I really have my gun with me? It would have been so easy: oops, sorry, officer, just went off in self-defense as he came after me with a poker…*

"We still only have the one killer," remarked Marcus absently, from the other side of the desk. "As Rennie has pointed out on several occasions. We still don't know for sure who killed Adam. We still don't know at all who killed Pierce."

He abruptly stood up, went over to the wall and raised the shades on the one-way glass, flipped an intercom switch. In the interrogation room thus revealed, Danny was half-sprawled across the table, weeping and slobbering, Brent sitting watchfully opposite.

Audie Devlin's voice came calmly and conversationally over the tinny speaker as he paced around the room. "But what were you thinking to use it *for*, Marron? You could never have shown it to anybody."

Danny was almost gibbering. "I've told you over and over! I just wanted to have some kind of leverage. In case my father-in-law shut me down. If I could control Hill, with the videotape, he would have to underwrite me from now on."

"Good plan," remarked Brent. "Too bad someone had to ruin it by tossing Pierce Hill off the cliffs at Otter Cove. Your leverage is gone, and you're left to face the murder rap alone. See, blackmail is tricky like that."

"I want my lawyers," he said sullenly, pulling into himself like a little snail. "No more questions. Get my wife, and get my lawyers."

Marcus shut off the intercom. "Won't do him much good this time. Stupid bastard confessed; we have the hard evidence, thanks to Rennie. Kind of wraps it all up. With bows on, as you say. He's finished."

"He's finished now, anyway." Rennie stared at the table. "He *knew* Pierce murdered Baz: he shot it, and then he sat on it. Until a time would come when he could use it. I hope he rots in jail, and then fries in hell." She started to shake. "Get him out of my sight, or me out of his, whichever you can make happen faster. Or I swear to God I will kill him right here in front of you. And there won't be any doubt whatsoever about who did *that*."

Marcus took her by the arm and conducted her

out, putting himself between her and the glass window, so that she wouldn't have to catch another glimpse of Danny Marron. At least not until he came to trial.

After a session with Devlin and Brent, to fill in details— naturally he had asked, even begged, to be allowed to see the incriminating videotape, and naturally he had been denied, but he had had to ask, what kind of crime reporter would he have been if he hadn't—Ken Karper headed back to the Highlands Inn to type everything up, and then to phone Burke Kinney and his own editor.

Audie Devlin had given him the official word to run with it. It was all going to come out, and sooner rather than later, the police figured; at least this way they had someone at a major newspaper to whom they could spoon-feed the story and be reasonably confident that it would come out right. None of the lawmen were surprised that Rennie wanted nothing whatsoever to do with it, and Marcus was the least surprised of any of them.

Unable to trust herself to speak, Rennie had been escorted out of the building by Marcus, very gently, and handed into her car. He'd offered to drive her back to the hotel or the festival, or if she wanted, he'd get a uniformed officer to drive her, but she shook her head and drove off, perfectly steadily.

In her room at the Highlands Inn, she collapsed onto the couch, staring in front of her at the rubble she'd left from the morning. It had been a long, long day, crammed with incident and drama and hell of several different sorts, and by now it was almost time for the final evening festival session to start. But first she'd take a nice hot shower and change her clothes. She wasn't tired—in fact, the farthest thing from it. But she needed something cleansing and purifying in which to steep her brain and spirit, something as far from murder and lies as she could get; and a shower and fresh clothes were a good start. After that, rock and roll would fill the bill. As it always did.

So yes, she would put on something new and pretty — that brown paisley tunic and pants outfit she made last week, maybe, very Grace Slickian — and she would drive to the festival field, and once tonight's bill began in earnest she wouldn't leave till it was over. None of her immediate circle of friends was on tonight: they'd all done their sets, so the performance anxiety was over, and they were now simply looking forward to being fans and spectators like everyone else.

And maybe the music could even take her mind off her fury and her grief, and start the healing process. Music had power: maybe it could even do that.

Sunday night

The Blues Project

Big Brother & The Holding Company
        (reprise; half a set)

The Group with No Name

Buffalo Springfield

Lionheart

The Who

The Grateful Dead

The Jimi Hendrix Experience

The Mamas & The Papas

Chapter 21

Sunday night, June 18

"IT'S HARD WORKING WITHOUT A STRAIGHT MAN—and nobody here is straight."

Comedian Tommy Smothers surveyed the crowd in front of him and waited professionally for the rolling laugh, a tiny, perfect smirk on his lips. Well, it was true, and everybody knew it. Even the cops probably had a contact high by now. But he was emceeing the closing evening alone—his brother, Dick, wasn't with him—and he knew he had to flatter his audience just that little bit more.

After everything that had gone on since Mojado, Rennie, down to her last nerve by now, was only desperately hoping for the festival to be over. Once she'd arrived in the arena, she hadn't told anyone about the

events of the afternoon, not wishing to spoil the last night
of Monterey for her friends. Plenty of time to tell them
later. They'd read about it in the bulldog edition anyway,
if there was one around—if Ken Karper got his story filed
in time.

For all the triumph floating around the field, right
along with the pot smoke, there was also a definite
valedictory feel in the air, something almost autumnal;
Rennie just hoped it didn't bode ill for the night's music,
or even the scene itself. As soon as she'd arrived, Gerry
Langhans had come over to crouch beside her seat, full of
heartfelt thanks that she'd cleared him of suspicion,
promising to take her out to dinner when they were both
back in San Francisco, before he went east again. He'd
already sent flowers to her room at the Highlands Inn;
Rennie, for her part, was just glad she could have been of
some help in what had been really just a mildly sticky
situation, and she'd told him so. They'd known each
other too long for anything else. But she found to her
surprise that she could not bring herself to tell him about
Pierce Hill and Danny Marron. Not just yet.

It would be hard to really bring anyone down
tonight, though: the place was packed and thrumming.
Looking around, Rennie estimated that there must be
upwards of fifty thousand people in the audience; and
later some would put the midnight Sunday night crowd
at almost ninety thousand, with a rough total of two
hundred thousand for the weekend. Biggest festival ever:
that should show everybody who thought this rock and
roll thing was merely a passing fad.

Old friends and new acquaintances alike were
there to see Monterey close out in glory: Belinda
Melbourne and Francie Nolting, Sledger Cairns, the
Powderhouse boys, Gray and Prue Sonnet, to whom
Rennie had at last been introduced, through the good
offices of her friend Carson Duquette and designer

Punkins Parker. Even Romilly Ramillies had driven up again from Mojado, especially to catch the festival's last night, though she hadn't brought Becca with her, as Rennie and Prax had hoped she might. She looked like Greta Garbo playing Eleanor of Aquitaine, draped and wimpled in dramatic and flattering rose jersey, and she spent all of her time backstage, talking to the Hollywood luminaries in attendance, Brandon Storey of course being the common ground upon which they stood to chat.

As Tommy Smothers ran his monologue and laughter tore up the arena in crosswise currents, Rennie forced herself to calmness. *Don't spoil tonight for anybody else, and don't spoil it for yourself, either. Just put it all aside, and let yourself enjoy it. This will never happen again. Oh, there'll be other festivals, sure, maybe even great ones. But nothing like this.*

After all that, the night opened dully enough, with the Blues Project. Huh. Where's the big improvisational power of blues when you really need it? Yet another reason why white boys should stay away from black music. Why hadn't they put these guys on with the Saturday afternoon blues-a-thon and not let them waste the leadoff slot here tonight? Uninspired, to say the least.

Too bad she couldn't have done the programming herself; her own personal Monterey last-night dream lineup would have rocked the socks off God himself. Evenor, Dead, Big Brother, Lionheart, Hendrix, Quicksilver, Turnstone, Who, Airplane...in no particular order except the Airplane as the closers. Ah, if only.

Unable to pay attention to a band that couldn't command it, and suddenly ravenous, Rennie took advantage of the dead air, as she considered it, to get something to eat. Foraging backstage at the Hunt Club buffet, trying to keep away from anyone she knew, to whom she might have to actually speak, she was careful

to keep one ear tuned to what was coming from the
stage.

*If I think about Baz, Adam, Pierce or Danny, I'll go
mad... I* will *concentrate on the music...I will* not *think about
what's going on back at the stationhouse...* She had dropped
half a Valium back at the Inn, and now she dropped
another, but they seemed to have as little effect on her as
if they'd been M&Ms. Maybe the music would be more
help. Maybe real M&Ms would be more help.

Big Brother had gotten their begged-for reprise:
only half a set, but at least they had managed to make
sure it ended up on film this time. And it was no less
intense than the previous performance, even though
Rennie had once been told by a member of Big Brother,
deep in his cups, that Janis planned out and rehearsed
every note she sang: every quaver, every swoop and
shriek, every stop, every slide. And once she had it
down, she never changed it. Not a spontaneous moment
in it. The Brother had gone on to say that Janis was a
nightmare to work with—not because she took so many
artistic risks and liberties, but because she took none.
Every take was exactly the same as the one before. It was
still glorious, of course; but perhaps a little less so once
you knew that. If you believed it, that is. But at least she
had her second shot now. This was one white girl,
anyway, who *could* sing black music. Only half a set; but
it would be enough to start a legend.

Rennie leaned over to put her lips up to Stan
Hirsh's ear, as he stood next to her in the wings, and was
surprised to hear herself speak with something
approximating a normal voice.

"Nice nipples on Janis."

Stan grinned. "Oh yeah, killer subtle. I saw her
tweaking them before she went on. I know a couple of
girls in North Beach who'd have been happy to lend her
some tassels if she really thought the nips wouldn't make

the, uh, point."

"It's no worse than Jagger stuffing his pants with a bar of Sweetheart soap before he goes onstage. Probably a lot less worse, actually." Rennie paused, shook her head, then laughed. " 'Less worse'? Man, I must be stoned…or else not stoned enough. Well, nipples or not, she looks beautiful. Even if she is wearing that dorky gold pantsuit. Not exactly what you'd expect from a Texan blues queen, is it. It's more like something a young faculty wife would wear to the English department's Christmas party. She was even laughing about it earlier: she called it 'gold lame', not 'gold lamé'. I'd have lent her anything if she'd asked, and Linda Gravenites made so many beautiful outfits for her… Still, she sounds like a freakin' goddess and that's all that matters. It's gonna happen for her, off tonight. I just hope she doesn't fuck herself up the way Tam and Fort did."

He turned to look at her, startled. "Tam and Fort! Of Fillmore Murders fame? You're not talking about what I think you're talking about? Oh God. You are."

"Yeah. Heroin. She started out as a speed freak but moved right along to smack. It's not widely known by the fans. Or indeed by most of the music press. In fact, we spend a good deal of time and ink denying it. Or just ignoring it. That and her girlfriends."

"*Janis Joplin* is BI?"

"Well, yes. And there's no Santa Claus, either. I'm so sorry." Rennie put a consoling hand on his arm; obviously some major illusions had been shattered here.

Stan looked mournful. "I've been to bed with her myself."

"*Have* you! I'm impressed. Well, there you are, then. So has Praxie, by the way."

"I really wish you hadn't told me that. Now I feel, in some strange way, as if I've been to bed with Prax."

"Nothing stopping you. In any way, strange or

otherwise. She thinks you're very cute."

"No, no. She's like my sister, that's just too creepy. Besides—"

Besides, indeed. Stan's girlfriend Marishka was standing a few feet away, watching and listening to the show with every indication of pleasure. She'd hit it off instantly with Rennie and Prax and the guys in both bands, and even with Tansy, which might easily have been problematic but turned out to be cool. Rennie gave Stan a knowing grin, and turned her attention back to Big Brother.

She was still backstage talking to friends when something billing itself as The Group with No Name came on—hey, if they couldn't be bothered to think up a name, she couldn't be bothered to listen to them. And consisting as they did of two pals of the Phillipses and a studio drummer, they were correct not to trouble themselves: nobody was ever going to hear from them again—no name, no music, no talent, no anything. So she went back for another bite to eat, surprised to find herself so hungry, while Buffalo Springfield—with David Crosby singing in, much to the Byrds' annoyance—delivered themselves of a set that, though good, could have been brilliant.

Returning out front just before Lionheart took the stage, half a sandwich in her hand, Rennie slipped back into her seat with high hopes of being knocked out of it. Well, it had happened before, right here, Friday and yesterday. It could happen again tonight, even more than once, before the evening was over. Maybe the music would save her, as it had not been able to save Baz Potter, or Pierce Hill, or even Adam Santa Monica. She closed her hands into fists, so tight that her nails dug into her palms, and fixed her attention on Lionheart as they waited in the wings.

Please…take my mind off everything…just do that for

me, can you guys do that…

Ned Raven had spoken so highly of this group as live performers that she had been deeply suspicious of his motives: he wasn't usually so professionally generous to other bands, not even friends, or especially not friends, and she wouldn't put it past him to be setting them up for a fall by overtalking them. Be that as it may, she'd been a fan of Lionheart's recorded work for years, and the progress from one album to the next had been truly impressive.

Like the Airplane and Evenor and the Dead, they were a sublimely talented six-man outfit: lead vocalist, lead guitarist, rhythm guitarist, bass player, drummer and a keyboardist who switched off to violin as often as not—all Brits except for the drummer, Jay-Jay Olvera, as Turk Wayland had mentioned at breakfast, dear God had it really been only that morning? Solid stars in England, though not on a Stones or Beatles or even Dave Clark Five level, by this stage in their career Lionheart could fill any venue in their native land except Wembley. And that supreme eminence wasn't very far distant. In fact, they were here straight off a gig at the Royal Albert Hall that had by all accounts blown the round red roof off the place; and now, lean and longhaired as championship salukis, they were ready to play America.

Now Turk, wearing a fringed brown buckskin shirt that made him look like a Viking Daniel Boone, stepped to his amp at stage left. He had a sleek black guitar slung on low, a model that Rennie hadn't seen very much of yet—a Stratocaster. Most of the major rock axemen were still married to their Gibsons, but from the first notes he played she could see why the switchover was beginning.

The pounding drums pulled everybody in instantly, then the Strat started to soar and Niles Clay opened his mouth and began to sing. And Rennie forgot her numbing grief and sorrow, forgot her weariness, forgot her sandwich, forgot even her critical impartiality—forgot anything and everything but what was coming straight at her from the stage.

This was it. This was what she'd come to hear: this, and Janis, and Otis, and Praxie, and Tansy, and whoever and whatever else wanted to make itself heard before it ended. The sound was incredible: the high ringing note of Mick Rouse's Rickenbacker under Turk's fiery Strat, Rardi Lombardi's violin skimming over the top of everything like a surfer on a wave, the close, strong harmonies, the lead guitar and violin like two extra voices, the powerful bass driving it all like a geyser. Plus Jay-Jay in the middle of it: the only other drummer who could fill up the front of the sound like that with rhythmic fatness was Ginger Baker of Cream. But Ginger *needed* to be up front—there was only Jack Bruce's buzzy Rumpelstiltskin bass and Eric Clapton's surprisingly scant guitar otherwise.

Lionheart had a richer sound. There were no holes—you could isolate any instrument in your head and something interesting would be going on all the time. In her review of their last album, Rennie had called their sound symphonic, and Turk himself, at breakfast that morning—only that morning!—had told her he'd been pleased and surprised that she, almost alone among reviewers, actually got what he was trying to do. It wasn't really symphonic, strictly speaking, she thought now, listening hard. But in the sense that the songs had a progressive construction—movements, if you will—yeah, it was. You could pick out what everyone was doing and relate to what everyone else was doing; after the first verse, sometimes two verses, it all went into masterful variations, each instrument taking a turn at being forward in the mix, doing something different, and it all hung together around Turk, even Niles Clay's clear lead vocals, on this brand-new song.

"Words can't trust
Thoughts'll trick
Feelings bust
Moods'll kick
Your mind and soul,
well, they don't al-
ways wanna try…
But the heart, no, the heart don't lie
It knows what it can't deny
Love may not always say what's true
or even know what's real
But the heart, no,
the heart don't lie…"

Turk swung round to his amp, and across the stage Rardi took off on violin. On Friday night, the Animals had used an electric violin on their acidified cover of 'Paint It Black', and it had been fantastic, but this was very different—violin as co-lead singer—and the audience was startled and pleased. Rennie found herself responding to the aching loveliness of the sound and how it carried the fed-back guitar right along with it.

Then the choppy stuttering distortion chords Turk was playing, with a heavy foot on the wah-wah pedal, suddenly lengthened and dovetailed and swung into the same long shimmering singing line as he kicked over to the Leslie, violin and lead guitar twining like two voices, one or the other going minor for a bar or two or throwing in a slur just for the hell of it. And Niles's voice rode over the top of it all, to complete the trifecta as they hurtled to the finish.

"Fate'll fool
Plans spell danger
Odds will rule
Hope's a stranger
When all is said and done

Only one thing's gonna run,
take wing and fly
'Cause the heart, no, the heart won't lie
It sees and it dares defy
Recant a million heresies
Love's the only one to keep
'Cause the heart, yeah, the heart don't lie…"

Rennie felt herself being pulled in, pulled under, wrapped in it like a rock and roll flag. No, the heart *doesn't* lie, does it…it can't. She had loved Lionheart since they were just a folk-rocky English group with one obscure album to their name, but this was a Lionheart she had never heard before. Maybe no one had.

It was yet one more new thing that had never been heard till now, something else that had never been done before; in after years Rennie and many other people who had been there watching and listening, and many, many more who hadn't, would swear that there must have been magic in the wood of the Monterey stage, major musical mojo, because so many artists who stepped onto it brought to it something greater than they ever had before, and stepped off it greater themselves. Yeah…who's got the Big Magic *now*, fellas?

Maybe it's Baz…being a guardian angel for the music…

Now Turk bent over his Strat, double-chording to fill, and when the vocal ended he took off on a rippling solo that sounded as if he was playing a twelve-string even though everybody could see he had only the usual six to work with. The sustain he was getting off the strings on the melody line was carrying the notes so long that he was chording and picking simultaneously, chiming arpeggios like a psychedelic carillon. God, he was *incredible*…the previous albums, great as they were, hadn't held a hint of this, and it wasn't just him either, the rest of the band was right there with him. Well, if that was what acid could do for you…

And then not even stopping for the signature change or for the audience to take a breath, let alone applaud, the band shifted completely to a godalmighty drum crash and pivoted on a dime into runaway cannoning hardline Delta blues. Turk slipped a glass tube on his fret hand little finger and slid so hard Rennie was amazed the strings didn't slice right through the glass, remembering that his English fans called him Slider, obviously for good reason.

For their closer, they opened up all the dials and punched everyone's lights out with something called 'Ozymandias', from the album released almost two months ago, *The Little Gentleman in Black Velvet*. It was languishing in the lower echelons of the trade charts' top 100 at the moment, but in three weeks — such was the power of word of mouth and FM radio — it would be second only to *Sgt. Pepper*, which had come out on the first day of June.

For their encore, though no one thought they could possibly top what they'd just pulled off, Lionheart dug into a song Niles informed them Turk had just finished writing for their next album, a gorgeous thing called 'Clarity Road', the first time it had ever been played, and Turk sang the vocal himself. Nailed to the back of her seat, completely paralyzed with joy, Rennie glanced aside and saw Jerry and Janis and Owen Danes, their eyes on sticks and their jaws on their knees. Oh good, not just her then…

When Turk brought it all to an end, not with the huge crashing orgasmic power chord that everyone was primed for but with a soft yet final run and pull-off that was ultimately far more satisfying, Rennie couldn't move. There she was, dumbstruck and shivering, right out there in front of God and everybody. She had been wrung out and hung up to dry. She had been beaten up and left for dead. She had been made love to. She had been to church. They all had.

Lionheart had done the impossible: for forty-five minutes they had made her forget, and more than that, they had filled the forgetfulness with something to remember. Plainly delighted with themselves and with their audience, the band now tossed off an instrumental verse of 'The British Grenadiers', out of sheer high spirits, just to not leave everyone completely adrift, and left the stage.

They all went backstage to offer congratulations, which the band shyly accepted, vivid with their triumph, flushed and giddy. Rennie talked a while with Rardi and Shane, then moved away as a new wave of visitors came in, and watched knowingly from the sidelines as Freddy Bellasca of Centaur Records cut out Turk and Lionheart manager Francher Green like a surgeon going in on a heart valve, and moved them aside for some serious talking. Oh yeah, *that* was a contract conversation if ever she'd seen one. She hoped it would work out: Lionheart could use a really high-powered record company behind them; Glisten was an honest little label with a nice roster, but they weren't in Centaur's league. It just sucked that Centaur also had to mean Freddy Bellasca.

A spoiled-rotten rich kid who'd been staked by a doting daddy to whatever he wanted to do in life, Freddy'd had a few failed ventures, but when he'd founded Centaur six years back, it had suddenly become obvious to all that running a record label was what he had been born for. To his credit, he had a brilliant sense of what would sell, and he wasn't stingy about throwing money at artists to get them to sign with him; it was what he did to them later that was the problem. Rennie, who'd met him about a year ago, sometimes wondered if he was living a vicarious life as a musician; he liked to think of himself as their real true friend, and indeed many of his artists felt that way about him. But by no means all.

Watching Freddy now, Rennie totaled things up in her head. Lionheart had done five albums, counting the current release. But now their contract was up, according to what Turk had said. Glisten, to which they'd signed six years ago, couldn't support them in anything remotely approaching the way they now deserved, and Centaur would buy them anything they needed — once it had bought *them*, of course.

Hovering not far from Turk, obviously waiting for him but equally obviously not wanting to claim his attention from the business he and Francher were clearly conducting, Tansy was a bright presence, a space gypsy in embroidered velvet and long silky sleeve fringe that touched the ground, fringe threaded with tiny bells and sparkles. She waved now at Rennie, and her smile could have melted permafrost. Rennie looked around guiltily for Bruno Harvey, but he was nowhere to be seen.

Prax had had a contract conversation of her own, all of Evenor had; first Dill Miller had enjoyed the enormous satisfaction of turning down Albert Grossman's somewhat condescending offer for the group, then he had arranged a serious meeting with Leeds Sheffield of Sovereign and another with Catherine Coachman of Palatine Records — the only female label prez in the business, and, weirdly enough, a former Benedictine nun. Both of them appeared to have a good deal more respect for Evenor than Grossman had shown, and were willing, nay, eager, to back it up with pleasingly substantial sums of cash.

But the night wasn't over. There had been a tense scene backstage that Rennie and others had been witness to, where Pete Townshend of the Who had furiously accused Jimi Hendrix of stealing his guitar-destructo act, a charge which Jimi had calmly denied. Neither band wanted to follow the other, understandably, and the row had been epic. Finally John Phillips had flipped a coin to see who would have to go on first, and Townshend called the winning toss. So Hendrix would follow the Who on the Monterey stage, which suited Pete fine, as he'd seen in London what happened to people who followed Jimi Hendrix, and he wasn't about to have it happen to his band. It had happened before. But it wasn't going to be a whole lot better going on ahead of Hendrix, either. Or following Lionheart.

As Rennie had told Marcus a couple of weeks back, like Lionheart and Jimi, the Who were mostly unknown in the United States except to the very hippest and best-informed music fans; they'd had a few singles out, good ones, but had barely cracked the charts. That was all about to change. Sulking because they won the toss but still had to go on after Turk and company, the Who took the stage to polite applause, then crashed into 'Substitute', a few more of their own songs, even a screaming cover of that old warhorse 'Summertime Blues'—the 1812 Overture of rock and roll. The audience remained unimpressed, and Rennie could tell the band was pissed off at the non-response—they wanted some of that awe they'd seen bestowed, and they set out now to get it.

"This is where it ends," Townshend snarled into his mike, and as he windmilled some crashing power chords, the fringe-clad Roger Daltrey began to stutter out 'My Generation.' *That* got the crowd's attention. With the sound roaring behind him like the throat of a volcano, the light show flashing gamely but ineffectively through the smoke-bomb haze, Pete began to whale on the stage itself, using his axe like, well, an axe. The neck cracked and came away from the body of the guitar, and he bowed it like a violin until the amps shrieked in agony. Stagehands, hoping against hope to save the equipment, and indeed the stage, were almost beheaded by the whirling guitar. The rest of the band joined in the mayhem, bashing whatever was nearest. Pete started clouting his amp like a blacksmith, giving it such a biff that it fell over, while Keith Moon, not wanting to be left out, kicked over a drum.

"Well, *that's* new," said Stan happily, and Rennie nodded, entranced.

So new that some of the deputy sheriffs, there to preserve the peace, uneasily wondered if they shouldn't be trying to preserve the pieces—from destruction, or at least from hitting the audience. But in the end, they wisely stood aside and let it all smash itself to bits, though a young, dark-haired rock writer from New York, covering the festival for the Saturday Evening Post, freaked out completely, thinking that the whole thing was real. So much so that she had to be rescued from underneath the stage, where she was cowering from the twin terrors that were Townshend and Moon, the Scylla and Charybdis of rock and roll. Well, even if the whole thing *was* bogus, which it absolutely was, who could blame her?

After that, the Grateful Dead had barely enough time to get their fingers warmed up, much less work themselves into their extended spangled wizardry. But first Monkee Peter Tork, who'd been hanging out all weekend cadging attention, felt the need to go out and inform the audience that contrary to wishful thinking, the Beatles really *weren't* there, *wouldn't* be there, had never *been* there. The crowd, by this point, finally drunk on what they'd been hearing, didn't care one way or another about the Fabs, but Dead bassist Phil Lesh was annoyed at what he perceived as Tork's attempt to bogart the energy. So he incited the audience, just a little, then bandmate Bob Weir happily invited the crowd to fold up the chairs and dance on them, and the crowd was delighted to comply.

Roadies were flinging people offstage like so many Frisbees, the cops and ushers were vainly trying to clear the aisles, and all the while Weir and Lesh kept insidiously coaxing people to dance. Enjoying the anarchy so typical of the Dead, Rennie caught a glimpse of Turk Wayland on the side of the stage: he was so tall and blond he was hard to miss, especially with Tansy's equally blond head right in front of his chest. She grinned: they looked as if they'd been carved out of the same bar of yellow soap, and they looked every bit as amused at the chaos as she was.

But the swirling energy didn't translate into Dead musical magic, not tonight. To everyone's keen disappointment; Rennie and many thousands of others had been anticipating the Dead's performance as the hearthstone of the festival—what it was all about, where San Francisco would show the world where psychedelic music was *really* at—and it just wasn't happening. The Dead generally needed at least an hour to seduce themselves and the audience into their trip, but they weren't going to get it tonight. The best they could get off was the ten-minute hurricane of 'Viola Lee Blues', and the Dead ended up leaving the Monterey stage frustrated and discouraged. They had not signed the film release, and so they would not appear in Pennebaker's movie; by all reports, they didn't mind.

After that, things took a while to settle down again. Rennie, looking around, holding on with both hands to the peace and clarity that Lionheart had given her, saw this brief hiatus as the calm before, during, between and after the storms. Because she knew what was about to happen, or knew a little, anyway—as it turned out, *nobody* could have suspected the full extent— and this crowd needed as much breathing space it could get, before Jimi Hendrix took all that breath away from them.

She'd met him the other day, when Garcia had brought her along to Jimi's room when he went to say hi. The Dead, the Animals and the Experience, among others, were all staying at the same business-traveler's-class motel on the edge of town, in a little motel row on the other side of the fairgrounds. Hardly the same level of sumptousness as the Highlands Inn or Otter Point, of course. But that would come.

When they arrived, they had seen him sitting cross-legged on the floor in the hallway, utterly absorbed, three guitars arranged before him like a giant Chinese fan. He had somehow gotten hold of a kindergarten paintbox, little tablets of watercolors; now he was carefully daubing abstract patterns on the quiescent instruments, as if consecrating them to his holy purpose—an apprentice shaman working his first war magic for his tribe, a young knight purifying his weapons before the quest.

As they shared a companionable and no less purifying joint, Jimi had talked amiably, in a voice as soft as clouds.

"I heard they wanted to work up a different color acid tab for every night of the week, man, but the festival's only three nights, so they just got to do but three colors—Monterey blue, Monterey red and Monterey purple. Far out."

Now he stood in the wings with his sidemen, bassist Noel Redding and drummer Mitch Mitchell, getting psyched up to go on in front of the hippest audience in rock and roll history. Brian Jones, who was announcing him, gave Rennie a quick peck on the cheek as he went by her and stepped out onstage.

"I'd like to introduce a very good friend," he mumbled into the microphone, "a fellow countryman of yours, he's the most exciting performer I've ever heard, the Jimi Hendrix Experience."

And yet again at Monterey, something new and rare shattered its shell, stretched damp wings and began to fly. This one gave a barbaric yawp as it went: a fierce tropical bird, probably dangerous and certainly spectacular, in full male display plumage—a ruffled orange poet shirt and a black and gold Indian vest and red satin pants, the hair puffed out over a pirate headband like a dandelion clock, jet to the amber of his skin.

That was what he looked like, and nobody had ever seen anything like him before. What he sounded like: well, nobody had ever *heard* anything like him before—notes like screaming tracer bullets, hitting the upturned faces and listening ears like sonic hailstones, like a hard rain falling. He covered Howlin' Wolf and Dylan and B.B. King; he cut the Byrds with a version of 'Hey Joe' that was from a whole other planet than the one that they had delivered the night before. He performed his own stuff, with power and with grace; he playfully riffed a few bars of 'Strangers in the Night' and even 'Wild Thing'—quick, witty musical allusions. Playing hard, he somersaulted across the stage and came up still playing. He flipped the guitar between his legs and he played it behind his back and he played it upside down and he played it with his teeth.

At last he fell to his knees on the stage, adoring his instrument, muttering thank you to the music and to whatever else he worshipped, and then he squeezed lighter fluid all over his guitar, holy chrism, and set fire to the hapless Strat, murmuring incantations, making come-hither fingers for the flames to rise from the sacrifice.

He threw pieces of the burnt offering to the astounded audience, who eagerly caught the relics from his hands. Even the Who hadn't matched that. Staggering offstage, he collapsed into Brian Jones's arms and they both almost went down. Hugh Masekela kept shouting "You killed them, you killed them!", and he didn't even look jealous. In view of three murders, Rennie wished he'd choose another less fraught verb to shout, but she couldn't argue with the sentiment. As was said by many thereafter, Hendrix, like the others before him, had gone onstage a nobody and he'd come offstage a star.

Bringing it all back home now... The Mamas and the Papas were supposed to be the big finish to Monterey. Not only were they the most popular and successful American band at that very moment, but they had been instrumental in getting the festival on. Now they couldn't manage to get their music off. After their handful of songs, Michelle left the stage visibly upset. Backstage, she confided to the commiserating Rennie that she'd just found out she was pregnant. She'd meant the festival to be so wonderful, and it had been, but her own band hadn't soared, at least not to the heights they'd wanted to; they'd closed out the festival the way big-time stars should, but after Jimi nobody was going to remember they'd even been there.

Rennie tried to console her, because she liked her and liked her band's music, but she was thinking privately that perhaps it was most merciful that no one but rock historians would remember that anyone had been on at Monterey after Hendrix, because Michelle was quite right. The Mamas and the Papas weren't the most creative or exciting band even at the best of times, though they did have a few genuinely immortal songs; and they had performed Herculean labors to make this festival happen. But their performance tonight had been more like Vegas hippies, and they knew it. Everybody knew it.

They had never been particularly happy onstage anyway: of all the top-line bands, they'd done by far the fewest live performances, and it showed. Tonight they'd hit all their musical marks, and they'd certainly *looked* like rock gods and goddesses in their regal attire, and had been hailed so by their people, and deservedly; but they had had fear on their faces, like deportees to some psychedelic gulag, time travelers from Avalon who'd gotten caught in rush hour and lost their luggage. Everything had changed, right there in front of them, and they knew that they and the kind of music they made were doomed. Oh, sure, there would still be light, pleasant poppy tunes to be heard, but from this moment henceforth, in the face of the newborn titans, such things would be irrelevant. The caravan had moved on.

Contributing to their own public execution, the band had actually dragged Scott McKenzie onstage to sing the excremental 'Flowers in Your Hair', and all over the arena the sound of San Franciscans being sucker-punched in the gut had reverberated like a cymbal shot. Again with the L.A. shtick…

But really it was a failure of imagination. No one could have predicted the lightning that had struck the Monterey stage six separate times—those acts couldn't be blamed for their own surprise brilliance, and the acts who'd disappointed couldn't be blamed that they themselves had failed to measure up to their own hype.

It was a real changing of the guard, and no one could have predicted *that*, either. Groups like the Association, Johnny Rivers, Lou Rawls, even the Mamas and Papas themselves: this was their swan song. The singers and the players and the music of the future had arrived, in no uncertain terms; the world had seen and heard it, and nothing was ever going to be the same again. Rennie felt it change before her eyes, beneath her feet, against her skin, inside her head. There would be no going back, and no one waved goodbye.

Anyway, Monterey was over. The last official note had been played, the last ovation roared out, the huge crowd was happily dispersing to do its own thing. In the little room under the stage, Jimi Hendrix was handing two members of Quicksilver Messenger Service a little pillbox filled with tabs of Owsley's Monterey purple. The Quicks each took one and Jimi gobbled a couple more, bringing his total, apparently, to half a dozen, according to awed onlooker Belinda Melbourne. Then he picked up someone's Fender bass that was lying around and started trading riffs with Jack Casady of Jefferson Airplane, the notes bubbling out from beneath the stage, spring water for the senses.

The post-festival mood was catching, and not limited to backstage: over at the Home Ec building, some of the Buffalo Springfield had joined some other Airplanes and Turk Wayland and Eric Burdon and Bruno Harvey in a jam, the sound arcing over the fairgrounds like heat lightning, or a musical aurora.

And not limited to the festival field, either: the playing and partying would go on all night at the Highlands Inn and the Inn at Otter Point and everywhere else musicians were. Somewhere Pete Townshend had found himself another guitar, and the Who played until dawn out of the back of a flatbed truck, on the football field that had been serving as a campground dormitory. No one got much sleep, but no one much cared, and those who did manage to get their heads down dozed off to a rock and roll lullaby.

Sitting exhausted on the end of the second row of seats as the crowd streamed past, having snorted a pinch of purple mesc that someone generously offered her — hey, the festival was over, she wasn't working now, she could if she wanted to — Rennie was thinking dully that tomorrow everyone would be out of here, herself included, and they still wouldn't know who had killed Adam and Pierce. Gradually she became aware of someone standing next to her, and a voice in her ear.

"Let's blow this joint, lass, shall we? And maybe blow *a* joint."

The someone had knelt beside her chair and was slipping his hand down the rear of her bellbottoms. She turned to look, and Finn Hanley smiled at her.

"Come on, let's get out of here."

So you can get in somewhere else? But she went with him anyway. Still with his hand on her ass, he started moving her to the back entrance and her car. As they went, she saw Marcus and Brent on the other side of an uncrossable tide of audience; they were shouting and waving at her, and seemed to be trying to convey something urgent, but she couldn't make it out and so she just smiled and waved back and left.

Chapter 22

"DO WE HAVE TO HANG OUT *HERE*? It's kind of — creepy."

Strong chilly sea breezes, roaring surf: Rennie had just realized that she and Finn were walking on the grass-topped cliffs above Otter Cove, not far from where Pierce's body had been found that morning.

Only this morning! It seems like a hundred years ago...

"Aye, I think we do. It's all right. Don't worry."

"What will you do now?" she asked after about a hundred years; the pinch of mescaline had kicked in, in that time-delay way it did — time stretching and plateauing, many minutes hanging fire, then the whole earth reeling over all at once, in a hurry to catch up. "Now that Pierce is dead, I mean. You might be able to renegotiate your deal with Rainshadow."

"You think?" His hand was out of her pants now, but he had his arm so firmly around her that it was hard for her to match his step and walk; he was almost dragging her at times. "Well, never mind that, we have other things to discuss. You told me you were a dear friend of Baz Potter. I think you ought to know that Pierce Hill killed him."

She turned to stare at him from a long, long, echoing way away. "I know that already. I've known all day. But how do *you* know?"

"Because he told me so before I pushed him off this very cliff. Right about here, in fact."

Rennie's ears had stopped ringing and her brain had suddenly cleared itself of the wisps of the drug, was as still and cold now as a winter night. It all was so inevitable, all of a sudden.

"I should have known... You seemed to be in and out of bed a lot last night. And a little too cold and wet—and recently scratched up—for just sticking your head out for a breath of fresh air the way you claimed."

Finn looked amused. "You really are as smart as they say."

"Not smart enough, or I would have noticed sooner."

"Well, don't fret yourself; it wasn't your fault. I knew who you were from the first, you see, from the pool at Mojado. But I didn't want you to know I knew."

"Now that's very interesting, 'cause that's exactly what I was doing with you. Not wanting to admit *I* knew who *you* were."

"I daresay we both had our reasons... Any road, last night I made sure you were asleep—just a little something in your milk, which you drank right up like a good girl—then once you were out, I went downstairs, met up with Pierce, got him out here and tipped him over the cliff."

"*That's* when your medal went missing," said Rennie in a burst of clarity. "You didn't care if the Blessed Mother saw us fucking, that was just a story. Pierce ripped it off you and gave you those scratches you blamed me for. But why did you kill him?"

"Because, as you heard at Waterhall, he was going to dump me from the label. Ironic, yes? He wouldn't let Baz and Roger go, clung to them like grim death, but me he wanted to cut loose. Me and Ushuaia and the rest. So I killed him. Pure revenge. Celts are big on that. I may still get dumped, but at least I got to dump him first. Literally. Right down there, on those rocks. Then I noticed the medal was missing. I went out to look for it—which is where you woke up briefly and thought I was coming back to bed from the loo—but I couldn't find it, so I figured it was lost forever in the cove below and hopefully no one would find it ever, or at least not until I was long gone. Which apparently no one has, at least not so far."

"And Baz?" she asked, when she thought she could trust her voice to ask it.

"Strictly Pierce's idea. He told me so himself before he took his little cliff-dive: at least he didn't plan it beforehand, the piece of utter bogshite, he said it was purely spur of the moment. I'm truly sorry," he added, and it sounded genuine. "I know he was your friend. But think of it like this: I avenged him for you and Hazlitt and his missus."

"Actually, I'm not so sure I see it that way…but why do you tell me all this now?"

"Because it doesn't matter now. I'm sorry, lass—"

Even then it didn't dawn on Rennie what he was saying, though it really should have been a no-brainer. Trying to make sense of it, she heard voices behind them, or maybe ahead, or rising up from the beach below. With an effort she focused. Oh, right, it was all three. People running and shouting, hmm, wonder why.

Finn pulled her across him, his arm on her throat like an iron bar. But she still didn't figure it out, not until she saw Audie Devlin and Brent Gilmore approaching with drawn guns, and from the other direction, other cops—the Monterey police, some of them still flower-bedecked, hands wrapped around their own weapons.

Hostage time…oh, man, do I never fucking learn? Marcus is right, it's Muir Woods all over again…see, again, if I'd really had my gun with me, I could have done something…

She made her mouth form words instead. "Finn? Why are you doing this? It's not going to work—"

"Best not to talk just now, my dear…" He raised his voice. "So you figured it out."

"We did," said Audie Devlin.

"And just for the sake of argument, exactly what is it that you figured, then?"

"Oh, *don't* waste our time, Hanley! That you're the one who threw Pierce Hill over the cliff, of course. We found your medal under his body. Very helpful having your name engraved on the back like that."

"Thank my godmother, the stupid cow, she had it engraved and gave it to me when I was a wee babby… Oh, I could claim I lost the medal while strolling on the rocks the other day, but I'll spare us all, shall I? Aye, I'm the one, right enough. I killed him. Threw him over the side like a sack of potatoes. More pressingly, I'm also the one who's going to throw Miss Stride here to follow him, if you don't step back right this instant like dear good lads and let us leave. Alone. With no one following. I'll let her go later, unharmed. Well, probably."

Audie stopped where he stood, and Brent casually drifted a little to cliffside in a flanking maneuver, just in case.

"We know why you did it, Hanley," said Devlin soothingly. "There's no need to hold Rennie hostage. We understand."

"Do you now? How is that possible, I wonder? Do you have any idea of what it felt like, being at that pig's mercy for years, then being cut loose by him, dismissed like an unsatisfactory stable-boy? Everything I put up with from him, only to be told I was to be pushed off for some still-wet-behind-the-ears noisy children? Of *course* I took the opportunity to push him off first."

"No," said Marcus, from where he had been standing, unnoticed, behind Finn twenty feet away; Rennie tried to twist her head to see him, but Finn's arm prevented. "We don't have any idea of that. How could we? But hurting Rennie isn't going to help you."

Finn scoffed. "Hill killed her great friend Basil Potter. He told me so himself—but I see from your lack of surprise that you already know all about it. You heard it from that little worm Marron, I shouldn't wonder. But I didn't kill Pierce for that. I killed him for me. Even so, I should think Miss Stride would be on her knees thanking me for it. Very talented on her knees she is, aren't you, my dear. Sorry, she can't talk just now, I'm choking her a wee bit hard."

Somehow Rennie found her voice. "Finn, let me go. This is stupid. You're not going to get away."

She felt the arm tighten as Hanley moved a step or two backward, closer to the cliff edge, and she tried to dig her heels into the soft, damp turf; but there wasn't much purchase, and nothing to grab on to. If he decided she was going over, with him or without him, then over she was going; hopefully it wouldn't hurt too much when she hit the rocks. Maybe the tide would be in and she'd fall into water, she might even survive if the water was deep enough... Then she felt the tension and intent go out of him like a sigh.

"Aye," he said ruefully. "I'm not, lass, am I. At least, not like that. I am sorry, truly. For all of it."

He flung her from him so violently that she sprawled to the ground; but he had flung her landwards. Then turning, before Brent or Devlin or Marcus could dash forward and grab him, he blew a kiss to Rennie, crossed himself, ran the twenty feet to the cliff-edge and was gone.

Rennie pushed herself up on all fours, a little dazed, but a white-faced Prax ran to her and caught her and pulled her away from the edge.

"No, don't look. Don't look, honey. Come with me. Come on. It's okay."

After Finn Hanley's broken body had been carried up from the rocks a hundred feet below, and Devlin and his officers had wrapped up the immediate police chores— including shooing away the hundreds of curious onlookers who'd come flooding out from the hotel and the TV crew who'd just showed up—Marcus came over to Rennie where she sat with Prax and Stan Hirsh on the terrace steps.

She was huddled in a big fringed shawl Prax had hastily commandeered from a solicitous and horrified Punkins Parker, and her hands clasped a cup of inn-supplied coffee brought out by an equally solicitous and horrified waiter; she was shaking only a little now, and hadn't spilled the coffee very much at all. Somewhere way far away, she made a note to herself of how much more lucid she was than she had been after the Clovis Franjo thing, but then she'd had so much more experience since then, hadn't she, yes she had…

"You okay?" asked Marcus presently.

"Don't I look okay?"

"Another day, another murder. You must be used to it by now."

"Yes. I suppose I must be."

"I don't mean to make light of it. It's still hard for me, every time, and I'm a professional. You don't have to pretend; it's all right to be freaked."

Rennie pulled Punkins's shawl closer. "I know."

Marcus tried again. "Much better for his image,

really. No sordid murder trial, however sensational, to dim his romantic luster."

"He'd probably have quite liked a trial," said Prax, who'd put her arms around Rennie, feeling her start to shiver again. "Another chance to show off. The Irish do love to be the center of attention."

"I have to admire how he did it," said Rennie presently. "I would have sworn to it in court that he was in bed with me all last night."

"All night?" Marcus's voice was flat and professional.

" —Guess not."

"Eat or drink anything before you went to sleep?"

"Some room-service sandwiches and milk. He just now told me he'd drugged the milk."

"You were out at least a couple of hours, I promise you. He was trying to establish an alibi, presumably, by being seen downstairs at the inn. They always try to fancy it up with some goddamn crap: he'd have done better to stay in bed with you the whole time. Alibi-wise, of course."

"Of course."

"Several people noticed him in the lounge during the time he was supposed to be upstairs with you. Hanley even asked them if anyone had seen Hill around—trying to be clever, I suppose, or maybe he'd just lost it completely by then."

"It must have been like that," Rennie said tonelessly. "I woke up and the window was open; he claimed he'd just wanted some fresh air, but obviously he had just come back in from the cliff and not latched it properly behind him. His skin was so cold, and there were scratches I didn't really remember giving him. And I did notice he wasn't wearing his medal. He ran me this lame story about how he'd taken it off because he didn't want the Blessed Mother to see him indulging in carnal activity. Which I totally believed, by the way. Because apparently I'm just that stupid."

Marcus shook his head. "You're not, you know... We think that by the time he took you upstairs, Pierce Hill was either already dead or just about to be. I'm sure Hanley properly appreciated your charms, but basically you were only there to give him a good solid alibi for the time of death, or as near as makes no difference, and to make sure he had explanations for the scratches on his neck and the missing medal. Which you supplied to his satisfaction. Even so, he couldn't resist dashing outside to check that Pierce was (a) still there on the rocks below, and (b) still dead. Scored on both counts. It was so wet and wild by then that no one would be out on the cliff edge who might notice the body in the dark, and the tide, though on the turn, was so far up the beach that nobody would be walking down there either. He was lucky Hill fell where he did, and didn't wash away."

"Or unlucky," said Stan, who'd just joined the little group with a thoroughly shaken Marishka; they'd seen the whole thing. "If the body had gone out to sea, it might not have been recovered until the festival was long over and Hanley was back in Ireland. The Monterey PD would have had a hard time getting him back to face the, so to speak, music."

"True. We lucked out there, at least."

"But how did you realize it was Finn who'd killed Pierce?" asked Prax, tightening her arms around Rennie. "Before he confessed, I mean."

"We didn't," admitted Brent. "But Sunday morning Rennie had come and told us a couple of things, one of which she was aware was a huge piece of information, the other not. The first thing she told us was that Danny Marron had been using a videotape camera Thursday night as opposed to the film camera he was using Friday morning, which was the big clue to the Baz

Potter side of things; and the other thing was that Finn
Hanley had been in bed with her Saturday night through
Sunday morning. Which just didn't sound right. When
other people told us they'd seen him downstairs at the
hotel when he should have been upstairs, we knew he'd
lied and hadn't been where he claimed to be. Where, if
he'd just stayed put, no one would ever have noticed him
and Miss Stride of the Clarion could have given him an
unbreakable alibi. And of course he had plenty of motive.
They always do something stupid and unnecessary,
thinking they're being clever."

Marcus nodded. "And then we found the medal.
In one of his outdoor excursions Hanley might even have
tried to get all the way down to the beach to see if he
could recover it, once he realized Pierce had ripped it off
his neck in their struggle. He didn't know where it was,
on the beach or on the lawn, but he couldn't get to the
rocks because the tide was too far in. We found it around
dinnertime, but we didn't let that little piece of
information out lest we tip him off. Which is what we
were trying to *tell* you, young lady" — Marcus whacked
Rennie on the leg, then gave her knee a little squeeze of
apology when she flinched — "when we saw you
swanning out of the fairgrounds with him. Maybe next
time — and yes, I admit with resignation and defeat, there
will most certainly be a next time with you, I've learned
that by now — you'll pay attention when cops yell and
wave at you in a significant and warning fashion."

"I might, then."

Presently Stan stirred where he stood beside the
terrace steps. "Hardly his intention, but just think how
valuable not only the Baz and Haz backlist will be now to
Elk Bannerman — the next president of Rainshadow
Records — but the Finn Hanley backlist as well."

Marcus laughed shortly. "It wouldn't be if Finn
hadn't killed Pierce. And if Baz hadn't been killed too. He

couldn't have it both ways. And he obviously knew we were on to him. That was why he grabbed Rennie just now. It was just a desperation move. Though obviously she didn't know what was going on."

Rennie looked up. "I'm sitting right here, you know. I *can* hear you." She glanced at the faces of her friends, so loving, so concerned, and took a deep breath, glancing aside at Marcus, who nodded impassively. *Okay, then, let's get it over with…*

"We have something else to tell you," she began. "Something that Marcus and Brent and Inspector Devlin and I know. Something about Pierce Hill and Danny Marron—and Baz."

Back at the Highlands Inn after the mandatory few hours at the Monterey stationhouse, where they had been greeted like old friends and indeed temporary personnel—and where Ken Karper had remained to glean as much as he could, along with Vince Bays to get more pictures—Rennie, Stan, Marishka and Prax, staggering their drained, exhausted way upstairs, ran into Bruno Harvey. He was so appalled at their appearance that he went with them to make sure they all made it safely to their beds. But as if by tacit agreement they crowded into Rennie's room, and while Stan poured out stiff drinks all round from his stash of single-malt whiskey, they told Bruno the whole story.

At the end of the tale, Bruno shook his shaggy dark head. "Unbelievable. Just—unfuckingbelievable."

"All *too* believable, my friend." Rennie lay back against the stack of pillows; her body was too wiped out to move, yet her brain wouldn't shut down, it was still zipping and sparking like some demented electric butterfly, flitting from flower to flower. *Fleurs de mal*, for sure.

Seeing this, Prax deftly changed the subject,

expressing to Bruno their guarded and sympathetic commiseration about Tansy's romantic defection.

Bruno smiled, with a kind of bleak gallantry. "Oh, you know Tanze, she's easily distracted by bright shiny new things. And just as easily bored with them. She'll be back. She'll get tired of Wayland soon enough. Or he will of her, more likely. I love Tansy, but I do understand her pretty well."

"And you'll take her back?" asked Stan.

Bruno looked surprised. "Of course I will. I love her, you know, as I just now said."

Rennie reached out a hand to him. "I know. We love her too."

When her friends had finally gone, hugging her, bidding her get some sleep, Prax last and most reluctant to leave, Rennie, so weary she could barely stand, brain dull as lead now, profoundly grateful for solitude at last, looked around the room. Hardly able to keep her eyes open, she noted the signs of the weekend just past, like landmarks or blazes on a trail: the flowers from Gerry, still vivid and fresh, and Prax's concert dress draped over a chair, and her typewriter, and the letter she had written to Basil Potter, lying on her nightstand. The two sheets of handmade paper, spangled with tiny bits of leaves and flowers—Rennie had purchased a box of it at a fairgrounds stall, to write her bread-and-butter note to Romilly Ramillies—lay half-concealing the strand of dark blood-colored beads bought from Keala Lopaka's stall. Memorial beads.

What a weekend: everything she had expected, and a ton of things she could never have seen coming in a million years. Nothing would be the same again. But then, nothing ever was.

After a while, she reached over and picked up the beads, curling them into her hand and curling up on the bed, her hair falling over her face, her fisted hand over her heart, the cold garnets touching her lips.

    *Now, Baz…*now *I can cry for you…*

Chapter 23

June 19 (Monday, Monday)

"WELL, YOU CAN'T SAY I WASN'T HELPFUL," Rennie pointed out, as she packed up her luggage the next afternoon, while Marcus sat in an armchair and watched. "Again. As usual."

"I've never said that," he objected. "I *would* never say that. What I've *said* is you have absolutely no business doing what you do."

"And?"

He sighed. "But you *do* do it and there it is and yes you have been helpful. Much as it pains me to admit. Reporters can go places cops can't go and get people to talk easier than cops can. Your trade has professional ethics — though in your personal case I sometimes wonder about that — but we have the law."

Rennie laughed and sat on the last suitcase to close it. "There now, that wasn't so hard, was it?"

He nodded at the cases. "Going back to town?"

"No, actually I'm not. I thought maybe I'd drive down the coast to Big Sur, if that doesn't conflict with your vacation plans or cramp your style, to have me local? Stay at one of those rustic little inns—or I might go back to Waterhall to help Romilly, who's probably completely freaked and would be glad of someone else around to help her cope. Or even go over to Tassajara: I could use a little Buddhist peace of mind myself right about now, and I think I could manage to forego meat and electricity to get some."

"And after that?"

She sat down on the bed, looking very tired, but very resolved. "After that—after that I'm probably moving to L.A. Dill suggested that Evenor make the move down there, depending on how they did at Monterey, and, well, as we all saw… So Prax is already asking around for a place to rent in Laurel Canyon, and she wants me to come with and be roomies. If I go, I'll keep my apartment in the Haight, at least for a while, and come up here a few times a month to do newspaper stuff."

Marcus spread his hands, looked down at his fingers, flexed them shut. "What about your job?"

"I'm working such a lot now out of L.A. and New York, it's much of a muchness. I doubt Burke will have a problem with it, and Fitz certainly won't. Besides, I think it will be really good for me to get out of San Francisco."

They sat silent for a few moments. Then Marcus: "Anything else you want to say to me?"

"Uh—I'm deeply embarrassed that I went to bed with a murderer who took me hostage and threatened to kill me?"

"Damn straight you are! Or should be. And for

the rest of our lives I'm never going to let you forget it."

"You and Praxie both."

They made a stop at the stationhouse to bid farewell to their new friends Brent Gilmore and Audie Devlin, and to give a final statement as well. It was so complicated, what with all the overlapping jurisdictions: the Monterey and Carmel PDs, the sheriff's department, the Highway Patrol, even the state police, whom most Californians didn't know existed—everybody had to have their oar in and their questions answered.

They were still in the middle of things when Rennie sat up suddenly, as if she'd heard something that the others hadn't, or remembered something important that she'd unaccountably forgotten.

"I have to go, I'm sorry," she said, scrambling to her feet and collecting her belongings.

"We're not finished yet," said Audie Devlin with some surprise.

"No, we're *not* finished, not at all." Rennie looked back at them from where she already stood in the doorway. "In case you've forgotten, we still haven't solved Adam Santa Monica's murder. I want to do it for him, and for his family. His real family. Whoever they might have been. And I think I know where to go. Who's with me?"

Rennie found the one she was looking for in Romilly Ramillies' sculpture garden, sitting in the smooth protective curve of a monolith of close-grained Grass Valley granodiorite, cradled in it like a child in its mother's arms or a surfer barreled in a wave. Her cheek rested against the speckled stone, still warm from the day's sun, and she made no move to run as Rennie lowered herself cross-legged to the grass a few feet away.

"I did it for Daniel," said Brandi Storey Marron in

a dreamy, high-pitched voice quite unlike her usual. "To take care of him. I like to take care of him."

"I know you do," replied Rennie after a moment. "How did it happen?"

"He was in the pool," Brandi continued, still in the unreal sing-song voice, clearly stoned on something. "That—*kid*. It was a couple of days before all the people came to Mojado. I was staying with Danny here, at my godmother's. I went up to the High Springs for a soak and I saw them there. They were naked in the pool and they were having an argument. I heard what they were saying. But I didn't really need to. I already knew all about it; it had started last year."

"What had, Brandi?"

"Their affair, of course! It was disgusting. Danny was begging him not to tell about it, not to leave him. I couldn't have that. I couldn't have Danny at the mercy of some pathetic teenage faggot. So I arranged to meet him at the café, the morning Big Magic opened. He was there waiting for me. I told him that I knew all about everything, that it was all cool with me. I told him Danny wanted to meet him at the pool the next night, and he showed up right on time, like a little dumb puppy."

"*You* were the one he looked so happy to see, that morning at the Springs café," said Rennie, suddenly sure. "Not Danny, you. That was when you talked to him. But he knew you were Danny's wife. Why would he trust you, or even talk to you?"

Brandi laughed, with the same unreality that her voice had held. "He wanted to tell me all about his affair with Danny; he said he'd even written me a letter, but I couldn't find it, after... Anyway, I told him I knew his parents, Elvis and Jackie, that they were good friends of my father's and they'd finally decided they wanted to meet him, and had asked me to drive him down to L.A. He couldn't believe it. He was so surprised I wasn't angry about him and Danny. I just said how cool it was that my husband's boyfriend was Elvis and Jackie's son, and he fell for it like a ton of bricks. He was so happy. He really thought it was all going to happen for him, that he'd be living with his mom and dad in Graceland."

"How did you get him into the pool?"

"That was the easy part," said Brandi confidingly. "He was right there next to me. I was sitting a little above him. I got my legs around his neck and just scissored him under, into the hottest pool. I was a competitive runner at USC, you know, I have very strong legs. He scratched me, see, all down along here."

She pulled up her long skirt, to show slim, muscle-grooved calves swathed round with thin gauze bandages, like young saplings swaddled in sacking for the winter. Partially unwrapping her right leg, Brandi revealed angry, shiny, tight-looking scarlet skin, welts and gouges on the shins and calves, the scalded epidermis already peeling into translucent, papery tatters.

"He almost pulled me in, and the water was so hot it burned me really badly. It hurts so much—I've been taking codeine for the pain, it's only just started to feel a little better. I couldn't wear pants, the fabric touching hurt too much, or even miniskirts, people would have seen. But in the end I kept him down long enough. Women have much greater lower-body strength than men do. It's all those childbearing muscles, you know."

"Yes," said Rennie, glancing up and behind her to where Brent, Marcus and Romilly were standing. "Yes, I do know."

Romilly pressed her hand to her mouth, and turned away into the garden, among her stones. Marcus met Rennie's eyes, and there was no expression on his face as Brent Gilmore and his deputy's assistant came forward to take Brandi into custody. She went with them like a lamb.

"But *how* did you know?"

Prax, Stan, Marishka, Marcus and Rennie were sitting on the terrace of Waterhall; Juha and Chet had returned to San Francisco from Monterey, hitching a ride with the rest of their band, anxious to get as far away from the murder vibes as fast as possible. But the others had stuck together. Romilly had pressed the hospitality of the house on them, then had calmly called the Revels family lawyers in San Francisco, ordering them to drive down, and a local lawyer friend to fill in till they got there. She'd just driven off to Monterey, following Brandi to her booking and arrest appearance: she was the girl's godmother, after all, and someone had to look after her until Brandon Storey could fly up from L.A. with heavy-duty legal muscle of his own.

Also, she'd told them, somebody was needed to stay with Becca until her brother Simon got there; the companion-nurse was devoted, and could certainly handle the situation, but Becca sensed the extra dimension of fraughtness, and she might be upset and afraid. They had readily agreed to keep their old friend company, and their trusted presence did seem to calm her down.

Rennie's eyes were on Becca now, where she walked with her beautiful English setter by the stream, under the nurse's watchful eye.

Maybe, just maybe — oh please, let something good come out of all this for her...

"How did I know?" she echoed. "That she was here at Waterhall? Romilly told me when I called her before we left the hotel."

Stan looked impatient. "No, how did you know it was Brandi?"

"Oh, that. Well, just something that happened Saturday night. It was so small and stupid I didn't even register it at first. Brandi was sitting on the edge of the stage between sets, talking to me and Praxie and Punkins Parker and Owen Danes. She had a long skirt on, but her legs were hanging over, and Owen wrapped his arm around them, just kidding, and she reacted as if he'd sliced her shins open with a boathook."

Prax rolled her eyes. "Always the drama queen. I noticed that too, and I just figured she was pissed at Owen for presuming to grope her sacred Storey limbs."

"Right? And we'd all been supposing Adam's killer would have burned *arms*, not burned legs, so I thought nothing of it either. Then after — after Finn, we were sitting on the steps outside the inn, and you smacked my leg, Marcus, and it made me jump, because I wasn't expecting it. And then I remembered that moment with Brandi and Owen."

Marcus looked impressed. "And you figured it out from that? I guess you really are a detective."

But Rennie was in no mood to be patronized. "I remembered something else too: when I went into the Mojado village drugstore the first day of Big Magic, when I drove in with Adam, I saw Brandi there. She didn't notice me, because I dodged her. But I was driving past there again the next day, and I saw her coming out of the drugstore. I remember thinking that she must have forgotten something the day before, she was such a flake. I told you and Brent and Devlin about it at the stationhouse on Saturday morning, and you wrote it down but you didn't do anything about it."

"How do you know we didn't? As it happens, any little scrap of information was welcome. But you're right, we didn't pursue the drugstore visit. Our mistake."

"Yes, well... Anyway, I checked with the clerk and the pharmacist just now, when we stopped in the village on the way here."

"And what did they have to tell you?" asked Marishka, though Marcus, who had accompanied Rennie and Brent into the drugstore and already knew the answer, was nodding.

"Oh, the clerk remembered perfectly what Brandi bought, that second trip of hers. A dozen gauze bandage rolls, six tubes of analgesic ointment and a big bottle of Vitamin E, which as we all know is alternative-medicinely good for healing skin stuff—scars and burns and such."

"Also the pharmacist told us she filled two scrips from a local doctor," added Marcus. "One for antibiotic burn cream, and one for codeine pills, for pain. Though she probably already had more than enough drugs on hand to take care of that."

Stan made a skeptical face. "Circumstantial."

"Indeed yes," Rennie conceded. "But nobody else at Waterhall needed any of those things; it wasn't as if she was thoughtfully restocking Romilly's medicine cabinet. So obviously she, or someone close to her, had something rather extensive that needed to be salved and bandaged and medicated for. She told the clerk it was a bad sunburn, and he saw no reason to doubt her."

"Bet he didn't see her legs, though," remarked Prax.

Rennie shook her head. "He did not. And of all the other possible suspects at Waterhall, nobody else's legs were blistered like coal-oven pizza and shredded like epidermal coconut. And we know this how, class? Because we saw Romilly and Becca in knee-length skirts and Danny in cut-off jeans and Simon in Bermuda shorts. Bare legs all. And Brandi wore nothing but long skirts all week. Also nobody else in the immediate circle of suspects had gone in for recent medical attention. Didn't take a house to fall on the fuzz to pick up on that."

"The doctor's already being questioned," said Marcus, stretching hugely, "and no doubt will be questioned some more in the very near if not immediate future, along with the drugstore clerk, before they hit the witness stand."

Stan smiled grimly. "And I should think it will not fill anyone with astonishment when the medical examiner matches the marks on Brandi's legs to Adam's fingernails."

"Exactly," said Marcus. "But it's Brent's patch and Brent's bust."

"And rightly so; he should get the collar." Rennie looked at him a little apologetically, though what she had to apologize for nobody was quite sure. "I just didn't believe Danny when he claimed he killed Adam. He was covering for Brandi, the only person he cared about more than himself. I guess he really did love her. But it made sense, his confession, and Brent and you and Devlin went with it, so I thought I must be wrong."

Marcus shook his head. "None of us believed him for a heartbeat. But you seemed to have something definite in mind. That was why Devlin agreed that we should just let you run with it—keeping an eye on you, of course, by which I mean 'following you at a safe distance in an unmarked car'—and give you as much information as we did. We had no idea it would go where it went."

"With her?" said Prax fondly. "You never do. You should know that by now."

Rennie shrugged, visibly uncomfortable. "More to the point, will anything happen to Romilly? Because of the rifle shots she lied about?"

"Oh, she'll get another stern talking-to, no more; no one's going to put Romilly Ramillies in jail for trying to protect her daughter, as she thought. But I'm sure you'll all have realized by now that it was indeed Brandi who shot at Danny, Pierce and Finn that morning, not Romilly. And certainly not Becca."

"I thought it might be," said Rennie. "Brandi, I mean. Either her or Simon Revels. But I didn't have any proof. Besides, little Brandi was right there on the spot, looking as if she'd just gotten out of bed. Perhaps a bit too *much* as if she'd just gotten out of bed, if you know what I mean. I should have picked up on that sooner. Well, she doesn't have show-biz bloodlines for nothing, does she. And she knew how to get her henna'd mitts on a Waterhall gun."

"But who was she trying to hit?" asked Stan, who with everyone else except Rennie had been jolted to hear Marcus impart this information.

Marcus threw him a quizzical look. "Danny, of course."

"But she loves him!" protested Marishka. "She'd just killed Adam for him!"

"All the same, she was the shooter. She'd come not from being asleep but from spying on the three guys in the sculpture garden; those were her damp, bare footprints on the slate path. But they dried up before we could match anyone's feet to them."

Rennie nodded. "Romilly was right: in spite of having stolen Danny from her, and being too insensitive to notice the fallout from her grab, Brandi did care deeply for Becca. She had found out from Adam that her marrying Danny had helped trigger Becca's initial freakout and worsening state of mind—or lack thereof, as she'd seen at dinner. No one had ever told her before. Maybe she and Danny finally discussed it later that night, who knows?"

Marcus took the thread back. "So, next morning, being the homicidal drug-besotted lunatic that she is—I doubt she was even capable of rational thinking by that point, or for a very long time before that—she just ups and grabs the first weapon she sees and indulges her always-uppermost selfish whims. And, at that moment, the ruling whim was to make Danny pay. For betraying Becca, and also for betraying her, Brandi, with Adam. And maybe, too, as a confused way to deal with her own guilt with herself for hurting Becca. So that was why she shot at Danny, and why she was so upset when we told her Danny was okay. She wanted to kill him, at that instant, but she didn't want him dead."

"That's nuts!" protested Marishka. "Surely that can't have been her only reason?"

"I doubt it was. I think she also panicked: she may be nuts, but she's not stupid. She figured she'd get caught eventually for Adam's murder, and she couldn't bear Danny to be out alone in the big bad world without her. Good thing she's such a rotten shot."

Prax nodded. "Or maybe she was just concerned that he'd find someone else to console him once she was in the slammer. Or once he was."

Rennie shook her head wonderingly. "She would rather have killed him herself than…well, maybe that's not true. Maybe she was only trying to scare him, keep him on the straight and narrow. Maybe."

"Do you think Danny knew all the time that his wife killed his boyfriend?" asked Stan.

"Oh yes," said Marcus grimly. "You bet he knew. He slept with her; he couldn't not have noticed the burns on her legs. Or the bandages she wrapped them in, or the codeine pills she was dropping for the pain. Must have hurt like hell; that water was really hot. She probably gave him some bullshit story about she fell asleep under the sunlamp, or she spilled the boiling pasta water, or the shower knob had gotten stuck. We'll find out eventually. But no, Marron knew exactly what she'd done. And he was glad. Now he didn't have to worry about Adam's blackmail."

Prax looked surprised. "How do you know there was blackmail?"

"That letter Adam was writing to the wife of his older-man boyfriend," said Rennie, before Marcus could speak. "The one in the little leather pouch that I found in my car. Adam wanted very badly to let her know. But what he hadn't realized was that she already knew all about him. True, the letter didn't give the names of either boyfriend or wife. But we know who was involved, and besides, we have her confession that she knew about the letter. She couldn't find it because when she killed Adam, the letter was under the front seat of my car."

"The photo of Adam and Danny together makes that pretty plain in any case." Marcus rubbed tired eyes. "He didn't really care for the kid, of course. There would always be some new starry-eyed prettyboy to come along for the great Daniel Marron."

Rennie shook her head in disgust. "The only person he really loved, besides himself, was Brandi. And as Stan said from the first, he might not have loved her so ardently if she hadn't been Brandon Storey's daughter. What a piece of utter slime."

"Well, Audie and Brent are busy at headquarters now, putting it all together," said Marcus, standing up to go. "There won't be any problem getting the charges to stick. We've got Brandi's confession for Adam's murder, and we'll get one out of her for the attempted murder, or at least reckless endangerment, of Danny, Pierce Hill and Finn Hanley; and Danny's for accessory to Baz Potter's murder and accessory after the fact to Adam's, concealing the identity of two murderers and whatever else we can get him on. And thanks to Rennie, we have the hard evidence to nail everybody to the wall, even posthumously. Though Brandi's so obviously off her rocker that I doubt she'll ever stand trial. The other two killers, hopefully, are even now being tried in a rather higher court than ours."

"Ahmen," said Prax, not without piety.

Heading back to San Francisco later that afternoon, having parted from Becca with many hugs and promises to return, and with the heartfelt thanks of the Revels family from her brother Simon, the occupants of the blue station wagon were unusually quiet. Once they were past Monterey again, though — Prax was at the wheel, as Rennie didn't feel up to driving, and she had carefully taken roads that kept them far away from the fairgrounds and Otter Point alike — they seemed to find themselves free of whatever inner constraints had muted them, and began to talk about casual matters, about music and other topics, a little too deliberately wide of the one topic that weighed them all down.

It was Stan Hirsh who dragged it out into the light, sitting in the back seat with his arm around his lovely and inscrutable Marishka.

"So, just let me go over it one more time before we write it up. Just so I'm sure I've got it straight when Burke asks us. Brandi Storey kills Adam Santa Monica because she knows about his affair with Danny and the blackmail attempt. Pierce Hill kills Baz Potter because he knows Baz is going to announce the breakup of the act onstage Friday night, Baz having foolishly boasted to him about it. Danny Marron secretly films the Potter murder, hoping to be able to use it as leverage with Pierce Hill. Brandi fires those shots in her godmother's garden; maybe she means to hit her husband, maybe she doesn't. Either way, Romilly Revels tries to take the blame to spare her daughter Becca, who *she* thinks had fired the shots trying to kill Danny. And Finn Hanley kills Pierce Hill out of plain old vindictiveness because he was getting dumped from the label, and takes Rennie hostage, and then kills himself. Complicated much?"

The former hostage nodded distantly, eyes on the road ahead. "I'd say that sums it up nicely. And now the *real* cutthroat killer action starts."

"You mean the murder trials?" asked Stan.

"No, I mean the contract negotiations. Between the hit Monterey acts and the bigtime managers and label guys."

"That's a bit—cold?" Prax was surprised; Rennie was a lot of unexpected and often contradictory things, but flip and cynical about murder wasn't ordinarily one of them.

Rennie turned to look at her, and Prax flinched at what she saw in her face. "Oh, what! If I start really thinking about it I'll have to go drown *myself* in the hot springs. Four people dead when it was all supposed to be music, grooviness, love and orchids. And so pointlessly dead."

Marishka's voice was somber."If dead ever has any point at all."

"So Brandi OD'd anyway," said Prax soberly.

They were having lunch at Annamaria's again, a month after Monterey. It had been all over the news that morning: locked up in a supposedly secure mental facility, confessed killer Brandi Storey Marron had somehow managed to get her manicured mitts on enough drugs to put herself out of everyone's misery. Deliberately or not, no one was sure; or, if they were, they weren't saying.

"Maybe she figured it was better than rotting in jail for the rest of her life."

Rennie nodded. "Romilly told me she absolutely flipped out when Danny was denied bail and carted off to the slammer, to such an extent that she was deemed too unstable to stand trial. But she was insane from the start. She should have been under care years ago, not running around loose. Her father was in the process of making, ah, 'arrangements' for her. Very private, very secret ones. Well, you can do things like that for your homicidal and loony daughter, if you happen to be Brandon Storey and a major political contributor. Serious strings were pulled all the way up to Sacramento—don't quote me or ask me how I know—and she was about to be shipped off to some posh bin in the French Alps, with no chance of release. The deal was, if she ever came out she'd be extradited back here and would have to stand trial for murder."

"So it wasn't jail, but a life sentence just the same."

"Or a death sentence, as I guess she saw it. Maybe she just thought it was better to take her own way out. Or maybe it really *was* an accident. I'd give a lot to find out who snuck her the drugs, though we'll probably never know."

"Could it be murder?" suggested Prax.

Rennie shrugged. "Sure it could. But if it is, I leave it to someone else to figure it out. They can have the glory. I don't want it."

"She might have gotten better eventually."

"She would never have gotten better." Rennie's voice was flat. "She didn't want to. You remember what Marcus said: she felt no remorse for killing Adam and none even for trying to shoot Danny." She broke off for a moment. "And that takes them all very neatly off, doesn't it. Brandi to—well, wherever it is she's gone to. Baz and Pierce and Finn to that great big recording studio in the sky. Danny will probably even get out someday; paroled after ten or fifteen years, if he behaves himself inside. He was only an accessory to murder, not a murderer himself."

"Maybe he can make a searing jailhouse documentary about the whole trip. Though probably he shouldn't try to get Brandon Storey to finance it." Prax's voice was a judgment, and after a while Rennie nodded.

"What about you?" she asked presently, voice and face both considerably lighter. "You Evenor, I mean. I noticed you yourself talking to Leeds Sheffield at the festival, and I heard that Elk Bannerman and Dill Miller and the five of you had dinner the other night. Doesn't take much to connect the dots: your contract is up, you've notched three hit singles, two respectably-selling albums and a firestorm performance at the greatest pop festival ever...you guys are one desirable rock property. Hey, come on, you must have a crumb you can toss a poor hungry reporter? Like, say, just f'rinstance, the exclusive announcement of red-hot San Francisco band Evenor signing a fabulous deal with Fill-in-the-Blank-Name Records? Or could that blank be filled in with, dare I say it, the name Rainshadow? Or perchance Sovereign?"

Prax's blue-green eyes sparkled. "When I am free to do any crumb-tossing, be sure that you will be the first and only one to whom I toss," she said with dignity. "And it will be more like a nice whole fresh-baked loaf than a tiny stale crumb, I promise you."

"Oh well, as long as it's good and loafy I guess I can wait. I hear Elk really wants to sign Turnstone to Rainshadow, once he's confirmed as label head, and I don't see any reason he won't be. Wouldn't it be nice if all of you ended up on the same label?"

Prax nodded happily, but she wasn't falling for Rennie's ever so artful lure. "Elk's the logical successor to the late unlamented Percy, really; I can't see Rainshadow *not* going with him as new label chief. He's maybe not quite so lavishly generous as he could be, but he's honest and he allows his artists complete creative autonomy, how's that for a big fancy critic word, and he doesn't jerk them around over things like publishing rights. Not like some I could mention, or would mention except for that nil nisi bonum crap."

"My goodness, now Latin! Better and better. You must hang out with some very smart friends."

"And Albert Grossman got Janis and Big Brother onto Columbia, just as Gerry Langhans said he would, and Quicksilver got signed by Capitol, as did the Steve Miller Band. The Quicks got a better deal than just about anybody, since Capitol didn't manage to land itself a 'hippie' band during the first rush of interest, so they were more willing to fork out now."

"So hopefully it will play out that way for you guys too, you and Turnstone and Lionheart. Reprise has Jimi, as we've seen, and it looks like Lionheart's going with Centaur, though Bellasca is going to get utterly outmaneuvered by Turk Wayland, who is one smart cookie. Or biscuit, as the Brits say. Being as that's never happened to Frederick before, he'll never see it coming. I am filled with delight to hear that this is even a possibility."

Prax's mouth went down at one corner. "Think of it as the last installment of Finn Hanley's revenge."

"I can *so* dig it."

Chapter 24

"YOU CAN GET A LOT MORE with a smile and an automatic than you can with just a smile. Or, indeed, just an automatic."

Rennie delivered herself of the line with the air of a professional pronouncing on a professional matter; which, really, she was, and Burke Kinney snorted a laugh.

"Some murderer teach you that?"

Rennie shook her head. "No, that would have been Detective Inspector Marcus Dorner, SFPD, actually."

She and Stan Hirsh were sitting in their editor's airy office at the Clarion. Rennie had just told her boss that she was thinking of moving to L.A., and they were discussing how the Clarion would handle it if she did.

"I'm just saying," she added pre-emptively. "Merely an observation. I'm certainly not planning on pulling an automatic on you if you won't let me go."

"Nor will you need to. I'm sure Fitz won't mind a

bit if you do your thing out of L.A. And Garrett and I certainly don't mind. You don't do so much day-to-day reviewing these days anyway; that's all over to Stan. You're the one who'll have to commute twice a month, not us. No, no, fine by me. Write from the mountains of the moon if you like. Just as long as you keep coming up with the goods."

Burke sat back in his beloved creaky old red leather deskchair and smiled upon them both with great benevolence.

"You two did terrifically well, I have to say. Garry is very pleased with you both, and so is Fitz. That wasn't just good writing, it was good music writing *and* good crime reporting. Even Ken Karper said so, and he should know."

Stan smiled shyly, but Rennie was suddenly silent.

"Problem, Strider?" asked Burke, seeing that she was troubled.

"—I know you're my editor, and Fitz is my publisher, but aren't the two of you getting just the least bit sick of it?" she asked in a low voice. "Rennie Stride, Murder Chick? And comes now her superhero sidekick from Cow-opolis, Stan Hirsh—"

"The Cowboy Wonder?" suggested Stan, straightfaced. "Listen, this kind of thing is what I moved to San Francisco *for*. I don't mean to suggest that I'm out to get bylines at the expense of your friends getting murdered, Rennie, but I have to say I'm damn glad we were able to do what we did, as much as we did, to get them justice. I'm quite happy to go back to reviewing Country Joe and the Fish at the Avalon, believe me."

Burke regarded Rennie for several long and sympathetic moments before he spoke, very gently. "You do realize it's not you, don't you? Not your fault? If you were a war correspondent, you wouldn't be responsible for all those flag-draped coffins coming home, any more than a traffic reporter is responsible for the car crashes or the TV weather guy is responsible for sixteen inches of mountain snow. Unless you have supernatural powers the like of which no human has ever possessed before, you don't make it happen. You just report on it. And I'm glad that you do, because you bring some very good sensibilities—journalistic and personal alike—to bad and problematic situations."

"Oh, I know," said Rennie bleakly. "My brother-in-law told me the same thing, last year. You're both right. And I'm glad too. If you can call it that."

"Are *you* sick of it, then?"

Another long pause. "No. Not yet."

"Good," said Burke, in a much brisker tone. "Then we have no problem."

Amazingly enough, Brent Gilmore, with Marcus's help, had finally tracked down Adam Santa Monica's parents. His real ones, not Jackie and Elvis. So the Durseys of Addison, New York, for such were they from whom young Adam, né Vincent John, had natally sprung, were reunited with their lost boy, and sorrowfully took him home to the valley of the Canisteo, to return him in death to the bosom of his family.

"It was horrible," Marcus said, relating the developments to Rennie later that week so that she could write a suitable follow-up story, give the young man some honor and fitting closure. "They had been out of touch with him for almost two years, frantic; had no idea where he'd been since he ran away or what he was doing or how he was living. Certainly no idea about him and— Marron."

He almost spat the name. "*Nice* people. Housewife mother, school principal dad, three older brothers and two younger sisters; they live on a farm in the hills outside this beautiful small town in western New York State, real rural heaven. They were absolutely devastated. Brent said he got the feeling they didn't give a damn that he was gay, even though they hadn't known about it and didn't really understand; they were just destroyed that he had run away and now he was dead and they hadn't been able to help him."

"At least he got to *go* home," said Rennie in a soft voice. "That's more than a lot of kids like him get."

"Well, that's something then, isn't it." But the snarl in the words wasn't meant for her, and Rennie knew it.

Indeed, there had been solemn and ritual closure all round: Finn Hanley's body had been flown back to Ireland, courtesy of his new label president, Elkanah Bannerman; the act had been viewed in rockbiz circles as Elk's way of atoning for Pierce Hill's many sins and offenses, even though Finn had been Pierce's actual murderer and was a suicide to boot.

In any case, the late singer had been given posthumous absolution by an understanding Franciscan from Mission San Carlos in Carmel. Rennie and a few others had attested that Finn had said sorry and been visibly contritional before going over the cliff. Which he had been, so that made it easier, at least in the eyes of the local bishop, to declare him a victim of his guilt and unsound mind, and allow for Catholic rites and burial. Then he'd been shipped home to County Galway, his Miraculous Medal once again around his neck, and local clerical authorities had looked the other way as he was interred with all due ceremony in an ancient country churchyard among the bones of his kin, with a splendid wake at three separate pubs over a twenty-four-hour time span.

And Robert Basil Potter had been cremated and brought back to his Welsh homeland, his ashes scattered by Pamina and Roger, alone, over his beloved Black Mountains, not far from the tiny village of Crickhowell, where he had been born. They'd brought Rennie's letter with them, and letters from each of them separately and both of them together; standing in a Neolithic stone circle on a high, empty mountainside, they had solemnly set all four missives alight, the loving words turning into ash to mingle with the other ashes, all blowing away on a cold wind across miles and miles of bare hills, into the heart of Wales.

Rennie didn't particularly care about how or where Pierce Hill had gone to his rest; all she knew was that he had been claimed by his nearest and presumably dearest, and, once his body was released from the Monterey County morgue, had been tidied into eternity as his people required.

Not for the first time, Rennie idly wondered where she herself would end up when she died. Maybe she'd be cremated like Baz, and have Prax or Stephen or whoever survived her divvy up her ashes and scatter them over a bunch of places she liked: a waterfall gorge in upstate New York, a Scottish glen or two, the shoreline of the Golden Gate, the Fillmore and Avalon backstages, the sidewalk in front of Cartier's. Probably it would all depend on whomever she was married to when she died, if indeed she ever got married to anyone again, which she didn't see happening.

But she really couldn't see herself pulling up the covers for the big sleep in some old marble vault or dreary suburban memorial park, either. Certainly not in the Lacings' private graveyard up in Napa, though Stephen and Eric would think it a hoot for her to be there among them, annoying the shade of Motherdear through all eternity, and if given the chance would certainly lobby for it.

No, she'd just wait for it, take it as it would come

to her and not think about it. Baz certainly hadn't; no more had Pierce or Finn or young Vincent Dursey. As friends and acquaintances and fellow scenemakers, from Tansy to Janis and Jerry and even Diego Hidalgo, were always telling her, death was merely the payoff for life, a perfect peach to be duly savored when it arrived and not fretted about beforetimes. It was just part of the trip; not better, not worse—but you couldn't have the rest without it. Given how frequently she seemed to be encountering the Reaper on behalf of other people these days, and with no reason to think that that would change anytime soon, Rennie considered that they had a point.

In other news, Turk Wayland and Tansy Belladonna had broken up a month after Monterey. Turk, being a gentleman, never said a word about it, privately or publicly, but Tansy, being no lady, cheerfully confided in everyone she knew, and in many whom she didn't, that the tall Englishman had unceremoniously dumped her, and she seemed completely untroubled by the development. True to Prax's prediction, Bruno Harvey had gladly and immediately taken Tansy back, so that was back to normal, or as normal as it ever got with those two.

Devastated by his daughter's drug death apparently more than by her murderous actions, Brandon Storey retired from Bluewater Studios. He visited her grave in Forest Lawn every day from his Beverly Hills mansion, but anyone could see that his springs of force and energy had dried up, and he soon became a recluse, handing the studio over to his sons and nephews to run, which they did with great success.

Becca Revels, on the other hand, seemed to blossom with healing and joy. Her mother generously credited Rennie and Prax with the lion's share of the unlooked-for and miraculous change, but those two privately thought that the truth was rather otherwise: that once the shadow of Danny and Brandi had been lifted from her world, Becca had begun to find her way home to herself. Whatever the cause or reason, the people who loved her were glad and grateful. Romilly had just taken her entire family off to spend a month in Maui, to further Becca's cure in a spiritual and lovely environment, and the word that came back on postcards was good, and better than good.

As Freddy Bellasca had boasted, Centaur did indeed sign Lionheart, Glisten catalogue and all; but as Rennie had predicted, the word on the street was that Turk Wayland's clever London solicitors had made a deal so advantageous for him and the band, and so rugged on Centaur, that Freddy had had to take to his bed for a week. Tough twinkies! Rennie had thought happily when she heard. Centaur would do just fine for themselves out of it. It was about time that an artist twisted a record company's tail to his own benefit; she was pleased to see that Turk had managed it.

Not to be left behind in the good-deal department, Evenor signed a fat new contract with Leeds Sheffield's Sovereign Records, label of the exalted Budgies themselves. Evenor was so thrilled that Dill Miller had landed this for them that they had been ill from joy. Rennie, who'd broken the news of the signing in the Clarion, as Prax had promised, cried happy tears along with them; great things were coming for Prax and Juha and the boys.

Turnstone too had done well. They'd gotten a multi-album deal from Rainshadow and Elk Bannerman, which, if it wouldn't pay them quite as much upfront money as other labels were paying, would give them a loose rein in the creative-control department and a really good publishing deal, and that meant much more to the band than mere filthy lucre. Not that filthy lucre wasn't nice, and not that they didn't get big old filthy heaps of it once the super-rush-released album took off in late August.

Flexing his new command muscle as Rainshadow president, Elk had also decided to keep Ushuaia and the other old folkies who had been scheduled for the chop, since Pierce Hill had died before they could be officially dumped. They'd given Rainshadow its start when times were tough, Elk warmly told the trade publications and anyone else who would listen; it was only fair and right that their label should loyally stick by them now.

Very pretty sentiments, thought Rennie cynically, when she read them in Billboard and Cash Box and Record World; of course, the trades made not even the tiniest mention of how the great sentimental publicity Elk got by sticking by those six acts after Pierce had been about to bin them *totally* outweighed the cost of keeping them. It was a pity that Finn Hanley wasn't around to enjoy the new regime and the stay of execution, as it were, that he would have enjoyed with the rest; but then again, if Finn hadn't killed Pierce, Elk wouldn't have been able to do as he pleased. Little Catch-22 there. The reaction in the business was mixed, to say the least. But Elk kept his reputation for honorable dealings, and in the aftermath of the reign of Pierce Hill that was no small thing.

So Monterey ended well after all.

Though not for absolutely everyone. Garcia and Gleason and Graham and the rest had been right about the charity rip-off: huge sharkfights began almost immediately about the festival money, and who got it, and where it had gone to, and the waters were roiled and bloody from San Francisco to L.A.

Down the road, *years* down the road, it would eventually sort itself out, though not without acrimony

and bitterness and many accusations none of them
entirely unfounded, and charities would indeed benefit
from Monterey bounty for decades to come. But for the
moment it was just more bad feeling, and Rennie,
understandably, was heartily sick of it.

At year's end, D.A. Pennebaker would release his
brilliant Monterey movie, to great acclaim. Rennie and
her friends were not the only ones who would note that
not only were the Grateful Dead and other bands shut
out of the final cut, but likewise shut out was all mention
of the deaths. Which was, perhaps, as it should be; either
way, in defiance of the laws of physics, Monterey was
both the zenith of what was being called the Summer of
Love and its absolute nadir also. But maybe too that was
karma. Or at least the karma mirror.

And no one would ever have to sit through Big
Magic as filmed by Danny Marron, so there was *that*
small blessing.

With all those matters settled at last, that left just
one loose rocknroll end to tie up.

"I hear you re-signed with Rainshadow," said Rennie to
Roger Hazlitt, at dinner one rainy night in September,
when she was in New York on a journalistic weekend, to
check in with Fitz and catch the Doors live on the Ed
Sullivan Show, which had been — interesting. "You and
Turnstone on the same label, Ushuaia and those others
still having a home there. All thanks to Elk — I like it."

He smiled at her. "Bet you were surprised."

"Not as surprised as I bet *you* were when Elk
returned the Potter and Hazlitt publishing rights to you,
and to Pamie as Baz's heir."

"No, not as surprised as that, I'll grant you. Elk
said it was a token of good faith, and for me it tipped the
balance to re-up. I was — oh God, I had *totally* given up
hopes of getting those songs back. I just wish — "

Rennie reached across the table to touch his hand. "I know, sweet boy. I wish he could have been here for it too. But I know Elk. He'll be a very different kind of label boss than Pierce, and that's a good thing. Besides, now you're label-mates, or stablemates, with not only Turnstone but Chris Sakerhawk and Owen Danes."

"Yes…it'll be nice having friends around. And I think you're absolutely right about Elk. But then you so often are so right about so much. You know, Pamina felt uncomfortable about inheriting all Basil's rights and royalties as his widow, so she's offered to share with his parents and brother and sister in England. Says she feels she owes them. Because of…well, because."

"She's always been a class act. Other chicks would have just bagged the money and run."

"Not *my* chick." Roger paused, with the air of someone about to impart Big News. "Now here's another surprise, baggage, and it's a pure scoop for you. Nobody else knows it yet except Elk and the lawyers and the other party concerned—but I signed as half of a new duo."

"No, *really*?" Rennie was delighted. "That's terrific! With whom? What's it called?"

"It's called—wait for it—Hazlitt and Potter."

"WHAT?"

He was enjoying her astonishment. "And I get top billing this time."

"But who—?"

"Haven't you guessed? It's Pamie, Ace. Pamie can sing. The most beautiful voice you can imagine."

Rennie was in tears and smiling from ear to ear at the same time. "I can't believe it—how amazing, oh Roger, how incredibly wonderful. And you're both cool with it?"

"We are. And we know Basil is, as well. And if anyone else isn't, too flippin' bad. Know what? We don't care."

"God's feet, why should you! But you do know there'll be talk? Still, nothing you can't handle. And I can write about it first, before anybody else? But you're both happy? Not just about that but about everything?"

"Yes and yes and yes and yes."

So that was all right then too.

When Rennie's story broke about the new phoenix rising from the ashes of Baz and Haz, Prax, just returned from Los Angeles, where she'd been house-hunting and recording with Evenor, had headed immediately to Rennie's place, to discuss it over dinner and joints.

"I don't know how it's going to go down with the fans, though," said Prax doubtfully. "They might want to think of a new name. Use Pamie's maiden name, maybe. Get married and make it Hazlitt and Hazlitt. Or something completely different. But I do like the idea, my God, who wouldn't. They were rehearsing the other day down in L.A., over at that place we're using in Culver City, studio next door to ours, and I listened in for a while. They sounded fabulous. And they are so in love."

"They do. They are." Rennie was silent for so long that Prax rapped her smartly on the back of her hand with a spoon to get her attention. "Ow! *What*? What the hell did you do that for? — No, I was just missing Baz all of a sudden. We were friends for so long, and now he's gone. There aren't a lot of people who know me from way back then. The guys in Powderhouse; some college roommates; Roger. But that's about it."

Silence again; but an easy one this time. Then Prax: "Not to change the subject, but to change, you know, the subject: did you hear that Janis has been getting it on with Jimi Hendrix?"

Rennie looked interested. "No, I hadn't. Well, I'm not surprised, since Tansy had already snatched, as it were, Turk Wayland, and she and Janis and Grace between them have scored all the local talent. Isn't it Grace who says that chicks in bands are the biggest groupies in the world? Yes, I do believe it is… But Jimi was a logical candidate. Unless Janis wants to go after Diego Hidalgo."

"Now that would be just creepy. I also hear that Bill Graham was pissed off with her? Janis, I mean."

"Oh, he was just mad about something she said a while back. I didn't print it, first out of protecting me from the wrath of Graham, and second out of protecting Janis from herself. But then she went and said it again to some underground rag and they did print it and Bill saw it and hit the ceiling."

"What on earth did she say?"

Rennie groaned theatrically. "She *said*, and I quote: 'The Avalon is the place for music; the Fillmore is where sailors go to get laid.' "

Prax roared with laughter. "Well, she should know!"

"You *think*?" Rennie was laughing herself. "Anyway, after that, Bill kept Big Brother out of the Fillmore for months and months; didn't you notice? But once the clear ringing money sounds of Monterey began echoing off the canyon walls of L.A. and New York, he changed his own tune and invited Big Brother back, to fill in for the Airplane on a bill with Hendrix as the opening act."

"And that was where the thing with Jimi started up. It's already over, apparently. Jimi is a cutie, but I bet Janis is kicking herself she didn't grab Turk before Tansy did."

"If she still wants to grab him, she can. Or can try, at least. Now that Turk and Tansy are splitsville, I mean."

"Didn't I say they wouldn't last two months? I'm surprised they were together even for one. Our Tansy's adorable, but that Turk's a genius. Tanze probably bored him to tears within three days. I doubt Janis could have hung onto him much longer, though."

"I don't think long-term is what anyone's thinking here."

"I'm sure you're right." Prax paused, not for as long as anyone would notice except Rennie, or someone else who knew her well. "Now stop rolling your eyes and listen. I talked to Dill the other day. Well, we all did. He said he needed to know what we want for ourselves, for us as Evenor, after Monterey."

"In what way did he mean 'want'?"

Prax looked a little tense, suddenly. "Oh, like did we want to be incredibly rich and famous big old stars, which would mean we'd have to work like, well, like very hard-working people and spend most of our lives on the road, or did we only want to work enough to be able to live comfortably and spend the rest of our time hanging out or surfing or whatever, and make an album a year and only go out on tour when we felt like it, or what exactly was it that we *did* want. He said he'd do whatever we told him to and whatever it took to make it happen. Guaranteed. For fifteen percent off the top, plus expenses. He'd handle everything. We wouldn't have to lift a finger except onstage or in the studio."

"What did you tell him?'

"We decided we wanted to go for it." Prax regarded her friend levelly, out of those astonishing aquamarine eyes. "All the way. You don't think less of us for it? I'd really love to be a huge rich famous star, you know."

"Me? Think less of you guys? Never happen! And you will be. A huge rich famous star. I can see it."

"Well, Dill got us signed to Sovereign; that's a majorly good start. Which means the move to L.A. is on, and right away. You know I've been looking for a house to rent."

"Then I'm coming with," said Rennie after a moment, but with decision. "If you still want me for a roomie?"

Prax beamed. "*Do* I!"

So that was settled too.

Something was in the air, or the cards, or the stars: all around, it seemed a time for breaking the patterns of the past and forging new ones. Chet and Rennie were over, quite amicably, with no discussion even: he was already deeply involved with Bernadette McMahon, the pretty brunette he'd met at Monterey, who as it turned out was a very gifted painter. Bernie was already at work on Evenor's next album cover, which would turn out lovely and artistic, not at *all* like some of the crappy covers you saw around, dumb collages that looked as if they'd been slapped together by someone with all the art skills of a Jerusalem artichoke; so that was fine with all concerned.

And on the heels of Rennie's decision to move to the Southland, she and Marcus decided not to continue to use each other anymore either, and he came over to Rennie's place to discuss it.

"Do we need to tell Stephen about us—about it? Whatever it was?" he asked after they'd gone over the pros and the cons and the whys and the wherefores; not that they'd really had to, it was all a foregone conclusion. "Now that we're officially finished, I mean."

"Ohhhhh, I think not," said Rennie on a long exhaled breath. "He never officially knew we were officially—doing what we were doing. Come to it, we were never even officially official. It's still the Icepick. He still doesn't deserve it."

"The *what*?"

She explained about the Icepick of Confession, and Marcus gave a short but amused laugh.

"You're absolutely right. As you so often are."

"So true. And we'll still be friends. Except of course when we butt heads over a case. Which you *know* is still gonna happen."

Marcus managed a creditable smile. "Friends, hell. We'll still be family."

"We were always family. In a totally non-incestuous way, of course."

"As you say."

Epilogue

Sometimes It Just Turns Out
That Way...

AT THANKSGIVING, Stephen brought Ling-ling Delphine
de la Fontange along on his holiday trip home to San
Francisco, to officially present her to the Lacings, whom
she'd known since her childhood but hadn't seen in
years, and to Rennie, whom she'd never met at all.

He had been a little nervous, understandably, of
broaching the subject of his possible future second wife
with his still lawfully wedded here-now-present first
wife. So there had been an intimate dinner at one of San
Francisco's best restaurants, just Stephen and Rennie, to
start off with, and two spectacular South Sea pearl
necklaces — one blue, one gold, and matching earrings —
to follow. Then the two of them had gone back to
Rennie's place for tea and talk. Just tea. Just talk.

"Her name, Ling-ling, means the sound that two
pieces of jade make against each other."

Stephen looked at Rennie for a reaction, but she
merely smiled, and continued embroidering the wedding

cloak she was making for Pamina Potter, soon to be Pamina Hazlitt, the beautiful sapphire velvet spread across her lap and pooling on the floor. They were sitting in the living room, fireplace crackling cozily away, stained-glass lamps throwing warm light all around.

"How lovely. Shall I just call her Ling, then? The way you do?"

"Ling is fine. Her father is French, Jean-Pierre de la Fontange, *Count* Fontange, and Mei-mei, her mother, is Chinese. But you knew that. She was born right here in San Francisco, lived in New York as a little girl, went to *lycée* in France. Then Vassar, and then she went home to Hong Kong with her parents. Since then she's spent a year each in London, Geneva, Amsterdam and Bangkok. Speaks five languages. She's a gem expert, you know."

Stitch stitch stitch. "I did know."

"We met as kids. Hadn't seen each other for years. And now we just—hit it off."

Thread knotted and clipped. Rennie drank some tea, then looked up at him, and in her face was nothing but calm affection.

"Why are you so nervous? Silly boy. I couldn't be happier. For both of you. It's not a problem for me. You know that. It shouldn't be one for you either."

It was true: it wasn't a problem at all. She was only sorry Stephen had to feel so jumpy about it. But that would get better as soon as she and Ling actually met, which was going to happen tomorrow, at lunch at Hell House.

Her brother-in-law Eric had had a bit more to say. "You should have *seen* what the General had to agree to, to keep Ling's father on the team. My mother can be *so* stupid...she's known these people for *decades*, they've been guests at Hall Place, my parents have stayed with them in Hong Kong many times. Anyway, she said something that *really* offended Jean-Pierre and Mei-mei—

I won't repeat it—and now the General has to seriously placate them. He needs Jean-Pierre to run the Asian business while Stephen is still new over there, and if Stephen and Ling eventually get married—once Stephen and you eventually get divorced—Motherdear will very much need to get along with Ling as her daughter-in-law, for business reasons as well as personal."

"Well, now that you and Petra have produced Thomas—sorry, Tizzy, to distinguish him from his godfather, your beloved and true spouse—the pressure to procreate is off Stephen for a bit. But he was meant to be a family man, and he will be. An adorable one."

Eric had smiled. "Petra's already pregnant again. We're hoping for a girl this time, to whom you will be godmother as promised. And you? Can we look forward to some Rennie print-offs in your future?"

"I hope so. I like kids, and I do want some of my own eventually. But I've never really thought of myself as a family woman."

"Oh, you will when the right family comes along... I thank God nightly on bended knee that my mother and Petra get on so well. Seeing as her record with wives of Stephen so far is 0-for-1."

"Let's hope her batting average improves, then."

Of course Ling and Rennie hit it off as soon as they set eyes on each other. Stephen, much relieved, even felt comfortable leaving them on their own together after lunch and going to the library to discuss business matters with his father and brother.

Alone in the conservatory, where they and Stephen had lunched, Rennie and Ling relaxed, kicked off their shoes and called for wine to accompany their discourse. In a burst of sisterhood, or harem solidarity, or something, Rennie commended Stephen into Ling's most excellent care and shield-like protection, while Ling

reciprocated by confiding that she and Stephen were in
no hurry whatsoever, and that as far as the divorce went,
Rennie and Stephen should take their time—in the East,
such matters were not hastily arranged. Rennie assured
Ling that there was no way in any universe that she and
Stephen would ever be getting back together to trouble
Ling's moon-fair countenance and glorious pre-
eminence, and Ling countered that Rennie would soon
find someone made as a match for her pearl-like
magnificence, as she would be to his, and they would be
blissful soulmates until the Twelfth of Never. Then the
two of them got drunk on Lacing Vineyards' best
chardonnay.

The day before she and Stephen took the Lacing
corporate jet back to Hong Kong via Honolulu, Ling
came to visit Rennie at the flat on Buena Vista, bringing a
house gift of a tall, beautifully carved, antique white
jadeite vase with her.

"This is fantastic," she said, walking around,
looking at everything there, much as Stephen had once
done, while Rennie happily admired her obviously
hugely expensive present and scanned the flat for the
best possible home for it. "I can see where you wanted
out of Hall Place."

"Hell House. Yes, I'm sure you can."

At Ling's recommendation, she placed the jade
vase on the left-hand side of the marble mantelpiece in
the living room. *Defeat with good feng shui some of the
residual fu left from the murders, if there's still any hanging
around...*

"Anyway, I'm sort of transitional at the moment.
My friend Prax, whom you met at the Avalon the other
night, just moved to Laurel Canyon, her band too, and
I'm going down there to be roomies with her. But I'm still
living here too. I love San Francisco, but I think I've been
too long at the fair. It will be good for me to be in L.A. I

have no history there. That's what I need right now: a clean slate."

Ling looked aside from her perusal of the framed concert posters. "You're keeping this apartment, though? It's much too nice to lose."

"Oh, sure. At least for the foreseeable future. Want to crash here next time you come? Little bolt-hole where you and Stephen can escape from Marjorie? Feel free. I'll have a key made."

"We may take you up on that. But it's good you're keeping it. You still need it. It's a symbol for you, in your growth and in your life, and you're not ready to let go of it just yet. Which is fine. You'll give it up gladly when the right time comes, because it *will* be right. Don't look so surprised! I know these things, and you do too, deep inside... The vase is for where you truly live, whether it's here or in L.A. or somewhere else entirely. You'll decide that. But I have something else, something just for you."

She took a tiny padded pouch of red Chinese silk out of her bag and held it out to Rennie.

"It's only a little thing. Go ahead, open it."

When she did, Rennie caught her breath. Well, Ling *was* a gem expert... In her palm lay a heavy oval pendant of dark-red jade with smoky-blue streaks, carved in the likeness of a very handsome dragon, fantastically three-dimensional, all scales and tail and curving lines of breathing fire.

"In Chinese culture, dragons are the symbol of yang."

"That's male energy," said Rennie, proud that she knew.

Ling smiled. "That's right, but not entirely. We all have both yin and yang energy in us, just as we all have both male and female hormones. And we all *need* both. Women's natural basic energy is yin—the passive, being energy—the phoenix power. And passive doesn't mean inferior: it's the energy that does not need to do, but merely *is*. It can move mountains simply by being. Literally. It's the energy that was before time and space."

"I can dig that."

"Well, men's natural basic energy is yang, the active, doing energy. The dragon power. But as I say, all of us contain both. Sometimes you'll meet men with really out-there yin energy, and women with equally out-there yang energy. And that doesn't mean they're unsexed or neuter or wussy or mannish or anything like that. It does mean they appeal bigtime to the opposite sex because of it. Some of the sexiest women around have yang to burn; it's a huge part of how they project their appeal. And some of the most masculine men you could ever hope to meet have the most subtle yin energy going; it's why chicks are attracted to them in droves. In your profession, look at the yin vibes of people like John Lennon and Mick Jagger; or, for yang, Janis Joplin and Tina Turner."

"You've studied this, then, have you?"

Ling returned the grin. "As a matter of fact, I have. Anyway, I can tell you that your own yang is very, very strong. Which you already knew. But to be realized, it has to meet its true mate with the matching yin, and that's why you and Stephen didn't work out. Your energies didn't fit, and there was nothing you could do about it. Neither one of you was to blame—simply two very decent, loving, good people who weren't made for each other after all."

Rennie smiled wistfully. "I know. We both knew, really. But it's nice to finally have it explained."

"It doesn't mean he's a wimpy emasculated pushover and you're a ball-breaking castrating bitch, if that's what you're thinking. It just means that you each have a great and particular strength and you need to get a matching strength and particularity from your mate. Stephen's wasn't it for you, and yours wasn't it for him. Nobody was at fault. You were like two right-hand gloves trying to make up a pair."

Ling leaned forward, her shoulder-length sheet of straight black hair shining like a raven's wing, and gently closed Rennie's fingers around the dragon pendant.

"Keep it close to you. Don't wear it, not yet. But that guy who's got the yin you need, who needs your yang? You'll know him."

And when, a couple of years down the road, the man Rennie had finally truly fallen in love with, and he with her, accompanied her to Stephen's wedding, Stephen's bride would notice something he wore around his neck, and she would smile.

"I *love* it! It's like a fairytale house. The good witch's house in a story."

Rennie and Prax were having a farewell lunch at Morton's Fork, the Sausalito houseboat-restaurant that was a longtime favorite of theirs—a last hurrah to San Francisco before they caught a late commuter plane down to L.A. with the final bits and pieces of their worldly goods—though Rennie was leaving most of her stuff in the Buena Vista apartment for continued use.

They were sitting at their usual table by the window, the city in the distance, its towers rising into a clear blue sky. And they were looking at a sheaf of color photographs of Prax's newly rented abode: a white Hollywood-French chateau halfway up the side of Laurel Canyon, with a sweeping view out front and a matching mini-chateau cottage guesthouse out back.

Prax grinned. "It *is*, isn't it? Wait till we get Tansy there, she'll flip. But what do you think?"

"Oh, I think I can manage to force myself to enjoy

living there."

"Either with me in the main house or by yourself in the cottage, whichever you like. Or both. You'll still have the place in the Haight; we can use it whenever we have to come up here. A pied-à-terre, isn't that what you snooty society types call it?"

"I wouldn't know. I just call it a crash pad. But this looks fantastic."

"I know," said Prax eagerly and happily. "Bit of a change from here. Not that it was terrible here, I mean. But it *is* a change. To settle down like that. I'm not used to it."

Prax's parents had been hippies before their time, intellectual bohos, and she and her younger brother Peregrin had been raised like gypsies, until the family finally landed back in Mill Valley where Prax had been born, and her mother got an English professor job at Berkeley and her father settled down to the designing and hand-crafting of gorgeously artisanal—custom-bespoke, at staggering prices—furniture of native California woods.

Becoming a musician had been Prax's sure and strong way of becoming who she was, who she needed to be, of keeping a center for herself in a shifting landscape. When she woke up the morning after Monterey and found herself famous, an overnight sensation—gosh, and after only about six years of 'overnight', too—her first decision had been to move down to L.A. with her band as their manager had suggested last year, and the second decision was to have him rent this amazing house for her. She would buy it, she had promised herself, just as soon as she felt secure and settled enough. An owned home had never been part of the McKenna family lifestyle, and as a rocker she was doubly wary of being tied down. But there was no need to rush into things. No need at all.

"What about the guys?" asked Rennie, shuffling

through the photos again, admiring the garden, the paved courtyard, the view, the tiled pool and fountain. "Have they found places yet?"

"Oh, sure. Mostly within earshot, too. There's a house across the road around the corner, on the other side of these trees, in this photo, here, where Juha and Chet are sharing, couple of doors down from Chris Sakerhawk. Jack and Dainis got a place up the road almost to the Valley, and Bardo is way up at the top of the mountain on Lookout Avenue, next door to Toy Tyler and down the block from Graham Nash. There's *tons* of musicians in the neighborhood: Byrds, Monkees, Buffalo Springfield, Doors, Judy Collins, Owen Danes, Cass Elliott, Frank Zappa, Megatherium, Diego Hidalgo. Turk Wayland just moved into the next canyon over. And Mireille is on the other side of the hill, up in Willow Glen."

Mireille was Prax's belle of the moment, a studious, dark-haired French screenwriter a few years older than they were; they'd met at Monterey, introduced by, of all people, Brandi Marron. Rennie liked her a lot, but she and Prax both agreed that there was major flakiness going on there, not just Frenchness. Still, Prax was happy, and that was enough.

"And Tansy, of course," Prax added. "As soon as she found out we were moving to L.A., she decided to come too. Bruno and Turnstone are already there, so it was a done deal. The whole canyon's full of musicians. The hills are alive with the sound of music."

"Is that a good thing or a bad thing?"

"I think, on the whole? Good."

"I do too." Rennie pushed her hair back over her shoulders and took a sip of wine. It would be new in Los Angeles, it really would be that clean slate she'd longed for. It wasn't New York, and it wasn't San Francisco. It had a whole different vibe and feel to it. Which was what she'd been looking for, and hoping to find.

Prax glanced up at her, knowing her thought. "Stephen won't be there, you know. Marcus won't be there. That whole Lacing trip won't be there. You're leaving all that behind. You'll be *you* there. You'll just— be you."

Rennie startled, then smiled, a great huge overspreading smile. "I know. And *we* will be there."

Prax flipped the photos like a deck of cards. "And the Rennie and Prax this place will make us, they're already there, waiting for us. Which, again, is a good thing." She paused a moment. "Marjorie tried again to get you back, didn't she. The lovely Ling notwithstanding?"

"Mothernotsodear? Oh yes, she tried. Briefly. But I surprised her." She stretched prodigiously, hands gracefully climbing the air above her head, then arms out to the side like wings, narrowly avoiding knocking over a candle in a tall glass vase. "I surprised me too, actually."

"Well, I know you'd never have gone back to Stephen. So in what way were you surprised?"

Rennie hesitated, not out of unsureness but a sudden desire to get it precisely right: how she felt, how she said it.

"I was shocked to realize how much I wanted what I wanted, how empowered it made me feel. And I was surprised by how hard it was, on every level, and also how utterly easy. I've had a good solid taste of it by now: to live alone, to write, to do what I want. To do what *she* wanted, what she asked me to do—even what Stephen wanted and asked me to do... Not in a million years. Not for anything or anyone. I could turn into a freakin' *pterodactyl* sooner than I could go back to that. I've always written, but suddenly I knew I was a writer. That I was meant to live a writer's life. I mean, I knew all that before, but now I KNEW it. Was it like that for you, when you realized you wanted to be a musician, that you *were* a musician?"

Prax smiled. "You bet it was. You and I stand on the same ground, only from opposite sides. I had nothing to lose and you had it all to lose. But also we had it all to win. For ourselves. Us for us. Sure it's scary, sure it's hard. Anything worth having always is. Women haven't ever really done this sort of thing before."

"No...do you ever wonder why we became friends in the first place?"

"I don't have to wonder. I know *exactly* why, and so do you. Because we already were, even before you walked in the door to talk to me that first time. It wasn't a question of deciding; it had already *been* decided, oh, a long, long time ago. As for the rest of it, you already know that too. Because you could have printed a *lot* more stuff about me, and you didn't, and you never have. Because those things weren't important to the music, and you saw that. Once I met you, talked to you, I couldn't *not* have told you. People just—tell you things. It's what you do. And what they do."

Rennie rested an arm on the railing below the window and leaned comfortably back in her chair.

"People tell me things, sure, but I don't have to write down, or indeed write up, everything they tell me. You said things on trust, I left things out on trust. Not every little fact, or big fact even, has weight in the larger picture. Not public weight, anyway. It's like an iceberg—you only see a piece of it, but you know damn well the rest is down there under the water. And it's what you don't see that can be the most dangerous—and the most interesting, too, because you don't see *it*, you only get to see what it *does*. As a journalist, I'm the one who gets to make the call about what's important to see and what stays submerged. That's the job. That's *my* job."

"Most rock writers I've talked to don't think like

that—it must be what you learn in journalism school. Or maybe it's just you. But that's why I'd never given anyone a real interview before. Not that swarms of reporters were swimming the Golden Gate like lemmings, pleading for one," Prax added with a grin. "But *you* remember how it was. I'd read your stuff and I liked where your head was at, and when you called me I thought, well, maybe the time was right. And *I* was right. I'm not the only one, either. Sunny Silver, Janis, Grace, Jerry, even Romilly..."

"You do the same thing in your music," Rennie pointed out. "When you compose the music, when you write the lyrics, when you perform for people. That iceberg trip."

"Because that's *my* job."

"Indeed it is... I don't mean to freak you out, and I wouldn't say it if I didn't know you felt the same, but as soon as I saw you I had the feeling we were meant to travel together, be friends forever."

Prax nodded sagely. "Karma mirror strikes again. But we always knew it was really the D'Artagnan thing, that musketeer trip. One for both and both for one."

"Can I be Athos? No, Porthos. No, Athos."

"You can be anyone, this time around—thank *you*, dear Dr. Timothy Leary. All of us can, and now you know it, too."

Yes, she did know, reflected Rennie, and looked across the water to the city she had loved and now was leaving. She did know. And she was.

Ozymandias

I met a traveller in an antique land
Who told me tales of cities fair and far
When I asked for more he took my hand,
Said Come with me, see how things really are

A broken giant of stone stands in the desert
The sand nearby half-masks a marble face
"My name is Ozymandias, king of kings"
Is carven deep upon the empty base

The lords of old thought they would live forever
Their names and titles never be forgot
Raised realms and statues out of pride and pleasure
Never dawned on them that they'd be not

Ozymandias thought he had it solid:
"Look on my works, ye mighty, and despair!"
King of all his eye surveyed
Lord of all he ordered made
Visions that would never fade
Now they're blank and bare

See how high pride has crumbled
Not even things of stone are set in stone
See how cold command has tumbled
However we may live, we die alone

[bridge]

Ozymandias never got the message
Look on his works, my people, and you'll see
Time shut down his masquerade
Fled and gone his royal shade
Nothing came of nothing made
Now the years run free

See how the once-chosen are forsaken
You can't trust time to do the work of fate
Don't stop giving to whatever you have taken
However long you've got, this trip won't wait

Ozymandias never learned his lesson
Look on his works, but not for us despair
He couldn't push the sands away
He never mended night or day
He didn't shape a world to stay
But we have learned to care

See how the powers have fallen
Not even kings and queens are built to last
Hear how the lone and level sands are calling
Boundless and bare, before the timeless blast

[out to fade]

~Turk Wayland